ENTANGLED VENGEANCE

An Alexis Snipperdoom Novel

Book 4

JD BROYHILL

ISBN- 9781737723264

Library of Congress Control Number:
2023918723

Printed in the United States of America

ENTANGLED VENGEANCE

DEDICATION

To James, Jeremy, and Stephen—may you
discover your truth.

To Rick—Forever in my heart.

Mom—I am eternally grateful for your love
and support!

Book cover design by:

Combar Cover Designs

CONTENTS

"I may be a Wizzard,
but true power lies in
knowledge and wisdom,
not just magic."

ARMBRUSTER PRESSTAN HEXTINGHTON

JD BROYHILL

THE BEGINNING

lexis blushed, grateful for the powerful and supportive members of her security team. She smiled at Andreh, happy he had been by her side when the attack happened. She noticed Armbruster standing next to Andreh. He acted stoically, saying little, allowing her the glory of attention. Alexis realized her life was filled with love and support. She felt appreciative and could not imagine this war ending her reign or life.

Alexis closed her eyes, listening as the group applauded. Though it was a somber moment, she felt relieved to know she would have their backing. Together, they would save Alstromia.

Armbruster placed his hand on Andreh's shoulder. "Thank you for all you have done today. It means a great deal to me. What do you think about that incredible Witch?" Armbruster asked, pointing to Alexis, beaming with pride.

"I believe war becomes her, Your Majesty. She will prevail. The Queen is the strongest Witch I have ever met in my life. She will undoubtedly discover who is responsible and obtain her revenge. It is just a matter of time!"

CHAPTER 1

War had been declared, or so it seemed to those surviving the initial, brutal attack. No official declaration had been publicly announced. Nonetheless, the sheer fact that the planet had been pelted with fire, burning rain, and other pernicious spells, causing catastrophic loss of life, gave way to the reality that it was the beginning of war.

The source of this evil and vile act was yet to be discovered. Alexis Snipperdoom refused to accept that this incident had been nothing more than just a warning. It was blatantly obvious that someone wanted Alstromia destroyed. She never imagined anyone or any group would have the audacity to attack her and Alstromia.

It was a bold move, one she was prepared to match. The enemy's onslaught of firepower seemed carefully planned and executed, but the Queen knew she would retaliate and end the war victoriously. Alexis intended to find those responsible, bring them to trial, and, hopefully, end their miserable lives. There was no excuse for the actions she witnessed on this historic day. It instantly changed the relationships between the planets and Clans, and in a way, she hated that. It was heartbreaking.

"Alexis, shall we head to the Security Command Team Chamber to discuss our strategy?" Andreh inquired. Armbruster stood next to Alexis but was preoccupied, holding a discussion with Yarlen. Neither seemed to notice the Queen's restlessness.

"Yes! Please arrange a meeting immediately. We must begin our war planning and response. We cannot and will not stand by and allow another assault," Alexis added.

"Yes, Ma'am, it will be done," Andreh declared, running off toward the Palace.

The day quickly turned to night, and the sky remained brightly illuminated by the green glow of the Protection Spell Shield. Nothing would penetrate it. Alstromia was safe for now. Unfortunately, the spell could not stay in place forever. It was a temporary solution. Yarlen had to research how to protect the planet in another way.

Armbruster and Yarlen entered the chamber first, followed by Rammadar Ximberton, Harshim Moonbliss, and Hamptin Coszor. Orin Vaxton conversed with Griffen Corilyn as they remained seated at the end of the conference table.

Rammadar Ximberton was stunned by the unexpected strike against the Queen and her planet. It was strange for him to realize he was about to go to war with someone he had respected. It seemed unfathomable to him that Zandorah, the Supreme Ruler of Iriss, could be behind the wave of spells and murder. Yes, it was murder. Innocent Witches, Warlocks, and Wizzards died on this tragic day.

Even Trixxie, the Queen's beloved pet Draghoon, had been brutally murdered before her eyes. The enemy sent clear and powerful messages to the Queen and her kingdom. It felt as if no one was safe from the unknown evil force.

Andreh hoped to speak with Pauto, who appeared more confused than angry. Pauto gazed around the room as if he were looking for someone. Andreh wanted to confront him and ask what was afoot, but figured it was best to leave it alone. Instead, Andreh approached Armbruster.

"Sir, we're all set to get started. Do you know if the Queen will be joining us for the strategy session as planned?" Andreh asked, but he didn't have to wait long for an answer. Soon after, Alexis and her Second-in-Command Aerianna entered, both dressed in their battle uniforms.

"All hail, our Queen," Andreh bellowed when he spotted her. Others in the room clapped and bowed respectfully to their ruler. Some remained silent, still not fully comprehending the severity of this life-changing event.

"Please, everyone, sit down," Aerianna commanded. "Our Queen wishes to address you."

"First, let me say thank you to all present in this chamber. I know most of us are at a loss for words following the cowardly act we witnessed. Rest assured. We will prevail! We will win! We must discover who is truly responsible for this spineless attack on our sovereign planet and hold them accountable. No one will escape punishment, trust me!"

Alexis quickly took her seat next to Armbruster. Yarlen sat on the other side of the King, followed by Andreh and Pauto. Aerianna sat across the table, facing Pauto. She appeared restless, fidgeting with her pen and tapping it on the table.

Armbruster jumped out of his seat and pounded his right fist on the table, gaining the attention of everyone in the room. Some flinched from the unexpected noise.

"We must ensure the planet's security. The current measures are only temporary. I will not allow my family or other Clan members to be harmed further. What has transpired is inexcusable." Armbruster swiftly took his seat. He wiped away the sweat, frustrated and angry.

The Queen remained silent, wondering if Yarlen would speak and share his plans for shielding the planet. Pauto looked down at his hands, avoiding eye contact with others. There was much more to discuss, but the conversation was stalled.

Andreh took matters into his own hands. "Your Majesties...please, we must formulate a plan. We cannot wait! Every second counts. The enemy's plans are unknown. We must be prepared and retaliate. Someone knows who is responsible, and finding them is crucial to our success! We should seek out help from Farla Summerstahr. Now that Florezzah has faded away, we must enlist someone with incredible potion-making skills. Sadly, there are only a select few we can trust."

The group contemplated his suggestion. Most were not fond of Farla and did not trust her. However, no one could deny that she was a skilled and creative Witch with an extensive array of potions and spells.

Armbruster agreed. "You may be on to something, Andreh. What do you think, Yarlen?"

"The shield will last for a while. But, as we all know, it is not a permanent resolution to our problem. I have consulted with other Wizzards and Warlocks. Most concur. Another form of magic might be in order. Farla may have a spell that could be more potent than the current one. However, her price is usually quite steep." Yarlen sat down, waiting for a response from the others.

Members of the group appeared deep in thought. Everyone had ideas but was reluctant to share them, afraid they would be considered silly or ineffective. Yarlen was a wise and clever Wizzard. He realized the timing was perfect, and the opportunity to bring about change was now! He stood up, grabbing his Ceptre.

"My Queen, Armbruster, and friends, please let us recall what has worked in the past. We need original spells, ones the enemy cannot challenge," Yarlen stressed, hoping to add to the conversation. He had someone in mind to contact.

Immediately, Alexis jumped out of her seat. "I know who can help. She is young, smart, and she creates unique spells. You may remember her from the Harvest Festival. I am referring to Cazzandra Whiddletoad. She is gifted, and I believe we can request her assistance, and she will oblige."

Yarlen waited for the Queen to take her seat. Once she looked comfortable, he spoke again. "Yes, Cazzandra is a new student of mine, and I will reach out and demand her presence. Shall she join us in our strategy session?"

"No," yelled Andreh and Alexis in unison. Both laughed. "I believe we do not require her attendance at this point. I want to meet with her privately, and then we can schedule a meeting with senior staff," Alexis clarified.

Andreh nodded. He felt it was the correct approach to use with a new and relatively inexperienced Witch.

Alexis leaned back in the large seat and closed her eyes. She recalled Cazzandra's superb spell from before. The young Witch was exceptionally skilled, and Alexis wanted to place her on the Command Staff immediately so no one else would have access to her.

Not far away, Cazzandra stood in the basement of the Palace, mixing up two newly created elixirs. Yarlen gave her permission to practice magic and concoct potions in the cellar. The enormous rectangular room was also where she lived. She placed a single, small bed in a corner. For added privacy, she surrounded the bed with heavy, dark red curtains suspended from the ceiling, draping down to the cold, stone flooring. Cazzandra preferred the quiet and darkness of the underground room. It provided her with a sense of security.

Since Cazzandra had lost her parents at a young age, she was used to solitude. Her grandmother, Sarmetta Whiddletoad, adopted and raised her. Sarmetta was a kind Witch but failed to provide the emotional support Cazzandra sought.

When Cazzandra was old enough to attend school, she begged Sarmetta to send her to learn in an environment filled with other Witches. Hesitant to relinquish the child to an institution, Sarmetta informed Cazzandra that she would educate her until she became older.

Upon Sarmetta's death, Cazzandra took the opportunity and applied to the *Vizzork Advanced Magical Exchange 1 (VAME 1) – School for Witches*. Predictably, she received notification that she did not meet the enrollment criteria since she had never been formally educated. Cazzandra assumed that would happen, but it was not all bad news.

Luckily, the board overseeing student admissions was so impressed by her resume, identifying a long list of potions and spells she had invented, that they allowed Cazzandra to schedule an appointment to appear before them to show off her current talents as a Witch. Her unique spells and abilities stunned the board members at the meeting. Later in the day, Cazzandra was unanimously accepted and invited to attend the prestigious school beginning in the Fall. She was honored and could not wait.

Now, a few years later, she was named the Honored Graduate of the Year at *VAME 1*, which included the opportunity to showcase one of her spells before the Queen.

Cazzandra was an overachiever. She loved Spellcraft and planned to become a famous Witch. Little did she know that her life was about to change again. This time, she would reap the benefits of her exemplary work.

During the Harvest Festival, she dazzled the crowd with her magical abilities. Immediately, Alexis knew this Witch could help her staff and Alstromia.

At that moment, Cazzandra received the opportunity of a lifetime. She was invited to work at the Palace for Yarlen and the Queen!

Yarlen contemplated Alexis' demands. He figured she would handle Cazzandra. It was best if he stepped aside. There was no reason for him to get involved.

Alexis rose, eager to locate Cazzandra. "Yarlen, before you leave, where may I find your student? I have new ideas to present to her, and I require her feedback," Alexis boldly announced.

"My Queen, Cazzandra, is in her chamber in the basement, on the other side of the Palace. She works and resides in my old experimental laboratory. I hope that is okay, Ma'am?" Yarlen responded.

"That is fine, thank you. Andreh, please accompany me. I do not wish to visit her alone," Alexis demanded.

Armbruster wanted to object and suggest he join Alexis, but figured there was a particular reason Alexis asked Andreh. Armbruster was not interested in finding out why. He had other things to worry about, and Andreh was not one of them.

After Alexis and Andreh departed, most of the group dispersed as well. Rammadar and Pauto stayed behind to discuss when to notify the SAow and AoE of the new orders.

Alexis led the way to the basement. Andreh walked behind her, wondering why she demanded his presence. It was not necessary. Halfway to their destination, Andreh abruptly stopped, pulling on the Queen's arm.

"Alexis, stop. What are your plans? Don't you think we should discuss it before we meet Cazzandra? Also, why do you need me?" Andreh released her arm, hearing her making huffing noises.

Alexis spun around and faced Andreh. She smiled, though it was not her usual sarcastic smirk. Instead, it was a pleading look.

"I do not want to be in the room alone with her. I am unfamiliar with the girl. You have conversed with her before. I assumed you were friends. Am I wrong?" Alexis asked him, placing her hands on her hips in a bossy manner.

"I would not say we are friends. We know each other. We have spoken a few times in the past. What do you want me to do or say when we meet with her?" Andreh wanted clear guidance and needed to determine what Alexis had in mind. Sometimes, she was hard to read. It was better to ask her straight out what she expected.

Alexis was tired of their conversation. She hated it when someone challenged her way of thinking or questioned her reasoning.

Getting frustrated, Alexis informed Andreh that she planned to ask Cazzandra to join the Command Team. Alexis would allow her to move into one of the Command Chambers. The offer, of course, benefited Alexis. It would ensure that Cazzandra was close by and that she could keep an eye on her.

"I see. So, you want her near you. Is that correct? Why are you drawn to this Witch?" Andreh complained. He could not understand her sudden interest in Cazzandra. It seemed odd.

"Andreh, I cannot comprehend why you are standing in the middle of the hallway, challenging me. As I told you… I plan to train her. She is brilliant and valuable. I am afraid someone could try to take her away from me or kidnap her. You really do not understand how very gifted she is, do you?" Alexis shook her head. She folded her arms and walked ahead toward the staircase leading to the basement.

Andreh chose to remain quiet. He could see that Alexis was becoming aggravated. It was not his intention to upset her further. However, he still thought it was bizarre that she was so obsessed with the young Witch. From their previous meeting, Andreh assumed Alexis was envious of Cazzandra's extraordinary talents and good looks. Now, he contemplated if there was something else. Most of the time, Alexis had an ulterior motive.

Making her way down the winding staircase, Alexis held on to the metal railing. The stone steps were slick. Andreh chose to walk behind her, holding his Ceptre high, providing additional glowing white light to the otherwise dark stairwell.

Reaching the bottom, Alexis approached the small wooden door on the right. She knocked. Andreh stood behind her, still holding the illuminated Ceptre. Cazzandra opened the door with a surprised look on her face. Immediately, she bowed before the Queen.

"Your Majesty, please come in." She moved aside, permitting Alexis and Andreh to enter the room. It was well-lit by candlelight. The large fireplace in the back of the room blazed. A round, heavy cauldron hung over the fire, suspended by thick, black Ozar chains. The bubbling concoction emanating from the pot was sweet and aromatic. Andreh rubbed his nose. The fumes made him nauseous.

"What a surprise, My Queen. What brings you to the Palace dungeon? Are you here to see Yarlen or me? Has he informed you that I reside here now? It is my laboratory. I am currently working on a new potion." Cazzandra babbled, feeling nervous. She spotted Andreh smirking.

"No, I came to see you, Cazzandra. I am aware of your living situation and presence in the Palace. We need to chat. May I sit?" Alexis plopped down on the only chair in the room, facing the young Witch, her legs crossed.

"Oh, okay. What may I do for you?" Cazzandra nervously asked Alexis, wondering why the Queen would come for a visit. It seemed strange and quite unusual.

"As I am sure you are aware, we have been under attack. For now, Yarlen and a group of his elite students have managed to secure the planet. However, it is a temporary fix for a problem that may not last much longer. I was highly impressed by your *Power Spell* at the recent event. Would you be interested in working for me directly on the Command Team? In exchange, you will receive a room in the Command Wing section of the Palace. Of course, you would still report to Yarlen as well. Andreh will be working with you, too." Alexis grinned cheerfully, assuming Cazzandra would be honored and eager to accept the generous proposal. There was no way the young Witch could refuse the Queen's generous offer.

"Well, that is quite a tempting promotion, My Queen. Respectfully, I must decline. As you know, I am inexperienced and may be unable to provide the services you request. I am still learning from Yarlen. I assume it will take time before I become proficient."

Alexis stood up and walked toward Cazzandra. "I am sorry, dear. I believe you misunderstand me. I am NOT asking you to accept the job. I am informing you that you WILL accept it. You do understand, right?" Alexis hissed, infuriated.

"Oh. I see. Yes, it isn't very clear. I thought you were asking me to join your team. Now, I understand. I am so sorry for the confusion. It is my mistake. When will I be starting, and precisely what are my duties?" Cazzandra inquired. She attempted to remain calm, though she felt her stomach flopping as she thought about working for Alexis Snipperdoom.

"Andreh will provide you with a detailed and outlined list of expectations. In the meantime, please join me for dinner so we can get to know you better. Armbruster, my husband, will also be in attendance. After all, you will be living a few doors down from us. It will be our pleasure to get to know you." Alexis stood and walked toward the door.

"Thank you for understanding, Cazzandra. I am so grateful to have you on the team." Alexis stepped out of the room alone. Andreh remained behind.

"Is she always so demanding?" Cazzandra asked Andreh sitting down on the hard chair.

"She is not that bad, really! Once you get to know her, you will like her. She comes across as gruff, but she is a very kind and loving Witch. Trust me. When I first met her, I was quite intimidated. I thought she was horrible. Now, we are great friends. You'd better hurry and change your outfit. Believe me, you cannot show up to dinner looking like that," Andreh advised.

Cazzandra wore a faded-out dark gray dress. Her hair was pulled back and braided to keep it out of her face. She looked dowdy for such a young Witch. Nonetheless, she would do her best to get cleaned up and impress the King and Queen.

"Thank you, Andreh, for your guidance. I appreciate it. Will you be at dinner?" Cazzandrah asked, hopeful. She thought Andreh was handsome, funny, and intelligent, and she hoped to spend more time with him.

"Not tonight. Alexis is requesting dinner with you and Armbruster. She did not ask me to attend. Sorry, you will be on your own."

"Do you have any other advice you wish to share with me? I have no idea how to act at dinner."

"Cazzandra, be yourself. The Queen will respect you more if you act normally. Do not pretend to be someone you are not. She will see right through you. She is clever. Also, don't be late. Good luck. I will see you later, Cazzandra." Andreh nodded and walked out the door. He planned to return to the Security Command Chamber to speak with Pauto and Rammadar. He also wanted an update on Trixxie's funeral plans.

Andreh had previously discussed Trixxie with Alexis. He suggested a proper funeral for the beast. Alexis broke down in tears, unable to speak. So, Andreh took it upon himself to talk with Yarlen, seeking guidance on this sensitive matter.

Yarlen informed Andreh that the Draghoon needed to be cremated, and its ashes should be sent out to the Sea of Miccay. Since most Draghoons were hatched in the caves by the Sea, they should return there upon their death. It was a necessary ritual to finalize their existence. It was considered bad luck to leave the body of the Draghoon on the grounds of the Palace. No one wanted to jinx the future of Alstromia or the kingdom. So, Trixxie would be cremated. Shortly after his conversation with Yarlen, Andreh instructed two of the

Palace Guards to move Trixxie to the center garden of the Palace grounds. They would hold a cremation service, scooping up her ashes and placing them into large Trimber containers.

Later, those boxes would be placed on a small boat, gliding down the river, and eventually ending up in the Sea of Miccay. Finally, Trixxie would rest in peace, the Sea taking back its magnificent beast. Andreh planned to inform Alexis of the cremation service once it was arranged. He did not wish to upset her further at this point. She was still mourning the loss of her precious pet.

Cazzandra washed up and dressed in a clean dress. This one was one of her newer gowns. It was long, almost touching her ankles. She loved the navy-colored dress embroidered with small white flowers. It had been a gift from one of her friends on Earth. Cazzandra had a few outfits. Fancy clothing had never been important to her.

In the past, she usually wore old frocks when working in the laboratory on concoctions. There was no need to get dressed up for work. She never went out to dinner or attended functions, so there was no reason to own anything pretty to wear. Now, she felt self-conscious. In a way, she felt ill-prepared to face the Queen. She worried she would be underdressed for the occasion.

Before leaving the chamber, she looked at herself in the floor-length mirror. She realized it was time to do something, as her reflection was underwhelming. Cazzandra picked up her skinny, brown wand and waved it over her head, casting a spell. Instantly, she smiled, looking at herself again in the mirror. *'Not bad,'* she said aloud. *'Maybe the Queen will approve!'* Now, she was ready!

Armbruster was not thrilled at the idea of Cazzandra joining them for dinner. He was unfamiliar with the young Witch. Frankly, he was uninterested in getting to know her. "Why the hell do I need to be there? If you want to become acquainted with her, that is your business. I have other things to do," Armbruster complained, staring at Alexis as she brushed her long hair.

"I already told you. We must find out everything we can about her. It would be better if we showed a united front. I want her to be aware that we are a team. Also, you may have questions for her. We need to find out more about her past. Relax, Armbruster. It is just dinner," Alexis began laughing. It was funny, he was so cranky and pissed off about having dinner with the young Witch.

"Whatever. Don't expect me to say much to her. I don't have time for this bullshit. We have other urgent matters to resolve. You know this."

"Armbruster, she will help us. That is why we must have this dinner. We can see for ourselves what kind of Witch she is and what she has to offer our Clan and Command Team. I am not stupid, and I am not wasting our time. On the contrary, I am working on getting us the help we need," Alexis articulated. "Now, please, get dressed and stop making excuses."

Reluctantly, Armbruster headed to his chamber next door to change into proper attire for dinner. He rolled his eyes, frustrated with Alexis. She always made things difficult. Armbruster believed there were better ways to address the current situation. In his opinion, this young, inexperienced Witch was useless to them. What could she do to help? Armbruster planned to grill Cazzandra over dinner, ensuring she got the message that he was unhappy about her moving into the Command Wing of the Palace.

As if Alexis read his mind, she yelled at him from next door, "Don't even think about making her uncomfortable. I warn you, Armbruster. We need her. You will see."

Minutes later, Cazzandra entered the dining hall, feeling anxious. She noticed two waitstaff members standing in the background, holding trays. One of the commoners approached, smiling. "May I help you?" he politely asked, noticing she looked lost.

"Umm, the Queen asked me to join her for dinner. I assume this is where I am supposed to be for that?" She apprehensively responded.

"Yes, the Queen informed us you would attend dinner tonight. You are Cazzandra, I assume? Please, take a seat here." The young commoner gestured for her to take a seat and placed a glass filled with a swirling blue liquid in front of her. After a quick bow, he hurried off, leaving her alone in the room. Cazzandra nervously scanned the area, taking in the sight of two, tall doors standing wide open, leading out to the balcony, where she could see leaves falling onto the Trimber deck.

The brisk breeze coming into the room caused her to shiver. She wondered if they planned to close the doors. It was getting cold. The second commoner approached the stone fireplace and ignited the stack of Trimber logs. Minutes later, a fire flickered in the stone fireplace, warming the room. The doors to the balcony were now shut, but the curtains remained open, allowing for a spectacular view of the valley below.

Suddenly, the two commoners stood at attention. The Queen entered, followed by Armbruster and Yarlen. Cazzandra rose from the seat, waiting for the Queen to take hers.

"Please, everyone, sit," Alexis commanded. Armbruster took his seat beside Alexis, and Yarlen chose to sit next to Cazzandra. He smiled at her, and she nodded, happy to be near someone she trusted and liked. It eased her nervousness.

"I am so glad you are here with us, Cazzandra. Are you warm enough?" Alexis noticed she shivered and rubbed her hands.

"Yes, my Queen. I am fine. It was a little chilly, but the fire is helping."

"Perhaps we need to provide you with a hot drink?" Alexis suggested, waving to draw the servers' attention, who instantly nodded and rushed toward the Queen.

"Your Majesties, what may I do for you?" he quickly asked, bent down, listening for instructions.

"You may bring us something warm to drink. Also, we are ready for our first course," Alexis responded.

"Right away, My Queen. We will return shortly." The two servers ran off to retrieve the Trillay with the meal's first course.

"So, Cazzandra, please tell us a little about yourself. I know very little about you," Armbruster began, giving Alexis a snide look. He turned his head and gazed at Cazzandra.

Alexis wanted to kill him. *'How dare he start shit this early?'* she thought, furious with him. "Oh, come on, dear. Let's eat first. We don't need to start with an inquisition," Alexis joked, hoping to lighten the mood.

"No, it is fine. I am happy to share anything you wish to know about me. Please feel free to ask," Cazzandra replied confidently.

"See, dear, she is okay," Armbruster said, giving her an evil look. "So, tell us about your childhood. Where did you grow up, and how did you end up here?"

"I grew up on Earth, specifically in Ireland. My mother and her family lived there for generations. After both of my parents died, my grandmother adopted me. Eventually, I attended school and moved to Alstromia. Now, I live here, in the Palace, and love it," she gleefully announced.

"Do you ever return to Ireland? Do you have any relatives there?" asked Armbruster, intrigued.

"After my grandmother's passing, I no longer feel the urge to visit Ireland. I am content to live on Alstromia and intend to remain here for as long as I am welcome. I look forward to learning from Yarlen. He is an exemplary teacher and Wizzard," Cazzandra expressed.

Alexis watched Armbruster and Cazzandra's interaction. It was a relief to her that they seemed comfortable around each other. The last thing she needed was someone new on the team, causing issues.

The wait staff placed food on the table and walked away, allowing them time to eat. Yarlen remained quiet, listening and observing. He ate his meal, wondering why Armbruster insisted he attend the dinner. But, since the meal was delicious, Yarlen didn't complain.

The four remained in the dining hall for a while. Unexpectedly, Andreh entered the room, followed by Rammadar. Alexis knew immediately that they were about to share bad news. Rammadar approached Armbruster and whispered in his ear. Armbruster shook his head and grabbed Yarlen.

"I am sorry, Alexis and Cazzandra. Please excuse us. We have an urgent matter that I must address immediately," Armbruster explained as he and Yarlen rushed out of the room, followed by Rammadar and Andreh. Andreh turned around briefly and shrugged his shoulders as he looked at Alexis.

Alexis felt tempted to leave, too. She was flooded with curiosity about what Rammadar had shared with Armbruster.

However, she ultimately decided to remain in the dining hall and get to know Cazzandra.

After less than thirty minutes, Alexis could not stand the unknown. She informed Cazzandra that she was needed in the Command Team Chamber. The fact that Andreh did not return to update her meant something serious had occurred. It infuriated her that Armbruster refused to inform her about what was happening. But she was not worried. She would get to the bottom of it.

Cazzandra placed her napkin on the table and thanked the waitstaff for the fantastic service. Believing dinner had gone well, she returned to the dungeon, eager to complete her project. In a way, things were a bit strange. Some of her life experiences were ending. Fortunately, now, there was a new beginning. It was exciting, and she was thrilled. Cazzandra could not wait to see what was about to unfold.

CHAPTER 2

*C*azzandra entered the laboratory, still in a fabulous mood. The night was memorable, and the dinner was delicious. She was unaccustomed to eating such fine food, though it was a nice change. She wondered when Andreh planned to fill her in on her job responsibilities. She was eager to spend more time with him.

Cazzandra planned to work in the laboratory until she knew what was required, concocting her new potion. It was a special item she wanted to present to the Queen. She hoped it would impress her. The Queen was a formidable Witch with high expectations. Cazzandra was intimidated but wished she could hide her nervousness from Alexis. She wondered if Armbruster felt satisfied with her responses to his questions. She had answered them truthfully, though she had left out some minor details of her life. Cazzandra did not feel the need to elaborate with the Royals, believing her privacy was essential.

Years ago, her grandmother had taught her not to divulge too much information. It was best to keep some things private. Now, Cazzandra felt more than ever that she needed to live by that rule. Until she knew the Queen better, she planned to be forthright with her answers but not volunteer any other details. After all, everyone had secrets!

Andreh observed Armbruster and Yarlen. They sat near each other at the other end of the conference table, whispering. He could not help but wonder what they were discussing. Rammadar approached the group with two of his aides, looking rather glum and quite tired.

His eyes were bloodshot, and he had dark, puffy circles under them.

"Armbruster, I have pertinent information to share!" Rammadar declared proudly.

"Okay, please, what is it?" Armbruster was eager to hear the news.

"Sir, I have spoken with several W3s from Earth. Rumor has it that Gardone, not Zandorah, is responsible for the attack. Supposedly, he has amassed a large group of Warlocks, working together to overtake Alstromia."

Armbruster contemplated his words, frowning. "And how reliable is your source, Rammadar? I cannot approach the Queen on the basis of hearsay. I must ensure the information is accurate. We cannot assume," demanded Armbruster. He stood up and faced Rammadar.

"My source is trustworthy. I have known her for years. Trust me. There is no one closer to him right now. She could be at risk if Gardone finds out she has shared this information. We must keep her out of this as much as possible. I assured her protection, Your Majesty. I plan to honor my promise." Rammadar glared at Armbruster. He wondered why he was in his face, acting so overly aggressive. Rammadar assumed that Armbruster feared repercussions from the Queen if the evidence proved false.

Armbruster felt confident that Rammadar would have prescreened his source. He would not allow someone to make false claims. Rammadar was resourceful and excellent at his job, with the ability to read between the lines. Therefore, Armbruster decided to listen to what Rammadar had uncovered. Afterward, Armbruster would decide whether to share it with his wife.

Unfortunately, there wasn't much time to reflect on the news. Alexis entered the chamber, followed by Aerianna. Both looked perturbed. Armbruster approached his wife, hoping to intercept her before she heard what they were discussing. But Alexis had a keen sense of what they deliberated. She noticed the serious demeanor on everyone's faces. Aerianna wondered why Pauto was not in the room or part of the discussion.

Aerianna made her way toward Andreh and gently pulled him aside, facing him. "Where is Pauto? He was not in his room earlier. Have you seen him?" Aerianna asked. Andreh squirmed around, acting odd.

"No, I don't know where Pauto may be at the moment. Sorry, Aerianna. I promise to inform him that you wish to speak with him, in the event we meet today."

Aerianna wondered what Andreh was hiding from her. He gazed out the window rather than look her in the face. She hoped nothing had happened to Pauto. Hopefully, he was not investigating the strike on the kingdom. It could put him in harm's way. She hated the idea of even thinking about it, but it crossed her mind more than once.

Pauto was headstrong and a fierce protector. Undoubtedly, he was actively seeking the truth about who might be responsible. It scared Aerianna to death. Aerianna rolled her eyes with impatience, walking away. She knew Andreh was lying. However, she couldn't prove it yet.

Alexis carefully observed Andreh, who appeared listless. She assumed he was pretty uncomfortable, which made her wonder about his conversation with Aerianna.

Andreh chose to flee the room, eager to locate Pauto. It was not like him to miss such a crucial meeting. Minutes later, Andreh approached the central Courtyard of the Palace. He saw Trixxie's lifeless body draped over a pile of rocks and Trimber logs. He assumed she would be cremated shortly. Andreh found one of the commoners and informed him to hold off on the ritual until he spoke with Alexis, asking if she planned to attend the ceremony.

The young Warlock acknowledged Andreh's request and informed the others standing by. It was best to wait for further guidance. No one wanted to cremate the

Queen's pet without her presence. That could lead to potentially serious repercussions. Andreh returned to the Palace, eager to speak with Alexis.

Trixxie's final send-off needed to be completed quickly. No one wanted the beast to stay on the Palace grounds longer than necessary. As he was about to enter the chamber, she opened the door.

"Alexis, may I have a moment with you privately?" Andreh requested.

"Sure. I was on my way out. What is it?" the Queen inquired impatiently.

"I have everything set up to cremate Trixxie and send her down the river toward the deep waters, allowing her to rest in peace. We want to begin the ritual right away. I assume you wish to attend?" Andreh explained.

Alexis contemplated his words. She wanted to scream. It broke her heart to think about Trixxie. She wondered if she could have saved her if she had not hesitated to cast a spell earlier. Now, it was a moot point. The enormous beast was dead.

Yes, Trixxie deserved a proper send-off to her final destination. Alexis agreed. She planned to watch the entire process and, afterward, properly mourn.

Andreh nodded, realizing how difficult this event was for Alexis. He walked beside her as they made their way to the Palace Courtyard.

Once Alexis spotted Trixxie, she dropped to the ground, crying. Andreh stood close to Alexis, unsure of how to proceed. He felt confused about her preferences. Should he hold her, cry with her, or remain standing next to the Queen? Alexis refused to speak.

Alexis looked up at Andreh, her face wet from tears. Her bottom lip quivered, and she grabbed his hand, pulling him down beside her. She held him and cried. Andreh remained stiff, not wanting to appear too close to the Queen. Others watched. Some snickered, finding it funny that Andreh tried to act aloof toward the Queen when everyone knew the two were having an affair.

Finally, Alexis released Andreh's hand and managed to stand. Shakily, Alexis approached Trixxie. She placed her right hand on the beast's giant head, inching closer and resting against Trixxie. At that moment, Andreh desperately fought back the tears.

It was too much watching Alexis suffer. Andreh could see how much she loved Trixxie, which honestly broke his heart. He turned his back, unable to stand the pain it caused him. He wondered how Alexis would survive this tragic event.

After a few minutes, she walked away from the giant creature. She nodded to the commoners, allowing them to light the Trimber logs, which would incinerate the

Draghoon. As the flames engulfed Trixxie, Alexis stood bravely next to Andreh. Strangely, she stopped crying. Alexis glared at the giant, glowing flames, emotionless. Andreh feared she was experiencing a nervous breakdown.

On the other hand, maybe she was contemplating revenge and retaliation for all who died that day. Andreh did not know what the Queen planned to do, but knew he would support her actions.

It did not take long for Trixxie's body to turn into dust. Alexis cast a spell to expedite the process, unable to stand the otherwise lengthy procedure. It was killing her to watch it. Alexis ordered Trixxie's remains to be placed into the four large Ozar boxes Yarlen had created for the occasion. The boxes were purple and numbered, with the Snipperdoom-Hextinghton names and logo engraved onto them.

Alexis, Andreh, and two commoners planned to accompany Trixxie's remains as she floated down the river on a long, flat boat. Andreh and Alexis would observe from the royal sailboat moored off the docks in the City of Miccay.

An hour later, Trixxie's ashes were carefully loaded onto the smaller boat and secured with Trimber tethers. Alexis and Andreh stepped onto the royal sailboat, the

Zintherdom, named after her Great-Grandfather, Westerthal Zintherdom, IV. The Queen chose to sit on a bench facing the boat's bow. This way, she could watch the smaller boat headed toward the Sea of Miccay.

The journey would take hours, but Alexis did not care. She enjoyed the brisk breeze and the smell of autumn in the air. Fall had always been one of her favorite seasons. Sadly, the memories of this day would ruin the Queen's future seasons. It would hang over her like a dark cloud. Alexis cringed at the thought.

Nonetheless, she stared ahead, thinking about finally releasing Trixxie back to the Sea. Trixxie's loss was catastrophic on every level. The beast had been exceptional, and Alexis doubted she would ever find another like her. She wept, watching the small boat drift down the river, gently rocking side to side as a commoner steered it toward the Sea. The dramatic final moments of Tixxie's send-off were heartbreaking.

Andreh held the Queen's hand. He did not care what others thought, realizing she needed his support. He knew this day was one she would never forget, which was heartwrenching.

Back in the Palace, Armbruster met with Rammadar, Yarlen, and a few others. They discussed potential scenarios for what could happen next. Pauto was still missing, which worried Armbruster. He pulled aside Yarlen and asked him about Pauto's whereabouts. Unfortunately, Yarlen was clueless. He had no idea where Pauto was or what he was doing. It was bizarre.

Andreh was also absent since he had informed Armbruster he planned to attend Trixxie's send-off, helping Alexis. For once, Armbruster agreed with his decision. It was better for Andreh to support Alexis. Armbruster did not care to witness Alexis falling apart because of a Draghoon's death. Armbruster felt it was ridiculous. Trixxie was just a beast. There was no need to get too emotional, as far as he was concerned. But then, he knew Alexis loved Trixxie. He felt a twinge of remorse for his lack of empathy. However, he quickly pushed that feeling aside, realizing that there were more pressing issues to address with the group.

Pauto approached the small, rickety Trimber door. It was painted an obnoxiously hot pink, peeling in a few spots. Nervously, he knocked on the door, hoping she would be home.

It did not take long for Farla to answer. She opened the squeaky door with a crooked smile on her face. She knew precisely why Pauto was there, and it thrilled her. "Hello, Pauto. I knew you would arrive. Please, enter my humble abode," she screeched, allowing him to enter. The hut smelled musky. There was an underlying, strange, putrid smell, too. He wondered what had caused that. He walked toward the fireplace, taking a seat on the stone hearth.

Farla watched him and leaned back in an old reclining chair, covering herself with a crocheted blanket. "So, the Queen needs my help? Why else would you be here?" she asked, feeling smug.

"If you know why I am here, then let us not play games, Farla. We need help securing the planet. You must be aware of everything that has transpired today. So, what can you offer us, and what do you desire in exchange?" Pauto demanded. He knew her price would be steep, but the Queen and Armbruster would agree, if for no other reason than to ensure the safety of all Clan members.

"Well, yes. I saw it all unravel before my ancient eyes. However, it was not unexpected. It was bound to happen. The Queen has ruffled many feathers. She has quite a slew of enemies. However, this move was quite bold. I presume you know who is responsible?" The old Witch inquired, glaring at Pauto, who shrugged his shoulders.

"Hmm, so you do not know. How interesting! Do you wish to find out? Or are you more interested in the planet's security? Please tell me specifically what you want. I am too old for guessing games. I want facts."

The Witch waited a moment for Pauto to respond. He stood up and locked eyes with Farla. "You know, it doesn't matter who did this. Our current focus is on security. So, if you want to help, that's fine. Do not waste my time if you don't wish to assist us. I will need to find someone else to help. Time is of the essence. I must return to the King with an update. What will it be, Farla?" Pauto asserted. He remained focused on her face. She lowered her gaze and focused on her bony hands, ignoring Pauto's fiery stare. She pondered his words, fiddling with the blanket.

"Sure. I can help. My price is the following: I want a job on the Royal Staff. It must be guaranteed. I demand the ability to continue providing support to the kingdom. I also want to live in my hut. I do not wish to reside in the Palace. It is too lavish for my lifestyle."

"Okay. I am confident we can work with those requests. Now, what can you do to help? You have not identified how you will earn your keep. Please, be specific," Pauto shot back.

"I can secure the planet with a spell using my original potions. I will require an assistant. Please find one for me. Return to the Palace and Armbruster and inform him of my offer. Come back once the deal is made. Until then, I will remain here. Please, feel free to leave," Farla clarified.

Pauto strolled toward the door, planning to depart. At the last minute, Farla shrieked, "I want nothing to do with the Queen. My dealings are with Armbruster and you. Is that clear?"

"Yes, it is understood, Farla." Pauto closed the door on the way out. He recalled that the Queen and Farla did not get along. It was best to keep Alexis out of the negotiations and allow Armbruster to make the final decision. Pauto jumped on his Torrin, flying back to the Palace. He was excited to share the news with the King.

At the base of the mountain, the river opened up and flowed into the Sea of Miccay, miles from the City of Miccay. The river became choppy. The small boat carrying Trixxie's ashes almost toppled over several times.

Alexis asked Andreh to retrieve the commoner off the smaller boat, allowing the craft to drift into the deep waters alone. Once the commoner was on board the Zintherdom, Alexis stood up, watching as Trixxie's vessel capsized. The giant waves of the ocean enveloped it. She ordered the Zintherdom to return to the city, unwilling to enter the treacherous water of the Sea of Miccay.

On the way back, Alexis sobbed. Though she was grateful to have witnessed Trixxie's final departure, it still broke her heart. She felt relieved that Trixxie would now become one again with the magical deep waters. Alexis began to smile as she thought about the completion of the ritual and wondered if she would ever find another Draghoon to love as she did Trixxie.

Andreh sat beside Alexis with his arm protectively wrapped around her shoulder. She trembled, and it was getting dark. One of the commoners approached, holding a lantern, and handed it to Andreh. He took it with his free hand and placed it on the deck in front of them. Alexis stared straight ahead, remaining silent on the boat for the last few hours. It worried Andreh. He wanted to speak, but felt it best to act respectfully and keep his mouth shut. Watching her hurt and being unable to do anything about it was difficult. Alexis mourned and was uninterested in idle chatter.

Inside the Palace, Armbruster leaned back in the comfortable chair in the chamber. Yarlen snoozed, his head snapping as he nodded off to sleep. He looked around, embarrassed. Armbruster smirked at him, finding it funny that the old Wizzard chose to remain in the room rather than head back to his chamber. However, Yarlen was a committed friend, and Armbruster was grateful.

Suddenly, Pauto appeared. He looked wide-eyed, quickly speaking to fill in the others on the news. Armbruster had difficulty understanding him.

"Pauto, for goodness sake, calm down. What about Farla?" Armbruster declared.

"I am sorry, My King. I was saying that I spoke with Farla. We have a plan. Please, allow me to share her stipulations," Pauto outlined the Witch's demands and what she offered in return.

Armbruster jumped out of his seat. "What the hell? Is she trying to blackmail us into accepting her help? NO! I refuse the extortion!" reiterated Armbruster angrily.

Pauto stared at Armbruster, biting his lip nervously, trying to figure out how to respond. "Sir, it is a negotiation. May I remind you that she has the upper hand? Please, let us find a way to work together," Pauto pleaded.

"Say what you will. Farla is using this tragic circumstance against us. What a wicked Witch! However, do you genuinely believe she can help us?"

"Yes, Your Majesty," Pauto retorted.

Yarlen agreed with Pauto. It made no sense to worry about Farla's price. Instead, they would focus on what the Witch could provide. It was more important. The payment could be renegotiated further later. The group unanimously agreed to hire Farla.

In the City of Miccay, Andreh helped Alexis off the boat. He held tightly onto her hand as the dock was wet and slippery. Once they stood on the cobblestone streets, he waved his wand, transporting them back to the Palace.

Andreh sat on the edge of the bed as Alexis gazed out of the window in her chamber. "Will you be okay, Alexis? Do you wish for me to stay a while? I am happy to remain here as long as you need me," Andreh offered.

Alexis continued to stare out at the valley below. She acted stoic, though she wanted to scream, cry, and pound her fists. She felt a tremendous loss, one she was unsure of how to survive. She knew Andreh meant well, but she wanted to be left alone.

"No, you may leave. I need time to reflect on my feelings. I am sure you can understand that. I do appreciate all you have done. Your support means the world to me." Alexis spun around and approached Andreh. She embraced him, holding him tightly, feeling guilty. The last thing she wanted was for him to be upset with her.

Andreh smelled her hair and perfume, as he ran his hand up her leg, eliciting feelings he knew were inappropriate during this time. Unexpectedly, there was a loud knock on the door. Andreh released her and moved to the other side of the room.

Armbruster entered. He scowled at the sight of Andreh. Alexis noticed immediately. "What can I do for you, Armbruster? I am exhausted and need my rest. We just returned from Trixxie's funeral." Alexis wanted Armbruster to know she was not ready for any form of confrontation about Andreh.

The Queen had suffered enough for one day and needed sleep. She hoped to forget the day's grueling, heartbreaking event.

"I am not here to start a fight. However, we must speak privately. Andreh, please leave," Armbruster ordered. Andreh bowed before the Royals and quickly exited the chamber.

Alexis remained standing, ready to hear what he had to say. Armbruster did not waste time. He outlined the potential new plan to help Alstromia using Farla. Alexis sneered, displeased at the thought of asking her for help. The Witch was talented but too demanding. Alexis chose to speak up.

"Alright, I understand your point. But I think I have a better idea. Let's reach out to Cazzandra again and let her know that we urgently need her assistance. I believe it would be more beneficial to involve her instead of Farla. What are your thoughts on this, Armbruster?" Alexis inquired urgently.

Armbruster vehemently disagreed. He did not feel that Cazzandra was ready for such an urgent task. She was too inexperienced. Even if Yarlen worked with her, it was still risky. The young Witch was just beginning her lengthy apprenticeship with Yarlen.

Alexis begrudgingly concurred with Armbruster's assessment of Cazzandra. Nevertheless, it was a risky decision that she was willing to make. Armbruster was shocked by Alexis's bold choice to entrust the planet's fate to an unfamiliar and inexperienced Witch, and he vehemently opposed the plan, making his displeasure known.

If Alexis planned to push forward with her plan, he would seek legal guidance from Head Legal Counsel (*HLC*) Jamessihn Shorttar. If need be, they would convene a Clan Council meeting and ascertain a way to bypass the Queen's ruling.

Alexis was not thinking clearly after the loss of her pet Draghoon. Her judgment was questionable, and Armbruster planned to take charge! He would rather give Farla what she requested in return for her services than allow Cazzandra the opportunity.

"Why are you so opposed to Cazzandra's help? She is a gifted young Witch. You are prejudiced against her. Stop it, Armbruster. I must insist. She is my choice. I will ask her to help us, and you have no say. Deal with it. Now, please, depart my room," Alexis asserted, walking him to the door.

Alexis was mentally exhausted from the arguments with him. Grudgingly, Armbruster left her chamber, shaking his head. However, he was not giving in so easily. He planned to visit HLC Shorttar and request feedback on how to proceed. Armbruster had worked with Jamessihn Shorttar before, resolving tricky situations. Armbruster felt that teamwork was essential in these circumstances.

It would be the best way to ensure everything was handled correctly and in accordance with the law. Jamessihn would also know how to legally control Alexis. That way, Armbruster would not have to overstep and further infuriate her. She would be forced to do what was best for the planet and not her ego. Armbruster grinned at the thought as he headed to the Palace gates.

He would transport himself to the Shorttar residence in the City of Miccay. It did not matter to Armbruster that it was getting late. Jamessihn would understand the urgency of his visit. Furthermore, Armbruster knew he had no time to waste.

Alexis was working to quickly implement her plan. Jamessihn had never been a fan of Alexis Snipperdoom. However, he was friends with her husband, Armbruster. They frequently attended meetings and met at Henrii's Potions and BrewHaus to indulge in a few of his famous potions and brews. He was highly concerned about the recent attack on Alstromia and wondered what was being done behind the scenes to protect it.

As Jamessihn relaxed in the living room, chatting with Shonderra Bluemount, his girlfriend, they were interrupted by an unexpected pounding noise on the front door. Staring at the clock over the fireplace, Jamessihn wondered who would come to his residence at this hour. It was almost 10 o'clock at night. He excused himself and left Shonderra alone while he marched to the entryway to confront the visitor.

Jamessihn opened the door and was shocked to see Armbruster standing on his doorstep. He looked disheveled and tired. Without hesitation, Jamessihn invited him into the lavish home. Once in the hallway, he immediately confronted him about his visit.

"Though it is always a pleasure to see you, Armbruster, I am perplexed about the timing of your visit. Why are you here? Are you okay? Is everything alright with the Queen?"

"Jamessihn, I seek your brilliant guidance with a touchy matter concerning my wife. It is quite complicated, and I need to know what I can do, legally, to stop her," explained Armbruster excitedly. He needed options presented to him ASAP.

"Ah, I see. Well, I guess we'd better head to the living room to chat. Please follow me," Jamessihn responded. The two Wizzards entered the room, ready to begin their discussion. Shonderra stood up, looking perplexed.

"Your Majesty! What a surprise," she exclaimed, bowing respectfully before the King.

"Please, Shonderra, no need to bow. We are friends and not in public. But I must speak privately with Jamessihn. "

Shonderra nodded and excused herself, heading to the bedroom, allowing them privacy to converse more freely.

"So, tell me what has happened, Armbruster. I assume it is related to the recent strike on Alstromia?" Jamessihn questioned.

"Yes and no. We require help in the form of new magic to keep our planet from being bombarded with fire, bombs, and spells. Yarlen has everything in place, for now, to keep things secure. Unfortunately, the spell in place is impermanent. It will dissipate in time. So, we must find another solution. I want Farla Summerstahr to aid us. Alexis is not keen on the idea and insists that we enlist the help of a young Witch named Cazzandra. She does not have Farla's experience or expertise. I worry that Cazzandra cannot concoct a potion and create a spell in time to save our planet. What can we legally do to stop Alexis and Cazzandra?" Armbruster stared at Jamessihn with begging eyes. He was desperate.

"Wow, that is a problem. I am so very sorry to hear about your disagreement with your wife. Unfortunately, I am not sure you can stop Alexis from enforcing her plan to utilize the younger Witch. She is the Queen, and the power to decide what is best for the planet and its residents lies with her. Furthermore, the only way to remove that power is to declare her mentally unfit. That process can take time. It sounds like this is an urgent matter and time-sensitive. Therefore, I am not sure you have the options you desire. I realize it is not what you want to hear," Jamessihn explained.

The two Wizzards looked at each other, remaining quiet. Armbruster thought about Jamessihn's suggestion. The implication was clear. He had to find a way to claim and prove that Alexis was mentally incompetent.

"So, let me ask you this, Jamessihn. Would her grief be enough to declare her mentally unsound? She is grief-stricken by the loss of her cherished pet, Trixxie. She is not of sound mind right now. Would that stick in court if we temporarily tried to remove her power?" Armbruster asked.

He wanted Jamessihn to know that he was desperate but clearly wanted to remain within the guidelines. Anything else would cause him problems.

Jamessihn tilted his head back, concentrating on the ceiling. He contemplated the options. "I do not believe that grief alone will be enough. You will need a stronger argument if we are to temporarily remove her from her throne. It is not an easy feat. To prove her inability to rule, she must be acting erratically, making bold, irresponsible decisions that are well documented. We need witnesses willing to testify against her. It is the only way."

"That will be difficult. Her staff is loyal. Even if they disagreed with her, they would never go against her, for fear of future repercussions. I doubt I can find witnesses willing to attest before the court to say Alexis is incapable of ruling her kingdom," Armbruster responded.

"I understand. What will you do?" Jamessihn questioned, noticing his friend looked nervous.

"Maybe it is better you don't know, Jamessihn. If I need you, I will reach out." Armbruster stood up, shook his hand, and marched toward the door.

"Armbruster, please stay vigilant. Alexis is brilliant. She will not allow you to take her kingdom away so easily. If you need anything, please do not hesitate to ask. I am always here for you, friend."

Jamessihn closed the door, returning to the living room. Shonderra was already seated on the couch, shaking with fright. She was unhappy after overhearing their conversation.

"Please don't get involved. It will end badly. I do not want to move back to Earth or Iriss. I beg you, James. I love you...Be careful!" Shonderra always called him James when she was either happy or mad, so he knew she meant business. He nodded, unwilling to be part of Armbruster's scheme.

Outside the Shorttar residence, Armbruster surveyed the area. It was a quiet night. There were dark clouds in the sky, hiding the twin moons. Occasionally, one of the moons tried to peek out, beaming bright light onto the Village of Miccay. Armbruster realized Jamessihn was correct. It was nearly impossible to face off against Alexis. However, he had a few things going for him. One, the affair with Andreh. Two, her grief from losing Trixxie. So, there could be a way to remove her from power, allowing him to step in and make the necessary changes.

First, however, he would enlist Farla's help and deal with Alexis later, once she felt better. Eager to begin, Armbruster planned to round up his team, including Yarlen, Pauto, and Rammadar, asking for their assistance in revising the plan. It would take careful development and secrecy. There were a few Wizzards and Warlocks that Armbruster trusted.

CHAPTER 3

lexis knew there was always more to a story. Armbruster liked to leave out pertinent information. At times, he did this on purpose. Other times, her husband felt it was in her best interest not to know specific facts. Nonetheless, Alexis believed that every tangled web of deceit would eventually disintegrate, leaving behind nothing but the cold, hard truth!

Armbruster felt hesitant to meet with Alexis, though she requested his immediate presence in her chamber. It was almost midnight, and Armbruster was tired. Plus, he felt guilty about his previous meeting with the other Wizzards. Most agreed Alexis was unstable and currently incapable of making wise decisions. Some were even willing to attest to that, but others disagreed. Many worried Alexis would end their lives if she learned about their participation in removing her from power.

Reluctantly, Armbruster knocked on the Queen's door. She yelled for him to enter, which he did, slowly approaching her bed. She sat upright, looking beautiful. Her long black hair cascaded down the front of her body, resting on her chest. Her lips were rosy, and her eyes were watery, probably from crying.

"Please, come closer, Armbruster. Sit next to me," Alexis insisted.

Cautiously, he obliged. Alexis reached for his hand as he sat down. She flashed a smile at Armbruster, which posed a challenge for him. She looked fragile, and he felt the urge to comfort her.

"What may I do for you, dear?" Armbruster asked, wondering why she had summoned him at this hour of the night.

"I need you! Please, stay with me tonight. I do not wish to be alone. I ordered Karita to ensure no one disturbs me." Alexis removed the blanket from her body.

Immediately, Armbruster saw that Alexis was naked. She looked sexy against the dark, red sheets. Her perfect body glowed by the only light in the room, emanating from the fireplace. His heart began racing with desire for her. She ran her hand down her body, teasing him as she watched his reaction. He wanted desperately to make love to her, but he knew that would complicate everything he was about to do.

Armbruster jumped off the bed. "No, I feel it is best to retire to my chamber. We had a horrible day. Neither of us is thinking clearly." He bent down and kissed her on the forehead, turning to leave the room.

"Are you serious?" Alexis screeched. "I am naked, ready to make love with my husband, and you say NO?" Alexis looked puzzled. She had never been turned down like that before. It infuriated her greatly. Embarrassed, she pulled the sheet up to her chest, now feeling self-conscious.

Armbruster turned around and faced her, standing near the door, ready to exit the room. "Alexis, you are out of your mind with grief. You need rest, not sex. Grow up!" He stormed out of the room, slamming the heavy chamber door. It was the only way he figured he could avoid having sex with her. Plus, he did not want to take advantage of Alexis when she was grieving. That seemed low, even for him. He headed to his chamber next door, hoping she was not too upset with him. She could get vengeful, and he did not need that.

Alexis pouted, feeling lonely and wanting to spend the night with Armbruster. She looked at the fireplace, wondering if she could fall asleep. She heard Armbruster enter the room next door, and his chamber door closed loudly. *'Pissed off, Armbruster?'* she thought. *'Oh well, join the club. I am angry, too.'*

Seething, she scooted down into the bed, hoping the warmth of the fluffy blanket would lull her to sleep. Before too long, she snored lightly, dreaming of Andreh.

On Iriss, Zandorah was still awake and unable to sleep. She had left the meeting with her staff an hour earlier, determining that Gardone and his goons were responsible for the War declared on Alstromia. Zandorah was still shocked. Her mother, Lorthana, sat across from her in a chair, eyes closed. The older Witch was exhausted and wanted to sleep, but knew her daughter was listless and unable to rest. So, she chose to stay with her.

"Darling, why don't we try to sleep? We need a break! You look bushed. You have dark circles under your eyes. In the morning, I will head to Alstromia and speak with Alexis, explaining that you are not responsible for the strike on her planet. Trust me, your sister will understand. I promise," Lorthana stressed.

"Sure, go ahead and retire for the night. I am not tired and cannot sleep. My mind is racing. I want to know what Dad is thinking. How can he do something like this? And worse, he made it look as if I were responsible! What a coward. I have always given him the benefit of the doubt, but we are done. I cannot condone his actions," screamed Zandorah.

Lorthana agreed with her daughter. Gardone was a coward. She was glad their Dismissal of Ceremony had been granted, and Lorthana was no longer married to the wicked Warlock. She sighed with relief. Lorthana informed Zandorah that she planned to retire to her chamber for the night. She was exhausted and could barely keep her eyes open. Plus, she hoped that if she left, Zandorah would eventually relax, too, and fall asleep.

Zandorah kissed her mother on the cheek and gave her a strong bear hug. Lorthana pulled away, looking at her child, who was now crying. It killed her to see her daughter so unhappy. Rather than get into another lengthy and time-consuming conversation, she smiled, kissed her back, and left the room quickly.

Now alone in the room, Zandorah walked to the window near the fireplace. She pulled back the heavy curtains and took in the scenery. She contemplated what Alexis was doing at that moment and whether she blamed her for everything that had happened.

Zandorah hoped not. She wanted her sister to believe her innocence. Nothing that had transpired was Zandorah's fault. It was all their father, Gardone! He truly was an evil Warlock. It took Zandorah a long time to come to this conclusion. She never wanted to believe the stories she heard from others regarding her father.

Even when Alexis insisted their father had kidnapped her, Zandorah did not believe Alexis. She was sure that somehow Alexis was responsible for what had transpired in the cabin at the top of Tullah Mountain. Unfortunately, now that the facts were revealed, Zandorah had to agree that Gardone was sinister and calculating. He did not deserve her trust or kindness. She planned to remove him from her life and never allow him to be part of her family again. Zandorah intended to protect her kin at all costs, including her stubborn sister, Alexis.

Shawnatar appeared unexpectedly. He smiled as he approached Zandorah, holding a giant bouquet of flowers. He looked handsome, dressed in black slacks, an emerald green tunic, and black shoes.

"What a wonderful surprise," Zandorah delightfully declared. Lately, he had been absent too much, and she missed him.

"How are you, beautiful? I can only imagine how much this day has worn you out. I am here now. How can I make things better for you, baby?" he lovingly asked, holding the flowers with one hand. He pulled her toward him using his other hand, embracing her. He whispered into her ear, "I love you so much!"

Zandorah took the flowers from his hand and carefully placed them on the round table beside her. She turned around and embraced Shawnatar, grateful for his support and love.

On the other side of the Palace, Armbruster stared at his bed. He thought about Alexis and fantasized about how he could be making love to her right now, feeling her sexy and firm body. Then it occurred to him why he had left her room so quickly. He was actively working to remove her from power, taking over as head of the kingdom.

Eventually, Alexis would hate him and retaliate, so it was best to keep his distance. In time, she would run back to Andreh, no doubt. The thought made him want to throw up. Armbruster changed into his long, old, and comfortable nightshirt. It made him realize how much he had aged, appreciating the simple things in the last few years. As his mind wandered, he realized it had been a while since he had spent time with his daughter, Lilah.

Armbruster flopped onto his bed and thought about it. It hit him hard to realize it had been over a week! How was that even possible? He had not spent time with his only child in a week. What kind of awful father was he? *'When did Alexis last see Lilah?'* he wondered. In the morning, he planned to eat breakfast with Lilah. He wanted to hold his precious daughter.

Armbruster vowed to become a better and more attentive father. He had been so focused on other things he had neglected his child. It was a terrible thing. Shaking his head in disgust, he crawled into bed, closing his eyes.

Pauto entered the room to find Aerianna asleep. He could hear her snoring. She faced the wall, away from the window, and pulled the blanket up to her nose. She looked peaceful. He quickly removed his clothes and slipped into bed, snuggling against her naked body. He was surprised. Aerianna usually slept in a long nightgown, preferring to cover her body. Happy she was not wearing it tonight, he rubbed her bottom, hoping she would wake up so he could spend quality time with her in bed. She moaned lightly, turning around to face him.

Aerianna smiled, then kissed Pauto and embraced him in bed. She loved him more than she had ever loved anyone and was about to prove it to him, making his night.

Unfortunately, the night was not over for Gardone or his team of evil-doers. They partied on Earth, feeling victorious. Some were intoxicated from drinking and celebrating too much. Gardone despised drunk Warlocks. He hated their rambunctious demeanor. Feeling disgusted, he left the party to head to his hut in the woods. He wished that Sharlottah Zipmound were around. He needed the attention of a female. He missed being intimate with someone.

Sharlottah, his girlfriend, was young and high-spirited. She had endless energy and wore him out. Nonetheless, he adored her. He entered the hut but felt disappointed when it was dark. He figured she had returned to her home on the coast. She did not enjoy the woods or the darkness. He made his way to his bedroom and undressed, feeling tired. It had been a heck of a day. After all, he waged war against Alexis and Alstromia. The thought thrilled him, and he smirked.

As he slipped into bed, he felt Sharlottah's body. She was asleep, and her athletic body was curled up against a fluffy pillow. The moment she felt Gardone beside her, she whispered, "Welcome home, lover." Sharlottah kissed him, reminding Gardone why he loved her so much.

The new day arrived, and Alexis yawned as she stretched, not quite ready to get out of bed. She heard her stomach growling and realized she was starving. Immediately, she summoned Karita, who appeared expeditiously with a Trillay filled with food.

'How does she always know what I want?' Alexis wondered in awe. The food smelled delicious.

After devouring the excellent breakfast, Alexis chose to shower and dress. She was eager to find Andreh and discuss her plans to enlist Cazzandra. Alexis was ready to make changes and hoped Armbruster and his team would agree to help. If not, she would fire those unwilling to side with her.

Armbruster joined Yarlen and Rammadar in the Security Command Team Chamber to strategize. War plans had to be implemented. Plus, Armbruster wanted to ensure Yarlen was willing to rally against the Queen. Realizing their complicated past, he wondered if Yarlen would agree. Rammadar was not on board with acting against the Queen's wishes, refusing to help remove her from power.

When approached by Armbruster, Rammadar threatened the King, stating that he would rather return to Iriss and work for Zandorah again than participate in the conspiracy to overthrow Alexis Snipperdoom. Rammadar felt it was sneaky and unethical, especially given the current crisis. Armbruster knew his support was lacking. Most Clan members preferred to keep Alexis as the head of the war team.

Armbruster and the Security Command Team were unaware of the presence of the *Ninety-Nightblade Brigade* (*NNB*), a group of ninety armed elite Warlock warriors who had already infiltrated the planet before it was secured. The stealthy *NNB* members managed to hide on Hexxton Mountain undetected and were planning a direct attack on the Palace when no one expected it.

Alexis entered the chamber as if she sensed something was planned behind her back. She squinted her eyes, glaring at Armbruster. He seemed to be deep in discussion, perhaps even plotting. When he noticed Alexis, Armbruster immediately stopped conversing with Rammadar and sat around the conference table, pretending not to see her.

"Did I miss something, Armbruster? You seemed quite animated until I approached. Please, do share, love!" Alexis barked. She was livid, wondering what he was hiding.

"Alexis, calm down. Nothing is happening. You are acting paranoid! We are discussing our war plans. Rammadar is very useful and has some brilliant ideas. Let us enact the Alstromia War Council and ask the Council of Peace & War to provide us with clear guidance on how to move ahead in this matter. We are at war. There is no denying it after what happened yesterday. Today, the enemy has made multiple failed attempts to take down our shield. Yarlen, thankfully, reinforced it by casting another short-term spell. We are running out of time, Alexis. Do something. You are in charge," Armbruster yelled, acting dramatic.

"I see. So, now that things are risky and out of control, you agree that I am in charge. I find that quite interesting," Alexis concurred. "Well, Armbruster, I am in control, and don't forget it. I already contacted the Council of Peace & War yesterday, stating we were under attack. Several representatives will be here today. Someone will have to get them through our protective shield. How you manage that is not of my concern. They will be here at noon, on the west side of the Palace. Make it happen, Armbruster. Yarlen, may I speak with you and Rammadar privately?" Alexis hissed.

Both Warlocks followed Alexis out of the room, heading toward the Landing Deck. Rammadar stood next to Yarlen. They waited for the Queen to speak. She sat on the stone bench, facing the balcony's barrier. Rammadar leaned against the railing, resting his hands on the cold stone surface.

"I want you to know I am not stupid. Before you say anything, I am aware of what Armbruster is plotting. Someone came to my chamber this morning, eager to tell me that my husband was a traitor. I am quite disturbed. So, cut the crap. I want the truth. What do you know?" Alexis demanded. She refused to allow them to lie to her. Not today. Especially after everything that had happened in the last 24 hours, which had been pure hell.

Yarlen figured it was up to him to fill in Alexis. He knew her better than Rammadar. "My Queen, Armbruster is not a traitor. He is worried about your mental capacity. You have been under extreme stress, given the death of Trixxie and the strike on Alstromia. He wants to help you by taking over some of the responsibilities. That is all! Believe me, Armbruster is not crazy. He knows he cannot remove you permanently from the throne," Yarlen explained.

He hoped she would believe him. It was a much kinder story than the truth. If she thought for one second Armbruster was attempting a coup, she would lose her mind. Yarlen was also reluctant to support Armbruster because he had worked diligently to regain Alexis' trust. He refused to allow their newly formed friendship to disintegrate.

"Okay, that is plausible, I suppose. What do you have to say, Rammadar? You and Armbruster are pretty chummy. Do you agree with Yarlen, or do you see it another way?" She wanted his honest opinion. Alexis knew little about Rammadar. She was reluctant to have him on the Security Command Team because he had previously worked for her sister, Zandorah. It seemed strange that he was eager to relocate to Alstromia.

When Alexis learned from Armbruster that he had hired Rammadar, she was leery of his intentions. She wondered if he was a planted spy from Zandorah and her team. She warned Armbruster to keep Rammadar out of all high-security meetings until trust had been established. Armbruster, however, never questioned Rammadar's motives. He knew why Rammadar wanted to reside on

Alstromia, and he missed his friends. So, Armbruster was less cautious about Rammadar than Alexis.

"My Queen, I realize we do not know each other well. My intentions have always been pure and aimed at securing the planet, the Palace, and your family. I believe Armbruster has similar goals. However, I must confess that I am worried about the manner in which he is trying to accomplish it. I have already voiced my displeasure over how he is handling it." Rammadar folded his arms, looking sternly at the Queen. He leaned against the railing, his back facing the valley.

Alexis nodded, seemingly agreeing with him. "Very well. I appreciate your candor. I will keep that in mind. Moving forward, I am assigning you to my team. You will no longer report to Armbruster. Do you understand, Rammadar? I do hope that will not be awkward for you. If it is a problem, let me know. I will speak with my husband and let him know it was my desire. Yarlen, make sure the representatives can get through the protective barrier. If you require any help, consider seeking assistance from Cazzandra." Alexis swiftly got up and departed from the Landing Deck, feeling that the discussion had concluded.

After the Queen's swift departure, Rammadar and Yarlen remained on the

Landing Deck for a few more minutes. Both were stunned. Rammadar was reluctant to report to Alexis but refused to complain.

Instead, he asked Yarlen for some advice. "So, Yarlen, you and the Queen seem to have a stable relationship. Why would she transfer me to her team? Is she trying to get back at Armbruster, or does she believe I can be of service to her? I am utterly confused."

"It is both, my friend. She is sending Armbruster a message that she is still in charge. Plus, she's probably hoping you will help secure the Palace and keep a watchful eye on her family. So, be flattered, but do your job. You do not want to upset Alexis Snipperdoom." Yarlen walked off, heading to the cellar of the Palace to speak with Cazzandra, leaving Rammadar alone.

Cazzandra worked in the basement, organizing her potion shelf. Two new concoctions had been added to her stock, and she felt excited about presenting them to the Queen. Cazzandra named one of the latest inventions the *Blockade Spell*. The spell would hopefully secure the planet from intruders. Though she had not yet thoroughly tested it, she felt confident in her abilities. As she was about to leave the chamber and head outside to test the potion's effectiveness, Yarlen appeared.

"Hello, Cazzandra. I am here to ask for your assistance. The Queen requests we secure the planet in a manner other than what is currently in place. I have also been tasked with allowing certain Council of Peace & War representatives to pass through our current shield. That is a problem. I am unsure about how that can happen without risking Alstromia's security. Do you have any ideas?" Yarlen inquired, hopeful.

Immediately, she flashed a smile and nodded. She handed Yarlen the newest magical potion in a #5 Potion Bottle. "Here, let's step outside and conduct a trial run, shall we? I will cast a spell and pour this liquid onto the ground. Hopefully, we will see tiny spheres fly into the atmosphere, orbiting the planet. They will help ensure no one can penetrate the invisible protective layer, which will be automatically enabled. What do you think, Yarlen?" Cazzandra asked, smiling.

"That is fantastic, Cazzandra. Let us assess it immediately," Yarlen responded excitedly. He could not wait to see if it worked. If it did, he was hopeful the Queen would no longer hound him about the planet's safety. "One quick question. Can we allow the representatives to pass through without disabling the current shield? Have you come up with a solution for that? It is imperative that they can pass through the barrier in place."

"I recommend executing a specialty spell to temporarily allow certain members to penetrate the shield. It will ensure that the planet remains secure while also accommodating the representatives. It is the most practical and effective solution. Shall I proceed with the implementation?" Cazzandra suggested.

"Fabulous! You are truly brilliant. I am hopeful your potion and chant will do the trick." The two sprinted up the stairs, thrilled to be able to try out Cazzandra's newest magic.

Further away, in the Palace, Alexis pounded on Aerianna's bedroom chamber door. She wondered why she had not yet visited her to give updates on the attack. Seconds later, Aerianna appeared, looking rather dreadful. Her hair was messy, and she looked pale as a ghost.

"Alexis, you may wish to stay away. I believe I am ill. I have been throwing up for two days. It is awful."

The Queen stepped back, putting a little distance between the two, and responded, "I will send a Healing Warlock your way. In the meantime, rest. I am so very sorry you are not well, friend. I will check on you later." Alexis left quickly to locate Edwinn Shivvers to ask him to check on Aerianna. He would ensure she received the help she needed to feel better.

Aerianna walked back to her bed, falling on the plush blanket. She felt woozy. The room spun, making her feel nauseous again. She curled up into a ball, wishing the horrendous feeling would subside.

Pauto and Andreh discussed security measures in the Courtyard. Andreh had just returned from Tullah Mountain and the Colosseum. He cast a spell from Yarlen, which allowed the Colosseum to be rebuilt and returned it to its former glory. However, the Queen insisted that some of the charred rubble be kept on the back side of the structure as a stark reminder of what had happened 24 hours prior.

The same magic worked on the Manor, too. It had received minor damage during the attack. Andreh was pleased with the final results and was hopeful Alexis would be as well. Pauto and Andreh chatted when Yarlen and Cazzandra appeared.

"What brings you two to the Courtyard?" Andreh asked, noticing both had their hands full with various magical items.

"We are here to test a new spell and potion, courtesy of Cazzandra," replied Yarlen. He looked proud and eager to begin. It delighted him that his protégé was so incredibly talented.

"WOW, that is awesome. Can we stay and watch?" begged Andreh. He found it fascinating. He could never invent an original spell. He was in awe of those who had such an ability. The only magical work he managed to perform was brewing potions, a craft he had picked up from Alexis.

"Sure. Just know we are experimenting. I cannot guarantee your safety," added Cazzandra with caution. She did not like the idea of others being present, but felt it was rude to ask them to leave.

Cazzandra placed the potion bottle on the ground and raised her wand into the air, chanting. A few seconds later, Cazzandra bent down and grabbed the bottle. She poured the blue and green swirling goo onto the stone pavers. Instantly, small, round orbs formed, shooting into the atmosphere, and a loud booming noise followed, with tiny stars falling from the sky. Cazzandra clapped and cheered. Yarlen nodded, assuming it had worked the way she intended.

"So, you were successful?" asked Andreh. He stared at the sky. He could not see any kind of shield like before.

"I presume so. There is only one way to find out. We have to discover if we can leave the planet. Who wishes to volunteer?" Cazzandra stared at the Warlocks, wondering which one would help.

"I will do it, Cazzandra. I will cast a spell to attempt to visit Earth. Let's see what happens," Andreh declared with confidence. With a swift wave of his wand and a powerful incantation, he attempted to transport himself to Earth. However, nothing happened, and he remained in place.

Cazzandra grinned. Her chant and potion worked perfectly. "Great. You are still here, Andreh. So, we can conclude the planet is secure. If we can't leave, others are blocked from entering. Yarlen, will you inform the Queen and Armbruster, or shall I?" Cazzandra asked, hoping to share it directly with the Queen.

"It is your work. Please share it with the Royals. I can accompany you if you wish. If not, you'd best be on your way and do it now," Yarlen retorted.

Andreh nodded. "I will join you, Cazzandra. I must speak with Alexis about the previous assignment she gave me and update her on it. Let's head inside the Palace."

The two disappeared, leaving the Yarlen and Pauto alone.

"That is one talented young Witch you have found, Yarlen. You must be proud," complimented Pauto.

"You give me too much credit. The Queen is the one who discovered Cazzandra. I am grateful for the ability to instruct her, though I feel she is actually teaching me at this point, " Yarlen replied, chuckling.

Pauto nodded and excused himself, eager to meet Aerianna for lunch. He was hungry and figured she would be, too.

★ ⁎.★ ⁎.★ ⁎.★ ⁎.★

Andreh and Cazzandra stood before the Queen's bedroom door. He knocked firmly, and together they waited for an answer. Andreh heard the Queen's voice commanding them to enter. He held the door open for Cazzandra to walk through first. She confidently stepped into the room and bowed respectfully.

"Your Majesty, I have some exciting news to share," Cazzandra announced. She stood a foot apart from the Queen, eager to share the update.

"Well, what is it? Do tell," Alexis asked, noticing how exuberant Cazzandra acted. She also gazed at Andreh, wondering why he remained silently in the background.

"Your Majesty, I have enacted a spell and used a newly formulated potion to secure the planet. We have tested the efficacy of both. No one can leave. It is also impossible to penetrate the invisible barrier to enter! However, I believe I can also allow the representatives from the Council of Peace & War to pass through securely, using a *By-Pass Spell.*"

"Really? Have you tried to leave the planet? How do you know it truly works?" Alexis questioned Cazzandra hesitantly.

Andreh stepped forward. "I attempted to leave the planet using magic. I could not depart Alstromia. I remained standing in the same spot. Her shield works, Your Majesty."

Alexis clapped her hands in excitement. "Congratulations, Cazzandra! I knew you would be able to do it. You are incredibly clever, and I am grateful for your hard work. Thank you so much. I am forever in your debt. Have you had the chance to inform Yarlen of the good news?" Alexis asked.

"Yes, My Queen. He was present during our trial run. Pauto was there, too. Is there anything else we need to do?" Cazzandra asked, stepping back. She hoped to return to the laboratory to work on a few other potions. She had some ideas and felt every second she stood in this chamber was a waste of her precious time.

"No, I believe that will do for now. Again, thank you for your work, Cazzandra. I will not forget all you have done. You may be excused," Alexis smiled, allowing the young Witch to leave. She sensed the girl was uncomfortable. Cazzandra nodded and sprinted back to the basement to continue her research work.

Andreh approached Alexis with a smirk on his face. "So, you like her, don't you? I can see it all over your face. You don't want to like her, but you do!" Andreh watched Alexis. Sometimes, she was challenging to read.

"I do like her. I never said otherwise. She is gifted, and I can see how useful she will become to the kingdom." Alexis concurred as she glared at him. "Why wouldn't I like her?"

"Jealously? Competition? I do not know, Alexis. You tell me," Andreh responded. He knew Alexis was the jealous type. When Cazzandra flirted with Andreh and Alexis noticed, she rolled her eyes with blatant disapproval. He found it funny that Alexis worried about his loyalty to her. His heart belonged to the Queen.

Alexis did not like Cazzandra's apparent affection for Andreh. She stepped forward, now inches away from Andreh. "Maybe I hate that she throws herself at you every chance she gets. I'm not particularly eager to share. You know that about me. I adore you, and she is not permitted to have you!" Alexis stared at him with a pouty face.

Andreh almost laughed. Instead, he pulled Alexis against his body, kissing her while playing with her long, black hair. She did not resist his touch. The two kissed passionately until Andreh pulled away to nuzzle her neck. Alexis moaned lightly and was about to undress when there was a disturbing knock on the door.

"Really? Who is it?" Alexis yelled, hating the interruption.

"My Queen, it is Pauto. I wonder if I could hold a quick conversation with you."

Alexis stared at Andreh. She realized it would look suspicious to Pauto that Andreh was in the Queen's private chamber.

"I am busy. Come back in an hour," Alexis responded, hoping Pauto would take his leave.

Pauto thought he heard voices before he knocked on the Queen's door. It sounded like Andreh. The thought bothered him. He hoped that Andreh was not still seeing the Queen. It was a dangerous game, one he would eventually lose! Not wanting to start trouble, Pauto acknowledged the Queen's request and departed to visit Aerianna.

Earlier, Pauto had wanted to share lunch with Aerianna, but she had a visitor, Edwinn Shivvers. It was highly concerning to Pauto that a Healing Warlock was tending to his fiancée. He wondered why Aerianna had not told him about any illness or injury. Pauto couldn't help but feel hurt that Aerianna hadn't confided in him, and he hoped everything was okay.

Seconds after Pauto left, Andreh asked Alexis, "What do you think he wants to discuss with you?" He held her in his arms. She moved away, grabbing his hand and leading him to her bed.

"Why do we care? That is not why you came to my chamber, is it?" she teased with a smoldering look.

"No. Absolutely not," Andreh agreed. He smiled, watching her undress before him. His day was about to get a whole lot better.

In another part of the Palace, Armbruster paced around the room impatiently. Yarlen watched him but fiddled with his long beard, pretending not to notice.

Rammadar entered the chamber and immediately noticed the scowl on the King's face. Obviously, he was in a foul mood. Rammadar quickly realized that all hell was about to break loose, and he began to fret. His working conditions were becoming challenging.

"Where have you been? I've been waiting for hours," hissed Armbruster.

"Your Majesty, I was with Yarlen earlier, then the Queen summoned me. I am here now. What may I do for you?"

"What does Alexis want from you? You work for me!" Armbruster bellowed. He was irritated that Alexis interfered with his staff.

"Well, about that, Your Majesty. The Queen demands I work for her now. She wanted me to inform you," Rammadar acknowledged. He walked to the open window to distance himself from Armbruster, worried about his reaction to the new information. Plus, he needed the fresh air, feeling stifled.

"What the hell? Absolutely not! That will not happen, Rammadar. You are needed here. I will speak with the Queen and let her know you are my staff member and work for Pauto and me. Is that clear?"

"Your Highness, I do not wish to come between you and your wife. Please speak with her and provide me with updated instructions about my position at the Palace," Rammadar requested, assuming this would happen.

Armbruster was displeased with the Queen's decision. Nonetheless, Rammadar refused to be used like a toy, tossed between the royals for their personal entertainment. It greatly irritated him.

"You can bet on it, Rammadar. I will talk with her now." Armbruster turned and

. * . * . * . * . .

stormed off toward the other side of the Palace, ready to confront Alexis. He was tired of her games and power trips.

Andreh dressed by the fireplace, though Alexis remained in bed. "You are truly gorgeous, Alexis," he declared, watching her.

"That is why you should come back to bed. I still need some private time with you, Andreh," Alexis replied with a naughty grin, sitting up and licking her lips.

"That is not a good idea, and you know it. It is the middle of the day. What if Armbruster came to visit you? Can you imagine? No, I have to head out and get some things done. You know I love you, but we must be careful." Andreh approached the bed to kiss her goodbye. She pulled him onto the bed, trying to pin him down, rolling on top of him.

"Come on...let me show you how much I love you," she began unbuttoning his pants.

"Stop, Alexis. I must leave," Andreh insisted, managing to jump off the bed. He kissed her full lips, his hands cupping her face.

"Fine. Be like that. I just miss you so much, darling. Oh, and did you mean it?" she asked Andreh, as he stood by the chamber door, ready to exit.

"Mean what, Alexis?"

Alexis rolled out of bed and ran toward him. She abruptly stopped, inches away from Andreh. She bit her fingernail and then yelled, "That you love me!"

Andreh planted a kiss on her lips. "Yes. I adore you. I love you. But I must leave. Please put on some clothes before someone visits your chamber," Andreh urgently insisted. He released her and quickly left, not wanting to be caught in a questionable position with the Queen.

★ ˙ ★ ˙ ★ ˙ ★ ˙ ★

Halfway down the corridor, he spotted Armbruster approaching. He seemed irritated, his lips pursed. Andreh looked down, hoping Armbruster would ignore him. However, he assumed there would be no such luck.

"Andreh, stop for a moment. Have you seen the Queen? I must speak with her. Is she in her chamber?" Armbruster grilled him. He looked at Andreh. *'Why does he look so happy?'* Armbruster frowned.

"I assume she is in her room or on the Landing Deck. I am on my way to meet with Cazzandra. Have a great day, Your Majesty!" Andreh did not wait for a response. He kept walking, praying that Alexis would be dressed when Armbruster entered her room.

Alexis felt elated. It mattered to her that Andreh acknowledged their love. She realized a long time ago that she loved him. It was not just a simple infatuation. However, he had never outright said that he loved her. It made her day. As she began dressing, she heard a knock on the door. Unfortunately, she believed it was Andreh returning. Alexis opened the door, only half-dressed.

The moment she realized it was Armbruster, she screamed, slamming the door. Perplexed, he pounded on the door, demanding she open it. Since she refused to respond to his request, he boldly pushed the door open and entered the room. He spotted her sitting on the end of the bed, facing the fireplace, wearing a black robe, arms crossed.

"What is it, Armbruster? Why are you here?"

"Let's start with…why were you naked when you opened the door? Are you expecting someone else? Don't tell me Andreh was here. I ran into him in the hallway, and he pretended not to know if you were in your chamber. My God. Why can't you two just stop this affair? Is it really so difficult to keep your hands off each other?" Armbruster yelled. He was livid with Alexis.

In his heart, he wanted to believe she had stopped seeing Andreh. Now, he knew better. The thought of the young Wizzard making love to his wife infuriated him. *'Why does she love him?'* He wanted to murder Andreh.

"Again, why are you here, Armbruster?" Alexis asked snippily. "And I was not naked. I had on some clothing," Alexis retorted sarcastically while attempting to hide a smirk.

"That is beside the point. Answer the question. Are you still having an affair with Andreh?" Armbruster knew the answer but demanded she say the words to his face. He felt she owed him that much.

"What I do, Armbruster, is none of your business. I told you before. I love Andreh. You will never understand our bond, and I really do not give a damn. So, again, why are you here? Get to it. I have a busy schedule today," Alexis replied.

She felt upset about the invasion of her privacy. Even more, she was furious that Armbruster was trying to start trouble with Andreh again. When would it end? It became apparent he enjoyed irritating her, and she flashed him a disapproving look.

"I am here to discuss Rammadar. You have overstepped, Alexis. He is my staff member. I hired him, and he works for Pauto and me. You will not be utilizing his services. Am I clear?" Armbruster screamed. He saw Alexis looking down at her hands. She remained silent, only slightly tapping her foot with impatience.

"Furthermore, I want a divorce. I will not allow you to continue an affair. It is disgusting. I thought we were past this Andreh fling. What the hell, Alexis?" Armbruster sat on the chair by the fireplace, waiting for her to respond. It did not take long.

"There will be no divorce. Not now. We have other more urgent matters to address. I understand your frustration with me, but I will ask you to wait for the divorce, please, if not for me, but for all of Alstromia."

"Alexis, I cannot believe you are asking me this favor. Sadly, I concur. This is not the time for a divorce. However, we will end this farce of a marriage in the future. I promise you this. Unless you stop seeing Andreh, nothing will change. I deserve better and should not be subjected to the stress of your infidelity!"

Armbruster felt used, but he knew Alexis was correct. A divorce in these circumstances would only make things worse. It would divide the kingdom and cause strife throughout the Clans and Alstromia. He didn't wish for that to happen. No matter what, right now, they had to display a unified front.

"Great. We agree. The divorce is on hold. You will not file for the Dismissal of the Ceremony until a later date. Once we concur that it is time, you may file, and I will not stop you," Alexis announced. "As far as Rammadar is concerned, keep him. I still have Andreh, Aerianna, and Cazzandra."

Armbruster rose from his seat and exited the room. He knew their marriage was over. Eventually, he would file the necessary papers to dissolve their marriage and set her free to love Andreh. It broke his heart. Feeling abandoned, he walked to Lilah's chamber, wishing to spend time with his daughter.

He entered the room and found Carmin clapping her hands, observing Lilah. The Princess sat on a chair, holding a short, icy blue wand. Immediately, Armbruster looked confused.

"What is going on here, Carmin? Are you teaching my child magic? We never discussed this before!"

"Your Majesty. Please allow me to explain. The Princess is quite gifted. I wanted to share the information with you and Queen, but honestly, she has not come by much to see her child. I have been working with Lilah. I hope that is okay?" Carmin replied nervously. She knew one day she would get caught. Hopefully, Armbruster would allow her to educate the Princess. She was eager to guide the *Young Witch in Training* (*YWIT*).

"Well, I never thought about it. I was under the impression that Lilah was too young. I suppose it is okay. There is no harm, as far as I am concerned. What is Lilah learning?" Armbruster asked.

"She knows how to levitate items, cast a few spells, and handle her wand like a pro! Sir, you should be so proud. She takes after you and the Queen," Carmin gushed, offering up a smile.

"That is fantastic news, Carmin. I am so delighted. Now, I would like to spend a little time alone with Lilah. Please, come back in an hour."

"Of course, Your Majesty!" Carmin left quickly, allowing the King time with his daughter. It warmed Carmin's heart that one of Lilah's parents still spent time with her. She wondered why Alexis chose to stay away. It did not make any sense.

Armbruster stood before Lilah. She smiled at him, and immediately, he was reminded of Alexis. Lilah was a mini version of his wife. She was beautiful and intelligent. Lilah had her mother's grin, and when her eyes sparkled, instantly, he saw Alexis. It was unbelievable how alike they looked.

"Hello, my precious daughter. How are you today? I hear you have been busy learning magic?" Armbruster spoke to Lilah lovingly. He took the wand from her tiny hand.

"Can you take the wand from Daddy without touching me?"

Lilah giggled. "Yes, Daddy. Look." Lilah closed her eyes and commanded the wand to come to her. The wand released itself from Armbruster's grip and floated in the air toward the Princess. Seconds later, she opened her beautiful lavender eyes and grabbed it.

"See, Daddy. I can do it!" Lilah proudly exclaimed.

Armbruster was amazed by Lilah's abilities. Despite the fact that she was only two years old, her vocabulary was equivalent to that of a five-year-old child.

Additionally, she had already gained the ability to control magic. Armbruster expressed his admiration by saying, "That's outstanding, Princess. What other amazing things can you do?"

"I can do this, Daddy," Lilah closed her eyes and instantly began levitating. She hovered over her chair. She opened her eyes and asked, "Done, Daddy?"

"Of course! How wonderful." He watched as the young Witch lowered herself onto the seat. "You are so gifted, my child. I am delighted by your magical abilities!" Armbruster hugged her tightly. She laughed and hugged him back. He loved his child more than life itself and wondered what would happen to their bond once he dissolved his marriage to Alexis.

Armbruster spent another hour with the Princess until Carmin knocked on the door, asking permission to enter the child's chamber.

"Carmin, the Princess truly is extraordinary. I am grateful you have taken the time to guide her. Please continue to nurture her talents. If you need anything from me to help her further, let me know. Yarlen is also a great source of information about magic and incantations. Please remember that."

Armbruster departed, leaving Carmin to tend to the *YWIT*. He felt pleased that he had the opportunity to spend time with Lilah. It meant a great deal to him, and he left feeling satisfied for the first time in months. The thought of divorce greatly bothered him, and he chose to push it into the deep crevices of his brain, hopeful to forget about it for now.

Carmin was grateful that Armbruster was not angry with her for teaching the Princess magic. His support was appreciated, and she planned to work with Lilah daily to help her grow her magic. Carmin realized that, eventually, she would need to inform the Queen about Lilah's exceptional abilities, and there was no way she could continue hiding it.

The sky on Earth was overcast and gray. It was gloomy and raining. Gardone felt restless. He pondered all the reasons why Sharlottah had left.

Searching the home for her, he eventually found the note propped up on the kitchen table. It read, *"I know what you have done. I need time to contemplate what to do about it. I'm afraid I have to disagree with you on these actions and cannot condone them. I love you, but I need space. I am returning to my home. Please, stay away. I will contact you when and if I am ready!" Love, S.*

Gardone dropped the note, letting it fall to the floor. He stared at it and shook his head, feeling disgusted. *'Another Witch, unable to stand my greatness,'* he figured. *'She will be back!'* Frustrated, he yelled, but no one heard him.

The Warlock slammed down his Ceptre, transporting himself to the hut, hoping to find Garlow. He demanded an update on what was transpiring on Alstromia, hopeful that Alexis was ready to negotiate and save her precious planet from further vicious attacks. If not, he would change his strategy. Alexis would learn not to mess with him.

Garlow lounged on the small couch near the fireplace. He sipped a hot brew, which warmed him. Nervously, he jumped, almost spilling his drink, when Gardone appeared, standing right before him.

"What are you doing here, Gardone?" he asked apprehensively with a shaky voice. He placed the mug on the table, watching his reaction.

"I want an update. What is your father doing on Alstromia? Has Alexis decided to give up her throne to me? What do you know?"

"Unfortunately, I have not been able to communicate with my father. There is a barrier keeping me from transporting to Alstromia. We cannot penetrate their shield. Though it is not visible, I know it is there," Garlow explained. "However, we have secured the *Ninety-Nightblade Brigade (NNB)*. They will strike when the time is right and make the Queen pay! It is just as you have planned."

"That's great news! But we need to increase our attacks on Alstromia immediately. I want more fire strikes! I want to see the entire planet engulfed in flames. And then, Alexis will have no choice but to come to me and plead for mercy! I just know it," exclaimed Gardone, his appearance resembling that of a deranged Warlock.

Gardone's eyes were wide, dilated, and bloodshot, while his hair looked greasy as if he hadn't taken a shower in days. His odor was equally unpleasant. Something was wrong, or so Garlow believed.

"Does the Queen know it was you, Gardone?"

"Oh, she knows. I heard it from others. It is exactly as I arranged. I am glad she knows it is my greatness that will destroy her! Sadly, Zandorah has banned me from Iriss. I cannot speak with her. Now, both daughters have turned against me. I suppose I have Lorthana to thank for that!" Gardone complained, frowning and swinging his fists in the air.

Gardone was curious about what Alexis and Armbruster were implementing to keep peace on Alstromia. He wondered if they had enacted the War Council. If they did, the Council of Peace & War would send a few select representatives to guide them through the process of responding to attacks and retaliating. It could either make things easier or overcomplicate the situation. Time would reveal which.

On the upside, if the representatives were headed to Alstromia, they would be granted entry. That would be an excellent opportunity for Gardone to sneak in Garlow and plant his spy on Alstromia! The *NNB* would do the rest. Gardone chuckled, thrilled at the thought.

The day was hectic, and everyone had a plan and purpose. Yarlen and Cazzandra were busy in the basement of the Palace, concocting various potions and spells. Yarlen was a dedicated and patient instructor.

Pauto and Andreh strategized with Rammadar on security matters concerning the arrival of the Council of Peace & War representatives. They would arrive shortly, and everyone was nervous about finding out if they could safely transport through the protective barrier. Cazzandra and Yarlen would be on standby, ready to open part of the shield near the Palace.

CHAPTER 4

The representatives attempted to penetrate the barrier without success. Yarlen noticed flashes of red and purple rippling across the sky. He immediately ordered Cazzandra to open a small portal to allow them to pass through, using her newly formulated spell.

Within seconds, three Warlocks and one Witch stood before them, holding their wands and books. The Witch also carried a large bag, which she had slung over her right shoulder.

Yarlen approached the group. "Welcome to Alstromia. We are pleased to have you. Thank goodness you were able to enter through our force field."

Luzindah Foggentin shook Yarlen's hand and surveyed the surroundings. "Where is Alexis Snipperdoom? Who is in charge of security?" she sounded snippy, and everyone immediately noticed.

Pauto advanced quickly. "I am in charge of security, along with Armbruster and Rammadar. May we escort you to our Security Command Team Chamber? I believe the Queen will be there shortly. Armbruster should already be waiting for us."

Without hesitation, the group followed Pauto inside the Palace. Yarlen remained behind for a few minutes. He wanted to congratulate Cazzandra on a job well done. After their short conversation, he excused himself to join the others in the chamber to listen to the briefing.

Miraculously, no one noticed Garlow had slipped through the portal, following the representatives right before the portal hole closed. He had consumed an invisibility potion and sprinted toward the back end of the Palace, hoping to evade others. The plan had been executed perfectly.

In the chamber, Alexis listened to Aerianna, unsure what to say. "I want you to stay in bed today and relax. I am glad Edwinn examined you. Though I must confess, the news is startling. Did you suspect what was wrong with you? What can I do to help?" Alexis offered.

"No. I wish to keep my diagnosis a secret. I will not be sharing it with Pauto or anyone else for now. I beg you to remain silent as well. I am not ready to share the news. I hope you can understand," Aerianna explained. She leaned against the headboard with the blanket pulled up to her waist. Her hands were folded on her stomach. Aerianna looked fragile and unwell. Alexis frowned, worried.

"Of course. I am more than happy to keep what you have shared with me confidential. It is not for me to divulge your secrets. I do believe you need to let Pauto know before too long. He is aware you are ill and will demand answers. Get your rest. I must leave you, as I have an urgent security briefing to attend. The Council of Peace & War representatives should be here by now." Alexis hugged Aerianna and rushed off to her meeting.

As Alexis strutted down the corridor, she couldn't help but wonder why Aerianna had decided to keep her diagnosis to herself. Sooner or later, Pauto would discover the truth, and he would likely be upset that she had waited so long to confide in him.

Alexis intended to hold a conversation with Edwinn about Aerianna at a later time. For now, she would keep her promise to Aerianna and stay silent about the information that had been entrusted to her.

The day was already quite a mess. The representatives were not as friendly as Armbruster had hoped, and the visiting Warlocks were overly aggressive.

The Witch, Luzindah Foggentin, seemed disinterested in attending meetings on Alstromia. Armbruster wondered why Alexis was late to such an urgent meeting. Pauto and Rammadar talked to the group to pass the time and keep them entertained. Luckily, Alexis finally appeared, acting flustered.

"Good day, everyone. I am so sorry for the delay. I encountered an emergency. I had to handle it first. We can get started now," she proclaimed.

Alexis chose the seat next to Armbruster. He gave her a strange look. He wondered what kind of unexpected event had occurred.

Pauto stood up and officially introduced Armbruster, then quickly sat beside Yarlen. Armbruster ceremoniously welcomed the four council members, then sat down, allowing Alexis to lead the rest of the meeting. He hoped she would be respectful, but figured it was unlikely.

"As you know, we have been subjected to an unprecedented attack on our planet. After a thorough investigation, we believe my father, Gardone, is responsible. Specifically, his new group of followers, identified as the *GRAW*." Alexis surveyed the room, waiting for potential questions from others. She continued. "Our security team enacted the War Council, as the Council of Peace & War advised. We also met with our legal counsel, Jamessihn Shorttar. As of this minute, we are at war. Regrettably, we have no means to respond appropriately, as the individual in question is believed to be residing on Earth. We have no intention of launching an attack on Earth and its innocent residents. Therefore, we seek your guidance and expertise in this delicate matter."

Luzindah stood up, placing her hand on the table before her. "Thank you, Your Majesty, for that detailed briefing. The Council members have previously met with our counterparts on Earth. We understand your enemy is potentially hiding on the planet. It isn't easy to locate him. Unfortunately, he has many allies. We cannot allow you to retaliate, targeting Earth. Therefore, we will find ways to sanction Gardone and his Clan of Warlocks. We realize it may seem like a slap on the wrist, but it is the best we can do at this moment. That does not mean we will not attempt to apprehend him. We have security teams scouring the globe. Once he is caught, he will be brought up on charges. As you know, the penalty for his actions is death!" Luzindah declared confidently.

The other representatives nodded and clapped in agreement. They wished for Gardone to be held responsible for his actions, realizing Alexis Snipperdoom and her staff would challenge the limitations of power. Still, they remained firm in their belief that this was the best way to address the situation.

Infuriated by the lack of urgent response, Pauto lept from his seat. He refused to keep his mouth shut. "That is outrageous! We have been pelted with fire, burn spells, hexes, and more. Due to this vicious attack, we have lost over 2,000 Clan members. How can you expect us to sit back and wait for answers or suggestions? It is unconscionable!" Pauto dropped into his chair, breathing heavily. He was fuming, pounding his fist on the table, and causing others to stare at him, shocked. It was unlike Pauto to react in such a violent manner.

Armbruster spoke next, though he remained in his seat. "I have to agree with our head of security, Pauto Vexxorth. We will not wait for another round of strikes." He watched the Council members as they glared at him. Armbruster continued. "Do you honestly believe allowing Gardone and the *GRAW* to continue waging war against us is acceptable?"

One of the Council Warlocks stood up to respond. "Sir, my name is Darnett Partle. I agree with you. However, we must follow all rules and regulations under the War Act, which is clearly set out as the Council of Peace & War's governing document. We cannot and will not allow you to engage in violence on Earth. Some humans would not understand. Many do not even believe in Witches, Warlocks, and Wizzards. You must trust us when we say we work relentlessly to locate Gardone."

Yarlen shook his head, feeling disgusted by the group of representatives' lack of support. He thought they were bureaucratic cowards. He pulled on Armbruster's arm, gaining his attention. Yarlen whispered into the King's ear, and Armbruster nodded in response.

Alexis was the next to speak her mind. She rose from her seat and approached the four guests. "I have been subjected to numerous attempted takeovers of my reign and planet. My father has repeatedly tried to take the kingdom away from me. It began the moment I took office. Clan members fairly elected me. I have fought again and again to overcome every situation thrown my way. I am sick and tired of it. You are supposed to protect us and provide ways to keep this from happening. Do your damn job! We are at risk of losing the planet and our way of life. You are tying our hands by telling us to use diplomacy and sanctions. What a joke!"

Alexis walked to the door, then turned to face the group. "Until you find a more effective way to support us, we have nothing else to discuss." She stormed from the room, causing a commotion.

Andreh, Yarlen, and Rammadar applauded the Queen's bold statement against the visitors. They felt the same. It was the correct way to handle the representatives who seemed only interested in peacekeeping.

Luzindah vehemently disagreed, shaking her head. "It is not true. We have enacted a tribunal on Earth and are ready to charge Gardone once he is apprehended. The Queen's words are not factual! We will return to Earth, seeking other options from Clan members and Council leaders to present to you in the future. It is clear we are not wanted here!" She folded her arms, glaring at the others.

Armbruster stood up next. "That is not accurate, Luzindah. My wife is frustrated with your current method of handling the state of affairs. It appears that you wish to apply diplomacy, which rarely works during war. We, as a Clan, beg you to consider what is happening. We do not want to contradict the current order of the Council of Peace & War, but we refuse to stand by and await orders. However, we must protect our planet at any cost."

Yarlen nodded in agreement. Rammadar spoke, feeling angry. "We have done what we can. If you cannot effectively aid us, we will be forced to ask others to join our coalition. I believe Iriss, our ally, will support our efforts." Rammadar knew the four representatives would take his words as a threat, but he did not care. It needed to be said. He was willing to deal with the fallout later. Hopefully, the King wouldn't be displeased by his assertive declaration.

"Exactly right, Rammadar," Armbruster added. "As a matter of fact, I will personally speak with Zandorah and ask for her help."

The four guests disagreed but did not reply, feeling the hostility aimed at them.

Luzindah approached Armbruster and asked for his help in departing the planet. At this point, all talks were halted. Armbruster tasked Yarlen with ensuring the group could leave Alstromia immediately.

After the representatives departed Alstromia safely, Alexis and Armbruster met in her chamber to discuss future plans. Alexis paced around the room restlessly. Armbruster sat in a chair by the fireplace, observing her.

"Well, what is our next step, Alexis? I wanted to speak with you before meeting with Pauto, Andreh, Rammadar, and the rest of the Security Command Team. I believe we can assume the planet is secure and safe. We must consider our long-term strategies. I don't think waiting and seeing what the enemy will do is in our best interest. Instead, we should formulate a retaliation plan."

"Armbruster, I don't think we have many viable options. Starting a war campaign on Earth to lure Gardone out of hiding is not feasible. Unfortunately, we are left with few choices due to limited resources. After consulting with Clan members on Earth, most agree that we should prioritize Alstromia's security and continue sending scout teams to Earth and Iriss to locate Gardone. There is a unanimous decision among the Clans not to attack or retaliate. The Council of Peace & War also supports this stance," Alexis stated firmly, expressing her frustration.

"We already know the Council lacks backbone. They want mediation. We should not give in, Alexis. They are not the ones faced with such tragedy," Armbruster shouted. He exhaled loudly, wringing his hands.

"I wholeheartedly agree. However, we must do our best to play the game. We must not act with aggression. Alstromia is a peace-loving planet, and we will act accordingly. We are the victims, not the perpetrators. I hope you agree with my plan, Armbruster. We must be careful how we present ourselves to the council members," Alexis asserted.

"Whatever you wish, My Queen. You know I support you as King and your husband."

"Great. I am thrilled to hear that, Armbruster. Please be so kind as to inform our staff of our new objectives. We will search for Gardone, but keep our planet defended."

Armbruster shrugged and rose from the chair. He exited the chamber, leaving Alexis alone, and planned to meet with his team and give them the updated war procedures.

On Iriss, Zandorah stayed in her room in the Castle of Zandor. She hoped to speak with

Lorthana but figured her mother was too upset to be bothered. Ever since the attack on Alstromia, Lorthana had been acting strangely. It seemed to Zandorah that her mother was holding her responsible for the instigation of war. However, that was far from the truth. Zandorah would never have started a feud against her sister or the planet Alstromia.

Zandorah preferred working with council members through tactful communication. She did not appreciate Alexis' threats against her and Iriss after the fallout on Alstromia. Though she tried numerous times to summon Alexis and speak with her, her sister failed to respond. Sadly, how her sister handled things between them was not unexpected.

Now, Zandorah was left wondering how to proceed. She knew Gardone would not try to enter Iriss since he was a wanted Warlock. Still, he could try sending some of his scouts to the planet to spy for him. Alexis could misconstrue that in many ways. Thus, Zandorah finally decided to send a message to Armbruster requesting a formal meeting on Alstromia. It was better to communicate with him. He would handle Alexis for her.

If necessary, Zandorah planned to message Pauto. Either way, she wanted to meet with the Command Staff on Alstromia to clarify that Iriss was an ally and not an enemy. Iriss was ready to aid Alstromia with their war efforts.

The day was beginning to frustrate Andreh. He yearned to see Alexis, missing their time together. It would be fun to take the Torrins out for a while, flying to Tullah Mountain. Unfortunately, Alexis had been keeping to herself. He heard Armbruster was taking up much of her time. It alarmed Andreh. He could not help but wonder if the two were reconciling their marriage. It elicited feelings he wanted to hide.

At times, he thought about returning to Earth, giving himself the opportunity for happiness. Andreh realized he could not remain on Alstromia and be happy. His heart was shattered. Alexis clarified that she was not ready to dissolve her marriage to Armbruster.

Sadly, it left very few choices for Andreh. He considered asking Cazzandra out on a date, hoping they would click. He believed a spark existed between them and was excited to explore it further. But his heart felt as if he was betraying Alexis. Perhaps that is why he had not yet asked Cazzandra out on a date. Plus, with the violent attack on Alstromia, there was no time for fun. Everyone had a mission to fulfill to ensure the planet's safety.

Andreh sighed, thinking about his life options. None of them made him happy. Reluctantly, he decided to head to the Command Chamber to speak with the others and find out if there were any new orders from the Queen.

Pauto and Aerianna remained in the chamber. They realized both had jobs to perform, but neither wanted to work. They were mentally and physically exhausted. Pauto gently held Aerianna's hand as she stared out the window.

Aerianna seemed preoccupied, uninterested in talking. After a few minutes, Pauto released her hand and walked in front of the window to gain her attention.

"Oh, Pauto. I'm sorry. I must have been in a daze. My mind is on a million things right now. I promise that I am not ignoring you. Please, forgive me," Aerianna pleaded, not wanting to alienate Pauto.

"Oh, darling. No worries. I know there is so much happening right now. What can I do for you, beautiful? I must return to work in a few minutes. I am sure Armbruster is already wondering where I am hiding." Pauto hoped Aerianna would ask him to stay a little longer.

Pauto awaited an answer, but Aerianna remained unattentive. Minutes later, he left the room, feeling it was better to focus on work. Aerianna would be okay. *'Maybe she just needs to be alone for a while to gather her thoughts,'* he pondered. He had no clue what was happening with her. Unsure of how to handle Aerianna's behavior, Pauto headed back to the Security Command Chamber to speak with others about the next plan to protect Alstromia.

Armbruster briefed Rammadar and a few others in the Security Command Chamber on the Queen's request. He stopped his speech abruptly when Pauto entered. Andreh followed him into the room.

"Ah, now that we are all present, let me recap my previous conversation," Armbruster announced impatiently. Apparently, he was unhappy that Andreh and Pauto were late to the meeting. After ten minutes, Armbruster settled down on a chair and patiently waited for someone else to speak. Meanwhile, Rammadar was eager to ask some questions and promptly stood up, heading toward the wall-mounted board.

"I believe our task is to maintain continuous surveillance of this entire area," Rammadar stated while pointing at a map on the wall, highlighting the extensive region that needed to be secured.

Armbruster chimed in, adding to the conversation, asking, "Do you believe that Gardone might be hiding on Tullah Mountain on Alstromia? I am worried that he could have established a base here. If so, we might need to change our objectives."

Pauto nodded and expressed his concerns. "Sir, I'm not sure how we can patrol the entire planet. We can cast all the spells we want, but it seems impossible to protect every inch of Alstromia. I don't want to sound negative, but it's a daunting task. I don't think we have enough security personnel unless we seek help from the Standard Army of Warriors." Pauto then leaned back in his chair, appearing defeated.

Armbruster had already foreseen this issue and knew the SAoW would be better equipped to help secure the perimeter. "Pauto, as the head of the SAoW, please brief and enlist your team for assistance," Armbruster instructed.

Pauto, Andreh, and Rammadar swiftly departed with a new objective outlined. They made their way to the Courtyard below, where they found the SAoW's Second-in-Command, Griffen Corilyn. Pauto was eager to share the King's new orders with him.

Despite everyone's hopes for the best, Pauto remained unconvinced. He couldn't forget how cunning Gardone had been in the past and how far he was willing to go to harm his victims. Gardone was a self-centered and egotistical being.

To ensure that Gardone would be brought to justice, Pauto decided to research complex *Reveal Spells*. He was determined to locate Gardone and make sure he paid for his crimes by spending the rest of his life in prison, unable to use his magic. Pauto believed that only then would true justice be served.

After the conversation, Alexis returned to her chamber, consumed with feelings of hatred towards her father. She couldn't help but wonder why he persisted in making everyone's lives miserable and what his intentions were concerning Alstromia. *'What does he believe he can accomplish? Most of all, will he ever stop the madness?'*

Years ago, during Gardone's initial bid for the position of ruler of Alstromia, many Clan members were hesitant to support him. They viewed him as a radical Warlock, more interested in seeking personal attention than fulfilling the Clan's needs and desires.

The Queen realized Gardone wanted to rule the planet to prove a point. His goal was to dethrone Alexis and force her to bow to him. That would never happen. Gardone lacked the mental acuity to hold such a powerful position, and she would rather die than pledge her allegiance to Gardone.

Gardone continually allowed his thirst for power to override the community's greater good. To Alexis, this was just another example of his blatant lack of integrity. For Gardone, it was about power and domination. It seemed he did not care about the fallout.

Alexis used her magic sparingly. She felt using magic for the sake of making a point was useless. She believed magic was to be feared and admired. It took years of practice and guidance by powerful W3s for her to gain her abilities. Alexis grinned, fully aware that Gardone stood little chance of taking the kingdom away from her.

She had amassed a large following despite her reputation as one who was cold and calculating. She preferred to be called decisive and intelligent, carefully choosing her moves with thoughtful intentions. Alexis never made any changes without contemplating the potential outcomes. She realized failing to do so could prove catastrophic. However, now that war had been declared, Alexis found herself up against not only her father but the entire *GRAW*.

Regrettably, the roster of active *GRAW* members remained well hidden, and no one could furnish Alexis with their names. To enhance her strategy against the rebels, Alexis aimed to identify the new members of Gardone's extremist group. She contemplated sending scouts to Earth and Iriss to obtain the list of the *GRAW* supporters. Since Aerianna wouldn't be able to work for the foreseeable future, Alexis understood that it was her responsibility to locate Gardone.

Aerianna remained in bed while her head ached, and she felt fatigued. She realized the need to formulate a plan to share her current health condition with Pauto. But she worried he would insist on dropping his current projects and withdraw from his Palace positions. Pauto would want to be there for her, even though Edwinn Shivvers made it clear Aerianna would eventually be okay.

She considered how to share the news. Alexis had kept her mouth shut, which was good, but ultimately, everyone would hear about her current state. Aerianna had to be the one to announce her condition before rumors began. She closed her eyes, believing she had to rest before she could do anything else.

Armbruster preferred to speak with Alexis privately. He knew she had a plan. Yarlen asked to join Armbruster because he still felt part of the team. However, Armbruster reminded him that Rammadar was now his Second-in-Command and that his services were no longer required. The words stung, enraging Yarlen. He detested his forced retirement. He felt there was much more he could do to help the kingdom and Armbruster. Feeling offended, he returned to the basement to work with Cazzandra. At least she still needed him.

Pauto tilted his head, attempting to understand Griffen Corilyn's plan. He was not making any sense. He suggested deploying half of the SAoW and keeping the rest of the army in place at the Palace. Pauto strongly disagreed. Griffen was young and relatively inexperienced. But he appeared to be motivated and talented in his magical abilities. Sadly, he lacked common sense. Pauto rose and approached Griffen.

"I understand your objective. However, it will be a complete waste of the SAoW power. We have a large army of warriors and security officers already in place at the Palace. The SAoW will be better utilized to secure the planet's perimeter, specifically around the Palace and the City of Miccay. Some members should deploy to the various mountains, Tullah as the primary objective, since it is close to the Palace," Pauto declared authoritatively. He had planned to allow Griffen to showcase his skills, but he quickly surmised that Griffen was not ready for such a grand task.

"Sir, I thank you for your guidance. I will do as you request." Griffen nodded and exited the chamber to locate the various SAoW group members. He disliked Pauto's need to interfere. Griffen felt his plan was solid and would be the right choice moving forward. Now, he understood Pauto would not relinquish his power completely to Griffen, demanding that his plan be implemented.

Pauto scurried from the building and headed to meet with Armbruster. He wanted to inform him of the progress with the SAoW. As he marched down the dimly lit corridor, he thought about Aerianna. He planned to speak with her at dinner, demanding she share news about her new medical crisis. Something was amiss. He worried about her well-being after hearing rumors that Edwinn had been visiting her numerous times lately. Aerianna was a private Witch, but she owed him honesty. He would demand it.

Alexis remained in her chamber, thinking about the Council of Peace & War. So far, they were unwilling to help at all. Their words were just that...words. They chose to remain focused on diplomacy and insisted Alexis follow their plan.

However, it became increasingly clear to Alexis that she would continue to reject their stance. It was soft and would not illicit the results she wanted to see. Therefore, Alexis put a bounty on Gardon's head and the entire *GRAW*. By doing so, the Hunters would surely find him. They would do the work for her. Ultimately, she was willing to pay their price, whatever it may be.

Blud-Trackers, also called the Hunters, were known to be ruthless. On Earth, they were called Vampires. They were a small and elite group, highly talented, able to use spellcraft and their natural instincts to locate just about anyone in a timely manner. There was one problem, though...the Hunters were challenging to find. They chose to remain out of sight, well hidden, and dispersed between the planets for security. It would take some time to locate one of the select few.

One of the great leaders of the Blud-Trackers was Magorr Bloodrup. He had been quite successful in locating missing W3s in the past. His hunt fees remained astronomical, usually too stiff for most to pay.

However, those with the proper resources could enlist his services. Magorr had never failed a mission. Alexis planned to find a way to locate Magorr. Her mother, Lorthana, would be able to help. She stayed in contact with some of the Hunters. At one point, she had dated Magorr just before meeting Gardone. It seemed conceivable that Magorr would agree to help them. Or, so the Queen hoped.

Alexis exhaled slowly, leaning back in the chair with her fingers interlaced, supporting her head. She tried to remain calm. Alexis figured that Lorthana would be upset at the prospect of locating Magorr. Alexis placed her hands on her lap and closed her eyes. Minutes passed, and she remained silent, meditating on the ideas swirling around in her head.

Suddenly, she opened her eyes and sprang from the chair. She dashed out of the chamber, ready to speak with Lorthana and locate Cazzandra to aid her in the departure. Alexis could not remain in her room, feeling restless.

In the Courtyard, Alexis waited patiently while Cazzandra lined up the necessary items to open a portal for her departure. She was ready to head to Iriss to speak with Lorthana.

Lorthana had planned to leave Iriss to head to Earth. She wanted to meet with the Council of Witches to discuss their views on what was happening on Alstromia. However, before she could transport herself, Alexis appeared, wearing her battle uniform.

"My goodness, child. I was not expecting you. Are you here to speak with your sister?"

"No. I have nothing to say to her at this point. I already know she is not behind the attacks. Actually, that is why I am here. I need your help, Mother," Alexis began.

"Okay. What may I do for you?"

"Mom, I need you to locate Magorr. I want to enlist his help in locating Gardone. Please, before you say no, think about it. Gardone must be found and brought up on charges."

Lorthana shook her head, feeling it was a horrible idea to hire Magorr. It was unlikely he would bring Gardone in alive. He did not care about the condition of the contract fugitive. All he wanted was to deliver a body to Alexis. No matter what had happened, Lorthana hated the idea of using a Hunter.

"Alexis, please, let us discuss this further. I believe you are acting rashly. Gardone should be held accountable for all his actions, but using a Blud-Tracker will not only cost you a fortune but could also result in Gardone's immediate death. Is that what you want? You will not get the justice you seek if Gardone is killed. Believe me. You will regret it," Lorthana warned.

"Furthermore, you realize what the Blud-Trackers are and what they do. Correct?"

"Mom, I'm aware of the Blud-Trackers and their peculiar characteristics. I don't understand how you could have been in a romantic relationship with someone like Magorr. His blood-red eyes and glistening blue skin give me the creeps. However, he's excellent at his job, so I guess that's something. Did it never bother you that his mother was a Witch and his father a Blud-Tracker? I heard he is more of a Blud-Tracker than a Warlock. Anyway, I'm okay with the Hunter using any means necessary to capture my father. Gardone made his decision, and now it's time for me to make mine." Alexis confidently stated.

"Alexis, if you intend to use a Hunter, I ask you to discuss it with Armbruster and the Command Team. Once everyone is on board with your decision, I will reach out to the Hunters. I promise," Lorthana retorted.

"To begin with, I don't require their approval to make decisions that benefit the planet of Alstromia or the monarchy. However, I will still inform them as a courtesy. I'll let you know my decision later," Alexis adamantly declared, slamming down her enormous Ceptre and vanishing.

Lorthana often felt that her daughter acted impulsively and was unwilling to listen to reason. The thought of seeing Magorr again didn't thrill her. It had been ages since they last met, and although she had heard about his accomplishments, she had chosen to stay away from him out of fear that she would fall for him all over again and find it hard to resist him.

Magorr was rugged, handsome, powerful, and irresistible, and according to others, he was still single. Shaking her head, Lorthana hoped Alexis would reconsider and not hire the Hunters to locate Gardone.

Alexis appeared in the center of the Palace Courtyard precisely as planned, and Cazzandra was overjoyed to see the Queen return unharmed. Alexis expressed her gratitude to Cazzandra for her assistance and assured her that she would need her help again in the future.

Afterward, Alexis strode confidently toward the Security Command Chamber, eager to discuss her plan to hire a Hunter with Armbruster, Rammadar, and Yarlen. Regardless of their response, she knew she would proceed with her new strategy. The Queen was informing them of her plan, not asking for permission. She demanded results.

The door flung open, and Alexis stormed into the Security Command Chamber, her head held high. She made her way toward the end of the enormous table and swiftly took a seat. Armbruster gave her a stern look, but

Alexis tilted her head to the side and met his gaze.

"Alexis, how nice of you to join us. To what do we owe this pleasure?" Armbruster mockingly asked. He figured she was there to start an argument. She appeared irritated.

"I have come to inform you and your team of my decision regarding Gardone's capture," Alexis declared assertively. "I believe hiring a Hunter is the best way to locate Gardone. It is time to take action and end his dangerous activities once and for all. As the Queen, I have made up my mind, and I expect your full cooperation in this matter. I will not tolerate any dissent or delay. We must act swiftly and decisively to protect our kingdom and its people. Please pledge your commitment and support to make this happen."

"I see," Armbruster responded sarcastically, squinting his eyes.

"Furthermore, I have already requested that Lorthana speak with Magorr Bloodrup since they are close. I don't know what the Hunter will charge for this task, but I don't care. It's a matter of planetary security, and no price is too high. Do we have an agreement?" Alexis declared, her tone firm and resolute.

She scanned the room, observing her team's reactions. Rammadar looked puzzled. His eyebrows furrowed while Yarlen shook his head and fiddled with his beard.

Armbruster remained silent, probably taken aback by her boldness.

Growing frustrated with the lack of response, Alexis spoke up. "So, what do you think?" she asked, raising her voice noticeably, unable to comprehend why the group refused to provide feedback. She had reached a point where she wanted to scream.

"Alexis, have you lost your mind? We cannot hire a Blud-Tracker. Hunters can be ruthless and violent. That's pure madness. Why would we even consider it? Let's be real, it's a radical idea," Armbruster exclaimed, unable to contain his disbelief.

"Ummm, Armbruster. I am not asking you to agree or disagree with my choice. I am informing you and your staff about my plan. It may or may not change how they continue to conduct their job as they attempt to locate him. Or if they even wish to bother. Perhaps it would be best if your teams focused on securing our planet."

Rammadar approached Alexis and bowed. He quickly looked up. "My Queen, may I have a moment with you?"

"You wish to speak privately?" Alexis asked, wondering why he had refused to express his feelings in front of the others. It seemed suspicious.

"Yes. Please," Rammadar replied.

"Alright, let's take a walk," Alexis agreed, rising from her seat and heading toward the door. Rammadar followed closely, and they promptly left the room, while the rest of the team wondered what was happening. It was unusual for Rammadar to request a private conversation with the Queen, and it piqued their curiosity.

Alexis and Rammadar arrived at the Landing Deck, and Alexis decided to sit on the stone bench that faced the Valley of Miccay. Rammadar joined her, sitting at the opposite end and holding his cloak firmly. Alexis couldn't help but notice his unease and became curious. *'Why is he so nervous?'*

"My Queen. I know Magorr. His price will be steep. He is known to be unethical and unyielding. Are you sure you want to put your father through that? I am not being disrespectful by any means. I am worried there will be no turning back once this is done. Magorr will bring your father to you. However, most likely, he will be delivered to you dead."

"I already know this. What is your point, Rammadar?" Alexis asked.

"Your Majesty, Magorr is a relative of mine. I wanted you to know. I have not been in contact with him for years. He is someone I feel I do not wish to associate with, ever. Yes, he gets the job done, but I don't particularly appreciate how he does it. I wanted you to know about my relationship with him. I prefer that you hear it from me rather than from someone else. I hope you are not upset, Your Majesty."

Alexis nodded. Now, it all made sense. He was apprehensive and worried that someone would broach the subject that he was related to Magorr Bloodrup, a Blud-Tracker and Hunter.

"I see. Well, I appreciate your candor. But I am keenly aware of what Magorr does for a living and how he accomplishes the feat. I have come to terms with my decision. My father made his choice. Now I am forced to make mine." Alexis stood her ground, shrugged, and walked away, leaving Rammadar alone on the Landing Deck.

He stared at the twin moons, wondering what Magorr would do. He assumed he would not care either way if Gardone lived or died. Magorr wanted the bounty, which would probably be paid in Victor Coins, and that was all that mattered. Rammadar hoped Gardone would be forced to face justice and not be allowed a quick death.

Rammadar departed from the Landing Deck with the intention of finding Armbruster and informing him about Magorr as a gesture of courtesy. However, he believed that this information need not be shared with everyone. In his opinion, it was a private matter, and he had the discretion to decide whom to share it with.

However, it was best for him to divulge the information before Alexis did. Entering the Security Command Chamber, Armbruster stood by the window, looking out. He heard Rammadar enter and turned around to face him.

"You have come to tell me something, Rammadar?"

"Yes, Sir," replied Rammadar. "I have already informed the Queen, and I believe you also have the right to know. However, I do not intend to inform anyone else about this private matter."

"Fine. What is it, Rammadar?"

"Sir, the Hunter, Magorr Bloodrup, is a relative of mine. Though we are not in contact, I felt it was imperative to share this information with the Queen and you!"

"Aha. I understand your reluctance to blurt out that information in front of everyone. I thank you for your honesty and respect you for it. It is no big deal, Rammadar. You are not responsible for others or their actions. However, I appreciate you coming forth and informing us about your relationship with a Hunter. It means a great deal." Armbruster placed his hand on Rammadar's shoulder, reassuring him, "You did the right thing."

Rammadar nodded, feeling grateful. The last thing he wanted was for Armbruster to lose confidence in him. The two stayed in the chamber for a while longer, discussing other important Palace business, while Alexis rested in her room, waiting to hear from Lorthana.

CHAPTER 5

Lorthana waited a few hours before finally mustering up the courage to locate Magorr. It was not an easy decision, and she felt sick to her stomach. She figured he would be in New England, on Earth. She transported herself from Iriss to his home with Yarlen's help and arrived outside the large mansion, wondering if he was inside.

Nervously, Lorthana tapped her foot, contemplating knocking on the door. Unexpectedly, the door swung open, and he smiled at her. Immediately, she noticed he was still as handsome as ever. Oddly, he did not appear surprised by her visit.

"Oh my! The beautiful Lorthana graces my presence after all these years! What brings you here, lovely?"

"Magorr, may I please step inside?" Lorthana asked, hoping to get to the point.

Magorr stepped aside and nodded, allowing her to enter the building. Her eyes roamed, exploring the area. It was dimly illuminated and smelled like lilies. She grinned, realizing it was exactly the same as before. He led her to the large and open living room. The tall stone fireplace roared with a flickering fire, adding ambiance. Candles graced every nook and cranny of the room, gleaming with light.

"Please take a seat," he gestured towards a group of sofas positioned near the fireplace. Opting for the first one, Lorthana gazed at him. He was dressed in black trousers, a white long-sleeved button-up shirt, and impeccably shiny black shoes. His dense, jet-black hair was neatly combed to the side. She also noticed a wide, white streak of hair mixed in with the stark black on the left side of his head. It was a new addition, and she felt it made him look distinguished. Magorr was extremely attractive for a 150-year-old Blud-Tracker.

"Magorr, thank you for meeting with me. I understand that it's unexpected for me to be here after so many years. Nonetheless, I need your assistance," she said, giving him a sideways smirk and feeling apprehensive.

"Does it have anything to do with Gardone? I have heard about his crazy antics, and I am sickened by them. He is a lunatic!" Magorr took a seat next to Lorthana.

"Yes. My daughter, Alexis, wishes to hire you to track him down. I was tasked with speaking with you since we had a previous relationship. I hope that does not upset you." Lorthana's heart raced. He still made her feel young and beautiful.

"Anything for you, my beauty. So, why me? There are other Blud-Trackers. I am only one of the exclusive groups. Though I am flattered, I have no idea why your daughter would specifically want me."

"She desires the best. You are that. I believe she is worried Gardone will be able to elude others. I reassured her that you would be able to capture him." She smiled, hoping he would accept her explanation.

"Really? Do you know why Gardone has attacked Alstromia? Is it revenge against your daughter or something else? I believe I heard they have a strained relationship, correct?" he desired clarification.

"My, my, Magorr. You've been keeping up with my family drama," Lorthana replied, feeling happy to be near him. In a way, she was surprised he still cared.

"Does it surprise you? I also heard that you have dissolved your marriage to Gardone. How wonderful. Are you seeing anyone?"

Magorr was quite blunt. It shocked Lorthana, but she was also flattered by his attention. Obviously, he was still attracted to her. He still looked young, and she instantly felt self-conscious, realizing she looked like an old hag compared to him. His skin still looked flawless, smooth as can be. His eyes were gigantic and mesmerizing. She felt drawn to him as before.

"Yes, you are correct. I could not remain married to someone who continued to do what he did. First, he kidnapped our daughter with the intention of taking the kingdom from her. Then, he had an affair with a younger Witch. Now, he is out to destroy Alstromia and Alexis again! My daughter has been through so much. I am doing everything I can to aid her," Lorthana explained.

"I understand." Magorr took Lorthana's hand into his. She pulled away instinctively, feeling his cold hand on hers. She had forgotten he was not warm-blooded.

He frowned at her action and quickly withdrew his hand, placing it on his lap. "What do you want me to do with Gardone once I capture him?"

"We prefer him alive, if at all possible. Alexis would like to turn him over to the authorities. We want him to suffer the worst of all fates…the loss of his magic. He shall live the rest of his life alone in the High Tower."

"Hmmm, I would rather put an end to his wretched life and make him endure my wrath," Magorr roared with an intense glare. Lorthana observed his trembling lip and hand rubbing. As soon as he realized she was observing him, he ceased his actions and opted to stare at the fireplace.

"Again, please, we need him alive. The next part is difficult for me, but I must know. Name your price." Lorthana stared at Margorr apprehensively. "Alexis is awaiting my response." She folded her hands and smiled at him.

Magorr nodded and contemplated Lorthana's words. It was simple for him. He could not charge for this task, wishing that Gardone had been caught. He had thought about finding him on his own before when he learned what Gardone had done. Given this opportunity, he had the perfect excuse to do so. Alexis and Lorthana had officially hired him to hunt down Gardone, and he was elated.

"I cannot take anything for this contracted Hunt Bounty. It will be my pleasure to bring him in. Gardone will know what it means to suffer. I promise you this."

"I will owe you, dear friend," Lorthana responded.

Unexpectedly, Magorr pulled Lorthana toward him and kissed her. She reciprocated, feeling the sweet, familiar sensation run through her body, making her weak. She scooted away, quickly withdrawing.

"As much as I am flattered by your kiss, Magorr, let's keep it professional for now," she insisted, feeling awkward.

"Does that mean you and I can explore where this leads after I hand over Gardone? I sense that you're still drawn to me, just as I am to you," he asked hopefully. Lorthana was stunning. Being around her made him feel different. She still made him feel wanted, and he had missed her immensely.

"You, dear friend, are getting ahead of yourself. I would think there are many beautiful Blud-Trackers, or Witches, for that matter, ready to enjoy your company."

"Perhaps, but my heart has always belonged to you, my beauty," Magorr replied. He was charming as ever. "You have not changed. You are just as stunning as before."

He brushed aside a few strands of her hair, gazing into her eyes.

Not wishing to become too distracted, Lorthana hopped off the couch. "Alright. I will contact my daughter and inform her of our plan. You have no idea how thrilled I am that you have agreed to help us. It means a great deal, and I am eternally grateful. I promise to make it up to you."

"Oh, you will. Trust me," Magorr chuckled, walking Lorthana to the front door. He took her hand and kissed it, staring intensely into her eyes. Lorthana looked down, feeling self-conscious.

Magorr's smoldering red eyes tried to mesmerize and capture her attention, and her heart raced, causing her to gasp for air. Lorthana ran out the door and slammed down her Ceptre, transporting herself back to Iriss. Her head spun. Magorr was still the true love of her life, and she realized why she had stayed away. She still desired him, yearning for his touch.

Magorr closed and locked the door. He stood in the foyer and looked around. Instantly, he noticed her smell. Still madly attracted to Lorthana, he closed his eyes, visualizing their previous kiss. He licked his lips, realizing how much he craved her. There was an undeniable force between them, pulling them toward each other, and he could not resist. Magorr could not wait to bring Gardone to Alexis. Hopefully, Lorthana would feel compelled to show her appreciation to him. The thought made him happy. He planned to summon his team, eager to begin the hunt.

Alexis paced around her chamber, wondering if Lorthana had been able to locate Magorr. She assumed her mother would find him. The two had been quite cozy with each other in the past. Alexis had heard the rumors in her youth about the torrid love affair between Lorthana and Magorr, long before she married her father. Alexis wondered if Lorthana was still attracted to Magorr.

Perhaps that is why she balked at the thought of contacting him. Maybe she was worried her feelings for him would interfere with the job she wanted him to accomplish.

Back on Iriss, Lorthana entered her room and plopped into the plush chair. She closed her eyes, remembering how Magorr had made her feel. She felt giddy and young. He had that powerful effect on her. She wondered whether they would rekindle their relationship, and she felt a flush of excitement.

However, first, she had to find a way to get a message to Alexis. She knew it was nearly impossible with the barrier protecting the planet.

Rammadar approached the Queen's Chamber, nervous about speaking with her. Their previous conversation left him feeling strange. Alexis appeared disappointed in him, and that was not something he liked. Reluctantly, he knocked on her door.

"Enter," the Queen shouted.

"Your Majesty. May we speak?"

"Rammadar, what a surprise. Do tell me why you are here. Has something happened? Is everything okay?"

"Yes, I felt awkward after our conversation on the Landing Deck. I wanted to ensure we were okay and that you were not upset with me."

"Rammadar, you have done nothing wrong. Why would I be mad? Magorr is a different breed, for sure. My issue has nothing to do with you. I must confess that my mother and Magorr had a previous romantic relationship. So, naturally, I was shocked to hear about your connection to him. Your comment took me aback."

"What? Lorthana dated Magorr? When?" Rammadar asked, intrigued. He also felt confused. It was the first time he had ever heard such information.

133

"It was a long time ago. It was before she married my father, Gardone. Supposedly, the two had been quite an item. I never could understand why she did not marry Magorr. But then, in those days, it was a faux pas to marry outside your kind. With Magorr's mother being a Witch and his father a Blud-Tracker, it was considered strange for them to intermingle. Now, it is more common. No one thinks twice about it."

"Yes, I knew about Magorr's lineage. I did not know about Lorthana's relationship with him. He never mentioned it. How odd!"

"Magorr is quite private, from what I understand, he's a bit of a recluse. Nonetheless, he is an excellent Hunter. I am waiting to hear from my mother. Hopefully, she found him and tasked him with bringing in Gardone. I believe he is the only one able to locate my father."

"Sounds good. I am glad we had this talk, Your Majesty. Thank you for your time." Rammadar excused himself and left to head back to the Security Command Chamber.

Alexis approached the large window. Worried about Alstromia's future, she looked outside. It was pouring rain. Once in a while, she spotted a flicker of light dancing across the sky. She wondered whether it was related to the magic cast by Cazzandra or to more relentless attacks against Alstromia.

On Earth, Magorr assembled his team. Three Blud-Trackers sat around the large table in the basement. "We have been tasked with locating Gardone Henrii Stainnard. He is wanted by Alexis Snipperdoom, the Queen and ruler of Alstromia. We must find him immediately."

Casstor Shadowlee squirmed uncomfortably in his chair. He disliked the idea. He was cognizant of the fact that Gardone declared war on Alstromia, pelting the planet with fire and spells. It was catastrophic, from what he heard. Though he believed Alstromia deserved justice, he wondered why Gardone felt compelled to initiate such a vile act against a peaceful planet. The idea of capturing Gardone worried him. He knew Gardone had a strong following and that his supporters would die for him. It would complicate the hunt.

"Sir, have you accepted the contracted Hunt Bounty? Gardone and his *GRAW* have certainly raised hell on Alstromia. But do we wish to interfere? It is not our battle. Do you believe it is possible to locate him easily?" Casstor inquired.

"Gardone is a fugitive. Though he may believe he is hiding well, we are Hunters. He is not a challenge for us. I have no doubt we will discover his whereabouts. We must apprehend him quickly and turn him over to the Queen. I have given my promise to her mother, Lorthana Snipperdoom, reassuring her of our aid. I will ask our friends to keep an eye out for the entire *GRAW*. In the meantime, let us plan for the day," announced Magorr.

Frustrated, he observed that Casstor seemed hesitant to join in the pursuit of Gardone, which was unusual given his typically eager and willing demeanor. This behavior prompted Magorr to wonder what might be causing Casstor to act differently and raised concerns that something could be wrong.

The room grew dark as Alexis moved away from the window. She planned to head to the basement to speak with Yarlen and Cazzandra about allowing her to leave Alstromia safely once again. She felt the need to transport to Iriss to chat with Lorthana about her meeting with Magorr, which she assumed had already occurred.

If Lorthana had made the arrangements, Alexis hoped it would just be a matter of time before Gardone was apprehended and brought before the Royal Court on Alstromia. Alexis prayed it would not take long. She yearned for justice.

In the hut on Earth, Gardone seemed restless. He sulked and flopped on the couch, making strange noises. It did not go unnoticed by several of the *GRAW* members. One member, Thornton Glowstone, sat beside Gardone, wishing to hold a conversation.

"Gardone, what is the matter? Everything has gone as planned. Yes, the current attack is on hold while the others attempt to penetrate Alstromia's new protective barrier. However, we successfully damaged Alstromia and killed many W3s. It is just as you hoped and planned. We even got lucky and killed the Queen's beloved pet, Trixxie, in the process. So, why are you acting strangely and restless? Is there something you need to share with us?" Thornton asked. He feared Gardone was withholding vital information.

"No. There is nothing that concerns any of you. I received a disturbing message from a trusted source that Blud-Trackers had been hired to find me. I fear I will be caught quickly. Magorr Bloodrup has been placed in charge. His team members are excellent Hunters. My days as a free Warlock are about to expire, I fear." Gardone fretfully announced. He lowered his head, feeling defeated. Though in his heart, he knew this day would come.

"I had hoped to destroy Alexis and Alstromia before my apprehension. I doubt I will see that happen. I believe Magorr will track me down. Honestly, I despise the idea of a blood-sucking Hunter using this opportunity to feast on my body to provide them with the nourishment they require to stay alive," Gardone bellowed, panic-stricken.

The rest of the group overheard the conversation and immediately became alarmed. Without Gardone leading them, they did not stand a chance against the Queen, Alexis Snipperdoom. She was powerful and had many allies willing to aid her. That fact frightened most. Gardone had always been the forceful one. If he were gone, who would take over? Who had the ability to successfully challenge the Queen?

"Just because a Hunter has been enlisted to locate you does not mean it will happen quickly. Perhaps you should move to Iriss? Maybe your other daughter will help keep you safe?" Thornton suggested.

"No. I am not allowed to set foot on Iriss. Zandorah has sided with her sister and mother. I have no other place to hide. Earth is my only refuge."

Thornton recommended, "In order to ensure your safety, we will have to relocate you to a different place every day." He found it unsettling that Gardone seemed to have accepted defeat even before being caught. Typically, Gardone was a picture of resilience, but now he appeared vulnerable. It was as if he was done fighting for his existence.

"I cannot continue to hide forever. I believe the time has come… I must place someone else in charge of the *GRAW*. With your expertise and leadership, the *GRAW* can continue to flourish. Will you assume the position?" Gardone inquired, offering him the job.

"Sir, I will be happy to take over the *GRAW* if that is your wish. However, I do not believe it is time for you to step down. You have much to accomplish. I will be happy to remain at your side until you are ready to relinquish your command," Thornton announced. He disliked the way Gardone acted. Gardone nodded, and the decision was made to keep him in charge of the *GRAW*, with Thornton aiding him.

In the meantime, they had to remain vigilant and move Gardone daily to make it more difficult for the Hunters to locate him. It was all they could do.

On Alstromia, Alexis approached the basement door. She did not bother knocking. Instead, she entered and found Yarlen working with Cazzandra, hovering over a steamy and bubbling cauldron. Both looked surprised to see Alexis.

"Your Majesty," declared Yarlen. "What an unexpected pleasure. How may we be of assistance to you?" Instantly, he worried. *'Why is she here?'*

"I must transport to Iriss to speak with my mother, Lorthana. I need your assistance. Please be so kind as to make it happen." Alexis felt restless and wanted to depart Alstromia as soon as possible.

"My Queen, I will happily accompany you to an outdoor location where I can place a temporary pass-through for you to leave. However, it will be impossible for us to communicate after that. So, we must schedule a time for your return, as before. How many hours would you like to remain on Iriss?" Cazzandra inquired.

"Until this evening. You may allow my return by 8 o'clock. Will that work for you, Cazzandra?"

"Whatever you wish, My Queen," she responded. "Let's head to the Courtyard. I will bring one of the vials filled with the necessary potion to send you through the portal," explained Cazzandra. Yarlen nodded in agreement.

A few minutes later, Alexis arrived on Iriss. Cazzandra's potion and spell worked perfectly. Alexis appeared by the main gate facing the Castle of Zandor. The moment security noticed Alexis approaching, they moved aside to allow her to enter the building. Alexis hurried past the guards, eager to locate her mother. She wondered if Zandorah was in the Castle and planned to speak with her if she had enough time. She wanted to share the news about the Blud-Tracker hire.

Lorthana dressed in her evening gown, hoping to relax before dinner. It had been an eventful day. The knock on the door was unexpected, and she quickly moved to answer it.

"Alexis! How wonderful to see you. How did you manage to leave Alstromia? Come inside, dear. I hoped to speak with you and share the news about Magorr," Lorthana hugged her daughter.

"Mother, get to the point. Did you locate Magorr? If so, did you ask him to track down Father?" Alexis did not want to waste time with idle chatter.

"Alexis, let us sit down and chat, shall we?" Lorthana insisted, pointing to two chairs in the corner of the room by a window. She could tell Alexis was eager to hear the news.

Reluctantly, Alexis sat on the chair and eyed her mother, awaiting her reply. With impatience, she tapped her foot. Lorthana folded her hands, appearing apprehensive.

"Alexis, I did manage to locate Magorr. Thankfully, he has graciously agreed to help us," Lorthana announced, watching her daughter's reaction.

"That is exciting news." Alexis jumped out of her seat enthusiastically, bending down to kiss her mother. "Thank you, Mom. I knew you would find him. I am delighted you were able to convince Magorr to help our cause."

"It was not necessary to convince him, Alexis. Once I explained the situation, he immediately offered to help us. He is not a fan of Gardone's."

"What is his fee? Did he share that with you? When will he start?" Alexis asked fretfully. She worried his price tag would be high and wondered how to pay him.

"You will be pleased to know he will do it for free! He claims it is his pleasure to come to our aid!" Lorthana announced proudly.

Alexis shook her head. "Aha! So he is doing it for you, right? He still has feelings for you, doesn't he?" Alexis interrogated. "He is aiding us because you spoke with him. If I had made the request, he probably would not have agreed, at least not right away, correct?" Alexis grinned.

Lorthana's irritation was evident as she snarled, "Why does it matter? He agreed, so I suggest we focus on that." Lorthana hated that Alexis made her so defensive.

"My, my… mother, you are getting quite protective of him. I am simply stating he is not doing it for me. He has agreed to capture Gardone to get into your good graces. It is quite apparent." Alexis began laughing. She found it funny that her mother vehemently denied that Magorr had an ulterior motive.

"Alexis, I am grateful Magorr vowed to locate Gardone for us. That is what matters, and we should keep that in mind. What he feels for me is beside the point. Yes, I am still very attracted to him. Seeing him brought back feelings I thought were long gone. Now, I realize they are still there. However, I have decided not to address my feelings for him until after Gardone is captured. Furthermore, I promise not to interfere or distract him from the job." Lorthana exhaled, glad she had made her position clear.

Alexis felt overjoyed at the prospect of Magorr chasing down Gardone. She closed her eyes and visualized his apprehension, which was a thrilling thought. He would finally face the consequences of his actions.

After another hour, Alexis realized it was time to head back to Alstromia. She did not want to be late and miss the opportunity to be able to pass through the portal. Her return had to be perfectly timed, and Cazzandra warned her that reopening the pass-through could take some time if she were late. Alexis

said goodbye to her mother, grateful for her accomplishments. Sadly, there was no
time to speak with Zandorah. Their chat would have to wait. It was a considerable relief that Lorthana had managed to hire Magorr. Gardone's days as a free Warlock were numbered, and Alexis smiled broadly at the thought.

At the center of the Courtyard on Alstromia, Cazzandra stood alongside Yarlen, anticipating the impending arrival. The moment was approaching, and Alexis was on the verge of needing the temporary portal to access the planet. Cazzandra usually didn't fret about her potions and spells, but today she seemed agitated, nervously adjusting her cape.

"What is the matter, Cazzandra? We are fully prepared. You are acting like a Cayley, fluttering around nervously. My goodness. Are you okay?" Yarlen asked, noticing her pacing in a circle.

"I am worried something could go wrong. After all, we are talking about the Queen. If I do mess up, she will have my head, guaranteed."

"You are crazy. The Queen adores you and has confidence in your abilities. It worked last time. Nothing will go wrong this time, either. You have the potion and spell, just as before, right?" He announced, attempting to put her at ease.

"Well, yes." She looked down at her feet, avoiding eye contact with Yarlen.

Yarlen frowned. "Okay, and why do you say it like that, Cazzandra? What are you not telling me?" He feared it was bad news. Instantly, he panicked, staring at the young Witch. His stomach was beginning to flip-flop.

"I ran out of one ingredient. So, I made a substitution. I am hopeful it will have the same effect." She confessed, scrunching her nose.

"Oh my goodness! Cazzandra! Why did you not inform me of this before? What ingredient are you missing? If the magic does not work and the Queen is trapped outside Alstromia, this could be catastrophic," Yarlen screeched, frenzied.

"I needed a variety of herbs from Tullah Mountain. In the past, I used to trade for them with Florenzzah. Now that she is gone, I have no idea where to locate the specialty herbs," confessed Cazzandra. She chewed on her thumb, worried about how Yarlen would react.

Yarlen became restless. He played with his beard as he walked back and forth. Finally, he stopped before Cazzandra. "We will see what happens. In the event the Queen does not manage to appear, you and I will make a plan to locate the missing herbs. Let's not panic yet," he suggested with an awkward grin.

It was too late. Cazzandra was already panicking, visualizing Alexis unable to penetrate the barrier she had put in place.

The idea of failing the Queen made her nauseous. Before she could say something to Yarlen, she noticed Andreh approaching.

"Have either of you seen the Queen? I must speak with her immediately. Armbruster has been frantically searching the Palace for her as well," he complained, arms crossed.

"As a matter of fact, Andreh, we await her arrival now. She should be here any minute," declared Yarlen, attempting to sound upbeat. He did not wish to share with Andreh that there could potentially be a problem.

The three stared at the sky, waiting. Cazzandra pulled on Yarlen's arm, indicating it was time. The two stood side by side as Cazzandra poured the liquid goo onto the stones before her. She closed her eyes, waving her hands, chanting. Yarlen looked up, waiting for the tiny portal opening. He noticed some flickering and purple sparks, which he assumed meant everything was working as planned. But minutes later, Alexis remained absent. Cazzandra stood next to Yarlen, her hands trembling uncontrollably.

Andreh began to worry. "Is this normal?" he asked, pointing to the sky, noticing it was a vivid, hot-pink color.

Cazzandra stared at Yarlen, rolling her eyes. Yarlen shook his head, realizing her chant and potion had failed. The sky had never been that color before. Yarlen roughly grabbed Cazzandra by the arm and pulled her away from Andreh, whispering in her ear. She shook her head, running away, fleeing to the dungeon of the Palace.

"I can only assume something is wrong," Andreh yelled, glaring at Yarlen. "Where is the Queen? Why is she not here? Did your apprentice screw up?" Andreh was furious and demanded answers.

"Yes, Andreh. We have a problem. The Queen cannot return. Let's head to the Security Command Chamber and share the news with Armbruster and the rest of the team."

Alexis frowned, staring at the sky, noticing the lack of a portal opening. She continued to slam her Ceptre down, hoping to transport herself back home, but nothing happened. She remained standing in place. Apprehensively, she lightly tapped the Ceptre, thinking she was too forceful. She laughed nervously. Five minutes passed, and the sickening realization hit her. She was stuck on Iriss! Alexis became terrified. What would happen in her absence? *'Will Armbruster take over?'* Alexis pondered.

Reluctantly, she returned to the Castle to speak with Zandorah and Lorthana. Alexis entered the Courtyard and looked around.

Finally, she located one of Zandorah's security personnel. Alexis quickly asked him to find the Supreme Ruler, her sister. She needed to figure out what to do now that she could not leave Iriss. Alexis also wondered about Andreh. What would he think when he found out she could not return to the Palace?

On Alstromia, the group of Warlocks and Wizzards met in the Security Command Chamber. Though Cazzandra was the reason for the discussion, she remained absent. She had retreated to the basement of the Palace to seek solitude.

Cazzandra was not used to failing. She feared the repercussions and wondered how she could fix the situation. It finally occurred to her that she could potentially locate the missing herbs on Tullah Mountain. If the search was unsuccessful, she planned to visit Farla to inquire if she would trade with her. The old Witch was known to have a large variety of magical herbs.

Armbruster screamed at the top of his lungs. "What do you mean Alexis cannot transport back to Alstromia? So, your apprentice botched the Queen's return? I knew she was incapable of handling such a critical task. Why did you not intervene?"

"Your Majesty," Yarlen began, "Cazzandra is gifted. The Queen absolutely did the right thing by assigning her this mission. It did not work properly because we ran out of the necessary ingredients. We attempted to gather more but failed to do so in time." Yarlen realized it was best to take the responsibility off Cazzandra. He hoped to save her.

"Furthermore, we are on our way to locate them now. Once we have them in our possession, we can concoct another batch and find a way to retrieve the Queen. Everything will turn out okay, Sir," the old Wizzard reassured the King.

"Do what you need to, but ensure my wife has the ability to return to her kingdom. In the meantime, I will call a meeting to inform everyone that I am in charge," Armbruster declared as he surveyed the room.

Pauto sighed and rolled his eyes. He was aware that Armbruster would seize the chance to assume control of the kingdom and Alstromia. Pauto hoped that Armbruster wouldn't misuse his newfound authority by implementing too many changes during Alexis's absence. It would lead to issues upon her return, and Pauto wasn't prepared to handle the aftermath. At the moment, he pledged to support the King and behave as usual, even though his allegiance lay with the Queen.

It was a dismal day for Alexis, and nothing could brighten her mood. She detested being stranded on Iriss. The room was adorned in cheerful pastel colors, and the fluffy white carpet was immaculately clean and uncomfortably bright. Alexis furrowed her brow, shook her head, and anticipated Zandorah's input.

Lorthana was reluctant to say much. She realized Alexis was worried about Alstromia's security during her absence and was probably frustrated that she needed to extend her stay on Iriss a bit longer.

"Alexis, you know you can remain here as long as needed. I will ask a few of my staff members to figure out how to break through Alstromia's barrier and return you. I am hoping someone can do something. I can only imagine how scared you are right now." Zandorah wished to keep the conversation positive.

"Zandorah, I am truly grateful for your support. However, I'm not afraid. I am furious. I want to understand what went wrong and who is accountable. I am hopeful it wasn't Cazzandra's doing. I trusted her to guarantee my safe return."

Alexis sank into the chair, gazing at the scenery before her. The blooming trees and overall cheerfulness only irritated her more. She loathed it and wanted to be back in her Palace. She found Iriss disgustingly picturesque.

As Alexis pondered what was happening on Alstromia, she became enraged. It occurred to her that Armbruster had probably declared himself in charge of the kingdom since she was unaccounted for.

However, what worried her more was what he would try to implement. Surely, Armbruster would use this time to assert his power. He disliked many things, and this was the perfect opportunity to make changes without any pushback. Alexis jumped out of the chair and paced around the room, mumbling to herself.

Lorthana rose from her chair and approached her daughter, gently taking her hand. "Alexis, please, sit down and take it easy. There is nothing we can do now, and it makes no sense for you to make yourself crazy. You cannot control what is happening on Alstromia. I can only assume that is your worry?"

"Mom, you know Armbruster. He will take over the day-to-day operations and ensure everyone knows he is in control. It makes me sick. He has waited a long time for such an opportunity. Also, I am worried about Lilah. I hope she is okay," Alexis removed her hand from her mother's and approached the window.

"Alexis, I will prepare a room for you next to mine. You will be near Mom, too. I hope that is okay," Zandorah offered. She realized Alexis was frustrated and nervous.

"Sure. That is fine. May I head there now?"

"Follow me, Alexis," Zandorah declared. As they exited the room, Lorthana remained behind, pondering how long Alexis would stay on Iriss. She was also curious if Magorr had the opportunity to gain information about Gardone's whereabouts.

Lorthana understood this was a pivotal time in their lives. Feeling exhausted, Lorthana decided to retire to her room for a quick nap. She needed some time to unwind and come up with a plan to assist Alexis further. However, her mind kept drifting, and she found herself thinking about Magorr in a sensual way, which greatly aroused her, and she smirked with delight.

CHAPTER 6

It did not take long for Alexis to fall asleep in her room on Iriss. She was mentally fatigued. Alexis thrashed around in the large bed, nightmares intruding on her rest. She was blissfully unaware of what was happening on Alstromia, which was probably a good thing. She would be furious if she knew what Armbruster enacted.

Armbruster proudly stood near the podium in the Courtyard. Half of the SAoW and other security members were lined up, ready to listen to Armbruster's speech. Yarlen remained standing in the back, allowing Rammadar to stand near the King.

"Good afternoon," Armbruster began. "I am here to inform you of a tragedy. Our Queen is on Iriss and unable to return to the kingdom. Our team is currently working on a resolution to bring her home quickly. In the meantime, I have taken over and will be in charge. I will notify the Council of Peace & War of the changes once I can relay a message to them. In the meantime, I will provide new plans to my team. They will inform you of your new orders shortly. Please keep our Queen in your thoughts. We are all very concerned for her welfare," Armbruster sat down, allowing Rammadar the opportunity to speak.

"I do not have much to add. Pauto and I will continue to work on security protocols and keep all supervisors in the loop. In the meantime, we must ensure our planet remains protected." He stepped back.

Pauto approached the podium. "We will do everything possible to bring the Queen home safely. I am working with Rammadar, the King, Andreh, and others to formulate a plan to expedite the process. Thank you." He moved aside since he was done talking.

Seconds later, Pauto excused himself to locate Aerianna. She had not returned to her duties, and he wanted to be the one to inform her about the Queen's unexpected leave. He knew she would be upset. Plus, he hoped to find out why she had been so ill recently. Something about the way she avoided his questions concerned him greatly.

Armbruster, Andreh, Rammadar, and Yarlen walked toward the end of the Palace to enter the Security Command Chamber. Armbruster planned to announce the new changes under his rule. He was thrilled to have the opportunity to make changes without Alexis whining about them.

Andreh strolled behind the others, feeling sick. He was frantic. When would the Queen return? Was she safe? What if he never saw her again? What if something worse had happened to Alexis? Perhaps she wasn't on Iriss, but instead, Gardone had captured her. The thought made him cringe as he entered the chamber.

The group of Warlocks sat around the oval table. Staring out the window, Andreh noticed two security members on Torrins patrolling the area outside. He wished he could get out of the suffocating room and fly his Torrin. He missed Alexis and could not concentrate on anything else.

Andreh heard Armbruster speaking but chose to tune him out, as his voice irritated him. He wondered if the King cared that Alexis could not return to Alstromia. Somehow, he figured Armbruster enjoyed her absence. He acted domineering and stern. Andreh frowned at the thought.

Before leaving the room, Armbruster placed Rammadar in charge of the new plan. Yarlen excused himself to join Cazzandra in the basement to figure out how to develop a new potion to return the Queen.

Cazzandra riffled through a giant pile of old spellbooks in the brightly lit chamber. She hoped for a different spell to help the Queen. At this point, Alexis was probably furious. Cazzandra worried she would be banned from Alstromia and sent back to Earth after Alexis returned.

Yarlen entered the chamber and noticed Cazzandra sitting on the cold stone flooring. Piles of books surrounded her. When entered, she looked up. He could tell she had been crying. Instantly, he felt terrible for her. She was young and alone. It could not be easy.

"Hello, Cazzandra. I am here to help you! Let us figure out how to remove the barrier so the Queen may enter Alstromia. What do you say?" Yarlen attempted to make her feel better, though he worried they couldn't pull it off.

His relationship with Alexis was finally in a good place. They were cordial toward each other, which was a vast improvement over their previous dealings. What would happen if things did not work out as he hoped? Would Alexis hold him responsible for Cazzandra's failures? He assumed she would.

Alexis was famous for blaming others. She should not have left the planet, as far as Yarlen was concerned. He wondered why Alexis had headed to Iriss in the first place. Why did she believe it was necessary? Could she have sent someone else in her place? Armbruster never shared with him why Alexis chose to leave Alstromia. It seemed like a strange thing to do, especially given the dire circumstances. Yarlen decided to focus on the current task, clearing his mind. Returning the Queen to Alstromia became Mission One!

On Iriss, Alexis heard the knock on the door and woke up. Irritated, she screamed, "Enter!" She wondered why someone would interrupt her nap.

Lorthana appeared. "Alexis, I have news. I have heard that someone used an Eternal Mirror and discovered what was happening on Alstromia. For some reason, nothing blocked the Mirror from revealing events. With that said, we need to get you back to Alstromia as fast as possible."

"Thank you for the information. If the Eternal Mirror works, there has to be a way to send me back safely. What else do you know, Mother? What is Armbruster doing?" Alexis assumed he had taken control of everything and was in the process of changing as much as he could. It was his one chance to do so. However, as soon as Alexis returned, she would make the necessary changes to revert to her rules. Armbruster was crazy for thinking he could do this to her. She would not allow it. Alexis did not wait for her mother to reply to her numerous questions.

Instead, Alexis jumped out of bed and dressed quickly. She was eager to meet with Zandorah and her team to assess the possibility of her return. She hated wasting time, and more than that, she despised remaining on Iriss. The planet and its environment annoyed her greatly. Alexis could not comprehend why Lorthana preferred to reside there. She offered Lorthana a room in the Palace of Snipperdoom, but she declined the invitation, stating she liked a more upbeat environment with abundant sunshine and less gloom and doom.

Alexis recalled the conversation a while ago with Lorthana. It was right after her Dismissal of Ceremony from Gardone. Lorthana felt lonely and stayed at the Palace with her family. One night, the two sipped various brews and reminisced about better times. Lorthana cried, stating she hated to return to Earth. Alexis offered her a room at the Palace, but Lorthana revealed she planned to live on Iriss. It hurt Alexis, but she knew her mother was like Zandorah, picking an environment with plenty of sunshine. She did not like the rain, thunder, or storms that frequently occurred on Alstromia.

That night, Lorthana departed for Iriss, leaving Alexis feeling abandoned by her mother. She could not understand why Lorthana constantly felt the need to be near Zandorah, casting aside Alexis. In a way, Alexis was used to it. It had been happening to her for as long as she could recall. Lorthana definitely had a favorite child, and Alexis was not the one.

As Alexis reminisced about that day, she began crying. Lorthana noticed, becoming alarmed.

"Oh, my goodness. What is wrong, Alexis? Do you miss your husband and child? Why are you crying?"

"Yes, Mom. I do. But that is not why I am crying. I remembered the night you moved to Iriss. It hurt. You have always preferred Zandorah. Why is that, Mother? Why am I never good enough for you?" Alexis asked tearfully.

Lorthana shook her head. "Alexis, stop. That is not it at all. I'm not fond of the weather on Alstromia. You know this. You prefer the darkness and the rain. Many of the Clan members do, too. I am not like that. I have always enjoyed the sunshine, warm breeze, and the budding trees and flowers. Iriss feels more like home to me. It has absolutely nothing to do with you. I promise. I adore you. I do not play favorites with my children!"

"Are you sure that is all there is to it?" Alexis asked apprehensively. "I wanted you to move in with me at the Palace. Not just for me but for Lilah, too. It would be nice to have you closer to your one and only grandchild."

"Alexis...I can always visit. I try to come and see Lilah once a week. You know this. Why are you blowing this out of proportion? I know you are stressed, but please, stop!" Lorthana insisted. She was not in the mood to get into some huge fight or drawn-out discussion.

Alexis contemplated her response. She knew her mother had spent quite a bit of time with Lilah. However, Alexis still preferred Lorthana residing in the Palace of Snipperdoom versus the Castle of Zandor.

"Okay, Mother. Whatever you want is fine with me. I just want you to be happy."

"Shall we join your sister for a late lunch? I am starving," Lorthana asked, hoping to change the subject.

"Sure, let's do that." Alexis followed Lorthana down the hallway.

★ *. ★ *. ★ *. ★ *. ★

As the day turned to darkness, almost everyone was in a foul mood. It was becoming apparent to Armbruster that no one wanted him to remain in charge. He received significant pushback on his new agenda. Rammadar was reluctant to follow his orders but obliged, realizing his job was at stake. Nonetheless, Armbruster noticed his lack of will to complete the assignments.

Andreh was absent from meetings and informed Pauto that he planned to take a week of personal leave to deal with some issues. Armbruster assumed it had everything to do with Alexis and her inability to return to Alstromia. He frowned, thinking about that.

Armbruster was not a radical Warlock or Wizzard. He was not attempting to overthrow Alexis or her rule. He simply wished to enforce a few things that he felt needed to be done.

One new change involved removing redundant staff members. He figured there were spies on the team, and Armbruster wanted to keep his circle small and secure. He had discussed this plan with Rammadar, who felt it unnecessary to make any changes until the Queen returned. Armbruster disagreed. He felt this was the perfect time.

Alexis disliked changes, refusing to listen to new suggestions. She preferred to run her kingdom the way she had from the beginning.

On the other hand, Armbruster wanted fresh blood. He knew there were talented Warlocks, Wizzards, and Witches who could prove themselves and aid the kingdom. He had previously discussed adding new personnel and thinning out the current ones, but Alexis denied his request. Naturally, now was the right time for such revisions, and Armbruster would not allow someone like Rammadar to stand in his way.

The only one standing up for him and his revamped proposals was Pauto. He seemed more than willing to go with the flow, praising the King for making such bold moves. Armbruster realized Pauto was an ally.

Pauto stared at the sky, watching purple and green sparks ricochet off an invisible shield. He wondered who continued to pelt the planet and why. He heard rumors that the *GRAW* was responsible, specifically Gardone. The thought caused him to flinch. *'Why would Gardone continually wage war against Alexis, his child?'* It seemed absurd. Pauto shook his head and chose to head to Aerianna's chamber. He wanted answers about her health and was tired of all the delays. He would force her to divulge her issues so they could discuss them.

Aerianna showered and dressed. It had been days since she had enough energy to do anything other than sleep. Edwinn had left her alone and reassured her she was on the way to recovery and would feel better soon. It was a huge relief to her to hear this. She wondered why Pauto had been absent, hoping he would visit her.

Five minutes later, her wish came true. Pauto knocked on the door and let himself into her room. She looked beautiful, wearing a long, flowing gown in pale pink. Her long blond hair was braided and fell down her right shoulder. Her cheeks had regained color, and she smiled at him.

"Hello, beautiful," Pauto said, kissing her on the lips. He pulled her against his body.

She smelled like flowers, sweet and fresh. Aerianna created her perfume with ingredients from Earth, such as essential oils, roses, lilacs, lilies, and more. She enjoyed working in the laboratory, concocting different scents. This specific perfume became her favorite, and she lovingly called it *Moonspellz*™ after her mother, Agnessa Moonspell. Aerianna has worn the perfume every day since its creation. Its captivating scent reminds her of her mother, who had been an avid gardener and loved flowers from Earth.

"I have missed you, love. Where have you been?" Aerianna complained.

"I came by, but Edwinn has been in your chamber. What is happening, Aerianna? I am dreadfully worried. Please, tell me. Are you okay? What can I do?" Pauto pleaded, releasing her.

She began crying. Instantly, his heart raced with fear. "What is it, Aerianna? Whatever is going on, I am here for you."

"Pauto, have a seat. We should talk," she responded, acting bravely. Pauto felt ill-prepared for the news he was about to receive. His hands shook with fright.

Suddenly, she felt ill, jumping up to sprint to the bathroom, barely making it before vomiting. Pauto followed her, watching. He became even more worried about her condition.

"Are you sure you are okay?"

"Yes, but our talk has to wait. I need to get cleaned up and rest. Let's chat after I feel better, okay?" she pleaded. Pauto agreed, though he was getting tired of the stalling. He wished to find out what was happening with her.

The dining room in the Castle of Zandor was quite spacious, and Zandorah picked a long table near the window for the luncheon with her sister and mother. The wait staff placed various potions, brews, and foods on the table. The room filled with delicious smells as Alexis and Lorthana approached Zandorah and the table.

Zandorah felt giddy. Hosting her mother and sister at her residence was an incredible feeling and a rare event. Alexis sat beside her, and Lorthana chose to sit across from the sisters.

" I want to discuss my departure. Have any of your team members discovered a way to transport me home? I am becoming restless," Alexis began as she stared at Zandorah.

Lorthana helped herself to food on the table and remained silent. She knew her daughters would do most of the talking, and she did not plan to say much. Alexis appeared frustrated, playing with the food on her plate.

"You know, Alexis, you should take this opportunity away from home to relax. My team is working around the clock to help you. It may be a while. I understand the barrier is still active and impenetrable. I am sorry. I know it is not what you wish to hear," Zandorah replied.

"It is not your fault, Zandi. I appreciate your help. I feel useless sitting around, doing nothing. To make matters worse, I have no clue what changes Armbruster is enacting on Alstromia," Alexis whined. She wished to leave, but had a feeling it would take a while. Zandorah's personnel were known to be slow and non-forceful. However, Alexis did not want to upset her family further by stating the obvious.

"Mother, you mentioned an Eternal Mirror. Who had it, and what specifically did they see? Please, I must know," Alexis insisted.

"Zandorah, are we able to speak freely in this room?" Lorthana inquired nervously.

"Absolutely. It is safe, Mother."

"In that case, I can share what I know." Lorthana spent several minutes explaining how the W3 came upon an Eternal Mirror and used it to help, though she failed to mention why. Lorthana then made a bold statement about another realm known as Xeagadale.

"Mother, please, stop. We know Xeagadale does not exist. There is only Alstromia, Iriss, Earth, and Draekidell. I do not understand why others insist on making up lies about it. No one has ever been to the elusive realm," Alexis retorted, laughing.

"You are wrong. I have been to Draekidell and Xeagadale, " she boldly declared. "Most of the Blud-Trackers and Hunters originate from Draekidell. Xeagadale is where one of our relatives was born," Lorthana rolled her eyes, perturbed that her children refused to believe her.

"So, why does no one ever discuss Xeagadale? It seems suspicious and downright odd," added Zandorah.

"It is a beautiful place. Witches, Warlocks, Wizzards, and Blud-Trackers live in harmony. The Supreme Ruler is named Krimaexx. He is a ThreeBlud. His mother was a Witch, and his father a Blud-Tracker. Krimaexx was the first Supreme Ruler whose direct lineage traced back to a Blud-Tracker family. His coronation was epic. Many of us attended the monumental occasion, including your father, Gardone. It was many years ago before you were born."

"I see, Mom. So, why have we never visited there? Most of all, why keep it hidden? It does not make sense, Mother," Alexis insisted. She did not believe the Realm of Xeagadale was real. She thought it was a fantasy, made up by lonely W3s with nothing better to do but create fiction.

"There is a problem with Xeagadale. That is why we have not visited. Most who reside there are not allowed to leave or share its location with others. A select few have traveled there and been granted permission to exit. It is real. " I promise you," Lorthana continued, "It does not matter, except...Magorr is from Xeagadale. His parents are from Draekidell. They departed Draekidell to raise Magorr in Xeagadale. It is where I met him."

"Ah...the plot thickens," Alexis added, now snickering.

"Mother, I am confused. What does any of this have to do with what is happening and the Eternal Mirror?" Zandorah wanted to know.

"All Eternal Mirrors have been created on Xeagadale by Krimaexx himself. Only a few W3s have one. I had one stolen from me years ago. That is why I was surprised when Yarlen gifted you one for your Ceremonial Exchange to Armbruster. I asked him how he came across such an unusual gift. I wondered if it was the one that had been stolen from me. Yarlen insisted it was a gift from a friend. I cannot tell you if he is telling the truth. The

Mirrors were created to help the owner *'see'* situations and locations."

The sisters were stunned. It was the first time in their lives that they heard such news. No one ever believed Xeagadale was real.

Lorthana leaned back in the chair and closed her eyes. She recalled the night she met Magorr on Xeagadale. He was young, handsome, and charming. The two were instantly attracted to one another. Lorthana knew he was a Blud-Tracker (ThreeBlud) but did not care. She knew they could be together. There was a way. Their love affair grew quickly, and Lorthana hoped to marry him and reside on Xeagadale.

But that is when tragedy struck. Magorr was tasked with tracking a fugitive from Earth. The hunt would keep Lorthana and Magorr apart. Sadly, months passed, and Magorr did not return to Xeagadale. After almost a year, most believed he was dead. No one knew what had happened to him. Lorthana gave up hope.

Reluctantly, Lorthana decided to live out her life on Earth. That is where she met Gardone, eventually marrying him. She still reminisced about Magorr, wondering if he was still alive and if he thought about her. Her heart yearned to be with him.

After her marriage to Gardone, she quickly acclimated to her new life, trying to forget about the love of her life, Magorr. A year after Alexis was born, she received a message from a friend residing on Xeagadale. She wanted Lorthana to know Magorr was alive. He had returned. She did not disclose where he had been, what had happened, or what had caused his absence. Lorthana felt torn. She wanted to reach out to Magorr but was scared.

If she reconnected with him, she would be tempted and perhaps even leave Gardone. It was unfair and cruel to her husband. She made the difficult decision to stay away from Magorr and Xeagadale, never attempting to communicate with him.

A few years later, Zandorah was born, and Lorthana was a mother to two Young Witches in Training (*YWITs*). She knew it was best to forget about Magorr. All that changed now. Seeing him again, she was instantly transported back to a time when her life was filled with love. She hoped they could rekindle their love affair in the future once he tracked down Gardone.

"Well, Mother, I guess we will see what happens. I can only hope that Gardone will be caught, and you will end up with Magorr if that is what your heart desires," added Alexis.

She wanted her mother to be happy, especially with everything Gardone had put her through. Plus, Alexis was painfully aware of what it felt like to be in love with someone and unable to spend eternity with them.

"If you need anything, Alexis, let me know. I am exhausted and plan to head to bed early. My home is your home. I am glad you are here, sister!" Zandorah hugged Alexis on the way out, which was a strange feeling for Alexis. She was unaccustomed to so much affection from her sibling.

Lorthana and Alexis chose to remain seated for a few minutes. Neither said too much, but Alexis could tell Lorthana wanted to say something.

"What is it, Mom? What's on your mind?"

"I have been thinking a lot. Specifically about the attack on Alstromia and your marriage to Armbruster. What else is happening between you and Armbruster? I have to tell you, I heard rumors. I tried to let them go, but now, I wonder if there is more to everything. I wish you would tell me."

Lorthana knew her daughter. Alexis was not forthright with her answers and quite evasive when confronted. When Lorthana had asked Armbruster what was transpiring in their relationship, he suggested asking Alexis. He did not want to speak on her behalf.

"Mom, Armbruster, and I have had marital issues for some time. I must also confess that I have feelings for someone else. Armbruster knows this, and he has asked me to agree to dissolve our marriage. I informed him we would not be doing that at this moment. Given the recent events, I informed Armbruster that we would not be ending our marriage for now. I did advise him at a later date that I would agree if he still wished to move forward with it."

Lorthana jumped out of her chair and paced around. "I think you are making a huge mistake. Armbruster is a catch. Any Witch would be lucky to have him. Why would you give him up? What the hell, Alexis?" she screamed at her daughter. "Furthermore, what will happen to Lilah? Armbruster adores his child! I believe you have lost your mind," she glared at her daughter.

"Calm down, Mom. I would never prevent Armbruster from seeing Lilah. I do not even want him to move out of the Palace. Nothing will change. He can stay. If, in the future, we move ahead to dissolve our marriage, we will implement a plan for Lilah. I do not want to think about that for now." Alexis stood up and walked toward her mother, her arms out. The two embraced, and Lorthana sobbed. Alexis realized this information was problematic for her to accept.

"I am heartbroken for the entire family!"

"Mom, it will all work out. Trust me. Please, let us focus on other things, shall we?"

Alexis suggested. She did not want this hanging over them like a dark cloud.

Lorthana released Alexis and stepped back, looking at her child. "So, who is it? Who do you love? I hope you realize he will be destroyed once everyone learns who he is and what he has done. He has wrecked the Royal Family!" Lorthana complained.

"Mom, you already know who it is— Andreh."

"For the love of all things wicked and wise. He is a child. He is so much younger than you," added Lorthana, flabbergasted.

"Mother, he is ten years younger. That is hardly so much...please! Andreh and I have a unique bond. It is something I cannot explain. Frankly, I do not feel the need to elaborate. We have been together for over a year, and we love each other. Armbruster and I have tried to make things work, but I am no longer interested." Alexis refused to justify her feelings or life to anyone. Her heart wanted Andreh.

"Very well. I do hope you are prepared for the fallout. It will happen, trust me. The Clans will be relentless. What if they ask you to step down? Will you? Have you sought out legal counsel? I would hope you find a way to protect Lilah, too." Lorthana became furious the more she thought about all the repercussions.

"Mom, we are done talking about this for now. Let us head to our rooms to rest. Tomorrow is another day. We can continue our conversation then if need be. Okay?" Alexis was already tired of the subject. She also hoped for a miracle, such as being able to return home to see Lilah and Andreh. Plus, her mother was seriously getting on her nerves.

The two Witches left the dining room and headed toward their respective rooms. Alexis walked with her head down, feeling overwhelmed. Lorthana was furious about the newly acquired information and refused to speak.

Once they were in their rooms, a storm hit Iriss, something quite unusual, causing a commotion in the Castle. Shortly after 1 a.m., someone knocked on Alexis Snipperdoom's bedroom door. Reluctantly, she opened it. Seconds later, her jaw dropped when she saw him. She wanted to faint.

CHAPTER 7

On Alstromia, Andreh felt restless. He could not sleep, concerned about Alexis. His conversation with Cazzandra was less than helpful. She managed to locate a variety of herbs that she felt could help her concoct the necessary potion to bring back the Queen to Alstromia. Nonetheless, she refused to guarantee any result until further testing was concluded.

The Palace bustled with working personnel around the clock, ensuring the planet's security. Armbruster retired to his chamber a little after midnight, hoping for rest. Unfortunately, sleep eluded him as his mind wandered to thoughts of Alexis, and guilt washed over him. Throughout Alexis's absence, he had been consumed by the desire to seize her power and reign. Now, an overwhelming and almost suffocating sense of guilt enveloped him. Sitting up in bed, he stared at the clock over his desk, noticing it was nearly 1 a.m. Armbruster's sole concern now was Alexis's safety as he moved forward.

Thunder boomed, and it rained more than usual. The streets in the City of Miccay flooded, turning into streams that filled rapidly. The river rose quickly and overflowed as well. Residents became alarmed as their homes were flooded, with water rushing into the buildings. Many left and fled for higher grounds, choosing to relocate to the Manor on Tullah Mountain. Some wondered if this was yet another unusual but planned attack on Alstromia. Once in a while, flashes of colored lights were visible against the gray sky.

The *GRAW* continued their assault on the planet, hoping to penetrate the barrier and cause more catastrophic loss of life. Unfortunately for the *GRAW*, Alstromia remained protected.

In the Palace's basement, Cazzandra worked feverishly to complete her potion. The liquid compound's coloring looked correct, giving her hope. She was eager to show it to Yarlen. He slept in a chair in the corner of the room, remaining faithfully by her side.

"Yarlen. Wake up, " she screamed enthusiastically. "We are ready to test the new batch I created."

Yarlen stretched and yawned, rubbing his eyes. "Are you 100 percent certain? We cannot fail," he staunchly reminded her.

"The potion is ready. I feel confident. We need a volunteer to try to breach the barrier once I temporarily remove it. Shall we do that now or in the morning? It is a little after 1 a.m."

"I will proceed through the portal and retrieve the Queen. Let us head to the Courtyard. It makes no sense to wait," declared Yarlen, eager to bring home Alexis.

The night was pitch dark, with the twin moons hidden by clouds. The rain continued to pour out of the sky relentlessly. Security teams discontinued their patrol flights on Torrins because the beasts slipped off the beasts due to the wetness. It became too perilous. Now, the safety of the planet would depend solely on spells and magic.

Though the weather remained turbulent on Alstromia, it was even worse on Iriss. Alexis stared at him, perplexed as to why he chose to visit her chamber. What would bring him to her this time of night? It was odd. He entered her room and walked toward the window. He wore black pants, a dark green tunic, and a long black cape that dragged on the floor, making a swishing noise. He briefly glanced at her, removing his cloak, before sitting in the chair by the window, facing her.

"I heard what happened. Are you okay? Is there anything I can do for you?" he offered as he fiddled with the cape in his hands.

"Why are you here? I'm certain your wife would disapprove of this visit. Why don't you just go? I will manage," Alexis said sharply. She stood before him in a long, semi-transparent white nightgown. He glanced down, reluctant to gaze at her distinctly fit figure. She, on the other hand, paid no attention and moved closer, standing less than a foot away from him. Nervously, he rubbed his hands and stole a quick glance at her.

"No matter what has happened between us in the past, I care about you. I can only imagine how worried you must be, unable to return to your home." He admired her beauty and felt strange. It had been a long time since they had been alone in a room together.

"I appreciate the gesture, but I am fine. My team will figure out a way to return me to Alstromia."

He stood up and approached Alexis, unexpectedly hugging her. He kissed her on the cheek, inhaling her scent. She pulled away, irritated.

"What are you doing, Shawnatar? Knock it off. You married my sister. It was your choice. I cannot believe you would show up in my room and try to seduce me. Really? Please leave my chamber," Alexis demanded angrily. *'The audacity!'* Alexis thought, disgusted.

"You will always be dear to me. I am sorry. I did not mean any disrespect. I will leave. I promise that I was NOT trying to seduce you. I am still your friend. If you need anything, let me know. The offer stands." Shawnatar exited the chamber, leaving the Queen wondering why he bothered to visit her. It seemed strange, and the timing was odd, too!

Shawnatar had a nasty fight with Zandorah half an hour prior, which was unusual for them. They were usually in harmony, without much disagreement. Today, however, he pushed her for information about Alexis. His wife became increasingly annoyed, noticing he appeared genuinely worried about Alexis. It instantly triggered feelings of jealousy, and she lashed out, making him regret asking questions.

After the awkward visit with Alexis, he marched back to his room. The sisters were a complicated pair, and he was tired of finding himself caught in the middle. Neither liked to give in. It was becoming a serious predicament.

Initially, what surprised Shawnatar the most was the fact that Zandorah offered Alexis a room at the Castle. He figured she would put Alexis up at the Inn near the river, preferring she stay away from her. Shawnatar assumed Lorthana had something to do with the decision to keep Alexis close by.

Lorthana had always been overly protective of her daughters. She did not enjoy the strife between them. Lorthana probably hoped the two would have the opportunity to work through their differences and reach an understanding. After all, they were family, and as family, they should stick together. Lorthana wanted peace.

Shawnatar retreated to his personal quarters, choosing to distance himself from the shared space with Zandorah. He sought solitude to clear his mind and reflect on the source of his distress. Perhaps he still harbored romantic feelings for Alexis.

It was probably best to find a way to reconcile those feelings once and for all. Shawnatar planned to make a point of locating Alexis in the morning and speaking with her privately. Hopefully, they could resolve the tension between them. It was time. Things could not continue this way.

Alexis stared at the door after Shawnatar's swift departure. She still felt irritated about his visit. Hopefully, Zandorah was unaware he had come to her chamber. It could elicit a new round of fights. Alexis was unable to bear more of Zandorah's accusations. If she was forced to remain on Iriss for a few more nights, maybe it was best if she found another place to sleep.

The Castle was becoming a hostile environment, and she was losing her patience. She wondered whether Yarlen and Cazzandra were working to bring her home. She prayed it would happen quickly. Alexis feared the longer she remained away from Alstromia, the more changes Armbruster would enforce during her absence.

It was almost 2 a.m. when Yarlen and Cazzandra entered the Courtyard. The Palace security teams watched the pair lay their potions, books, and other magical items on the wet cobblestones. Cazzandra sighed as she gawked at Yarlen. He seemed eager to test the new concoction. She, however, was quite reluctant. What if she failed? Would the Queen remain stuck on Iriss?

The thought frightened her. She felt nauseous, and immediately, her knees buckled, unable to hold her up. She almost toppled over. Yarlen noticed her struggling to remain standing. He swiftly moved toward her.

"Cazzandra," Yarlen took her hand. "Everything will be fine. I know this potion will work. I believe in you! Stop second-guessing what you have created. Now, let's begin the process. I must rescue the Queen," Yarlen urged.

"If you are certain, Yarlen. I'm petrified. If I mess up, the Queen will dismiss me and possibly banish me from the Palace. I will never find another Wizzard as skilled as you, Yarlen, to mentor me." Cazzandra sobbed, feeling unsure of her abilities.

Yarlen shook his head. "Do not talk like that. It will be okay. You are an exemplary student. Do your part, and let me do mine. Once the Queen is home safely, there will be nothing else to discuss."

"If the magic is successful, when shall I reopen the portal? Do you want two hours or do you believe you will need to stay behind longer?"

"I am confident that I can locate Alexis within two hours. Please ensure that we can return within that timeframe." Yarlen smiled, hopeful she was prepared. He gave her a thumbs up, letting her know he was ready.

Cazzandra nodded. While chanting, she picked up one of the vials and poured it over the cobblestones. The liquid bounced off the cobblestones and shot into the black sky, producing a loud booming noise. Tiny stars dropped down from above, reminiscent of sparkly glitter. A second later, Yarlen nodded as he slammed down his Ceptre. He became enveloped in a green fog and disappeared.

Enthusiastically, Cazzandra clapped, jumping up and down with joy. She was about to head back to the basement of the Palace when she noticed Andreh approaching, and his scowl instantly elicited new fear.

"It looks like you were successful. So, Yarlen is off to locate Alexis and bring her home? Why not Armbruster?"

Cazzandra shrugged her shoulders. "You will need to ask Yarlen when he returns. He did not share that with me. I assumed the arrangements had been made with the King. It is really none of my business," she asserted. Cazzandra showed no interest in conversing with Andreh, as he appeared upset and acted bossy. She chose to walk away without a word, unwilling to waste more of her time.

"Hold on, Cazzandra," he began. "Does the King know?"

She spun around. "As I stated, I have no idea. It is my job to help Yarlen leave Alstromia safely. It is not my responsibility to inform the King."

"I see. Fine, I will speak with Pauto. Cazzandra, do not let your new power get to your head. You are still accountable for your actions. The King will be furious if he finds out he was left out of the decision-making. I cannot keep protecting you."

"Andreh, you are not my babysitter. I do not require your protection services. I greatly appreciate everything you have done for me. However, I now work for Yarlen. I report to him. He can deal with the King and the possible repercussions. Have a good night."

Cazzandra gathered her potions and books and left briskly. She felt annoyed that Andreh had doubted her intentions and decisions. However, she was relieved that Yarlen was finally able to travel to Iriss, which felt like a fortunate turn of events. It seemed like things were finally starting to fall into place.

Upon arriving at Iriss, Yarlen approached the Castle gate and recognized the two security guards, who let him in without hesitation. Yarlen was eager to locate Alexis and return within the designated two-hour timeframe. The thought of being stranded on Iriss, like Alexis, made him feel uneasy and ill. Therefore, he prioritized finding Alexis as soon as possible, knowing they had a limited time to depart Iriss successfully.

In the hallway, Yarlen focused his mind and raised his Ceptre of Argin, allowing it to guide him to Alexis. As he approached a chamber door, he pounded on it loudly, hoping to awaken her. The noise initially annoyed Alexis, but her irritation vanished when she saw Yarlen standing before her. Overjoyed, she embraced him tightly, realizing that her return to Alstromia was imminent.

"Oh, thank the stars! You are here. Yarlen, how did you manage such a feat? Did Cazzandra help you in any way? I know the girl is talented, come on...tell me," Alexis was hyper and ready to hear all the news.

Yarlen politely asked, "My Queen, may I enter?" He couldn't help but notice that she was wearing a sheer, almost transparent nightgown. His face flushed with embarrassment, but he maintained his composure.

Feeling self-conscious, Alexis turned and ran toward the bed, picking up a robe. She threw it over her nightgown, hoping Yarlen could no longer see her nakedness. It was an awkward moment for both.

Yarlen entered and closed the door. He quickly walked toward the only chair in the room and promptly took a seat. The Queen sat on the edge of the bed.

"Yes, Cazzandra is the one responsible for my departure from Alstromia. She managed to concoct a new potion, allowing the portal to appear. We only have two hours. Well, technically, it's about an hour and forty-five minutes. The portal will be open for only a minute or two. We must leave Iriss shortly, Yarlen explained. He did not want her to waste more time.

Alexis crossed her legs and nodded. "So, what is Armbruster up to on Alstromia?

Please do not lie to me, Yarlen. We have had our ups and downs, but are now in a good place. There has been honesty and understanding between us." She dropped the belt from her hand. Nervously, she clasped her hands and rubbed her thumbs. Yarlen noticed.

"Your Majesty, I have no intention of lying to you about anything. I wanted to retrieve you from Iriss and ensure your safety. I have not informed the King of my actions. He does not know I have managed to leave. He keeps our planet protected while ensuring our armies are ready if this situation escalates. No one knows what is happening and why. We have concluded that Gardone and the *GRAW* are to blame, but we lack proof."

"Yes, I assumed my father was behind the attack. I am sure the *GRAW* is involved. I would love to know if he will ever stop. He has taken lives, and it is unforgivable."

"Alexis, have you thought about how you wish to proceed upon your return to Alstromia? I believe Armbruster will do whatever you feel is best for the planet. He is dedicated to you. Please believe that." Yarlen hoped to sound upbeat, painting Armbruster in the best light possible. Unfortunately, it was a lie. Armbruster was not working to help Alexis. He did everything to shine a light on himself, hoping to regain a stable position of authority that others would respect. Yarlen assumed Armbruster wanted more power. He had discussed running for Head of Alstromia, as ruling King, thereby dethroning Alexis.

"That is not the impression I have from what has been relayed to me. I hear Armbruster wants to take over Alstromia. He feels I am incapable of continuing as Queen. Have you heard such rumors, Yarlen?" Alexis interrogated.

"Armbruster always wants to be in charge. That is not news. Yes, he mentioned his plan to run against you in the future, declaring his wish to be the ruler of Alstromia. I told him it was a horrible idea. He never listens to me." Yarlen lowered his head, feeling like a traitor.

"I see. Well, thank you for your honesty. Let him do what he wants. In the meantime, I have something I must share with you. It must stay between us. Promise me!" Alexis stood up and folded her arms. She gazed at the elderly Wizzard, wishing that he would continue to safeguard her secret.

Yarlen rose from the chair, looking into her eyes. "Okay, what is it, Your Majesty? I am all ears."

"Armbruster and I will seek to dissolve our marriage in the near future. I am in love with someone else. I am not interested in staying married to Armbruster. I wanted you to hear it from me. Please do not share this information with anyone else. I beg you not to betray me."

"I assumed as much, My Queen. I have heard the rumors about you and Andreh Darkhill. I hope he is worth it. It will become an issue for you later. I hope you realize this."

"Andreh is my future. I am not worried. I am strong and in control. Now, step outside while I dress for our departure, please," Alexis insisted. He obliged, leaving her alone.

Yarlen leaned against the wall in the hallway, smirking. He was elated that Alexis confided in him. He vowed to keep her secret until she announced the separation from Armbruster. He held his Ceptre for support, feeling tired.

Alexis exited the room and closed the door. She nodded at Yarlen, indicating she was ready. Without giving notice to her mother or Zandorah, Alexis followed Yarlen to the Castle's main gate, eager to head home.

With a determined look on her face, Cazzandra ascended the staircase from the dark dungeon, determined to reach the Courtyard. She had spent well over an hour and a half preparing for this moment, and the time was almost upon her. Soon, she would attempt to open the portal for Yarlen and Alexis, and she couldn't help but feel a sense of trepidation. Would it work? She prayed for success.

Armbruster shouted at Andreh. He was livid. "What the hell? Yarlen left without talking to me. Why would he do that? Are you absolutely sure, Andreh?"

"Your Majesty," Andreh began, his voice measured and respectful. "I spoke with Cazzandra earlier today, and she reassured me that Yarlen's decision to keep everyone out of the loop regarding the Queen's retrieval was intentional. Yarlen believed it was best to keep such information private, and I must say, I agree with him."

Andreh paused momentarily, allowing his words to sink in before continuing. "Furthermore, I believe that Yarlen has the kingdom's best interests at heart, and we should trust him to do what's right."

Armbruster's anger dissipated as he took a deep breath and stretched his back, lost in thought. "I suppose you're right," he finally conceded. "It was probably for the best that not too many people knew about the plan," he continued, his voice tinged with frustration, "I am still the Queen's husband. I should have been notified." He turned to Andreh, his eyes narrowed in contemplation. "Don't you agree, Andreh?"

"Sir, I would have told you if I had known," Andreh replied with genuine remorse. "I only found out a little while ago, and I am deeply sorry. I can only imagine how blindsided you must feel."

Andreh's heart went out to the King, who had been dealing with many drastic changes lately. He hoped that Yarlen would succeed, not just because he wanted Alexis back, but because he knew it would bring much-needed stability to the kingdom.

"Sir, I am retiring to my room. I have requested a week's leave. Pauto approved it. I will be back in a few days. I hope that is okay."

Armbruster seemed to take the news in stride, giving a slight nod, but as he turned his back on Andreh, he let out a heavy sigh. He was already aware of Andreh's leave request and, frankly, did not care.

CHAPTER 8

Yarlen's hand reached out for the Queen's, gripping it tightly as he slammed his mighty Ceptre down. Both of them closed their eyes, holding their breath, fearing it would not work. Suddenly, they found themselves enveloped in a green cloud, and before they knew it, they were transported back to Alstromia without any complications.

As planned, they arrived in the middle of the Courtyard, where Cazzandra was waiting for them with a broad grin on her face. Yarlen breathed a sigh of relief. He was thrilled her magic had worked. Finally, the Queen was back in the kingdom.

Alexis let out a shriek of excitement. "You've done it, Cazzandra, you brilliant Witch!" she exclaimed, giving her a tight hug. Cazzandra felt slightly uncomfortable with the sudden embrace, so she gently pushed back to create some distance between them.

"I am so glad it worked, Your Majesty," Cazzandra said, relieved. "I'm not entirely sure what happened before, but please accept my sincerest apologies." She bowed her head slightly, showing her respect for the Queen.

"No need to apologize, Cazzandra," replied Alexis, her voice filled with gratitude. She then turned to Yarlen, pulling on his sleeve. "Come on, let's head to the Security Command Chamber. I wish to face my husband," she snapped with a determined look on her face.

With a sense of purpose, Cazzandra picked up her items and returned to the Palace's dungeon. She hoped to develop new concoctions and discover an innovative method to prevent the enemy's infiltration attempts. She planned to develop a new magic that would ricochet and hit the enemy, causing catastrophic damage. She believed it was the best way to deter further attacks. Cazzandra knew the enemy was relentless and that it was only a matter of time before they struck again. She was determined to be ready for them.

Andreh lounged on his bed, his eyes closed. He wondered whether Alexis had managed to return to Alstromia or was still trapped on Iriss.

Unexpectedly, Andreh heard shouting and loud noises coming from outside his room. Curious, he jumped out of bed and quickly reached the chamber door. As he opened it, he was surprised to see one of the Security Commoners staring back at him.

"Sir, did you hear? The Queen has returned! Yarlen has brought her back to the kingdom. Isn't that fantastic?" he ran off before Andreh could respond.

Andreh's face lit up with a smile as soon as he learned that Alexis was safe, and he felt a sense of relief wash over him. He wondered if he should head toward her chamber. Thinking about Armbruster and the rest of the staff, he decided it was best to lie low and allow Alexis to approach him. He closed the door and headed back to bed. Finally, he would be able to take a nap without worry.

The Queen and Yarlen entered the Security Command Chamber. Armbruster spun around the second he recognized Yarlen's voice. He spotted Alexis and nodded, relieved she was okay.

"I am back! Armbruster, please call a meeting with Rammadar and the rest of the staff. I want an update on all the changes you have made! I am taking over the day-to-day operations, as before. Do you wish to fill me in now or wait until the rest of the staff arrives?" she hissed, furious with Armbruster.

"Alexis, darling, I am thrilled you are okay," Armbruster said as he approached her and planted a quick kiss on her cheek. Alexis felt a wave of nausea wash over her from the unwanted gesture. She thought it was a blatantly fake display of affection, and she forcefully pushed Armbruster away, rolling her eyes at him.

"Good try. Now, shall we sit?" Alexis insisted.

"Of course," responded Armbruster.

Word swiftly spread throughout the Palace that the Queen had returned unharmed. The majority were taken aback to learn that Yarlen had come to her rescue yet again. It seemed that Yarlen had taken on a rather protective stance toward the Queen.

Within a short time, residents of Miccay received the news about the Queen's return as well. Most had been horrified to learn of the earlier news that the Queen was stuck on Iriss and unable to return. Now, however, they could celebrate. Their ruler was back. Many residents did not like how forcefully Armbruster attempted to change things the minute Alexis was gone. It seemed underhanded rather than strategic. However, they kept their thoughts to themselves, not wanting to be considered troublemakers for expressing their feelings.

Rammadar entered the chamber and saluted the Queen. It was a good day, in his opinion. He was glad she had returned. Maybe now, things would revert to the way they were. He was less than thrilled at having to make the changes the King requested during her absence. Now, it would no longer be necessary. *'Thank goodness,'* Rammadar thought, relieved. It was as if a cloud had been lifted.

The hut was quiet and dark. Gardone rested his head against the back of the recliner, exhaling deeply. His eyes were closed. A fluffy blanket was draped over his body, keeping him warm. It was cold, and he despised it. He preferred the warmth and sunshine. His mind replayed the news he had been given less than thirty minutes before as he attempted to rest. Alexis was back on Alstromia. *'How did she penetrate the barrier securing her planet? Hmmm, I need to find out more,'* he said to himself, opening his eyes.

Unfortunately, it was not the only news Gardone received. The Blud-Trackers were closing in. From what he gathered, Magorr was sighted not far away, the next town over. Gardone shivered at the thought of Magorr catching him. He wondered if he would kill him or allow him to live. In a way, Gardone wished to die. It would be a kinder way to end everything. He feared facing a trial, realizing it would be far worse for him. So, he hoped Magorr would appear quickly, ending the drama once and for all.

On the outskirts of a small town, a few miles away from where Gardone was hiding, Magorr and his team searched through several small cabins in the woods. They had received information that Gardone was staying in a hut covered in thick ivy and moss. It provided camouflage, making it difficult to locate the building in the woods. Regardless, it was just a matter of time before Magorr would find Gardone. The thought was thrilling, and he considered meeting with Lorthana to share the news with her. Of course, she would be extremely grateful. Hopefully, she would want to show her appreciation romantically. Magorr could not wait! It would be his prize for bringing in Gardone.

Back on Alstromia, Alexis listened to the team. She mindlessly chewed on her lip, frustrated. Armbruster had been quite busy in her absence. Alexis glared at him, and he, sensing her anger, lowered his gaze. Armbruster understood that he had crossed a line and opted to keep quiet. Armbruster was well aware of Alexis's displeasure, and the thought of the potential repercussions frightened him.

"Thank you for the updates. As of this minute, I am reversing all previous changes made by the King. Though I am sure he had every intention of helping during my absence, I prefer to keep my policies in place. Now, I must retire for a while. It has been a horrible day for me, and I am exhausted."

With a determined look, Alexis stood up, her eyes locking with those of others in the room. Their nods of agreement only fueled her conviction.

Without wasting another moment, she briskly exited the area and sprinted toward her chamber. She had a sense of urgency in her steps, hoping Andreh would be there waiting for her. But even if he wasn't, she knew she had to speak with him to discover what he knew about what happened with Cazzandra's first attempt to bring her back to Alstromia.

Despite her reluctance to blame Cazzandra, something unexpected and terrible had happened, leaving Alexis stranded on Iriss. Frustration and anger boiled within her, and she knew she could not let this slide. She demanded answers and clarification about the incident, determined to ensure it never happened again.

At the same time, the Council of Peace & War met on Earth to discuss the newly acquired information about Gardone. They realized there was much pressure to find a solution to help Alstromia and Alexis Snipperdoom. They had received immense pushback from elite W3s. They were displeased about how the Council was handling the current situation. They wished for less diplomacy and more force. Some of the older W3s even threatened to vote to remove most of the current representatives and place new members in charge. It was a heated situation that seemed to worsen by the second.

Luzindah Foggentin pounded her fist on the table. She appeared furious. "I do not care what others think. We must continue to enforce the laws and regulations. We will not be bribed or threatened by influential W3s. I will hire legal counsel if necessary to ensure we are protected. Apparently, these W3s are attempting to push their agenda, and I will not allow it," she screeched.

Several of the other council members applauded. However, others remained silent, knowing they would soon be out of a job if Alexis had any say in the matter. In fact, many were surprised that she had not already raised hell to get her way. They knew that Alexis Snipperdoom was not one to be trifled with when it came to the kingdom's protection.

Darnett Partle, a senior representative of the Council of Peace & War, jumped out of his seat. He refused to remain silent.

"Luzindah, I feel your approach is way too reserved in handling this urgent and tragic matter. We must enact a much more aggressive plan. Alexis Snipperdoom has sought out legal counsel. I was informed today. I do not believe she will continue to wait for us to decide how we will support

Alstromia. Let's not play games. Alstromia has been attacked. They are at war with the *GRAW*. We must make it clear that we will do more than just threaten Gardone and his team of Warlocks. We must formulate an aggressive plan and implement it immediately. We must also bring the Queen and her team into our planning. It is the only way!" Darnett slumped down into the chair, breathless.

"And how do you propose that happens? We cannot allow her to declare war on the *GRAW* and retaliate on Earth. What choices do we have?" Luzindah retorted. She shook her head and squinted her eyes.

"I heard Alexis has hired a Blud-Tracker to bring in Gardone and the *GRAW*. Maybe we can announce support for her actions?"

"Absolutely not! We cannot condone such actions. It goes against everything we stand for, you know this," screamed Luzindah. She flinched, her eyes twitching under the stress.

"Policies are made to be amended. This certainly is the time to do so. We do not want Alexis Snipperdoom as an enemy. It would be better to have her as an ally," insisted Darnett.

The other group members agreed with Darnett, which only seemed to infuriate Luzinah more.

"Fine. The majority vote will be enforced. Members, you may cast your vote to amend our current policy and enact a more lenient one in order to appease Alexis and Alstromia," she announced snippily.

Darnett instantly bellowed, "That was not what I meant, and you know it. I am not implying we should be more lenient. I am saying that we must adopt a policy of support for Alstromia and back the Queen's decisions. Alexis Snipperdoom knows what is best for her planet and kingdom."

The room fell silent, and all eyes turned to Darnett. He stood tall and confident, his voice firm with conviction. Clearly, he believed in the importance of supporting the Queen and her decisions.

The remaining members stood, applauding Darnett's response. Luzindah realized she had to back down and allow voting to commence. She would also have to accept and support the outcome if she wanted to keep her current position as the team's head representative.

"Fine. Let us vote," announced Luzindah. "Those members who wish to support Alstromia and Queen Alexis Snipperdoom's efforts declare, aye. Those opposed say, nay!"

A minute later, it was announced that the Council of Peace & War would support the Queen and start the process of adding an addendum to the current guidelines.

Luzindah was furious about the change but realized there was little that she could do. Reluctantly, she moved forward to begin the process of notifying Alexis and her command staff.

Magorr stood beside Casstor Shadowlee, his friend, and a Hunt Warrior. He noticed his restlessness. "Casstor, what is wrong? Ever since I accepted the job to hunt down Gardone, you have acted strangely. It is not like you. Do you wish to bow out of this particular job? If so, it is fine, but please share with me why," Magorr insisted, staring at Casstor.

Before answering, he faced Magorr. "It is not that I don't wish to partake. With all due respect, I must remind you that we are dealing with a highly skilled and malevolent Warlock. Gardone is known not only for his dangerous magic but also for his cunning ways of evading capture. If we are to bring him to justice, we must be prepared for the worst. I cannot stress this enough…this will not be an easy task. Gardone is not one to surrender easily. I can only hope he does not try to either kill himself or us. But if we succeed in apprehending him, we will have taken down one of the most wicked Warlocks of our time," replied Casstor.

"Well, let me worry about Gardone. I plan to deliver him to Queen Snipperdoom alive. But if he decides to retaliate and we lose members in the process, I will end his miserable life swiftly. I have no problem doing so. You know this."

Magorr instructed the others to continue searching for Gardone. He placed Casstor in charge during his brief absence. Magorr planned to head back home to contact someone he thought would greatly help them in their hunt for Gardone. However, he had to act quickly and keep her out of the spotlight as much as possible. He did not want anyone to know she was a planted spy.

Alexis reveled in the moment, realizing Armbruster was displeased she had returned. Though he pretended to be happy about it, she knew better. As she lounged in her room, there was a loud knock on the chamber door.

"Come in!" she shouted.

Andreh entered the room. His smile was gigantic, and he quickly approached Alexis. He grabbed her and pulled her close. "You have no idea how much I missed you. I have been so worried about your welfare. Thank goodness you are back," he exclaimed before kissing her. She grabbed him and held him tightly, never wanting to let him go. Alexis leaned her head back, lost in the moment. Andreh tried to move away, but she snagged his arm, pulling him towards the bed.

"Show me how much you missed me," Alexis teased with a seductive smirk.

"Of course, my love," Andreh responded, ripping off her clothes and kissing her gently on the stomach. Alexis arched her back, enjoying the familiar feeling of ecstasy. There was no one like Andreh, and she knew he would be hers forever!

While the lovebirds enjoyed their tryst in the bedroom, Aerianna stood over the toilet bowl in her chamber, throwing up her last meal. She was tired of this awful feeling. Aerianna's legs felt like rubber. Her energy level was depleted, and she wished to feel 'normal' again. *'How long will it take before I feel like myself?'* Aerianna pondered. She wiped her mouth with a towel and approached the sink to brush her teeth and wash her face. Maybe she would take a nap. She felt exhausted, becoming aware of the fact that her condition was getting worse. She had to finally tell Pauto everything. He had a right to know.

In the dimly lit basement of the Palace, Cazzandra worked with focused determination on crafting new spells. Her mind raced with ideas on how to impress the Queen and make up for the circumstances that had left her stranded on Iriss. The last thing Cazzandra wanted was to lose the Queen's faith in her. Just the thought of it was devastating. She knew she had to work harder and faster than ever before to prove her worth and make an impact. As she poured all her energy into her work, she couldn't help but feel a sense of urgency to succeed. For Cazzandra, failure was not an option.

Yarlen entered the laboratory and found Cazzandra near the large table. She looked up when Yarlen approached.

"Hello," Yarlen greeted her as he stepped into the room. "How are you doing? I assume you are busy working on something new?" he asked, noticing her deeply concentrating on a task. "I hear the Queen wants a complete update on what happened. I have already written a report. I want you to read it and tell me what you think," he added, shoving a large, brown folder toward her. He assumed she would not like the report's findings.

Cazzandra paused her work, took the folder, and removed the stack of papers. She stared at him, feeling apprehensive about the contents.

"That seems like an in-depth and long report. Once the Queen reads it, will I be in trouble?" she asked apprehensively.

"Why don't you read it? Then, we can discuss it. If you feel some changes should be made, I will consider it."

"Do you wish for me to read it now?"

"Yes. The Queen and I have a meeting later this evening. She demands I hand in my report by then," Yarlen clarified.

Cazzandra nodded. She began reading the document while Yarlen leafed through the spellbook on the table. It did not take long for Cazzandra to stop reading.

"NO! This is not okay, Yarlen. I will not allow it," she screamed, infuriated.

"What do you mean, child? Everything I stated is reasonable and mostly factual. What specifically do you disagree with? I thought I was quite thorough. I am not sure why you are upset."

"For one, you are NOT responsible for the issues that arose earlier. I was. It was my fault the potion did not turn out because I failed to gather the correct herbs. You cannot allow the Queen to punish you. I am not okay with that. Please, change your report, or I will be forced to meet with the Queen and tell her the truth," Cazzandra insisted. *'Why is he doing this?'*

She was not used to others protecting her. It was an uncomfortable feeling. Cazzandra placed the papers back into the folder and stood up.

"Cazzandra, the Queen will take the news much better if it comes from me. I must take the blame. She will be skeptical of your abilities in the future if I tell her you failed to concoct the perfect potion in time. Trust me. I know how Alexis operates. She will yell and scream, but that will be the end. If she thought it was your fault, there could be severe consequences. Let me take the blame. I am an old Wizzard with little time left. You have your whole life ahead of you. You are talented. You made a mistake, one that should not define or end your career," Yalen explained. He sat on the stool and watched the young Witch. She absentmindedly played with her long, red hair, staring at the fire.

"Yarlen, I am not sure I can live with that."

"Cazzandra, you must. I insist," Yarlen reiterated.

A heavy silence hung in the air as the two remained lost in their thoughts. Each tried to formulate different outcomes and hoped to discover the best course of action. Eventually, Cazzandra reluctantly realized she had to agree with Yarlen's request. It was better for him to take responsibility for the failed potion, even though it felt wrong. The thought of living with the reality of that lie made her feel sick to her stomach. Cazzandra shook her head disapprovingly, wishing that there was another way.

"Okay, Yarlen. I suppose we can provide the Queen with your report, but I want you to know that I disagree with this decision. It's a bold lie, and it goes against everything I believe in. But I trust your judgment, and I hope that this will be the right decision in the end," she said emotionally. A tear ran down her cheek, and she forcefully wiped it away.

Yarlen practically sprinted out of the room, clutching the report tightly in his hand. He was confident that Alexis would be impressed with his findings and would accept his story without question. As he walked down the corridor of the west wing of the Palace, however, his confidence began to wane. Doubts crept into his mind, and he couldn't help but worry about how Alexis would react to the report. Despite his best efforts to remain composed, nervousness began to take hold.

Not far away, Pauto entered the room and found Aerianna in bed. She was awake, reading a book.

"How are you feeling, Aerianna? Can we chat?" He would not allow her to sidestep their conversation again. She would finally disclose her illness. He was prepared for the worst.

"Of course," she placed the book on the nightstand and gestured for Pauto to sit beside her on the bed.

"Tell me what is going on. I know it is something awful. I am your future husband. Do you not trust me? I have to tell you, I am hurt. I would think you would want me to know what is happening with you right now," Pauto declared.

Aerianna sighed. She realized it was time to tell him, though she felt ill-prepared. She took his hand into hers and smiled. "Alright, Luv. Here it goes...I hope you know how much I love you. I was not sure how to tell you. The reason I have been so sick is..."

Just as she was about to share the news, there was a knock on her chamber door. "Aerianna, it is Armbruster. I must speak with you. May I enter?"

Pauto and Aerianna stared at each other. Neither appreciated the interruption, especially when Aerianna was finally about to disclose the reason behind her illness. However, they knew it would be an urgent matter if Armbruster arrived in person without prior notice. With a heavy sigh, Aerianna called out, "Enter."

CHAPTER 9

The King immediately noticed that Pauto and Aerianna looked upset about his unexpected visit. Regardless, Armbruster knew he had to share the news. Waiting was not an option. He chose to offer up a smile and advanced, ready to talk.

"Hello, Your Majesty. Are you okay? What brings you to my chamber at this hour?" Aerianna inquired. She hoped to move the conversation along so she could finish the urgent discussion with Pauto.

"I received news from a friend on Earth. The Blud-Trackers are closing in on Gardone and the *GRAW*. Also, the Council of Peace & War officially declared that they are supporting us. They will seek volunteers to help hunt down Gardone. In the meantime, I did not want to disturb the Queen. She needs her rest after her ordeal. Will you be back at work soon, Aerianna? I heard you have been ill. Are you better?" Armbruster stared at her. She looked pale and thin.

"Well, that is great news about the search for Gardone and the *GRAW*. Also, I am delighted to hear that the Council of Peace & War has had a change of heart. They seemed uncooperative in the past. As for my health, I would like to keep it private for now, if that is okay. Pauto and I were just about to discuss it before you arrived." Aerianna wanted him to know she preferred that he leave her room.

"I am so sorry to have come at an inopportune time. Please accept my apology. I would appreciate it if you could attend the meeting in the morning. Pauto, please be there as well. It is a senior officer meeting."

Armbruster excused himself and left swiftly. Outside the chamber, he noticed Yarlen approaching. He held a folder and walked with his head down.

"Hello, Yarlen. What brings you to this side of the Palace? Are you here for the Queen or me?"

"I wanted to speak with the Queen but thought I would first meet with Aerianna," Yarlen explained.

"NO! Do not do that. She is about to hold a conversation with Pauto about her illness. I am unsure what is wrong with Aerianna, but she needs privacy. Why don't we head to my room, and we can talk," Armbruster announced.

Reluctantly, Yarlen agreed. It would be a good idea to run the report by him and receive feedback.

★ *. ★ *. ★ *. ★ *. ★

Finally, alone with Pauto, Aerianna turned to him and sweetly smiled. "As I was saying before we were interrupted, I hope you know how much I love you," she said softly. "I've wanted to share some news about my health for a while now, but with our recent engagement, I have been worried about how you might react."

"Nothing you can say will cause me to love you any less. I adore you. You know this,"

Pauto reassured her, wishing she would hurry and tell him the news.

"I know. I love you, too. Still, it may be a shocking revelation to hear what I have to say. Pauto, I am pregnant. I am eight weeks along. Everything is okay, according to Edwinn. He said I need rest for a few more days. I will be fine."

"Oh, my gosh! Are you serious? Of course, I am thrilled. I love you and cannot wait to meet our baby. Oh, Aerianna. What wonderful news!" He kissed and embraced her.

Aerianna whispered, "Are you sure you are okay with it?"

"Of course! It is our baby. Now, we must expedite our wedding! We need to talk with Edwinn and determine the expected date of the baby's arrival. When will we know the gender? Gosh, I am so excited!" Pauto yelled.

Aerianna felt relieved that he was happy. At first, she worried he would be upset, but his reaction was genuine. He was beyond thrilled.

"Edwinn will check on me tomorrow. We can both talk with him then. I want you there," Aerianna reassured Pauto.

Pauto walked around to the other side of the bed and began undressing. Aerianna watched him quietly, feeling a sense of calm wash over her.

He scooted in beside her, pulling her close. She rested her head on his chest and felt his heartbeat, which was steady and strong. With Pauto by her side, Aerianna realized their new journey was just beginning. Feeling safe and loved, she closed her eyes.

Alexis wondered if she should get out of bed and speak with Aerianna. As she gazed at Andreh, she changed her mind. She scooted next to him and wrapped her arm around his body. He pushed himself against her, wanting to feel her close. The two fell back asleep, unaware of the horrible event about to unravel.

It was getting late and dark on Earth. Gardone was alone in the hut. Most of his friends had returned to their families for the night. He tossed and turned in bed. Gardone's mind was on Alexis and Magorr.

Suddenly, he heard a strange noise. He sat up in bed and looked around apprehensively. He knew it was Magorr, though he could not see a thing.

Ten seconds later, the entire room was brightly illuminated. That is when he saw his pale, icy-blue face, with the eerie, red-glowing eyes, watching him. His fangs were exposed, and he laughed as he noticed Gardone shaking.

"Finally, I knew I would find you. It did not take long. Your buddy outside is gone. I gave him a choice: Leave or die. Guess what he chose?" Magorr informed Gardone.

"End it now! Just do it!" Gardone shouted, adrenaline pumping through his veins. He was ready to face his fate, knowing that this moment was inevitable. The tension in the air was intense. This was the moment he had feared, the one he hoped would never come. But now it was here, and he was ready to meet it head-on.

"NO. I will deliver you to Alexis. She can do with you as she wishes. I do not care. You are a coward, and I hope you spend the rest of your life alone in a dungeon without any magical abilities. You truly are the scum of the universe," declared Magorr. He approached, ready to apprehend Gardone.

Gardone had already made up his mind, and he had chosen to embrace death. He smiled at Magorr, then closed his eyes as a bright, purple mist enveloped the room, filling it with magical energy. The silence was broken by Gardone's agonized screams, and then suddenly, he collapsed onto the floor, motionless. His eyes stared blankly at the ceiling, and one last breath escaped from his lips before his chest finally fell still. Gardone was no more.

Magorr shook his head. What had Gardone done? Was it sorcery? He was utterly confused. Magorr shrugged without care and picked up Gardone's limp body. He flung it over his shoulder, heading back to the estate to summon others.

As if she sensed something, Alexis awoke with pain in her chest. Nervous, she clutched the left side of her body, sitting up, frightened.

"Oh, my God, am I dying?" she screamed, waking Andreh.

"What has happened, Alexis? Are you alright?" He quickly cast a spell, causing the fireplace in the room to roar to life and illuminate the area.

"I suddenly had an excruciating pain in my chest. I felt as if I was suffocating. It was alarming. I feel okay now," she responded, sitting back in bed and resting her head against the headboard.

Andreh took her hand. "Should I call Edwinn to check you out? That is so scary."

Alexis shook her head. "No. I want to try to sleep. I am still tired. I believe that I am okay. Go to sleep, Andreh." Alexis reassured him. She saw the apprehensive look on his face. He was not convinced all was good.

Nonetheless, he did not argue with her. He watched as she curled up and closed her eyes. Andreh stayed awake observing her. He wondered what caused the pain. Was it a panic attack? So much has happened recently. It would not surprise him if it had been. She was under extreme pressure.

As Alexis began snoring, Andreh assumed she was okay and felt relieved. He closed his eyes, hoping to catch a few more hours of sleep before the busy morning ahead. Armbruster had called for a meeting with all senior officers, and Andreh knew he had no choice but to attend. He couldn't help but wonder what was in store for them.

Magorr nonchalantly dropped Gardone onto the oversized couch in his spacious estate and approached the window. He gazed out at the harvest moon, shining brightly in the night sky. As he contemplated how to summon Alexis, he knew that he couldn't make a direct request due to the protective shield that enveloped the planet of Alstromia.

A few minutes later, he sat down next to Gardone, wondering why the Warlock had taken his own life. Maybe he was frightened of the impending trial and reprisals for his actions.

Yet the GRAW was still intact, which meant someone would have to locate the new leader and disband the group before more attacks against Alexis and her kingdom continued.

A smile spread across Magorr's face as he thought about Lorthana. He decided to contact her, hoping she could find a way to relay a message to Alexis. After all, seeing the love of his life again was all that mattered to him.

Magorr closed his eyes and chanted, hoping his magic still worked. He was more of a Blud-Tracker than a Warlock and realized his powers were relatively weak. However, to his surprise, she appeared minutes later, dressed in a long gown, her hair pulled up, looking tired.

"Hmmm, I guess you can still summon me," Lorthana teased.

"I tried. I wasn't sure if it would work. Again, I am a ThreeBlud. My powers are fairly evenly distributed, but I feel my biggest strength lies with my Blud-Tracker abilities. I am less of a Warlock, you know this," Magorr responded.

His heart skipped a beat as he gazed at her. He adored the twinkle in her eyes that made them sparkle. Her full head of long, black hair contrasted beautifully with the strands of gray that shone like silver tinsel. He wanted nothing more than to ravage her body.

"Why the urgent matter?"

Magorr moved aside, allowing Lorthana to see Gardone on the couch. As she caught sight of him, she gasped and covered her mouth in shock. His arm dangled off the side of the furniture, and his eyes were closed. Instantly, she felt nauseated and unsteady.

"Is he alive?" she asked fretfully. In a way, it did not matter, but the idea of his death was an unwelcome thought.

"No. I am so sorry."

"I suppose he left you no choice," Lorthana added.

Magorr explained, "He did it himself, using sorcery. He produced a purple fog and died instantly. I've never seen anything like it."

"I see. He must have used the *Purple Reckoning Spell*. It is painful but swift. It is a self-destructive spell. I have never heard of anyone actually using it. How sad."

Lorthana sobbed, holding Gardone's cold hand. Though she no longer loved him, she still hated that he was dead. She disliked death and knew Zandorah would be deeply affected by his passing.

"I am sorry, Lorthana. I planned to deliver him to Alexis alive. He chose to die. There was little I could do. It happened too quickly," Magorr attempted to justify the circumstances.

"Yes, well, the *Purple Reckoning Spell* is irreversible anyway. So, he knew he would die. That is probably why he chose such dark magic in the first place. It was his choice, as you stated. Obviously, he had it planned. He never intended to face a jury and trial," Lorthana concluded.

The two remained in silence for a while. Eventually, Lorthana released Gardone's hand and approached Magorr, who stood near the window. She hugged him tightly, and he held her, taking in her intoxicating scent. She always had such a powerful effect on him. Magorr couldn't help but wonder what was going to happen now. A few moments later, she stepped back and looked at him intently.

"Now what?"

"We must find a way to deliver Gardone to Alexis on Alstromia. Any ideas how?"

"Yes. I believe I have a way," she replied confidently.

"Okay," Magorr said, still observing her.

"First, I should show you my appreciation for what you have done for Alexis. Don't you agree? I believe you need to show me your bedroom, Magorr," Lorthana whispered, removing her gown and dropping it onto the rug.

His eyes flashed with lust for her. "Yes, yes indeed." Excitedly, he scooped her off the floor, holding her in his burly arms. Magorr sprinted up the stairs with her as she giggled, kicking her feet, acting like a young Witch in love.

The rest of the night was uneventful. Most W3s slept soundly. Armbruster, however, was still wide awake. He had fallen asleep briefly but awoke feeling strange. His head hurt, and he had difficulty breathing. Armbruster wondered what was happening. He took another swig of tea and placed the cup on the nightstand.

At first, he assumed it was a panic attack. However, he had not had one in years. He sat up in bed, rubbing his temples, feeling nauseous. Ten minutes later, he contemplated whether it was wise to summon Edwinn. Maybe something was wrong with him.

On the other hand, Armbruster did not wish to appear weak to others. After all, he was King. He was the epitome of strength and wanted to continue to portray himself as such. He thought about researching a spell to heal his headache, but he fainted before he could do so. His body slumped down in bed, and his breathing slowed. Armbruster was not okay!

The night quickly turned into a new day. Alexis was awake, showered, and brushing her hair when Andreh opened his eyes. He watched her. She was so beautiful, and his heart felt as if it was about to explode with love for her. He could not imagine a life without her.

She heard him pull back the heavy blanket on the bed, making huffing sounds. "Good morning, handsome. I hope you slept well," Alexis dropped the silver brush onto the vanity table and rose to approach the bed. Andreh held out his hands.

"Come back to bed."

"Andreh, get up. We must attend the meeting in the Command Chamber. Don't waste time. Armbruster will be upset," Alexis reminded him.

"Fine. But, I want it on record that I would rather remain in bed with you," Andreh teased.

"Aha. I will meet you there. I am heading to Aerianna's room to speak with her before the meeting begins. Don't be late, Andreh, I mean it." Alexis shook her head, frustrated with him. She did not want to get into another fight with Armbruster about Andreh. She was tired of it.

Rammadar was the first member to enter the empty chamber. He took a seat and closed his eyes, wondering what Armbruster would implement today. He assumed Alexis would attend the meeting, too, now that she had returned to Alstromia.

Yarlen entered the room and approached Rammadar. "Armbruster wanted me here. Yes, I know you are still his Second-in-Command. However, he ordered me to attend the meeting. So, here I am," the old Wizzard explained, sitting beside Rammadar.

Rammadar nodded but said nothing. He closed his eyes again, now worried even more than before. *'Why would Armbruster ask Yarlen to join the meeting?'* Something was off.

Aerianna and Pauto were dressed. She finally felt better and more relieved after informing Pauto about the pregnancy. The two were about to head to the meeting when Alexis knocked on the chamber door.

Once in the room, Alexis smiled. "I see," she began, noticing the smirk on Pauto's face. "You told him. Good for you. Congratulations to you both."

"Wait, you told Alexis before you told me?" Pauto shouted, instantly furious.

"Umm, she was here when Edwinn arrived. I had to tell her. Stop it. I had every intention of informing you as soon as possible. I also wanted the timing to be right." Aerianna explained. She hoped he would stop with the hurt feelings. It was getting on her nerves.

"Fine," Pauto responded, rolling his eyes with displeasure.

"Alexis, why are you here?" Aerianna asked.

"I need to discuss a few things with you. Pauto, why don't you head to the meeting? We will be there shortly," Alexis advised.

Pauto realized it was not a suggestion. He acknowledged the request and departed the room, allowing the Witches time alone.

"Okay, so?" Aerianna began. "What is it?"

"I received communication via the Eternal Mirror this morning. Mother needs us to head to Earth. I do not know why. I did not see further details. We are to meet at Magorr's estate. I assume he has news about my father. Please accompany me. I don't want to show up alone, and I certainly do not want Armbruster to join me."

"Sure. Have you spoken with Yarlen or Cazzandra about getting us there without complications? I mean, there was that issue before. I would hate to be stuck on Earth!" Aerianna reminded Alexis, reluctant to join her on the trip.

"No, not yet. I thought we could speak with them after the meeting. I first wanted to confirm you would come with me on the trip. I wasn't sure if you were feeling well enough. Thank you for agreeing to go. It means a great deal to me!"

"I am always here for you, Alexis. You know this. I will be there as much as possible… until the baby is born. I may need to take some leave after the birth. I am sure you understand. So, when will you want to depart?"

"As soon as possible. In the next few hours. Do you feel well enough to travel?" Alexis asked her, concerned for her welfare.

"I feel great, thanks!" Aerianna gleefully announced. "I am travel-ready!"

The two left the chamber to attend the mandatory meeting called by Armbruster. Neither was in the mood but knew it was essential to appear.

Andreh entered the chamber and was surprised that Armbruster was not there. He wondered why. It was very unlike him to call a meeting and be absent. Sitting next to Yarlen, the two began conversing to pass the time.

Within a few minutes, Aerianna and Alexis entered. They approached the table and quickly took their seats, wondering the same thing as Andreh. *'Where is Armbruster?'*

They surveyed the room. Rammandar stood. "Has anyone seen the King? I haven't heard from him since late last night. Perhaps we should send someone to check on him."

Alexis responded. "No. That is not necessary. Everyone, stay here. I will head to his room to find out if he is there. Hopefully, I will return swiftly with him." She jumped out of the chair and exited the room.

The hallway was empty, and she strode down the corridor, heading to the King's chamber. Once she stood before the large door, she knocked loudly. After waiting for him to answer for more than a minute, she impatiently pushed open the door. It was dark inside, and the heavy, velvet curtains were drawn. The fire in the fireplace was almost out, providing no light. She called out his name.

Frustrated at his lack of response, she cast an *Illumination Spell*, and instantly saw him slumped over in bed. He had landed on his side, and foamy-looking drool dripped from his halfway-opened mouth. His eyes were partially open.

Armbruster's skin looked pale but glowed a strange, icy green. "Oh, my God, Armbruster. Can you hear me? Honey, hello?" Alexis screamed, violently shaking him. Armbruster failed to respond. Without hesitation, Alexis closed her eyes and began chanting. She released his hands as she examined the rest of his body.

"I am here, Armbruster. Edwinn will arrive shortly. Hang in there," she reassured him. Sadly, he was unable to hear her words as he was unconscious.

Edwinn appeared with an oversized bag in one hand and a Ceptre in the other. He stared at Armbruster and Alexis, perplexed.

"What has happened?" he asked, dropping the bag and leaning the Ceptre against the wall.

Alexis was now in a state of panic. "I do not know," she screeched. "I found him like this. He was late for a meeting that he had organized. I was worried when he didn't show up, so I went to his chamber to find out why. Edwinn, what has happened to my husband?" shrieked Alexis.

"Alexis, Your Majesty, please...move aside. Allow me to examine the King," Edwinn insisted with a stern stare.

As Alexis nodded and reluctantly walked away, Edwinn rushed to the King's side. He listened to Armbruster's breathing and touched his skin, which felt ice cold. Armbruster's breathing was labored, indicating that his condition was deteriorating quickly. Edwinn carefully pulled up one of the King's eyelids to examine his eyes and instantly jumped back, his face filled with fear. It was terrible news. The situation was dire.

"Alexis, please locate Yarlen and bring him here quickly. I need him."

"What is it?" she screamed hysterically.

"There is no time to explain. Hurry if you want to save Armbruster," yelled Edwinn.

CHAPTER 10

lexis wished she had brought her wand or Ceptre to transport herself instantly to the others. However, she had failed to do so. Unable to think, she did not cast a spell either. Instead, she ran from the room to the Security Command Team Chamber (*SCTC*) to locate Yarlen and alert the others to Armbruster's medical condition. Her heart raced, making her dizzy.

She pushed open the door, breathless. "Yarlen, help! Edwinn needs you in Armbruster's chamber. Please, quickly. The King is in trouble." She managed to yell before collapsing onto the ground.

Andreh lept from his chair, running toward the Queen. He bent down, aiding her. "Can you stand? What about the King? Are you okay?" Andreh knew something awful had occurred. The Queen looked wild-eyed. Her breathing was erratic.

"Something is wrong with Armbruster. Yarlen, go! NOW!" She screeched again. The old Wizzard slammed down in Ceptre and disappeared.

Alexis dropped into the nearest chair, sobbing. "I found him. He was a strange pale green color, drooling, unconscious in bed. Oh, my God. If you had seen him." Alexis explained, with an elevated voice, sounding frantic.

Rammadar approached. "My Queen, we must raise our security level immediately. With the recent attacks on our kingdom and now the King's new mysterious health crisis, it seems like clear indications of foul play. It's time to take decisive action to protect you and our people. As Armbruster's Second-in-Command, I urge you to act without delay and authorize the necessary measures to ensure our safety. Trust me, we cannot afford to wait any longer."

"Yes, do what you must. Take Andreh with you. I want an update as soon as possible," Alexis commanded. She contemplated what had occurred. She remembered the look on Edwinn's face. He saw something when he looked at Armbruster's eye. Yet, he refused to tell her. Obviously, it was something horrific.

"Aerianna, please join me. I need to speak with you privately in my chamber," Alexis announced.

Aerianna took Alexis by the arm and guided her out of the chamber. She was shaky and unable to walk on her own.

As Yarlen entered the King's room, he immediately noticed Edwinn chanting over Armbruster. Edwinn turned around to face the old Wizzard when he heard him approach.

"Good. I need you. Armbruster has been poisoned. It seems he has been fed the *Venomous Wyndroot*. He has the telltale neon green ring around the iris. Here, look," Edwinn stood up and moved aside, allowing Yarlen to verify his diagnosis by looking at Armbruster's eye. Yarlen agreed, nodding.

Yarlen was puzzled and asked, "Yes, you are correct. But why do you need me? You are the Healing Warlock. How can I be of any help to you?"

"The *Venomous Wyndroot* is quite rare. The antidote must be concocted. I require leaves and seeds from the *Crimson Inferno Bursting Heatberry*. As far as I know, it only grows on Hexxton Mountain. We both know it is difficult to harvest because of its explosive properties. That is why I need you. I must remain here with Armbruster," explained Edwinn. "Hopefully, you have someone who can help you with this urgent task."

"Understood. Yes, I can take my apprentice, Cazzandra. We will retrieve what you need. How much is required?"

"I would think at least 10 leaves and 20 seed pods. So, probably a few plants. They must be fresh, non-wilted leaves. Since it is fall, they may be difficult to locate. They tend to die back this time of year. Sorry, it will be a challenging hunt!"

"No worries. We will not fail you!" Yarlen reassured the Healing Warlock. Not wishing to waste time, he slammed down his Ceptre and transported himself to Cazzandra's room in the dungeon.

Cazzandra placed two vials of new potions onto the long, Trimber shelf over the fireplace. Feeling accomplished, she grinned. It was good to be able to work on magic whenever she wanted without interruptions.

She spun around when she heard Yarlen's voice. "Cazzandra, we have an urgent mission to complete. We must head to Hexxton Mountain and harvest several fresh *Crimson Inferno Bursting Heatberry* bushes. I know what you are thinking. No, it cannot wait. Armbruster has been poisoned, and Edwinn Shivvers requires these plants to make an antidote before it is too late for the King," Yarlen yelled.

"Oh my goodness! That is awful. You know, most of the plants will have already died back. Hopefully, we can locate enough of them to help," Cazzandra responded. She picked up her cloak and secured it around her neck. She grabbed her dark, purple sack, flinging it over her right shoulder, and quickly snatched her wand off the desk.

Yarlen and Cazzandra stood before the fireplace, holding hands as Yarlen chanted. Suddenly, they appeared on Hexxton Mountain, standing near a narrow pathway. Despite the rain and cold wind, Yarlen appeared unfazed while Cazzandra frowned, clearly unhappy about being outside in such horrible weather.

"I've located the freshest plants near the waterfall in the past. Let's head there. Hopefully, we will be able to find them," Yarlen said, leading the way down a rocky and muddy path. A few minutes later, they arrived at a noisy waterfall. The sound of the water rushing down the steep incline and splashing onto the rocks was deafening. Yarlen pointed to an area off to the right, near a small cave entrance, and Cazzandra nodded, following him once again.

Yarlen pointed to the bright red and orange plants. "Look. There are at least ten here. They look fresh. Let's get ready to take what we need. I will remove the leaves, and you need to harvest the pods quickly. Be careful not to touch the thick stem. It burns and causes horrible blisters," Yarlen advised.

"Now you tell me," she whined.

Yarlen moved swiftly. His senses heightened as he carefully plucked the leaves from the stem. His movements were precise, and he made sure not to disturb the pods or the stem. Once he had gathered a heaping pile, he quickly stashed them in the satchel, his heart beating fast from the thrill of the action.

As he looked up, he noticed Cazzandra gracefully maneuvering her way through the field. Her hands were wet from the rain, but her focus was unwavering. She held a small dagger, and with each swift movement, she removed the pods with utmost care. She knew that even the slightest mistake could cause a catastrophic explosion, releasing a toxic gas that would spell doom for them both.

Cazzandra was about to turn around and remove the last seed pods from another plant when she heard a sudden thud. She spun around to see Yarlen lying on the wet and soggy ground, having slipped on a patch of mud.

Without a second thought, Cazzandra released the dagger and rushed to Yarlen's side. She helped him stand. But just as they thought they had avoided disaster, the sharp dagger ruptured a large bunch of seed pods. In an instant, there was a deafening explosion, and red glittery dust flew all around them, blinding them momentarily. Cazzandra panicked as she realized the gravity of their mistake. The sound of the explosion echoed through the field.

"Hold your breath, Cazzandra! Do not inhale it," Yarlen screamed. He quickly covered his mouth with a cloth. She nodded, moving away from the plant and placing her hands over her mouth while her eyes began to water.

Once the dust had dissipated, the two picked up their bags and headed toward the pathway. Feeling confident they had what they needed, Cazzandra reached for Yarlen and placed her arm on him while he chanted.

It did not take long for them to reappear inside Cazzandra's laboratory. "Here, let me place all the items on the table. You retrieve Edwinn and find out how to concoct the antidote. I will ensure the pot is boiling and ready," Cazzandra advised.

The old Wizzard nodded, rushing to speak with Edwinn. Once he entered the chamber, he instantly stopped in his tracks. Alexis stood on one side of the bed, holding Armbruster's hand while Edwinn chanted. She looked frantic, her entire body shaking.

"We located an ample supply of plant leaves and pods," Yarlen announced happily, standing before Alexis and Edwinn, still covered in mud. But he was elated to share such splendid news.

Edwinn shook his head, releasing Armbruster's hand. Yarlen cocked his head, observing the Healing Warlock, confused. "Tell me how to make the antidote, Edwinn. Cazzandra is waiting. We can get started right away," Yarlen announced.

By now, Alexis was crying uncontrollably. She managed to crawl onto the bed, shaking. She scooted in next to Armbruster. "NO!!!!! WHO did this to you? OH MY GOD! My beloved husband, how did this happen? It is MURDER! My husband, the KING, has been MURDERED! I will avenge your death!" Alexis screamed. She was furious and heartbroken. She continued to sob, resting her head on the King's chest.

Edwinn moved away and pulled Yarlen aside. "The King took his last breath a few minutes ago. There was nothing we could do. The poison was too strong. Please alert our security team at once. The King has been assassinated!"

Speechless, Yarlen approached the bed. He bent over and moved near Armbruster, noticing he was not breathing. He really was dead. Yarlen was in shock and denial. The Queen cried, refusing to leave the chamber or her husband's side. The pain was too new, something she had never felt. It was a loss beyond description. The pain was so intense that it felt like her heart was going to burst out of her chest.

Alexis couldn't bear to open her eyes and face the reality of the situation. What had once seemed like a bad dream was now a harsh and painful reality. Her gut instinct knew the truth, but her heart struggled to accept it. The weight of the situation was suffocating. Armbruster Presstan Hextinghton, the King of Alstromia, was dead.

The two Wizzards chose to leave, allowing the Queen time alone with her deceased husband. Once outside the chamber, Yarlen slammed down his Ceptre and transported himself to the Security Command Chamber.

Rammadar spoke to Andreh and others, pointing to a map on the wall when Yarlen entered. The moment Rammadar saw him, he knew something horrific had happened. Yarlen looked as if he had been crying.

"Rammadar, we must ensure NOBODY can leave the planet. I mean, NO ONE! The King has been MURDERED!!! He is dead in his chamber. The Queen is with him. Someone must head there now and protect her! Please send a guard to the Princess's room, too. We do not know if the killer is still inside the Palace," Yarlen bellowed. He gripped the back of the chair, feeling his legs grow weak and rubbery. The reality sank in quickly. The situation was dire.

Andreh responded, "I will head to the chamber, secure the scene, and protect the Queen. Send reinforcements." Andreh waved his wand and disappeared.

"What? How did this happen? Are you sure?" Rammadar wanted clarification before initiating the highest security level.

"Yes. Armbruster is dead. Cazzandra and I were on a mission to retrieve plants to concoct an antidote. Edwinn said it was a *Venomous Wyndroot* poisoning. The King had the telltale neon-green circle around the iris of his eye. There was no denying it." Yarlen explained.

Rammadar pounded his fist on the table. "How could this happen? We must have a traitor in the Palace. When was the last time someone left or arrived on the Alstromia? You and your young apprentice helped make that happen, no?" Rammadar questioned.

"Are you implying we had something to do with his death?"

"Of course not. I am saying someone managed to infiltrate our barrier unnoticed and killed Armbruster. I will summon the AoE and ensure the Torrins are in the sky searching for anyone, not from Alstromia. We will search each hut along the river banks until we find the intruder. It will be a difficult task. Can you locate a useful spell to help expedite the process?"

Yarlen tilted his head to one side and said, "I will head to the basement and join Cazzandra in the laboratory. She's been waiting for my return and might know a chant that could come in handy. Cazzandra is gifted and could be of great assistance to us. I'll update you when I have more information. In the meanwhile, please remain vigilant."

The breaking news did not take long to circulate in the Palace. Once the AoE and the SAoW were enlisted to secure the Palace and City of Miccay, commoners grieved the loss of their King.

However, the King's death announcement had not yet reached Earth or other realms, as the security bubble over the planet of Alstromia hindered communication. Yet, somehow, someone had managed to penetrate the barrier and end the King's life. It seemed unfathomable, but sadly, it was reality.

Standing before the chamber door, Andreh felt a sense of apprehension wash over him. He felt reluctant to face the deceased King and his wife. To make matters worse, the guilt of his ongoing affair with Alexis weighed heavily on his conscience. It all felt so wrong, but there was no undoing it now. He knew it was imperative that he put aside his feelings and be there for Alexis during this tragic time.

Andreh entered the chamber and found Alexis curled up next to the Armbruster on the bed. She sobbed, making huffing noises. His heart sank at the sight of witnessing her pain. Alexis looked up when she heard the door open. She stared at Andreh, her eyes black from her smeared makeup.

"Who did this, Andreh? Armbruster and I may have had our differences, but I never wanted him dead. We planned to divorce in the future, but now, he is gone! Just like that, he was murdered by a coward." She began crying again, but managed to lift herself off the bed. She approached Andreh and collapsed into his arms. He held her while she cried, unable to bear the pain. Andreh felt her body quiver, and he pulled her tightly against him, attempting to comfort her.

Andreh allowed her to grieve. He wondered what the security detail managed to discover about the intruder. Had they located the person responsible for the King's death? It was just a matter of time. Yarlen and Cazzandra would find a spell to expose the murderer. Then, the trial would begin!

After a few minutes, Alexis pushed herself away and walked toward the window with her head down. Andreh observed her, remaining in place. She stared out and wondered how to tell her child that her father, the King, was dead. Alexis needed her mother, Lorthana, and wished she were there. She desperately wanted her backing.

"Andreh, it's crucial that we find a means of informing my mother about everything that has happened. I need her here with me during these trying times. Could you please fetch the Eternal Mirror from my chamber? I'll try to contact her through it. Even though I'm uncertain if it'll work with the protective barrier in place, it's the only method that was capable of sending messages from Alstromia in the past."

Alexis dropped into the chair near the window and cupped her face with her hands. She sighed, feeling a crushing pain in her chest. Alexis winced.

Andreh noticed and immediately began moving toward her. Alexis shook her head, not wanting Andreh near her. She had to remain focused on the tasks that lay ahead. He could not become a distraction. She knew he meant well, but she had to stay firm. Andreh could act as her security only, or he needed to go.

"I am uncomfortable at the thought of leaving you alone, Alexis. It is not safe. Can we head to the chamber together?" he asked cautiously, knowing she would most likely refuse.

"I cannot leave Armbruster. It is not right." Alexis stared at Andreh angrily.

"Your Majesty, respectfully, he is gone. You, however, are still alive and potentially the next target. I am sorry. I know it sounds harsh, but it is imperative we ensure your safety." Andreh figured she would argue and become belligerent, but she surprised him.

"Yes, you are correct. We must keep our working government and head of the kingdom in place. We cannot risk more upheaval. I will accompany you to my chamber and attempt to communicate with Lorthana. Once we are successful, I will return to Armbruster's side."

Alexis held her head high, approaching her deceased husband. She gently touched his arm. He looked ashen, and she felt tears well up instantly. She forced herself to be brave, marching toward the door, ready to depart.

The rainy and gloomy day matched the somber mood that had befallen the Palace. The dim lighting only added to the already melancholic atmosphere. As the news of the shocking event spread throughout the Palace, many chose to avoid the Queen. Despite this, a few commoners still offered their respect by bowing as she sauntered down the hallway.

One Security Commoner glanced at Alexis with teary eyes. The staff in the Palace cared for the King. He had been a fair and powerful ruler. The loss was heartbreaking. This day would be remembered. In time, perhaps, they would honor Armbruster's life with pomp and circumstance. For now, most mourned, still unable to make sense of what had just occurred.

Rammadar ensured the Princess was secured in her room and assigned two AoE soldiers to her security detail. The Princess was unaware of what had happened. The Queen had not yet spoken with her child.

Carmin heard the news and sat on a chair in her chamber, crying. She was unable to face the *YWIT*, knowing the Queen had not shared her father's passing with her. The young Witch had to be shielded as much as possible.

★ ˙. ★ ˙. ★ ˙. ★ ˙. ★

Andreh opened the chamber door and ensured the area was secure before allowing

Alexis to go in. After entering her room, Alexis looked around, wondering how much her life had changed in a matter of hours. It was not easy to comprehend. She shook her head and approached the Eternal Mirror, hoping for answers.

Without hesitation, she stuck her head inside, feeling the familiar, icy cold sensation run through her. It sent chills through her, and she immediately shivered. As she looked around inside the mirror, she saw her mother on Earth speaking with a Blud-Tracker. She assumed it was Magorr. He was handsome and sat beside her mother on a couch, holding her hand. Though Alexis could not hear what they discussed, she felt an urge to join them. There was a reason her mother had summoned her to the estate earlier.

Alexis turned her head, hoping to see something else. She spoke loudly, asking her mother to listen, but sadly, she did not hear Alexis. Frustrated, Alexis withdrew her head, which was beginning to ache from the cold. She touched her hair. One large section of her long, black locks was frozen and felt stiff.

She chuckled, finding it amusing. Andreh stared at her, wondering what was so funny. Alexis picked up her silver brush and ran it through her hair, hoping to keep it from getting damaged by the ice.

Andreh chose to remain silent, observing Alexis as he sat on the edge of her bed. He was about to say something to her when she pushed back the chair and stood. She looked regal and sexy as hell. He was tempted to kiss her. Sadly, Andreh realized the timing was all wrong. It would seem cold-hearted to take advantage of the Queen. She was mourning, and their relationship would be placed on hold. Andreh would have to support her without displaying romantic feelings, which would be a considerable challenge. He loved her dearly, beyond anything he had ever experienced.

Alexis noticed his look. She quickly began the conversation to move things along. "I was unable to communicate with Mother. We must find another way to reach her. Zandorah must be informed as well. Let us speak with Yarlen and Cazzandra," Alexis forcefully announced. She walked toward the door, expecting Andreh to follow.

"Are you sure you wish to do that? Perhaps it would be better if I asked for their assistance. You look exhausted and are in mourning. No one expects you to do much right now. Take your time, Alexis." Andreh advised. He advanced and took her hand in his. She looked into his eyes, attempting to make sense of his advice.

"No. I must remain strong. This isn't just about me anymore. I must speak with them. I cannot head to Earth to see Mom and Magorr without their help," Alexis insisted. She did not want pity. As Queen, she had to portray undeniable strength, even during such a sorrowful time.

Those who disliked Alexis would take her mourning as a sign of weakness and attempt to sabotage anything she tried to accomplish. Alexis Snipperdoom refused to give her enemy any leeway. Alexis was made for moments like these. She was at her best during challenging times, and she would emerge even stronger than before! Regardless of what others believed, she would portray a vision of strength and had no problem boldly announcing she would not back down until Armbruster's murderer was brought to trial.

"Andreh, please ask Aerianna to join me. I require her help. I must seek out Edwinn's help to move Armbruster to Visitation Hall. I want his body ready for the Mourning Ceremony. We must begin the process. Everything we do from now on will be scrutinized. Let us not give anyone a reason to doubt our sincerity or loyalty to the King," Alexis adamantly declared. It was the first time she acted like royalty in hours and displayed forcefulness.

Once the Mourning Ceremony for Armbruster was over, there would be a private funeral. He would be buried in the Royal Garden near the Courtyard in the center of the Palace grounds. Protocol had to be followed.

Andreh nodded and quickly hurried from the chamber to locate Aerianna. He knew Alexis wanted to be alone to deal with the grief. Andreh also figured she planned to visit Lilah and find a way to explain to her daughter that her father was gone.

Armbruster had not faded into the *Eternal World of Guidance*. Though Armbruster was a powerful Wizzard and Warlock, he was by no means exemplary. Alexis realized this the moment he died. If Armbruster had been an extraordinary W3, he would have immediately faded away, disappearing before her eyes. Then, he would have become a *Guiding Force*. Sadly, none of that happened. But it was not unexpected.

CHAPTER 11

One tragedy stood out more than the others. The residents of Alstromia quickly forgot about the recent attack on the planet once the news reached them that their beloved King had been murdered. Though the Palace had not officially announced it, the information had been leaked. Residents took to the streets, holding candles and chanting the King's name, wondering how the Queen would handle the situation.

Surprisingly, the most discussed topic in the land revolved around the young Princess who had experienced the most inconceivable loss of her father. It was a harsh and sad reality. Everyone felt awful for the *YWIT*.

Commoners gathered at the Palace entrance to stand in solidarity and honor the deceased King. The crowd grew as the afternoon advanced. Luckily, the rain stopped, and the twin moons peeked out from behind the dissipating clouds.

As Alexis gazed out the window, she observed the situation unfolding. Realizing that a statement needed to be issued, she waited patiently for Aerianna to arrive. When Aerianna finally appeared, Alexis couldn't help but notice that she seemed in better health than she had been in weeks, with more color in her cheeks.

"Alexis, My Queen, I am so very sorry for your tragic loss. What may I do for you?" she offered as she entered the room. Given the situation, she wore the Red Robe of Tears, which was appropriate.

"Aerianna, thank you for coming so quickly. We must release a statement to share with the entire kingdom. I will be the one to read it. It will take place in the Courtyard, so everyone who wishes to attend can do so. Though we do not have much to go on, we can announce that the King's demise was murder.

We will not divulge the details, of course. I do not want anyone to know about the poisoning. We must act as if we do not know. I do not want to tip off the responsible party, as that would allow them to gloat about their accomplishment. We will pretend he died suddenly of an unknown illness and hint at a potential murder. The rest of the information will remain our secret," Alexis boldly declared. She sat in the chair in the room's corner, her legs crossed. She wore black pants and a long tunic. Aeiranna was surprised Alexis was not dressed in her robe. It seemed odd.

"Furthermore, I need to speak with my child. Though she is young, she knows and understands death. I already explained it to her when Trixxie was killed. So, shortly, I will head to Lilah's room. I do not wish to be disturbed. If you can begin writing my speech, I will be grateful."

"It will be done, Alexis. I will complete it quickly. Please take care of Lilah! Do not worry. I will do the rest." Aerianna reassured the Queen.

Alexis rose from the chair and nodded. She headed out the door to meet with Carmin before speaking with Lilah. She had no idea how to say the words to her young daughter.

She located Carmin in her room. The middle-aged Witch opened the chamber door, looking disheveled. Her hair was soaking wet around her face, probably from crying. Her hands shook as she invited the Queen into her chamber. Carmin was not surprised to see Alexis. She knew this moment would come. She could barely look at the Queen, feeling dreadful.

"Carmin, I am so sorry this has affected you so deeply. Please know I am here for you!" Alexis announced, sounding proper.

"My Queen, you are the one in need of support. I cannot imagine the excruciating loss you feel. How may I help?" Carmin inquired.

"I am heading next door to speak with Lilah. Do you know if she has heard anything about the King so far? I hoped to be the one to inform her about Armbruster's death."

"No. We shielded Lilah by keeping her in the room. I figured you wanted to tell her about her father before too long." Carmin looked away, feeling a tear roll down her cheek.

"Thank you, Carmin. I will head to see the Princess now." Alexis opened the door and left to enter Lilah's room next door. She stopped briefly and took a deep breath, praying she could keep it together and not fall apart in front of her child.

Lilah flicked her wrist while holding her wand, asking her books to rearrange themselves on the shelf. She smiled, feeling proud to have learned another spell. The second she heard the door open, she turned around to face her mother.

"Hello, my darling. How are you today? My, you look so pretty wearing your purple dress."

"Mommy!" Lilah screeched, excited to see her mother. She dropped the wand and ran toward her. Once Alexis held her tightly, she began talking rather quickly. "Mom, did you know I learned a new spell today? I am getting so good at it."

"What do you mean? What magic? I did not realize you were learning spells. Who teaches you? Daddy?" Alexis inquired with curiosity.

"No. Daddy said Carmin could!"

"I see. Well, precious, let's sit on your bed. Mommy must speak with you about something. Okay?" Alexis felt her throat tightening at the thought of divulging the news.

Lilah jumped on her bed and waited for Alexis to join her. She giggled, happy to see her mom. Alexis took Lilah's tiny hand into hers, looking at her daughter. "Darling," she began. Instantly, she felt tears flowing from her eyes. Lilah looked at her, concerned.

"Mommy, are you okay?" Lilah asked lovingly.

"Sweetheart, something very sad has happened. You must be brave. Okay, Princess?"

"Okay, Mommy, I promise," the young Witch replied, smiling sweetly at her mother while Alexis wiped away more tears.

"Lilah, your Daddy is gone. Something happened, and he died. He will not be coming to see you anymore. Do you understand?"

Lilah looked at her mother and frowned. "Do you mean like what happened to Trixxie?"

"Well, sort of. Trixxie is dead. Daddy is dead, too."

"Mommy, no! Daddy is not dead. He was here yesterday. We talked, and we played. He read from the new spellbook! No, Daddy is okay!" Lilah insisted. She looked at Alexis, pouting, convinced her father would appear at any moment.

"My precious child, I know this is hard to understand. I am so sorry. I loved your father very much. But I was there when he died. We will move him to the Visitation Hall. I will take you there later. But you must be brave. It will be hard for you. Daddy is not coming back. I am so, so sorry." Alexis observed her child, unable to find any other words of comfort.

Upon jumping off the bed, Lilah quickly grabbed her spellbook and made her way toward the carpet by the fireplace. There, she began to rock back and forth, muttering under her breath. Now and then, Alexis could hear the word "Daddy" coming from Lilah's small voice. The sound tugged at Alexis' heartstrings, and she couldn't help but feel pained by her daughter's words.

Alexis continued to observe her child, feeling guilty about having to share such horrible news. Lilah self-soothed, rocking back and forth, clutching her book. After a few minutes, she released the book and stood.

"Mommy, I wanna see Daddy. I want to see my Daddy now," she forcefully yelled. "My Daddy is NOT dead. Mommy, you are wrong!" The young Witch insisted angrily.

"Okay, darling. In a little while. I will check and let you know when everything is ready. You stay here. I will send Carmin in to watch you. I will return soon." Alexis kissed her daughter on the cheek and left the room. Her heart ached, and she wanted to die. It was the worst day of her life. She had not anticipated the child's reaction. Should she allow Lilah to see her father's dead body? Would it scar her for life? How should she proceed? Alexis decided to get advice from Edwinn Shivvers. He would know how to handle the situation. He was familiar with death and dying.

As Carmin entered the Princess's chamber, she noticed Lilah seated on an oval, fluffy carpet near the fireplace, clutching a pink blanket that Armbruster had given her for her last birthday. Carmin didn't know what to say to comfort the young girl, so she sat down next to her and watched Lilah stare blankly at the flames dancing in the fireplace. It was clear that the child was not okay, and Carmin couldn't help but feel a sense of sadness for her.

Edwinn knew Alexis would eventually come to speak with him. There was much that needed to be done to prepare Armbruster's body for viewing.

"My Queen. How may I be of assistance to you?" he offered as she entered his room.

"I have a problem. I hope you can guide me. I am at a loss. My child wishes to see her father. I am not sure if I should permit it. Is she too young? I mean, it is just a body. His spirit has long moved on. How would you handle such a situation?" The Queen looked at him, desperate for his advice.

"Alexis, if it were me, I would not allow it. I believe it is unwise. It might be better to let her see him once his body is completely covered and in the glass coffin. She is young and impressionable. I would hate for this to slow her growth and learning. It is a horrible thing, Your Majesty."

"I understand. Part of me feels the same as you. However, I am unsure if, by denying her closure, I am helping her. I may actually be damaging her further. Gosh, I wish my mother were here to help me." The weight of the situation seemed to overwhelm Alexis, and she couldn't hold back her tears any longer. They cascaded down her face, adding to her already heavy burden. It seemed like the tears refused to stay away. They were relentless, waiting for a moment of weakness.

To Alexis, grief was an evil force that stripped away everything good and left one spiraling down a dark and empty stairway of despair. She couldn't stand the feeling of being out of control, knowing that the black veil of death was waiting, ready to destroy what was left of her love for her husband. Regardless of what she decided to do next, she knew her life would never be the same again.

Death had won. Armbruster had departed from their lives forever, leaving behind a void that could never be filled. The absence of his bedtime stories for Lilah was only the beginning. The tragic loss had also extinguished any hope for a better future. The cowardly act that took Armbruster's life left Alexis with an overwhelming desire for revenge.

"Well, what will you do, Alexis?" Edwinn asked. Alexis stood before the large window overlooking the Valley of Grandu, lost in thought. Edwinn's question brought her back to reality. She tried to appear calm and collected, but deep down, she knew she was not yet ready to take the necessary action. She wanted to protect her child from the pain of their loss, as any loving mother would.

"I do not know. Perhaps it is best to wait and see if I can speak with Lorthana. After that, I will make my decision. Nothing will change between now and then. So, can you help me prepare Armbruster's body for the ceremony and viewing? If you need help, I believe Yarlen can assist you."

"It will be done, Alexis. Yes, I will ask Yarlen for help. He is a great Wizzard. Armbruster would want him there to help prepare his body. I know it. They were good friends."

Alexis nodded. Then it hit her. She still had to deal with the attacks against her and Alstromia. Also, there was an unresolved issue with locating Gardone. She had been summoned to Magorr's estate before all hell broke loose on Alstromia. Alexis decided it was time to speak with Aerianna and make plans to depart for Earth. There was nothing she could accomplish on Alstromia in the meantime.

Alexis felt a sense of relief knowing that she had a dependable team to support her. Edwinn would handle the ceremony and ensure Armbruster's body was prepared. Yarlen would assist him in the process. With Armbruster gone, Rammadar would take charge and keep the Security Command Chamber running smoothly. Andreh would be there for her whenever she needed comfort. Lilah was safe in her room, under the watchful eye of Carmin and the AoE soldiers. Alexis trusted her team to handle things while she focused on her next steps.

Aerianna opened the door when Alexis knocked. She squinted, wondering if the Queen was ready to make the announcement.

"Did you speak with Lilah? How did it go?" Aerianna cautiously asked.

"The child understands what has occurred but is in shock. She is unable to deal with the news. She demanded I take her to see Armbruster. I am at a total loss and unsure how to proceed. Is the speech ready?"

"Yes, it is. Here," she handed Alexis a handwritten one-page piece of paper.

Alexis took it from her and sat in the chair by the desk. She read it and felt another round of tears trying to escape.

"It is perfect. Thank you. It means so much to me. Under these circumstances, I could not have put together the correct words."

"Of course. It is my job. I am happy to help."

"Yes, it is your job, but you are also my friend. I appreciate your support."

"I am always here for you. You know that," Aerianna responded, sounding upbeat.

"Okay, then. Let us head to the Courtyard. A large crowd is gathered. Please, let us stop at the Security Command Chamber and enlist the help of a few Security Commoners to keep us safe, just in case!"

"Absolutely, Alexis."

On Earth, Magorr sat on the other side of the couch near Lorthana. She twiddled with her long, braided hair. "What will you say to Alexis when she arrives?" asked Lorthana. "I planned to tell her the truth. What else?"

"Alright, and what exactly will you say?" Lorthana asked, hoping for more detail.

"I will explain how I attempted to deliver Gardone alive, as we agreed, but before I could do so, he cast a spell ensuring his quick death. That is the truth." Magorr's nose crinkled. He appeared upset. It did not escape Lorthana.

"I am not questioning you. I wanted to hear the exact words. I know my daughter. She will ask me if it is true. I want to feel confident and be able to say YES!" Lorthana explained, now feeling awful about making Magorr upset. The last thing she wished was to hurt his feelings.

Magorr laughed, noticing the look on her face. "My beauty, I am not angry with you. I am a bit confused. You usually do not question me. I am unfamiliar with such actions from you. That is all," he reassured Lorthana.

"Well, we have not been around each other for a very long time. I suppose we are getting to know each other all over again. Right?"

"Indeed, my Luv. I am grateful we were brought together once more. Fate intervened. You and I were meant to be. There is no denying it. I feel it, and I believe you do too. Am I wrong?" Magorr asked her.

His fiery red eyes stared at her, exploring every inch of her soul. She could feel him, and goosebumps rushed down her arms and legs. She leaned back her head, exhaling slowly, attempting to remain calm. Her entire body tingled. Magorr had stirred up some long-suppressed desires within her.

"No. You are not wrong. I believe in fate. I still have feelings for you. I tried to dismiss these emotions for many years. I believe you are the love of my life," Lorthana boldly declared. Overcome with embarrassment, she covered her mouth, caught off guard by her own words. Magorr pulled her onto his lap. His hands gently cupped her face as he kissed her like never before. She surrendered, savoring his touch, grateful for another chance with him.

CHAPTER 12

lexis and Aerianna stood on a raised platform erected solely for the announcement. The crowd could easily see the Queen. Security Commoners surrounded her, and Torrins circled above with AoE members holding the reins, watching ever so closely. Everyone knew what was at risk.

The Queen had to remain safe at any cost. No unauthorized person would gain access to the remaining ruler of Alstromia.

"Welcome, everyone," Aerianna shouted for all to hear. "Thank you for your attendance. The Queen will now make some remarks." Aerianna moved back, allowing Alexis to stand in the front.

"My friends and residents of Alstromia: it is a grim day. I stand before you to announce the passing of my beloved husband and your King, Armbruster Presstan Hextinghton. He died in the Palace earlier today from unknown causes. At this point, we have not ruled out foul play. Once we have more information about his death, we will share it with you. In my heart, I believe it was murder. Perhaps he was a victim of the relentless cowards who have attacked our planet, causing the death of thousands of innocent victims. We still do not know for sure, so I will bravely wait for more information and try not to jump to conclusions. My daughter, Princess Lilah, and I request privacy while we mourn the loss of our beloved. Please stay vigilant. If you hear anything about the King's death that you believe will help us solve the mystery of his passing, please contact our Security Command Team in the Palace. I will be forever grateful. Thank you for your love and understanding." Alexis stepped back. Aerianna quickly advanced.

"All Hail, Queen Alexis Snipperdoom. May the spirit of Armbruster rest in peace. Forever, we will remember you, King of Alstromia!" Aerianna waved her arms in the air as the group chanted Armbruster's name. Some cried, others appeared shocked, still unable to truly believe he was gone.

Alexis held back the tears, remaining stoic by Aerianna's side. She wanted to portray resilience and power. Crying would have made her look weak, so she refused to let the public see her vulnerable side. Instead, she waved to the crowd and walked down the stairs to leave the podium. She wanted to return to the Palace and make plans with Aerianna to head for Earth to locate Lorthana and Magorr.

The crowd finally disbanded. The Warlock wearing the long black cape walked away, trying not to laugh. It pleased him immensely that the Queen believed her husband may have been murdered. Indeed, he had, and it had been his job to complete.

It had been effortless. Everyone knew him, yet no one suspected him. Bringing the King his favorite after-dinner drink and potion was not a problem. The King's chamber had been unprotected. The Security Commoner on duty that night was at dinner and had failed to appear before he did. With a spiked drink in hand, he entered the King's room.

Armbruster had been pleasantly surprised to see him. The two chatted, catching up after months apart. Armbruster drank the toxic tonic, unaware he would be dead within hours. The poison worked quickly and effectively. There would be no cure concocted in time to save his life.

As the poison spread through his body, Armbruster suddenly felt his mouth become numb. Confused, he tried to swallow, finding it difficult. He began to feel woozy. The world spun around him, and he felt light as air. His chest tightened, and his legs refused to support his weight. Armbruster stared at the ceiling as he noticed his eyes closing. He knew he was dying. His last thought was of Lilah, which brought about a smile on his face. Armbruster never knew what had happened, and he began to fade away, his spirit slowly departing this realm.

Finally, Alexis would suffer and feel the pain Gardone felt when she murdered Loggane. The murderer had avenged Loggane and Gardone single-handedly! The feeling was exhilarating. He felt an unbelievable sense of pride in what he had achieved.

Now, he would visit his father and pretend to be shocked by the King's passing. He was a great actor and could certainly pass it off with little effort. The pride of his accomplishment energized him.

Gardone had known for a while that his time was running out. The Blud-Trackers were closing in. He begged him to finish one last step in their great rebellion against the Queen and Alstromia. Of course, he was honored and agreed without hesitation. Gardone told the assassin how to sneak into the planet with the Council of Peace & War representatives.

Surprisingly, the plan worked. Elated to finally be back on Alstromia, he executed the final step of the plan to kill Armbruster. Once the King was dead, he would reintegrate himself into the Clan on Alstromia, as he did before. Months later, he would depart for Earth, never to return. Or at least, that was his plan.

Sadly, he was unaware that Gardone had cast a spell to end his life. The wicked Warlock refused to be subjected to a lengthy trial, which he would lose anyway. The thought of life without his magic or freedom was unbearable to Gardone. It was easier to die a quick and efficient death. He had made all final arrangements with his team, anticipating that he would have to use a climactic spell on himself.

Gardone would have loved his life to have a meaningful ending. Sadly, it did not. He died before Magorr, Casstor, and a few others. Gardone had gone out on his terms. That was the only heroic part as far as Lorthana was concerned once she learned of his death. The rest was cowardice, in her opinion.

Gardone chose the easy way out without facing any repercussions. It made her angry. Lorthana had longed for revenge. Gardone selfishly took that option away. That is what made his death hard to accept. In a way, he had won, and he did not deserve such a victory!

Aerianna led the way to the Security Command Chamber. Plans had to be implemented to secure the Queen and allow for safe transport to Earth. Yarlen and Cazzandra had been summoned, too. Their services were essential in the next step. Alexis slumped in the chairs, twirling around like a child, playing absentmindedly. She consciously tried to steer clear of any thoughts about her current situation.

Andreh entered the chamber and laughed when he saw what she was doing. She smirked as he approached and stopped the chair from moving. She wanted his support, though she assumed he would fiercely disagree with her newly formed plan.

"NO. That is not a good idea," Andreh screamed after listening to the detailed course of action Alexis wanted to implement. Rammadar gave him a stern look.

"Andreh, it is my decision. There will be no further discussion about this matter. Aerianna and I will be back before too long. I promise. I need to see my mother and ascertain what has happened on Earth. I assume it has everything to do with my father, Gardone!" Alexis retorted.

"I do not care. It is not a smart move. Rammadar, back me on this. Tell her she is wrong. It is too risky!" Andreh bellowed.

Rammadar had every intention of staying neutral, but he had to agree. After all that had happened in the last 24 hours, it was unwise for the Queen to depart Alstromia unprotected.

"My Queen, respectfully, I must agree with Andreh. I feel it is rash for you to leave. Can you wait a little longer and postpone your departure? Perhaps until we know more about the King's death. I fear for your safety. Your Majesty, what would become of the Princess if anything happened to you?"

"That is a low blow, Rammadar, using my child against me. She will be fine. My mother

and sister will provide for her in the event something happens to me. I am not worried."
Alexis crossed her arms, glaring at Rammadar. He felt her wrath and flinched, wishing that he had kept his big mouth shut. Andreh, on the other hand, was far from done.

"See, Rammadar agrees. You cannot leave. I forbid it. You must think of Lilah and the kingdom. I insist," Andreh vehemently announced.

Ever so calm, Alexis approached Andreh. She raised her finger, almost touching his face. "Ummm, you will not allow it? You must insist? Andreh, who do you think you are, telling me, the Queen, what to do? Screw you! I will do as I please. I suggest you BACK OFF!"

Andreh grabbed her by the sleeve as she tried to escape the room. She spun around. Her green eyes flashed with hatred.

"Let go, Andreh. If you know what is good for you, release me immediately. Do you hear me?" Alexis screamed. She was tired of everyone telling her what to do. She was determined to see her mother and Magorr on Earth. Nothing would interfere with her plan.

Andreh reluctantly dropped his hand. He knew she would do what she wanted, and his concerns meant nothing to her. She did not seem to care.

"Andreh," Alexis began. Her voice softened. "I know you and Rammadar mean well. However, I must do what is right. I am leaving. If you are so worried about my well-being and safety, feel free to accompany me as my security officer."

"Great, I will," he responded, following her and Aerianna out of the chamber. Rammadar stayed behind, shaking his head. He was surprised the Queen had been so easy on him. Perhaps the rumors were true. Maybe Andreh and Alexis were having an affair. He sighed, not wanting to think about that. It was too much to face in one day.

Instead, he bellowed out orders for others in the room to ensure the planet remained protected. The last thing he needed or wanted was another fatality. *'Not on my watch,'* Rammadar said to himself.

Inside Alexis' chamber, Aerianna shook her head, rolling her eyes at Andreh. She was furious with him for the outburst in the Command Chamber. It was uncalled for as far as she was concerned. However, she knew it was best not to make a big deal about it in front of Alexis. She loved Andreh and would protect him, even if she was mad at him for what he had said. Alexis was fragile from all the horrific events. First, the attack on

271

Alstromia, followed by Trixxie's death, and lastly, Armbruster's murder. Though the Queen refused to acknowledge her feelings, Aerianna knew she was struggling.

The knock on the Queen's chamber door was followed by Yarlen's voice asking for permission to enter. He had brought Cazzandra with him. Andreh had requested their presence.

"Great, you are here. So, Aerianna, Andreh, and I wish to depart Alstromia. Given what has happened, we must be careful to close the portal as soon as we have gone through it. We must keep the protective shield over Alstromia until we know more about the attacks and Gardone's whereabouts." Alexis declared. She was uninterested in excuses. She was ready to leave.

"Your Majesty, Cazzandra and I are ready to assist you. We must head to the Courtyard and open the portal. How much time will you require this time?" Yarlen asked. He hoped there would be no repeat of the last time.

"I thought about it and figured four hours is ample time."

"Aerianna, are you sure you wish to join us? You could remain at the Palace," Andreh suggested. He had heard the rumors that Aerianna was expecting a child, and she was still weak and tired from morning sickness.

"The Queen has asked me to join her. I do not mind accompanying you."

Alexis shook her head. "No, now that Andreh is coming along and can protect me, you should stay on Alstromia. Plus, I need you here as my Second-in-Command. It is better this way. Okay?"

"Of course, whatever you need, Alexis," Aerianna agreed. She had a pounding headache and was grateful for the opportunity to remain at the Palace. Hopefully, she could get some well-deserved rest once the others departed. It was better that Andreh would be there to protect Alexis.

"The decision has been made. We will head to the Courtyard. See you in about four hours, Aerianna! Get your rest." Alexis hugged her friend on the way out of the chamber, eager to meet Lorthana and Magorr. *Hopefully, they will have excellent news to share about Gardone,'* thought Alexis.

The team of four stood in a circle. Alexis and Andreh held hands. Cazzandra followed the same routine as before. Luckily, the magic worked, and Andreh and Alexis disappeared, passing through the portal and arriving on Earth.

Alexis leaned against Andreh as he knocked on the large door. She was tired and highly irritated. Luckily, it didn't take long for Magorr to answer. He recognized Alexis but was confused about the Wizzard who accompanied her. He had never seen him before, and he frowned.

"My goodness, Alexis. You are stunningly gorgeous, just like your mother. Who is this with you?" Magorr inquired, his eyes taking in the stranger, seizing him up. He wondered why he looked at Alexis in such a way. *'Are they romantically involved? No, that cannot be. She is married to Armbruster.'*

"Magorr, this is Andreh Darkhill. He is my security detail for the day and a close friend. May we enter? I understand Mother is here?" Alexis refused to waste time with chit-chat.

"Yes, of course. She is in the living room, drinking tea. Please, come in," Magorr watched as the two entered the estate. He closed the door.

"Please, follow me," he added as he led the way to the living room.

Lorthana jumped off the couch when she heard the voices. She knew it was Alexis. "My child! You made it. Thank Goodness. I am so thrilled you are here. We have so much to discuss. Ah, Andreh, nice to see you, too," she added, attempting to be civil though she did not like him. She knew about the affair, and it sickened her. Even so, she wanted to be kind and not make a scene in front of Alexis.

Magorr politely offered the visitors a seat. He chose to sit beside Lorthana, eager to hear why Alexis was there. He assumed it had something to do with Gardone, her father.

"Mother, I have horrible news to share," Alexis began. Andreh grabbed her hand and squeezed it, providing her with support. Lorthana noticed and flinched, disapproving of their public display of affection.

Alexis felt the tears running down her face, dripping onto her robe. Lorthana looked perplexed, wondering what kind of horrible news there was now. It seemed as if there had been nothing but bad news lately.

"What is it, Alexis? It must be something awful. Tell me, my darling."

"Mother, it is Armbruster!" Alexis blurted out.

"What about him? Is he okay?" she asked nervously.

"No, Mom. He is not. Tragically, he is gone."

"Well, for goodness sake. Gone to where? I knew he disliked Alstromia. Is he here on Earth? What the hell, Alexis? Is it because of him?" she pointed to Andreh.

Andreh jumped up, releasing Alexis' hand. "Ms. Stainnard-Snipperdoom, I had nothing to do with what has happened to Armbruster. Rest assured." He shook his head, tired of the judgments.

Alexis pulled on Andreh's arm, asking him to sit beside her. He took a seat and attempted to regain his composure. Alexis took a deep breath and exhaled.

"Mother, Armbruster has not gone away. He is dead. He was murdered. We believe he was poisoned." Alexis began sobbing again.

"Wait, what?" Lorthana screeched. She could not believe what she had heard and scooted to the edge of her seat, staring at Alexis in disbelief.

"Hold on, did I hear you correctly? Armbruster is dead? Are you sure? No, that can't be right."Lorthana refused to believe the announcement. Tears began to flow. Magorr quickly placed his arm around Lorthana.

Alexis pulled herself together. "Yes, Mother. You heard me correctly. He is gone, deceased. The final funeral arrangement will be made soon. Yarlen and Edwinn Shivvers are working on preparing his body for the Mourning Ceremony. I have already informed Lilah and the residents of my planet. I wanted you and Zandi to know, too."

"Oh, Alexis. I am so sorry," Lorthana said, standing up and approaching her daughter. She sat on the other side of her, ignoring Andreh. "What can I do for you? This is the most horrible thing to happen ever. My goodness! What a loss. He was a good Wizzard. He was handsome, talented, and he loved his family. He will be greatly missed. What will you do now?" Lorthana was shocked. It was heart-wrenching to realize Armbruster was dead.

"As I stated, we will hold all ceremonies required. Armbruster will be laid to rest at the Palace grounds near the Courtyard. It will happen in a day or so. I hope you will be there, Mother. I want Zandi there, too!"

"Of course, Alexis. Your family will be by your side to support and comfort you and Lilah!" Lorthana reassured her daughter. It broke her heart. Armbruster was gone! It was incomprehensible.

"Alexis, we have news, too," Magorr began, realizing it was not a great time to bring up Gardone's demise.

"Okay, what is it, Magorr? Did you locate my father?" Alexis asked, hopeful.

"Yes, indeed."

"And where is he? Is he here with you?"

"Yes, he is here. Alexis, I had every intention of delivering him to you alive. However, Gardone refused to come with us willingly. He killed himself by casting a spell. It was quick. There was nothing we could do. I am so sorry." Magorr waited to see her reaction. He assumed she would be upset.

Andreh was unsure whether she was in shock or simply did not care. Alexis looked unaffected by the declaration.

"Where is his body? I want to see it," Alexis insisted, standing up.

"Follow me," Magorr said, leading her to the parlor, where Gardone's body was displayed on a table. Half of his body was covered with a long, black velvet blanket. His hands were folded, and he looked peaceful.

Alexis stood beside Gardone's body, her hand resting on his. "So, this is the way you wanted it, Daddy? You were such a coward. You've never faced anything hard. You ran away from everyone and everything that challenged you. I wish I could say I will miss you, but I will not. I am only sorry that I am your daughter. I am deeply ashamed to have called you my father. You have disgraced our family." She bravely walked away.

Sadly, Alexis did not shed a single tear. Her heart was conflicted. She had wanted Gardone brought up on charges for what he had done. However, she did not want him dead. Ironically, death seemed like an extreme measure, even though he had taken so many lives. Alexis had lost her husband and father a few hours apart. It was inconceivable. Andreh watched her with worry, contemplating whether she would ever forgive Gardone for his actions.

Alexis returned to the couch. "Mother, we have a few more hours before heading back. Let us discuss Armbruster's ceremony. Also, I need your advice regarding Lilah. She wishes to see Armbruster's body. She insists he is not dead. What should I do?"

Lorthana addressed her daughter. "Okay, Alexis. Let us talk." Lorthana scooted in beside her on the couch, grabbing her hand.

Andreh followed Magorr to the balcony off the living room. The view was spectacular. Below the bluff, the water was dark blue and looked cold. The breeze was frigid. Andreh slightly shivered, wishing for a warmer cloak and some gloves.

"Your estate is beautiful, Magorr. Have you lived here long?"

"Pretty much my entire life. It is a serene place. I do love it here. So, how is Alexis, really? Who murdered Armbruster?"

Andreh shrugged. "We do not know who killed the King. We are still investigating. It is a horrible situation. Someone managed to cross the protective barrier and enter Alstromia. Then, they managed to infiltrate the Palace. Since the King had no visible wounds, I believe he knew the killer. Perhaps Armbruster even invited the murderer inside his chamber!"

"WOW. That is an unpleasant thought. Do you want my help locating the assassin? I would be happy to accompany you to Alstromia and use my skills as a Blud-Tracker to hunt down the one responsible," offered Magorr.

"I would say yes, but Alexis will most likely decline the offer. I am not sure she wants others involved. I know she is grateful that you found Gardone. It is truly regrettable that he is dead."

The two remained on the balcony chatting while Alexis and Lorthana summoned Zandorah from Iriss.

CHAPTER 13

andorah arrived alone minutes after receiving her mother's and sister's message that her presence was requested on Earth due to a family emergency. She strode toward Alexis, happy to see her. Once she stood near her sibling, she noticed she had been crying. Alexis did not allow others to see her cry. *'Something horrible must have happened!'* Zandorah thought, instantly panicking.

"Alexis! What is it? Are you okay? What is happening on Alstromia? Have the attacks stopped? I hope you know I had nothing to do with them. It was all Daddy and the *GRAW*," Zandorah shouted.

"Zandi, stop! I know it was Daddy. Mom, don't you want to tell Zandorah about Dad?" Alexis announced.

Magorr entered the room and took responsibility for informing Zandorah, which made things less uncomfortable for Lorthana. He initiated the conversation by saying, "Zandorah, my job was to locate Gardone." After explaining the events that resulted in her father's death, he took a seat.

"What? Is Dad really dead? Are you sure?" Zandorah shouted.

"Yes, Zandorah. He certainly is. Now, let us not dwell on Gardone. Alexis is here because something far worse has occurred. Isn't that right, Alexis? Do you want to tell your sister, or should I?"

Alexis did not respond to her mother. Instead, she blurted out the news. "Zandorah, Armbruster was murdered. No, we do not know who is responsible. My team on Alstromia is working on finding out the facts and arresting the killer."

Zandorah shook her head. "Hold on. Is this a twisted joke? Dad is dead? Armbruster has been murdered. Ummm, right. Blatant lies!"

Magorr responded. "All information is factual. Gardone's death was his fault. None of us could have predicted it. Armbruster was poisoned. So, yes…sadly, it is all true, Zandorah."

The realization finally dawned on her, and she couldn't contain her emotions. She started shouting, "NO! Not Armbruster! He was a kind-hearted man, an exceptional father, a great King, and he loved you, Alexis!"

"I know, Zandi," Alexis wrapped her arm around her sister. "Zandi, please come back to Alstromia with Mom and me. I need you there. Plus, Lilah would love to see her auntie! Okay?" Alexis asked.

"You know I will not say no. What will happen to Father? What will you do with his body, Mom?" Zandorah figured he had to be buried somewhere.

"Magorr offered to bury him near his hut in the woods. I believe it is best. We do not need a ceremony. Though I believe someone should notify his mistress." Lorthana rolled her eyes, still bitter about Gardone's marital infidelity.

Alexis and Zandorah agreed. Magorr could proceed with the burial. Neither planned to attend. Lorthana wanted to be there with Magorr. If for no other reason, she wanted closure. However, Alexis preferred that her mother accompany her to Alstromia for support during this difficult time.

Lorthana felt torn. Ultimately, she chose to join Alexis. It was far more important to her to be there for her daughter and grandchild than to watch Gardone's burial on Earth. It meant very little to her. As difficult as it was to admit, she did not feel any remorse or regret over his passing.

In Lorthana's opinion, Armbruster deserved a proper burial, unlike Gardone. She stood and motioned for Magorr to join her in the parlor. She wanted to wrap up a few loose ends before departing with her daughters and Andreh.

"Thank you for promising to take care of the difficult part. I appreciate you taking the initiative to bury Gardone. I am grateful and in your debt."

"My beauty, I will do whatever you desire. You should not have to face such a difficult task, especially alone. It will be done today. Rest assured," Magorr responded. He wrapped his arms around her small waist and drew her against him. He kissed her passionately and then pulled away, realizing Gardone's body was a few feet away. It felt wrong.

"I will return when I can, Magorr. I must help my child and grandchild. Hopefully, you can understand. They need me. I promise to come back! We still have much to discuss," she reassured him.

"I understand, Lorthana, and I will be here waiting! Hurry back, my beauty." Magorr released her, and she returned to the living room.

"When do we depart?" Lorthana asked the group.

Andreh quickly replied. "We have less than an hour. We cannot miss the timeline, or we might be stuck here. It is time to say goodbye."

"I already have. Magorr is taking care of Gardone's burial. We can leave when you are ready. I did not bring items besides my Ceptre and wand."

Alexis nodded, feeling relieved that her mother and sister would be joining her in returning home. Despite her eagerness, her mind wandered as she listened to the others. She started to reminisce about Armbruster and found it hard to accept that he was gone. It all seemed so surreal.

The previous day, they had talked about planning a trip to the cabin on Tullah Mountain, hoping to make amends and spend quality time with Lilah away from the Palace. Armbruster had been a hopeless romantic. He also wanted to keep his family together for as long as possible. He knew about the affair but still made an effort to spend time with Alexis.

Feeling guilty, Alexis wondered if she should have tried harder to make things work with Armbruster. But then, she could not deny her love for Andreh. In the end, Alexis knew that Armbruster's untimely death was not her fault, and she couldn't change what had happened in the past.

As the group chatted for a bit longer, Alexis recalled the night she gave birth to Lilah. Armbruster had been there, holding her hand, supporting her. It was a time when they were deeply in love and a united front. Alexis wondered what caused them to drift apart. It happened long before her love affair with Andreh.

Suddenly, Andreh lept off the couch and headed toward the door. "It is time. We must not be late!" The others agreed and joined him, heading out of the house. They gathered on the grass, standing in a circle, ready to depart.

Alexis held onto Andreh and Lorthana. Zandorah took Andreh's other hand. Alexis began the chant. Lorthana used her free hand and slammed down her Ceptre.

Yarlen and Cazzandra clapped when the group appeared in the Courtyard of the Palace as planned. It was a huge relief. The Queen advanced, followed by Andreh. Lorthana and Zandorah walked side by side, stopping beside Yarlen.

"Thank you, Yarlen and Cazzandra. I am thrilled we could return on time without complications."

Alexis headed for the Palace entrance to find Rammadar and Aerianna. Cazzandra excused herself to head back to the Palace's dungeon to complete a new project. Yarlen wanted to meet with Edwinn in the Palace to help him prepare the King's body for the scheduled public Mourning Ceremony in the morning.

Most of the *GRAW* members heard the devastating news about Gardone's death. Many were upset, while others realized it was not unexpected. Gardone had caused much upheaval and was personally responsible for the death of thousands of innocent victims. The question remained: Should the *GRAW* discontinue the attempted attacks against Alstromia and the Queen?

An invisible, protective shield secured Alstromia. The *GRAW* members knew this, making their efforts redundant. They could not cause the catastrophic damage or harm they hoped for.

Thornton Glowstone, the current leader of the *GRAW*, felt reluctant to continue such war tactics. He preferred to stop all actions. However, he knew such a decision would be best discussed with the entire group. He planned to call a meeting and ask the *GRAW* members to vote to officially end the War.

In the Palace's dungeon, Cazzandra dropped onto the bed, expelling a huge sigh. She felt relieved that the Queen and her entourage had returned safely and on time to Alstromia. Now, her worst fears could finally be buried. She had an abundance of herbs and other ingredients in case it became necessary in the future to transport the Queen or others off the planet. Yarlen was a supportive friend and instructor. He never gave up and displayed more patience than any of her previous teachers.

Alexis entered the Command Chamber and noticed Rammadar sitting in the corner near the tall window. He seemed to be staring out, lost in thought. Alexis placed her hand on his shoulder, causing him to jump.

"Your Majesty! I did not hear you enter the room." He quickly stood and bowed.

"I just returned. Please, sit," Alexis announced.

"So, what are our plans? I assume we will move ahead with the Mourning Ceremony and burial immediately? What will you do, My Queen? How may I be of assistance?"

"Yes, Yarlen and Edwinn are preparing Armbruster's body. We will hold the ceremony at 10 a.m. There will be a public viewing after. We will open the Palace gates, allowing W3s to view his body. I will need you to enlist your SAoW for extra security measures. I believe we will also hold a viewing in the city. I have asked for the Royal Carriage to be prepared to hold Armbruster's body. He will be covered in the glass coffin. But, I believe it will allow for closure for those mourning the loss of their King."

Alexis slumped in the chair beside Rammadar. She was tired and wanted everything to be over. Her heart ached, and Alexis felt as if she were drowning in sorrow. It hit her hard to realize she still loved Armbruster. She had hidden those feelings when she fell in love with Andreh. Now, as she prepared to bury her husband, she felt remorse. She should have been kinder to Armbruster. Unfortunately, it was a moot point. He was gone, as was her opportunity for amends.

"I will head to my chamber. If you need me, you can call on me anytime. I know there is much to be done. Please, do not disturb Aerianna. She needs her rest!" Alexis rose from the chair, feeling her legs fail her. She fell back into the chair, looking embarrassed, but stood a few seconds later.

"My Queen, are you okay?"Rammadar took her hand, trying to steady her. She swayed, her eyes fluttering.

"It is all too much," she began, sobbing. "How will I make it through the next few days? Rammadar, I do not believe that I am that strong," she boldly declared.

"Your Majesty, we are all here to support you. Rest assured. You are not alone. Please, let me accompany you to your chamber," Rammadar said firmly.

"Okay," Alexis concurred. She knew it was one of the few times in her life when she required assistance. She was weak, and her body was rebelling. Standing before her chamber door minutes later, her eyes locked with Rammadar's.

"Thank you for your help and support. It means so much." She closed the door, leaving him wondering if she was okay. He had never seen the Queen so vulnerable. It worried him greatly.

Rammadar left the area of the Palace and headed to locate Yarlen and Edwinn. He wanted an update on the King's body preparation and felt an urgent need to see Yarlen. He approached the old Warlock's chamber door and knocked. Yarlen shouted for him to enter. He noticed Edwinn leaning over the King's body. Armbruster's clothing had been changed, and he now donned his royal attire, including his purple cloak. His crown was placed on his head, and his Ceptre lay next to him. His body glistened in a magical and surreal way.

"Is the King prepared? Will we move him to Visitation Hall tonight? Why does he look sparkly and strange?" inquired Rammadar.

Yarlen spoke up. "We have finished the process. He is petrified and ready. It is the way we preserve elite W3s. It is a magical chant used with a specialty potion. Most W3s on Earth do not use it, but the Queen wishes it for Armbruster. So, we have done it," Yarlen elaborated.

"I see. I did not know. That is quite interesting."

Edwinn added to the conversation. "Since he will be in a glass coffin, we want to ensure he looks his best. He will not be covered until we bring him to the City of Miccay for the viewing."

"Will there be a funeral procession?" asked Rammadar, still highly intrigued by the King's new physical appearance.

"Yes," Yarlen responded. "The Royal Carriage will hold His Majesty. He will be followed by the Queen's Carriage, the AoE, and SAoW."

"Very well," Rammadar noted. He moved next to Armbruster and touched his arm. "He is cold and hard. It is odd."

"Yes, it is very different now that his spirit is gone," agreed Yarlen. "But we can still pay our respects."

"I wonder why the Queen wishes him to be petrified. Does this process apply to all royalty, or is it a preference?" Rammadar added, still filled with curiosity.

"Most of the time, high-ranking members of Clans and heads of government are petrified. Actually, the official process is called *'Memorialed.'* It is a way of ensuring the body of the W3 is completely preserved for eternity."

"I understand," Rammadar concluded.

The two Warlocks remained standing near Armbruster. Both were heartbroken over the unexpected loss of their King. He had been a wonderful friend.

"We must deliver Armbruster to the viewing. Will you and your team accompany me and his *'Memorialed'* body?" Yarlen inquired.

"Whatever you need, Yarlen," Rammadar responded with a heavy heart. He turned and called for members of the AoE to help move the King's body. It was a somber moment.

On Earth, the vote was unanimous. The decision was made to cease all actions against Alstromia and the Queen. The *GRAW*

members agreed with their new leader. Thornton planned to send a message to the Palace announcing their ceasefire. Hopefully, the Queen and her armies would not retaliate further. Thornton wanted this campaign to be done. He was exhausted and ready to flee the planet, seeking refuge elsewhere, realizing his life was now in danger.

In the woods near the Warlock's hut, Magorr buried Gardone. He stared at the corpse in the deep hole, wondering if things could have ended differently. Moments later, he filled the grave with a large mound of dirt covering the dead body. Magorr wished to finish the process quickly so he could focus on his relationship with Lorthana. He wondered how Alexis was holding up now that she had lost her father and husband. It was unprecedented, something she would never forget.

The night arrived quickly. The two moons shone in the sky, which was clear and also bitterly cold. Alexis dressed in her Robe of Tears and joined Aerianna in Visitation Hall.

Andreh and Pauto arrived within minutes, standing beside the two Witches. They awaited Armbruster's *'Memorialed'* body.

Trumpets blared, and Alexis felt the release of her tears as they rolled down her cheek.

By now, the Hall was filled with W3s. She noticed Lorthana and Zandorah sitting in the front row, facing them. Her mother cried as she held Zandorah's hand. Next to her, Shawnatar sat with his head lowered. Alexis was surprised he had made the trip. She was grateful to Yarlen and Cazzandra for their magical talents in safely bringing her family to Alstromia and bypassing the shield.

All eyes turned to the heavy double doors, which swung open. Two AoE members entered. The first one held the Alstromian flag. The other carried the family crest flag. They stopped by the stairs beneath the podium, where Alexis stood. The two AoE Commoners placed the flags into the metal holders and moved aside.

Next, the glass coffin holding the King floated through the air and advanced to a raised stone table placed in the center of the room. With a loud bang and crunch, the coffin settled onto the sturdy structure. Alexis sobbed, unable to contain her emotions.

Several other AoE and SAoW entered the room and stood in the back of the room, their heads lowered. Yarlen arrived with Edwinn and approached the ornate coffin, waving his Ceptre, causing the side of the glass to slide down.

He nodded to Alexis. She made her way down the stairs and walked toward the table, holding her husband's body. She stopped before the structure and stared at Armbruster. He sparkled under the light in the room, and his skin looked iridescent. She thought he looked beautiful and placed her hand on his.

Instantly, she flinched, feeling the cold and stiff fingers as she brushed over them. Armbruster was gone. His body was a shell. She knew this and withdrew her hand, diverting her gaze. Aerianna joined her and placed her arm on Alexis, who looked unsteady, swaying slightly. Pauto noticed and quickly dashed toward the Queen, catching her before she fainted.

Andreh panicked and ran toward Alexis, helping Pauto carry her to a chair. She opened her eyes, confused. "What happened?" she asked Andreh, feeling embarrassed.

"Alexis, My Queen, you fainted. I believe we should get you back to your chamber. You require rest." Andreh added, hoping she would agree.

"Okay, I am so sorry. Yes, Andreh, will you escort me to the room? I need to walk and clear my head," Alexis responded, wishing to leave the area. Seeing Armbruster's remains was too difficult for her.

Andreh nodded in agreement and extended his hand to help her stand up. He held onto her arm and led her out of the room. Pauto attempted to follow, but Andreh shook his head, indicating that he should stay behind. Andreh realized that Alexis needed privacy. Pauto understood the message, nodded in acknowledgment, and returned to Visitation Hall to rejoin Aerianna and the rest of the group.

Standing next to Armbruster, Edwinn chanted, holding his wand high up in the air. Doing so caused purple and gold glitter to rain down from the ceiling, landing on the coffin. Meanwhile, others watched silently. Aerianna also pointed her wand at Armbruster's casket and called out his name as red sparks emitted from her wand, making zapping noises. Overcome with emotion, she dropped her wand and broke down in tears.

Lorthana advanced with Zandorah behind her. She raised her wand and forcefully declared:

"Beyond this world and into the next, may your spirit travel without pretext. With this spell, I call upon the light to guide you through the darkness of night."

Lorthana stepped back. Zandorah raised her Ceptre and chanted:

"Life and death, beyond the veil, spirits hear my breath, without fail. Open wide the gates of the afterlife, allowing Armbruster to journey without strife."

Finally, Yarlen raised his Ceptre of Argin, aiming it at Armbruster, and said:

"By the power of the spirits beyond, let these words of magic bond. Grant Armbruster's passage to the afterlife, where souls of the departed thrive. May he journey safely to the other side and find peace in eternity to abide."

Yarlen lowered his head, loudly exhaling and closing his eyes. The ritual was complete. Sadly, Alexis missed it. She sat on the edge of her unmade bed while Andreh knelt before her, holding her hands.

After the Command Staff departed, the room was opened to commoners who worked in the Palace to pay their respects to Armbruster. The AoE and SAoW members remained in the room, keeping an eye on everything and ensuring that nobody interfered with the King or his coffin. The next morning, the funeral procession was scheduled to run along Main Street, allowing the other residents to bid farewell to their esteemed ruler.

CHAPTER 14

On the first official day of mourning, Alexis awoke to find Andreh asleep and snoring in the chair by the window. He looked peaceful with a fluffy blanket draped over his body. She jumped off the tall bed and made her way toward him. She slightly touched his left arm. His eyes fluttered open, and he smiled.

"Alexis, are you okay?" Andreh   asked, concerned, noticing her black nightgown flowing to the tile floor. She looked tired, with messy hair and dark rings under her eyes, matching her lingerie.

"Yes, I am alright. We must dress and head to the Courtyard. The carriage with Armbruster will be departing in a few hours. I should probably try to eat something. I feel weak, plus it will be a long day."

"Should I call for Karita, or would you like me to bring you breakfast?" Andreh asked as he waited for her reply. She ran her fingers through her hair and absentmindedly stared at him. "Alexis, did you hear me?" Andreh asked, noticing she looked zoned out. He realized today would be one of the worst days of her life.

Alexis stood by the window, captivated by the scenery. Feeling stifled, she unlocked the window, leaned back, and took a deep breath of the fresh air. "Please, bring me something to eat. I am famished. I will shower and dress in the meantime." She spun around, kissed him on the cheek, and then made her way toward the bath chamber.

Andreh left her room. He knocked on Karita's door. She answered immediately, wearing a long work gown with a crisp white apron. "Andreh, how may I be of assistance?" she asked.

"The Queen needs breakfast. Please deliver it to her chamber. I will be back in a bit." He swiftly left to find Yarlen to inquire about Armbruster's final viewing in the city.

Karita arrived in the Queen's Chamber with a trillay overflowing with Alexis' favorite breakfast foods, including fluffy pancakes and eggs, just like the ones she had enjoyed on Earth. Alexis had a particular fondness for blueberry syrup as a topping for her pancakes. To wash it all down, she usually opted for a cup of *Shadow Rose Tea*, a brew her mother had created for her during her childhood in New England. This unique tea combines various ingredients to make a pink and black brew that evokes the shadows and roses of a magical garden. At the same time, its strong and melancholy-healing properties add to its spellbinding effect.

Alexis was seated at the small round table near the window, sipping her tea, when Lorthana entered the chamber. The moment their eyes met, Lorthana felt a wave of sadness. She had no idea how to support her daughter during such a challenging time.

In the stables, Essten readied the Torrins. They would pull the Royal Carriage with the King's Memorialed body. The Torrins were restless on this day, which was unusual. It was as if they sensed the reason for the day and revolted. Essten tried his best to calm them down by talking to them lovingly. His wife, Marittaz Spellwin, remained in the background, watching. She briefly thought about Collan and felt a twinge of sorrow.

Quickly, she brushed aside the hurt and approached another Torrin to prepare it for departure. She wished to aid Essten as much as possible. He refused help, desiring to do this one last thing for the King as a gesture of love and respect.

The sky roared with thunder, and the lightning flashes illuminated the atmosphere. It was a somber day on Alstromia, and Alexis chose to wear a black gown and cloak, avoiding the Robe of Tears.

Meanwhile, Carmin readied and dressed Lilah for the viewing of the King and his send-off to the city. It would be the first time Lilah would see her father's *'Memorialed'* body. Carmin was concerned about how the Princess would respond to the sight of her deceased father.

As Lorthana and Zandorah entered the Queen's Chamber, they were dressed in subdued colors. Lorthana's red, swollen eyes suggested that she had been crying a lot and looked awful. Standing beside Alexis, she immediately hugged her tightly, feeling her daughter's trembling body. While Zandorah watched them, tears streamed down her face. Just as Alexis was about to say something, there was a loud knock on the door. Alexis sprinted toward the door, shouting, "Enter."

Lilah screamed, "Mommy!" as she ran toward her mother and hugged her legs tightly. "Carmin told me that we have to be brave when we see Daddy today. I promise to be super brave, Mommy," Lilah declared. She wore a dark-purple dress with a black cloak, and her hair was braided and tied back. Alexis found it strange that Lilah's usually bright lavender eyes looked gray today.

"I'll be with you the whole time, my precious. We need to be courageous. Grandma Hana is here too," she said, giving a wink to her mother. Lorthana approached the child, picked her up, and hugged her tightly.

"You're such a big girl now, Lilah. Don't worry, sweetie. Zandi, Mommy, and I will always be here for you," Lorthana comforted the young Princess.

"I know, Grandma. I'm going to miss my Daddy," Lilah replied, closing her eyes and allowing Lorthana to embrace her. It was a challenging moment for everyone present in the room.

"Shawnatar is in the Hall, waiting for us. The others are there, too. We should head out." Zandorah took Lilah from Lorthana and held her hand. They left the chamber, strolling toward Visitation Hall for the last ceremony before Armbruster was moved to Miccay.

Alexis stared at her mother, feeling frozen in place. Suddenly, she could not move, and it was difficult for her to keep walking. Lorthana saw Alexis's face and immediately came to her aid.

"Hold my hand, darling. I got you! Let's pay our respects."

The two Witches moseyed toward the Hall, with three security officers following. Alexis kept her gaze low while a few commoners curtsied, noticing the Queen as she passed them in the hallway.

In Visitation Hall, the mood was subdued. The Command Staff was present and seated in the second and third rows facing Armbruster's transparent coffin. The first row was reserved for the Queen and her immediate family.

Yarlen stood on the left side of the podium while Edwinn Shivvers remained on the right. They planned to oversee the entire process.

Andreh watched from the doorway, peeking down the corridor, hoping Alexis was on her way. The room was packed beyond the capacity limits of 250 W3s. There were many more than that. W3s squeezed in the area, choosing to stand along the wall. Most had come from Earth and Draekidell. The only representative from Xeagadale was Magorr Bloodrup. Lorthana had invited him, and he was delighted to accept her invitation.

Rammadar stood beside Yarlen, playing with his cloak. He felt quite uncomfortable standing with Yarlen. The two had a strained relationship since Armbruster offered him Yarlen's job, forcing the old Warlock into early retirement. Nonetheless, Rammadar knew it was essential he watch over his boss one last time, if for no other reason than for respect. He would miss Armbruster. The King had been a well-respected Warlock.

Finally, Andreh spotted Alexis and Lorthana making their way toward the Hall. He smiled, but the Queen continued to look down. Lorthana gave him a nasty look, puckering her mouth in disgust. She was still furious about Andreh and Alexis's affair.

"All Hail, Queen Alexis Snipperdoom, Ruler of Alstromia. Wife of our beloved deceased Ruler, King Armbruster Hextinghton!" Andreh screamed. He moved aside, allowing the two Witches to enter the Hall. He quickly took his reserved seat beside Pauto Vexxorth.

The double windows in the room were open, letting in a refreshing breeze. Although the rain had stopped, the lightning remained brilliant, and the thunder added to the gloomy atmosphere.

Armbruster's body was placed in a transparent coffin, with only the bottom half of his body covered by the Death Sheet, as per custom. His head was adorned with the royal crown, and his hands were folded, resting on his stomach. On his left-hand ring finger, he wore his Ceremonial Ring, which Alexis believed was appropriate for him to wear to his grave. His substantially long Ceptre was placed next to him.

Alexis quickly sat on the cushy purple chair. Lorthana sat on the right side of her, and Lilah was on her left. They held hands. Lilah looked up and noticed the coffin holding her father. She pulled on her mother's sleeve.

"Mommy, do we get to say goodbye to Daddy?"

"Not yet, baby. In a little bit. First, we must listen to Yarlen. Hush, okay?"

Lilah nodded and stared at her lap, beginning to feel the pain of the loss of her father. She sobbed, and Alexis rubbed her hand lovingly.

Yarlen approached the center of the podium. "Welcome, friends and family. It is a grim moment for us all. Our beloved King is gone. I had the privilege of working with him for years. He was a fair, loyal, and gracious

King. He will be missed. I extend my deepest condolences to the Snipperdoom family. You are in our thoughts during this tragic time."

Edwinn spoke next. "Today, we gather to mourn the loss of our esteemed King. He was a great leader and a true friend to all who knew him. His legacy will live on through the countless lives he touched and his many accomplishments. We will remember him for his strength, courage, and unwavering dedication to his people. He led with honor and integrity, and his memory will continue to inspire us all. As we say final goodbye to our dear Armbruster Presstan Hextinghton, we take comfort in the knowledge that he will always be with us, in our hearts, and in our memories. We honor his life and legacy and pledge to carry on his vision for a better world. Rest in peace, dear friend. Your spirit is free, and your legacy will never be forgotten."

After taking a deep breath, Edwinn spoke again, "Now, let's allow every W3 present to pay their respects. However, please refrain from touching the glass enclosure. You can view the King from here, but kindly limit your viewing time to under a minute as we have a large crowd today." Edwinn then descended the three stairs and positioned himself on the right side of the coffin to keep a watchful eye.

Alexis stood, glancing at her child. "Come, it is time, Lilah." She stoically led her daughter toward the glass casket. Lorthana followed. Zandorah rose from her chair and made her way toward her mother to support her. Shawnatar remained seated, allowing the women to view the King first. The Queen remained composed while gazing at her husband through the glass. The tears were absent, and it appeared as though she had already shed enough of them to exhaust her supply.

Lilah, who was trying to comprehend the situation, observed her mother with a tilted head. Although she found it hard to believe that her father was no more, she eventually broke down, sobbing uncontrollably. Lorthana held her in her arms, consoling her.

Alexis remained standing in place. After a long pause, she finally spoke. "My beloved husband, I am deeply sorry for what has happened to you. This needless tragedy has shattered our family. However, I promise you that I will not rest until the person responsible for your death is brought to justice. Every day, I will pray that your spirit roams freely. Please don't worry about Lilah and me. We will manage. You will be missed forever!" She leaned forward, kissed the coffin's side, and picked up a dark red rose from the metal urn, placing it on top. Finally, she stepped back, giving Zandorah and Lorthana a chance to say their final goodbyes to the King.

Lilah glanced at the glass coffin intently. She wanted to take in every detail of her father's face. It was devastating. Her dad, her hero, was gone! She blew him a kiss. "Goodbye, Daddy. I love you so much. Please don't forget me. I won't forget you!" Lilah hugged Lorthana as she sobbed, unable to stand looking at her father anymore. The child was overwhelmed by waves of heart-wrenching emotions.

Lorthana nodded to Armbruster. "May your spirit be at rest, Armbruster. I loved you, dear son-in-law. You were one of the strongest Warlocks I knew. You were a loving husband and father. You will be missed, dear one." She stepped away quickly, hoping to contain her sorrow. Lorthana followed Alexis out of the chamber, still holding the crying child. Zandorah remained behind.

With courage, Zandorah faced Armbruster. The flickering candles floating around the room cast a shimmering glow on his body, making him appear almost serene. The windows were now shut, and everything was quiet.

Zandorah couldn't help but think he looked just as rugged and handsome as he did when he was alive. Since his eyes were closed, she couldn't see his dark blue, sparkly eyes. The thought of never seeing them again made her sad. His thick eyebrows looked well-groomed and perfectly framed his masculine features. Zandorah felt a more profound sense of loss than she had expected. She gently placed a rose on his casket, struggling to find the right words to say before walking away.

One by one, the W3s took turns saying their final goodbye to the King. For some, it was a difficult time. For others, it was part of the ceremony and meant less. Finally, after everyone else was done, the Command Staff had their turn.

As Andreh stood before Armbruster, he felt overwhelmed with guilt. Despite their recent differences, he never wished for the King's death and still held great respect for him. He regretted that their relationship had to end this way. Andreh laid a rose on top of the pile of others and stepped back, saluting the King. With tears streaming down his face, he shouted, "My King, with honor, I will protect your family. You will be deeply missed." Andreh quickly left the room, still sobbing.

Pauto stepped forward onto the stage, and he couldn't help but feel emotional. Tears welled up in his eyes, and a lump formed in his throat, making it difficult for him to express his thoughts to the King. Despite this, he respectfully lowered his head and whispered to the King, "Your Majesty, I am grateful for your love, endless patience, and guidance. Your departure leaves a void in my heart that cannot be filled. May your spirit roam freely."

Yarlen and Edwinn chose to remain behind to ensure the King's body was guarded until later in the day, when he would be moved to the City of Miccay for the final viewing by the local residents.

Alexis, Lorthana, and Zandorah took Lilah to her room. Alexis wanted her to rest because the child was distraught.

"Mommy, what happens to Daddy now?" Lilah inquired.

"A procession is scheduled in a little while, and the Royal Carriage will carry his coffin through the City of Miccay along the river so everyone can pay their respects. Once it ends, we will lay your father to rest in the Courtyard next to my great-grandfather, Zintherdom, and your great-grandmother, Grimleah Maggica Snipperdoom."

"Do I have to be there, Mommy? I don't want to see Daddy put in the ground," Lilah complained. She had been through too much already.

"Of course not. If you do not want to be there, there is no need to be. I will be there for both of us. How does that sound, precious?" Alexis asked.

"Thank you, Mommy. I am tired." She kissed her mother on the cheek and slid down into the bed. Alexis drew the covers up to the child's chin.

"Get your rest, darling."

After putting Lilah to bed for a nap, she left the chamber, and the other two women followed. Alexis plopped on the bed in her chamber, kicking off her black high-heels. She rubbed her right foot, which ached. Lorthana sat in the chair by the fireplace, and Zandorah leaned on the window ledge to face the others.

"That was far more brutal than I anticipated," Zandorah announced.

"I agree," added Lorthana.

After removing her cloak, Alexis asked, "What is the appropriate way to feel in such a situation? I have no clue!" Her utmost concern was Lilah. As tears streamed down her face, she looked up with a sorrowful expression. Her chest felt tight, and she was in pain.

Lorthana stood and approached Alexis. "There is no proper way to feel love. Everyone is different. We each must deal with the grief in our own way. I am so sorry. I wish I could remove the heartache and pain."

Zandorah found herself at a loss for words and was unable to react appropriately, leaving her silent. She sensed that Alexis was trying to act tough, which made her emotional state even more concerning. Zandorah wasn't sure if Alexis would be able to recover anytime soon, which made her question how she would handle her relationship with Andreh, who had been absent.

Zandorah wondered if he had chosen to stay away or if Alexis had asked for a break. Finally, she decided to speak with Alexis because she didn't wish to appear heartless.

"Alexis, I plan to return home tomorrow after Armbruster's burial. If you need anything at all, please do not hesitate to ask. I am happy to stay longer if necessary and lend a hand with Lilah. Your well-being and comfort are of utmost importance to me, and I am here to support you in any way that I can. I hope you know how much you mean to me."

"Zandi, thank you so much for offering to stay. However, there is no need. Mom will remain here for a few days to help. Everything is fine. I know you have a kingdom to run. Thank you for your moral support during this difficult time."

Zandorah smiled and bent down, kissing her sister on the cheek. "I love you. See you in a bit." She quickly departed the chamber, wishing to escape before bursting into tears. The emotions were high, and she could not stand another minute of it.

Lorthana decided to take her leave as well. She knew her daughter needed rest before the event in the city. It would be the most challenging part of all ceremonies to finally lay Armbruster to rest.

Alone in the chamber, Alexis stripped down to her bra and underwear before slipping into the tall and fluffy bed. As she drew the covers up to her neck, she couldn't help but gaze at the fireplace ahead, lost in her thoughts.

The tragic event that had occurred kept running through her mind. She wondered why there was no way to save Armbruster and why no cure or magical intervention was possible. It all seemed so unbelievable to her. Eventually, the rattle on the windows from the mighty thunder lulled her to sleep, but she still sobbed lightly, her heart torn into pieces. She needed this respite. The parade would begin in less than two hours.

CHAPTER 15

Aerianna dressed and smiled lovingly at Pauto. He remained in bed, watching her. He loved her more than words could express. This afternoon would be tough on everyone, and he contemplated how she would bear it. She had been close to the King and worked on a few projects with him.

Now, she would stand beside Alexis and watch as Armbruster's remains were paraded through the streets of Miccay for all to see. Thereafter, a private funeral would be held.

"I should head to the Queen's Chamber," Aerianna announced, snagging her wand off the dresser.

"Okay, Luv. I will meet you on the Landing Deck later. You seem to be feeling better. You look amazing. Your color has returned!" Pauto asked, noticing her blush.

"I feel wonderful. I believe the morning sickness is over. At least, I hope so. Please do not worry about me. Alright, see you later." She dashed from the chamber, finally feeling like herself again. It was a relief. She had been feeling ill for over three weeks, which seemed like an excessively long time to be miserable.

The AoE and SAoW lined the streets of Miccay in preparation for the King's funeral procession. A few AoE members mounted Torrins and flew overhead, ensuring the highest security level.

The decision had been made to remove the protective shield after Alexis and Rammadar received communication from the *GRAW* that they were permanently halting all war efforts against them.

At first, the command team was reluctant to believe it was true, fearing it was a trap, but after a lengthy conversation, Yarlen convinced Rammadar and others to take down the shield. He assumed the *GRAW* members were running scared now that their original leader, Gardone, was dead.

The day was filled with sadness, but there wasn't a single cloud in sight, and the pair of moons above shone brilliantly. Alexis had enjoyed her nap and was prepared for the event. She studied her reflection in the tall mirror and couldn't help but notice the dark shadowing under her eyes. At first, she contemplated using makeup to conceal them, but then she decided it was better to let them be. She wanted others to see her pain in the hope that it would quash the rumors about her relationship with Andreh.

It was exhausting to hear about it, especially now that Armbruster was no longer around. The Royal Carriage stood ready with the Torrins harnessed to it, waiting for Armbruster's coffin's arrival. Essten was present to ensure that the Torrins remained calm, but today, they appeared restless and were pacing around unnecessarily, which was unusual and strange.

316

After knocking on the door of the Queen's Chamber and receiving no response, Aerianna attempted to open it. She found the door unlocked and entered the room, where she discovered Alexis sitting in a chair by the fireplace, holding a handkerchief.

Alexis appeared to be in a terrible condition, with puffy, red eyes and her hair disheveled.

"Alexis, shall I call Karita to help you get ready for our trip to Miccay?" Aerianna asked kindly.

"Why would we need to do that? I am ready," Alexis replied confidently, wondering why Aerianna had even suggested it.

"Not to be disrespectful, Your Majesty, but your hair looks unkempt, and the rest of you looks awful, too. I am not sure you should be seen in public like this," Aerianna suggested cautiously. She noticed Alexis squinting her eyes. Aerianna hoped she was not about to start a tirade.

Aerianna flinched as Alexis let out a scream, "Listen, I am grieving, and I don't care how I look. So, no, I plan on attending the occasion looking like this. You and everyone else can deal with it," Alexis retorted angrily.

"I am deeply sorry, Your Majesty. Please accept my sincere apologies. It was not my intention to upset you further," Aerianna said as she bowed her head, avoiding eye contact with Alexis.

"I'm sorry, Aerianna. I didn't mean to lash out at you. I'm just hurting right now and lacking patience. Please don't take it personally. I know you meant well," Alexis said, offering up an awkward smile.

The two were about to head out when Lorthana and Zandorah appeared, dressed for the occasion, looking glum. Lorthana hugged Alexis and held her hand.

"Shall we head to the Landing Deck? I've been notified that there's a carriage waiting to take us to the city. Armbruster is currently being loaded onto the Royal Carriage in the Courtyard," Lorthana announced.

Alexis nodded, rendered speechless. Her throat constricted, making it difficult to breathe. Despite this, she miraculously composed herself and settled into the carriage a few minutes later, taking shallow breaths to prevent herself from losing consciousness.

Opting to close her eyes, she braced herself for the demanding part of the day that lay ahead. The mourning of the commoners would be overwhelming, and she wasn't prepared to manage their emotions. Despite understanding their sentiments for Armbruster, Alexis hoped to move forward quickly and lay him to rest.

Alexis felt the chill in the air as the carriage sped toward the city. Looking down, she saw a large gathering of W3s near the open field by the river. Although she was accustomed to handling crowds, the sheer number of commoners caused her to feel anxious. She wondered what they would say and if she was ready to face them. She hoped Aerianna would step forward, allowing Alexis to stay in the background.

Lorthana and Zandorah were deep in conversation, seemingly unaware of Alexis's anxieties. They contemplated bringing Lilah to Iriss to give Alexis a reprieve and the opportunity to grieve in solitude. It could be challenging to care for her child amid such heartbreak.

The carriage finally landed in the City of Miccay, near the river's edge. Alexis exited first, followed by her mother and sister. Immediately, they were surrounded by AoE and other security members. Seconds later, they were escorted toward the Royal Box, stationed in the middle of the town. Alexis and her family and friends would watch the procession and allow the commoners to approach and provide caring words of comfort.

When Alexis was finally seated, she noticed the growing group. She felt her heart skip a beat when she saw him. Alexis wondered if he would show up at the event. He neared the Royal Box, lowered his head, and then offered up a gentle smile.

"Your Majesty, my deepest condolences to you, Lilah, and the rest of the family." Andreh seemed in a hurry to leave before Alexis could utter a word. He turned around and headed across the street, standing near the BrewHaus, watching Alexis. Andreh maintained a professional but detached demeanor, which was quite strange.

Lorthana was visibly displeased, rolling her eyes. She believed it would have been wiser for him to avoid Armbruster's public viewing today. She hoped that his appearance would not spark any new rumors.

The night before, Zandorah had a lengthy conversation with her mother, during which she learned that Alexis was romantically involved with Andreh Darkhill. With Armbruster no longer in the picture, Zandorah found it puzzling that Andreh did not keep his distance for a while, giving the family some time to mourn in peace without any added drama.

As Viollah Grackenbone held the microphone, the trumpets suddenly blared, announcing her performance. Her enchanting voice filled the air as she began singing the famous song, *"The Crown's Last Fall,"* dedicated to the deceased ruler. The crowd hushed as they listened to her heartfelt rendition, with some even shedding tears.

Alexis, too, was moved by the performance and the solemn procession of the Royal Carriage carrying their beloved King, Armbruster, through the City of Miccay. As the commoners tossed Victor Coins and roses at the carriage, some shouted, "Forever in our hearts," while others declared, "May his spirit rest in peace," a testament to the ruler's legacy and the love he had earned from his people.

After the Royal Carriage passed, the AoE and SAoW members marched behind, slamming down Mesmer Ceptres to show respect for the loss of their Commander and King.

Viollah stepped off the stage and joined Alexis, who hugged and thanked her for the touching tribute to her husband. The two Witches briefly conversed while the parade of soldiers came to a stop. Eventually, the crowds dispersed, signaling the end of the somber occasion.

The Royal Carriage was airborne, heading toward the Courtyard of the Palace. Alexis and the family were seated in another carriage, following behind. Within minutes, they touched down on the lawn outside the

Palace. The gates were wide open, ready to receive the King.

As the Royal Carriage moved toward the garden on the right side of the Courtyard, Alexis and Lorthana walked behind it, heads lowered, bravely holding hands. Yarlen, Edwinn, Pauto, Rammadar, and Andreh were waiting for the group. Chairs were arranged in two rows with a metal stand in the center. The glass casket was to be placed on it, and the final words would be spoken before Armbruster was laid to rest in the ground.

It was early evening, and it was getting darker. It was also cold, and it began to drizzle with rain. Alexis courageously stood in front of Armbruster's casket while the rest of the group sat in the upholstered black seats, observing the Queen.

Alexis nodded to Yarlen, who waved his wand, temporarily removing the top of the glass enclosure and allowing Alexis to touch her husband.

Slowly, she pulled the Death Sheet up and over the top of his body. She stopped before it reached his neck. Alexis bent down and kissed Armbruster on his cold cheek. A single tear dropped onto his face, rolling down and landing on the dark-purple pillow beneath his head.

The Death Sheet was finally covering his head, and she bravely declared, "Rest in peace, my love. Until we meet again."

Armbruster's body was now fully draped, and Yarlen brought down the glass top over his remains, causing a resounding thump, indicating that the coffin was now sealed. The whole procedure was completed in under five minutes.

Edwinn and Yarlen then approached the casket and lifted their wands. With a loud cry, they uttered in unison, *"May you rest in peace and not be forgotten, buried deep into the earth until we reunite."*

Armbruster slowly descended into the open hole in the ground. Once his coffin was no longer visible, dirt fell from the sky, landing on his casket, covering up the King and allowing him his final rest. It was done.

Yarlen and Edwinn walked away, having completed their part of the ceremony. Andreh stood and aided Alexis, who could not walk on her own. Aerianna, Lorthana, and Zandorah followed them into the Palace.

The burial of the King of Alstromia felt like an unending nightmare and was difficult to accept. Even though his legacy would endure, his physical presence had now been laid to rest in the Palace grounds.

Alexis and Andreh entered her chamber. Meanwhile, Lorthana joined Zandorah in her room, intending to hold a conversation before she departed for Iriss.

"Should I return to Iriss later this week? I'm planning to spend some time with Magorr on Earth and will bring Lilah if Alexis agrees," Lorthana announced.

Zandorah quickly responded. "Yes, in the meantime, I will set up a room near mine in the Castle for Lilah. Why don't you bring her in a few days? You can also ask Magorr if he wishes to accompany you. I would love the opportunity to get to know him better."

The decision was made. Lorthana hugged Zandorah and wished her safe travels back to Iriss, promising to be there soon. She left the chamber and headed to see Alexis to inform her of the idea of taking Lilah to Iriss for a few weeks. It seemed like the best plan, given the circumstances.

Andreh held Alexis and kissed her gently on the forehead. He could feel her shaking. As he was about to suggest changing into more comfortable clothing and heading to bed, Lorthana entered the room with a snarky look on her face.

"Well, I am not surprised to see you, Andreh. However, I need time alone with my daughter. Please leave," she insisted, refusing to take no for an answer. Alexis squeezed his hand and made it clear she agreed with Lorthana.

Andreh boldly kissed Alexis on her lips, telling her he loved her, before leaving the chamber. He ran to his room, hoping to rest and forget the horrific, challenging day.

"Sweetheart, Zandi and I would like to take Lilah to Iriss for a few weeks. It would give you some time to grieve and get your thoughts in order. I know there is much to think about now that Armbruster is gone."

Though she felt it was a good idea, she hated thinking her child would be away from her. "That is fine, Mother. I appreciate it. When will you take Lilah?"

"I am departing for Earth in a little while. Once I meet with Magorr, we will discuss it further. We should take her sooner rather than later," Lorthana added.

"Agreed. Let me have some time to chat with Lilah and explain the situation. I want to ensure she is comfortable with leaving. I do not want to make her feel unwanted or scared. She is fragile and grieving, too."

Lorthana wholeheartedly agreed. It was not an easy time for the Princess. She had never dealt with such a tragic loss. Nonetheless, her mother needed time to heal on her own.

"I am grateful to you and Zandi. Your support means a great deal to me. Thank you, Mother! Now, if you don't mind, I want to shower and retire for the night. I am emotionally and physically drained. I simply cannot function much longer." Alexis kissed her mother and walked to the bathroom, ready to let the shower's hot water soothe her aching body.

CHAPTER 16

The dreams that haunted her were terrifying. She thrashed in bed, screaming his name. In her nightmare, he stood in a pitch-black pool, his rotting arm extended toward her, pleading for her to rescue him. His eyes, once a dark blue, now appeared black, dull, and enormous.

327

He was dressed in a long, ripped cloak that flapped violently with every gust of wind, accompanied by the deafening sound of thunder in the background.

Panicking, she desperately reached out to grab his zombie-like, bony hand, but it slipped through hers, leaving her feeling utterly confused and terrified.

He looked evil, nothing like before. The flesh was falling off his body, and his bones stuck out. Alexis was forced to look away, unable to look at his disintegrating corpse.

Suddenly, she heard a rapidly bubbling noise, which caused her to look in his direction. She saw the black goo envelope his remains, much like a giant monster sucking him down into the abyss. However, before his head disappeared into the darkness, he screamed, "*It was MURDER!*" Then, there was silence.

Alexis sat up in bed, drenched in sweat. Her hair was damp, clinging to her cheek. She brushed it aside while she shook with fright. She shivered in the cold room, seeing her breath. *'How did it get so cold?'* Panicking, she waved her hand, reigniting the flames in the stone fireplace. Seconds later, it roared, warming the chilly room.

Apprehensively, she slid back down into the sheets and pulled the comforter up to her nose. She was too scared to try to sleep. Had it been a nightmare, or was Armbruster truly communicating with her in some magical way? How could this be happening? Was she losing her mind?

One of the Security Commoners pounded on her bedroom door. "Your Majesty, are you okay?" he yelled, hearing the screams.

"I am fine, thank you," she responded, unwilling to elaborate on the event that had caused her to cry out in fear.

The room was quiet, except for the noise from the fire crackling. She stared out, noticing it was calm. How had she heard thunder? Was it in her nightmare? She believed it was real. Then, the visions of his dead body came to mind, and she flinched, almost throwing up. She forced herself to close her eyes. As she did, she heard the words, "*It was MURDER,*" again. This time, they were spoken more forcefully, implying urgency.

Unable to remain in the room, Alexis quickly jumped out of bed and picked up her long robe. She threw it over her gown, fastened it with the belt, fled the chamber, and ran as quickly as she could toward Andreh's room. She pounded on his door numerous times. As she was about to try to open the door, he appeared, staring at her, perplexed.

"Are you okay? It is the middle of the night, Alexis." She looked wide-eyed and frantic.

Alexis quickly pushed him aside and entered his chamber. He closed the door, following her to his small bed. She sat on the edge, rubbing her hands nervously, wondering how to share the detailed and awful nightmare with him. She worried he would believe she was insane.

"What is it? What has happened? Goodness, you are a wreck," Andreh noticed Alexis looked crazed.

"I had a vivid nightmare about Armbruster. It seemed so real. He was shriveled skin and bones, telling me he was murdered! It was horrible and traumatic. I heard the thunder and felt the icy cold wind on my skin, bringing chills to my body. I watched Armbruster become enveloped by a black, gooey substance while he screamed! Andreh, do you think it could have been Armbruster communicating from the other side?"

"Hold on, Alexis. Armbruster is gone. We buried him. You were there! It was just a nightmare. You are upset and mourning. I am sure your reaction is normal. Maybe you should try to sleep. Tomorrow, things will be better," Andreh tried to rationalize, though suddenly he felt uncomfortable.

"I don't know, Andreh. It felt surreal!" Alexis insisted, staring at him. She forced herself to look away, feeling embarrassed.

"Come to bed. I will hold you and watch over you. Nothing will happen, I promise," Andreh reassured her.

Reluctantly, she climbed into bed, allowing Andreh to comfort her. Before too long, she fell asleep, feeling secure in his arms.

On the other side of the Palace, Rammadar entered his room. It had been a long day. He wondered how the Queen fared after the burial. Rammadar had spoken with Yarlen, who seemed eager to assist him in running the Security Command Team. Since Armbruster was gone, and Rammadar felt he needed more experienced guidance, he gladly accepted Yarlen's offer to temporarily step out of retirement to aid the Palace.

Rammadar ensured that Pauto's leadership position would be maintained, recognizing the value of his knowledge. Additionally, he realized that Andreh deserved more responsibility as he had repeatedly proven himself and showcased his abilities as a skilled Wizzard.

Finally, as the morning approached, Rammadar chose to sleep. He was exhausted and knew implementing a new Palace security system would be hectic and energy-zapping.

On Earth, Thornton Glowstone shared the news with the rest of the *GRAW* that he planned to disband the group. After the loss of Gardone and the realization that the Queen was stronger than ever, he refused to continue on a path that was ineffective. Though many disagreed with his plan, no one fought him.

Thornton reluctantly locked the hut in the woods one final time. He did not plan to return. As far as Thornton was concerned, their mission was over. He would return to his girlfriend on Draekidell and hopefully start a new life without strife.

Regardless of all the drama and sorrow Alstromia experienced in the last 48 hours, there was a glimmer of hope for better times. Aerianna knew this more than most. She rubbed her growing belly, eager to meet her child. Pauto entered the room and noticed Aerianna facing the window. She quickly turned around when she heard him.

"You are back! I missed you," she gushed, rushing toward him. She kissed him and placed his hand on her belly. "Our baby missed you as well!"

"So, I was thinking," he began. "We should accept Alexis's offer to move into Armbruster's room. It is much bigger, and the reading area would be great for a nursery. I know it may seem cold and heartless to some extent, but life goes on. We have to think about the baby and our future."

"I suppose you are right. Maybe we can hold off a few weeks. I do not want to seem too eager to others. It might send the wrong message," Aerianna reasoned.

"Agreed! I would like to offer your room to Rammadar. He will need more space now that he will be taking on more responsibility. Andreh could move into my room. It is much bigger than his tiny chamber. He deserves it. I believe Andreh has proven himself to the kingdom," Pauto rationalized.

With Armbruster's death, the Palace roster would change, and the improvements would allow the kingdom to run more effectively. Aerianna concurred. She felt Pauto's suggestions were valid and planned to endorse them. She also wanted to speak with Alexis to get final approval before moving forward and offering the rooms to others.

Following a lengthy conversation, Aerianna and Pauto came to a mutual decision to call it a night. They knew that the next day would be packed with activities, starting with the preparations for their wedding. Since they were expecting a baby, they could no longer delay the ceremony. Thus, it was imperative for them to begin the planning.

On Earth, the weather was nasty. It rained, but snow was forecast. It was chilly and gloomy. Nonetheless, Magorr's mood would not be swayed. He grinned when he opened the door for Lorthana. She was dressed in a black cloak. She planned to seduce him and hoped to move their relationship forward. Lorthana licked her lips with a lustful glare.

Quickly, she untied the cloak and stepped forward. The garment dropped to the floor, leaving her standing in the middle of the foyer, naked. She swayed her hips, drawing attention to her slim waist and voluptuous body. His eyes flashed with desire for her as he ogled her firm breasts. Magorr picked her up, cradling her in his arms as he rushed up the stairs with her, ready to make passionate love to his soulmate.

W3s discussed the King's final farewell throughout the land. Some had attended the event, while others chose to stay back. However, most were curious about what would become of Alstromia and the kingdom. Alexis had always been the figurehead, but everyone knew Armbruster was the driving force behind her. His passing left many feeling insecure about Alexis's ability to run the planet independently.

Even on Alstromia, many discussed Alexis stepping down and allowing a new election. One name kept coming up repeatedly in conversations, and it was Yarlen Granderview Raventon II.

Another name mentioned on numerous occasions was Pauto Vexxorth. He was a superior Warrior and an excellent Wizzard. He was able to run the security team without Armbruster on many occasions and handled himself admirably. He was also engaged to Aerianna, which was a plus. They would undoubtedly make a commanding pair.

Many W3s figured this was the perfect time for new blood. A new lineage of royalty in the Palace would be an excellent change. Something good could come out of the tragedy. Unfortunately, Alexis still had many supporters who vehemently opposed those seeking to undermine the Queen's current rule. It became apparent there would be more disagreements on the horizon. Armbruster's death had stirred the proverbial pot, causing a rift in the Clans.

As morning arrived, Alexis stretched, almost falling out of the small bed. She shook Andreh, waking him. "Listen, this bed is way too small for the both of us. From now on, we will sleep in my chamber. My neck is literally killing me from sleeping twisted like a pretzel."

"Sleeping in your bed? Does that mean I am moving in with you? Isn't it a bit sudden?" Andreh asked, concerned. The last thing Alexis needed was to be scrutinized more.

"Yes, why not. Everyone already knows about us. Why does it matter at this point? We have nothing to hide. We love each other. I stood by Armbruster until his death. I did nothing wrong. Our love is important to me. I am unwilling to hide it. If it costs me the monarchy, so be it. My existence will go on," Alexis proudly announced. It had taken her a long time to realize how vital Andreh was in her life. No one would take him away from her.

"Okay, Luv. If you say so. I will support whatever decision you make and remain faithfully by your side, always." Andreh glanced at her lovingly, taking in her beauty. His adoration for her grew stronger with each passing day.

Without warning, Alexis sprang out of bed and stood in front of Andreh. She then knelt down, gazing up at him, and took his hands in hers. "Andreh Thommaz Darkhill, will you marry me?" she boldly asked.

"What? Alexis, no! It is too soon. I love you, but let's allow things to calm down. We should not do anything to spotlight our relationship." Andreh pleaded, feeling awkward as he looked down at her. Instantly, Alexis' green eyes welled up with tears.

"Marry me! Please don't make me beg. I can wait, but not forever. I want to marry you. I want us to have a family and grow old together," she insisted, with a pleading look on her face while tears dripped off her cheek, landing on her chest.

Andreh joined Alexis on the floor. He squeezed her hand. "Okay, darling. We will be married and hold a Ceremonial Exchange. I will be your husband and love you forever!" The two kissed, sealing their future union. Both were elated and ready to move their love story forth.

After a while, Alexis made her way to her chamber to change before her meeting with Rammadar and Yarlen. She was thrilled to hear that Yarlen had returned to the Command Team, as he had more experience than most. Despite their past differences, they were now good friends and supportive of each other. She planned to inform him that he would also be involved in her upcoming Ceremonial Exchange with Andreh, and she hoped that he would agree to officiate their wedding.

Andreh was lying on his bed, contemplating when he and Alexis could get married. He knew that, according to the

Ancient Books, a six-month period of mourning needed to be observed. He hoped that Alexis would respect this time and not challenge it. If she chose not to follow the mourning period for royalty, it could potentially draw unwanted attention to Armbruster's mysterious death.

Unfortunately, some W3s had already started to theorize that either the Queen or Andreh had some involvement in Armbruster's demise.

Although it was utterly absurd, these rumors needed to be put to rest to prevent them from spreading recklessly throughout the Clans, as it would harm the realm of Alstromia moving forward. Andreh planned to discuss everything with Alexis later in the evening.

After a long day of meetings, Alexis found herself standing near the window in her chamber, feeling utterly exhausted. Just then, Aerianna walked in with a broad smile on her face.

"Oh my, you look absolutely radiant, my dear friend! Pregnancy seems to suit you. What brings you here?" she inquired.

"Alexis, Pauto, and I have decided to accept your generous offer to move into Armbruster's room in a few weeks. However, we believe it would be best to wait for two to three weeks before making the change.

Additionally, we would like to offer our current rooms to other members of the staff. Rest assured, Andreh will receive a new room as well," explained Aerianna.

Alexis raised her hand, stopping the conversation. "There is no need to worry about Andreh. He will be moving into my chamber. We have decided to marry in the near future after the shock of the King's death dissipates."

"I see," Aerianna responded. She felt it was a horrible idea for the Queen to remarry so soon. However, she didn't plan to say so.

"It seems like you disagree, judging by the disapproving look on your face. However, I believe that I deserve happiness just as much as anyone else. I want to move forward with my life, and I am not getting any younger. Having another child in the future is something I desire, and I would prefer it to happen sooner rather than later," expressed Alexis with irritation. She was tired of constantly feeling the need to justify her life and decisions to others.

"Your Majesty, whatever you decide is entirely up to you. You already know that I will support your plans, no matter what they are. On the topic of marriage, I actually need your assistance. Pauto and I plan to hold a Ceremonial Exchange in the next few weeks. I understand that it may seem rushed, but given the circumstances, I would like to get married as soon as possible."

"It sounds like a good idea, Aerianna. Would you like to hold your ceremony during the WinterFrost Festival? It's only a few weeks away, but I can handle all the arrangements. The Manor would be a beautiful venue for the celebration, or we can hold it here in the Palace's Ballroom. Just let me know what you prefer, and I will make it happen." Alexis was eager to plan their wedding and create a memorable event for everyone on Alstromia.

"Thank you so much, Alexis. If you're up for it, I would be happy to let you take care of everything. I greatly appreciate your help and support. You're an amazing friend!" Aerianna hugged Alexis tightly and then turned to leave.

"You have nothing to worry about. I promise! Your Ceremonial Exchange will be epic," Alexis teased.

Alone again in her room, Alexis pondered her future wedding to Andreh. She had hoped to marry him during the WinterFrost Festival. Now, she was planning Aerianna and Pauto's union instead. It made her happy for them, but she felt a pang of jealousy.

Andreh appeared without notice. He held a bouquet of pink and white Peruvian lilies, her favorite. "I heard about Aerianna and Pauto's wedding plans. It is very kind of you to plan it for them. Does it bother you that we will need to wait to marry?"

"No, it doesn't. I thought about making it a double wedding, but I refuse to take the spotlight off them. They deserve this special celebration. It has taken them a long time to realize how much they love each other," Alexis confided. She knew it was the right thing to do, and she was prepared to make it spectacular for her friends.

Andreh's heart was filled with love for Alexis as he spoke with excitement, "I cannot wait for the day when we are united, and our family grows, no matter how long it takes. I hope to make you happier than ever before and be a friend and guide to Lilah as she grows up. However, I do not intend to replace her father, Armbruster."

"Andreh, you are a loving and affectionate partner. I cannot believe how fortunate I am to have found you. How about we have dinner and unwind? We have a lot to catch up on, and I need to start preparing for my friend's wedding."

The rest of the night was uneventful on Alstromia. However, Zandorah received disturbing news about her planet's security. She had hoped that since the *GRAW* had discontinued waging war on Alstromia and officially disbanded, all would finally return to normal. Unfortunately, this was not the case.

"How can this be?" screamed Zandorah.

"My Esteemed Ruler, we have intelligence that he has started a new group. He plans to attack us. We are not as powerful as Alstromia. The premise is he believes our planet has many resources, and his group would love to overtake us and make this their new base of operation!" replied Carhlston Hillstrom. He was the newly appointed head of security for Iriss. It bothered him that he faced such an overwhelming crisis at the beginning of his new job. He felt apprehensive that things could go wrong and that he could be blamed or fired.

"That is quite alarming if it is true. How do we know this is not an unwarranted rumor? Have you been able to verify the threat?" Zandorah continued to grill him.

"Yes. It has been verified." Carhlston realized Zandorah was not sufficiently equipped to stand up to a new threat. She was still rebuilding her army and personnel after Rammadar's unexpected and swift departure from her staff. In the past, he had handled the most urgent matters pertaining to planetary security. The job had been passed on to Carhlston, and he disliked the pressure.

"Okay. I will reach out to my sister to see if she can help us prepare for a potential attack on our planet. Maybe she could send half her AoE to train with our warriors? I will let you know what I find out. Lastly, who is planning to attack us?"

Zandorah figured Alexis would be willing to help out in some way. However, she was unsure if that aid would include members of her elite group of warriors. Maybe she could spare a few Dark Guardians. Within the ranks of the Alstromian AoE resided an elite force known as the *Dark Guardian Wizzards*, who were feared and revered as the most powerful beings in all the land. Their iniquitous powers were sought after as they were the ultimate weapon in AoE's arsenal. These Wizzards could be dispatched on covert missions deep into enemy territory to eliminate even the most formidable foes.

"The *Dark Earth Legion (DEL)* is a newly formed army headed by *Ventorroh Grimstock*. He has come from Draekidell to wreak havoc. I am unsure how many are on his force. Currently, he has made his home base on Earth in the northern region. Ventorroh is a ThreeBlud. I believe he will enlist Blud-Trackers as well as Warlocks and Witches," elaborated Carhlston, standing at attention before her.

"That is bad news. We have never faced a Blud-Tracker or ThreeBlud army before. This is craziness!" Zandorah screeched nervously.

Carhlton nodded. "Indeed. We need to contact a trusted Blud-Tracker for advice on any potential ways to engage this new type of enemy. Do you know of anyone? I will reach out to Clan members on Earth for guidance."

"I actually do know someone, Magorr Bloodrup. He happens to be a friend of my mother," Zandorah suggested. "I will have a word with Mom to see if we can arrange a meeting with Magorr. It is quite disheartening to see all this commotion. Why can't things be peaceful for once?"

"Because there is always someone unethical and tyrannical willing to steal and destroy," explained Carhlston, shrugging.

"True. Let's schedule our next meeting for tomorrow afternoon. By then, I will have had the opportunity to contact my mother."

"Yes, Zandorah. It will be done." Carhlston bowed and exited the chamber.

CHAPTER 17

With most of the wedding plans already set, Alexis was thrilled that it took less than two days to complete. There were a few minor items that still needed to be addressed, but it did not worry her. She eagerly looked forward to sharing the good news with Aerianna later that afternoon. Yarlen had agreed to officiate the wedding, after which two days of festivities were slated to take place on Alstromia, including Aerianna's official name change ceremony.

345

Aerianna dressed and headed to the Queen's chamber since she had been summoned for an urgent meeting. She wondered what the Queen planned to discuss with her.

Alexis was lounging in her room when Aerianna arrived. The table beside her overflowed with samples of flowers, Bloomitz, accessories, and more. Along the wall hung three dresses.

Aerianna curtsied and entered the Queen's room. Instantly, she noticed the dresses and items. "Ah, you have summoned me to discuss the wedding plans, right?" she surmised.

"Yes, that is correct. I asked two sewists for help. These are the most stunning of all the dresses. I hope you like them. I only picked one white dress, as is tradition on Earth. I assumed you wanted to stay within our traditions and wear a colored gown."

Aerianna admired each gown. The materials were exquisite, and she knew they were expensive. "My Queen, I am not sure I can afford such lavish attire."

"Pick one, Aerianna. It will be my wedding gift to you. If you do not like any of these, I will request more be brought to the Palace."

"Oh, no. Each one is breathtakingly gorgeous. I prefer the pink one. It is exactly the way I envisioned my gown," Aerianna beamed, standing before the mirror, admiring herself.

"That is the one I picked! Carmin helped me choose the others. Great. You will wear the pink. It has a gorgeous golden cape that is lacy and sparkly. I will have it delivered by tomorrow so you can see it," Alexis explained.

"How can I ever thank you, Alexis? It is like a dream come true," she gushed. She admired the sparkly pink gown. The tiny crystals were scattered throughout the bodice. It was also a modest gown and showed minimal cleavage. The long train was adorned with a delicate, feminine rose-shaped lace pattern.

"There is no reason to thank me. Now, let us sit down and pick out the rest of the wedding items. The venue is set. This is the final step in completing the wedding plans. I wasn't sure if you wanted local Bloomitz or flowers from Earth?"

"I would like to combine the hot pink Bloomitz with white and golden-yellow roses from Earth. What do you think?" Aerianna asked, looking for guidance. She was not a professional planner and hoped Alexis would guide her in the right direction.

"Sounds stunning! What a great idea, Aerianna. I love the idea of combining the two."

"What will you wear? I am hopeful you will agree and become my Wedding Ambassador. I prefer not to use the earthly term, Maid of Honor."

"I understand. I am honored to accept the position of Wedding Ambassador and will do it justice."

Aerianna placed the dress on the bed. She hugged Alexis, thanking her for the gorgeous gown. The two friends spend the next few hours wrapping up the final details of the Ceremonial Exchange event.

Once dinner time arrived, both were elated to sit around the large table in the dining hall overlooking the serene Valley of Grandu with Pauto and Andreh.

Pauto began the conversation, "I hear that our wedding has been planned." It felt strange for him to discuss it in front of Andreh and Alexis, since he always thought they would be the first ones to get married, not him and Aerianna.

"Yes. It will be spectacular. Rest assured, Pauto," Alexis declared confidently.

"I have no doubt, My Queen. Aerianna and I are grateful for all you have done for us. We will never forget it," Pauto informed her.

Andreh observed Alexis and witnessed her right eye twitch. Instantly, he realized she was jealous, and he felt overwhelming guilt. He wished he could change things and marry her right away. The night before, he had brought up the fact that they needed to wait six months, according to the *Ancient Books*, and Alexis lost her temper, yelling at him and stating she would do what she wanted.

It took him hours to calm her down and reiterate why it was necessary to obey the rules for royals to remarry. Reluctantly, she agreed, but he knew her heart was not inclined to be pleased about it.

The night came to an end, and Alexis was ready to return to her room and forget about the wedding for a while. She was tired of the subject. Andreh accompanied her as they strolled down the corridor, heading toward her chamber. Alexis remained silent, and he chose to walk without saying a word. He knew anything he would say would most likely upset her further.

"Andreh, do you mind if I stay alone tonight?" Alexis asked, arriving at her chamber door.

"Umm, okay. Did I do something, darling?" His feelings were hurt, and he wondered why she did not want him to sleep in her chamber, as they had previously agreed.

"I have a lot to think about and need a night by myself. I am not upset with you at all. Please, do not think that." Alexis reached for him and drew him close. She flung her arms around his neck. "I love you. I am furious that we cannot get married. I need to contemplate all the options, that is all. Please do not be angry." She let him go and opened the door. Planting a kiss on his cheek, she observed his expression.

"I understand, Alexis. I love you, too. I will see you tomorrow," he managed to say as he watched Alexis enter her room. She closed the door. He was troubled because he assumed she would lean on him during difficult times. Instead, she chose to pull away.

Disheartened, he meandered down the corridor, wondering if she could let things go and accept the situation for what it was. Their hands were tied. No matter what they desired, rules were rules, and they had to be obeyed. Going against the standard could potentially cause more problems. With everything that had happened already this year, there was no need to stir up more trouble, or at least that is what Andreh believed.

Once inside his chamber, he jumped onto the bed and stared at the blank wall ahead. He wondered if Alexis would accept the situation. After all, six months to wait to get married was nothing. Plus, realistically, it would take time to plan a large wedding.

The Queen's remarriage would be an epic event. It would not be scheduled on a whim. Security protocol alone was a nightmare.

Andreh knew this for a fact. He sighed as he removed his clothes and crawled into bed, exhausted. He drew the blanket up to his chest and wished he were not alone, missing Alexis beside him. Erotic thoughts breezed through his mind, and he fantasized about making love to her as he exhaled deeply, squirming in bed.

In her chamber, Alexis tossed and turned, feeling restless. Her mind was too active, and she wanted to scream. Suddenly, she heard the message from Zandorah, summoning her urgently. Alexis jumped out of bed and dressed, ready to head to Iriss. She wondered what could be so critical that Zandorah sent a *"Draghoonfire Dispatch,"* meaning it was the highest level of urgency. Alexis considered, *'What else has happened?'* She hoped Zandorah was okay and that Iriss was safe.

Alexis closed her eyes and slammed her commanding Ceptre to the ground, transporting herself to Iriss. She arrived outside the Castle of Zandor, and the commoners moved aside, allowing her passage when they recognized her. She briskly strode down the hallway, eager to make it to her sister's room.

She knocked and entered without waiting for a response. What she saw shocked her.

Zandorah sat in a chair near the window, crying, while Lorthana held her hand. Her greatest fears seemed to have come true.

"Goodness, what is wrong? You have never sent a *Draghoonfire Dispatch* before!" Alexis squinted, examining the Witches and noticing their listlessness. "Mom, you are here?" she asked, worried.

"Alexis, sit down, please," Lorthana requested, pointing to the bed.

Alexis placed her Ceptre against the wall and took a seat, bracing herself for what she was about to hear.

"Okay. Tell me the horrible news."

"Yes, Alexis, it is tragic," agreed Zandorah, blowing her nose and wiping it. She looked up, embarrassed. "Alexis, I am afraid someone is trying to initiate war with us. I do not have the proper resources to retaliate and do not wish to surrender our planet or my reign. What can you do to help?" she quickly asked her sister.

"Tell me everything you know, Zandi. I will do my best to help," Alexis reassured her. Lorthana smiled, happy the sisters would work together.

"I summoned Mother, and she suggested I get you involved. She was on Earth with Magorr. I feel awful for having to interrupt their time together, but this is an urgent matter. Supposedly, there is a Warlock,

Ventorroh Grimstock, who has come from Draekidell to try and steal our resources and overtake the planet. Also, he is a ThreeBlud with a lot of backing. I am worried. Can we secure the planet before he invades it? I do not know much about the sinister Warlock."

"Yes, I will enlist Yarlen and Cazzandra to help. They will lock down Iriss immediately. I have never heard of Ventorroh. I find out all I can." Alexis closed her eyes and chanted. "Okay, Yarlen will be here shortly. Hopefully, Cazzandra will be with him. Let's wait and see. So, what is your army's strategy to protect the planet? What have you implemented?"

At the start of her briefing, Zandorah discussed the protocols in place for Iriss and informed Alexis of the recent change in the Head of Security position. She reminded her that Rammadar had left the job and joined her team, which forced her to hire Carhlston Hillstrom to replace him. Although Hillstrom was capable, Zandorah expressed concerns about his lack of experience in handling urgent matters and feared that he might not be as effective as required.

"First off, I am sorry. I know you miss Rammadar. He and Armbruster discussed his employment a while ago. Armbruster offered him the position without consulting me. I had nothing to do with it. I promise. Yes, I understand it left you in a lurch. I will do what I can to aid you. Please do not fret."

Alexis neared her sister and knelt before her. "I am here for you, Zandi!"

Lorthana started sobbing. It was the moment she had waited for a long time. The sisters were finally working together and getting along. It was a true miracle!

Yarlen appeared, looking crazed. His hair was tangled, and frizzy, and his eyes were bloodshot. "My Queen, I received your urgent request. What has happened? Cazzandra will be here shortly. I notified her that she must join us."

"Yarlen, we are in desperate need of your magical abilities. Zandorah and Iriss are in trouble. Let me explain," Alexis recounted the events that led up to the moment. The old Wizzard shook his head. He fiddled with his beard, tapping his foot.

"Hmm, that is not good news. Yes, I heard of Ventorroh Grimstock. I know his parents. He was a student at *AMLA* years ago. I find it strange that he would turn against Iriss. Very worrisome indeed!"

Cazzandra appeared wearing her green gown and cloak. She held her wand in one hand and a large black velvet bag in the other. "I bought many potions and supplies," she gleefully announced.

"Great, Cazzandra," Alexis shouted. "You are amazing. Please work with Yarlen to find a way to secure the planet. Zandorah, please ask Carhlston to join us in the briefing room. We will discuss the military backup. After that, I will return to Alstromia and speak with Rammadar, asking for his guidance. He will know what we can provide."

The plan was set. Alexis hoped they could ensure Iriss's safety. After all, it was just a little while ago that she was faced with a similar problem with Alstromia. She was getting tired of the relentless attacks on their planets. It had to come to an end. Alexis planned to contact the Council of Peace & War and inform them of this matter.

An hour later, Alexis hugged Zandorah goodbye. She promised to send an update about providing her with military help. In the meantime, Alexis wanted to hurry back to the Palace to speak with Rammadar and Pauto. Hopefully, they would have ideas on how to proceed to aid Iriss and Zandorah.

Lorthana tried to comfort Zandorah. She sat in the chair, sobbing, but was grateful Alexis agreed to help. However, she was still frantically worried about the implications of future attacks on her planet. Lorthana realized there wasn't much she could say. So, she chose to excuse herself and return to her room. The entire day was way too exhausting.

Zandorah strutted toward the window, feeling claustrophobic. She quickly opened the side window and stared at the expansive Courtyard below, noticing the military personnel lined up, holding Ceptres. She wondered if Carhlston held a briefing. Hopefully, he was preparing their warriors.

Zandorah chose to rest, realizing she had to wait to see what Alexis could do to help. Her head pounded, and she worried about the uncertain future that lay ahead.

Upon returning to the Palace, Alexis felt energized and ready to speak with Rammadar, informing him of the dire situation regarding Iriss. She needed his support and hoped he would be willing to aid her sister. Since, at one point, he worked on Iriss and for Zandorah, Alexis felt confident he would do all he could to render aid.

Aerianna felt sick, experiencing a bout of heartburn, and her back ached. She wondered if it was normal to have these problems early in a pregnancy. This was her first, and she had no clue about what was expected and what wasn't. Once she rested on the bed, she rubbed her belly, wishing the miserable feeling would subside.

She was about to close her eyes when she tasted bile making its way up her throat.

Panicked, she jumped off the bed and ran to the bathroom, throwing up her lunch. She rested her head on the wall beside the toilet, wondering if she should shower.

Unexpectedly, Pauto entered her chamber, calling her name. "Aerianna, where are you, love? Are you here?"

Aerianna sat up and wiped her mouth with the hand towel nearby. "Pauto, I am in the bathroom. I will be right out!" she shouted as she stood, looking at herself in the mirror. Aerianna noticed that she looked pale. She hoped nothing was seriously wrong.

"There you are, beautiful," Pauto declared as she emerged from the bathroom, holding a towel. "Umm, are you okay? You look awful. What can I do?" Instantly, he panicked, noticing her pallid complexion. She looked sickly.

"I have been feeling ill most of today. I just vomited. I plan to stay in my chamber for the remainder of the day. I don't think I can work." She placed the towel on the nightstand, sitting on the edge of the bed. Pauto approached and knelt before her with a look of concern on his face.

"Tell me how I can help. Should I stay with you for the rest of the day?"

"I will be okay. I just need some rest. I assume it is normal to be so sick during the first few months of pregnancy. Gosh, I hope it passes. It is unpleasant. I keep smelling things that are not there. Then, I throw up! Goodness!" Aeiranna added, embarrassed.

Pauto nodded, understanding her feelings. He also felt horrible for her. "I could stay and keep you company. Or, I could bring you some soup. Maybe that might help?" he offered.

"No. I will probably continue to be sick. I really do not want you here witnessing it. It is disgusting." She smiled at him, hoping he was not hurt. Having him in the room was nice, but she refused to puke in front of him.

"Okay, darling. I will check on you later. I have a few things that require my attention in the Command Chamber. Please, summon me if you need anything, promise! I love you." He kissed her, observed her for a moment, and departed the room.

Aerianna dropped onto the bed, closing her eyes as the world spun, making her feel woozy all over again. Unable to bear the feeling, she quickly sat up. "So, I will not be sleeping, I see," she complained, realizing the nausea persisted. Accepting her circumstances, she opted to read by the fireplace. She was cold and miserable.

Hopefully, the warmth of the fire would help her feel better. She pulled the fluffy blanket up, covering most of her body, and placed her feet on the ottoman. Surprisingly, she fell asleep minutes later, blissfully warm in her room.

Pauto entered the Command Chamber and immediately noticed Alexis standing near the map on the wall, conversing with Andreh. He frowned, wondering what they were discussing.

"Great, you are here," Alexis announced as Pauto advanced.

"Yes, I just visited Aerianna. She is extremely sick and unable to work. She will be staying in her chamber," Pauto explained.

"OH, NO! Will she be okay? Should I send Edwinn Shivvers her way? She probably needs a Healing Warlock," Alexis offered.

"No. Let's allow Aerianna to rest. She prefers to be left alone. I plan to check on her later. If she is still not well later this evening, we can ask Edwinn to visit her chamber for a medical check-up."

"Sounds good, Pauto. So, now...we have to discuss a critical matter concerning my sister and her planet. Please sit. I have already shared this information with Andreh and Rammadar."

"Hmm, where are Yarlen and Rammadar?" Pauto inquired.

"Rammadar will be here shortly. Yarlen is with Cazzandra on Iriss. I promise to fill you in on everything," Alexis declared.

Rammadar appeared seconds later with three other Wizzards. He looked official, wearing his battle uniform, bowing before the Queen, and quickly taking a seat beside Andreh.

"Now that everyone is here, let me explain the dire situation with Iriss," Alexis began. Twenty minutes later, she sat down by Andreh, waiting for questions from others.

Andreh made a strange face and jumped up, walking to the large map on the wall. He pointed to a section of Alstromia.

"Our AoE is currently training here," he announced. "We should send someone to retrieve them. Zandorah needs at least twenty-five percent of our SAoW and a handful of our AoE."

Rammadar nodded. "Agreed. We can spare that. Maybe we can send three of our Dark Guardian Wizzards, too. They can help the AoE with covert operations. Zandorah will require all the help we can provide."

Alexis smiled. She felt relieved that her team was willing to support her sister and Iriss.

"Great. We have a plan. Rammadar, please coordinate with Pauto and Andreh and begin the process of sending troops. Also, I believe the remaining warriors left behind should be placed on high alert. We must ensure our security as well," she added.

"It will be done, My Queen," Rammadar responded, nodding.

"Wonderful. I will head to my chamber and summon my sister and mother. I will find out about the security field that Yarlen and Cazzandra were tasked to enable over Iriss. It is imperative that our forces can penetrate the barrier to enter the planet. I will get back to you soon." Alexis left quickly, wishing to speak to her family.

The others remained behind, strategizing and preparing to implement the new plan. The SAoW and AoE would be recalled and ordered to deploy to Iriss.

CHAPTER 18

erianna woke up feeling sweaty. She swiftly removed the blanket and tossed it onto the floor. She noticed the fire had burned out. Feeling unsteady, she managed to stand and walk to the bathroom, the cold floor causing her to shiver. It was dark in her chamber, and she could not wait to take a hot shower and then slide into her welcoming bed.

Pauto arrived not long after. Aerianna was in bed, holding a spellbook, when he entered the room. "Ah, you are awake! How are you feeling?" he asked. He sat beside her and reached for her hand.

"I feel so much better," she reassured him. " I took a nap and just showered. I even have my hunger back."

"I am so happy to hear that. What do you want to eat? I can get you some food," Pauto offered.

"I already ordered a meal. It will be here shortly. I am starving!" Aerianna smiled.

"That is excellent news. So, let me fill you in on what is happening." Pauto began disclosing everything that had occurred up until this point. He wanted to ensure she was briefed, as he assumed she would return to work shortly.

"Great, I am listening," Aerianna responded, eager to hear the update.

In another chamber of the Palace, Alexis and Lorthana chatted while Zandorah fiddled with her gown. She rolled her eyes with impatience, wishing she were back in the Castle of Zandor.

"Zandorah, isn't that fabulous? Alexis and Alstromia will help protect you and Iriss. I am so happy to hear such wonderful news," gushed Lorthana, thrilled about the offer.

"Yes, that is extremely generous. I need to return home. Yarlen and Cazzandra reminded us that we had to return to the planet within an hour. The shield will be up by then. Though we will still be able to communicate with each other, no one will be able to enter without Yarlen and Cazzandra's *By-Pass Spell*."

"Great. Why don't you and Mother head back to Iriss? I will ensure that my troops arrive shortly. Then, Yarlen can resecure the planet," Alexis added. "Please ask Yarlen to stay with you and provide assistance as needed. Have Cazzandra return to the Palace on Alstromia. We may need her."

"Thank you, Sis. Yes, I will inform them of your requests. I appreciate your help. Mother, are you coming?" Zandorah inquired.

"Yes, let's head home, Zandi. See you later, Alexis. We will talk soon." Lorthana hugged Alexis and grabbed Zandorah's hand. She slammed down her Ceptre, the Staff of Itma, and the two disappeared.

Alexis contemplated whether the threats against Iriss were real. In a way, she felt the information could be fabricated because it was strange that both planets had been targeted. Maybe Zandorah had made up a crisis, hoping to bring the sisters together?

Nonetheless, Alexis did not want to withdraw her offer if there was even the slightest chance of a genuine problem. In the meantime, she planned to send scouts to Earth to learn more about Ventorroh Grimstock and his followers. Perhaps Cinderillah Winterbloom, one of the senior-scouts, would be able to provide vital intelligence.

On Earth, Ventorroh Grimstock glared at one of the Warlocks as he questioned his motives. It was apparent that the Warlock had no clue that his actions were about to get him killed. He sat down the second he noticed Ventorroh's snarling look and furrowed eyebrows. Worried about his well-being, he looked away nervously.

"We must move swiftly. My team has informed me that Zandorah has asked for reinforcements to secure her planet. I assume she has requested her sister's help. I wonder how prepared Alexis Snipperdoom and Alstromia could be, considering they have been dealing with the *GRAW* and Gardone's relentless attacks. Regardless, we must hurry. If Zandorah fortifies her planet, it will be much more difficult to overtake Iriss. We need her resources and could use her troops for our next move," declared Ventorroh. He stood at the head of the table, his head held high. Ventorroh Grimstock was a striking ThreeBlud, famous for his looks. He had long, pitch-black hair, icy blue eyes, and a prominent jawline. Standing over six feet tall, he exuded a muscular build. His mother was a skilled Blud-Tracker and Hunter, while his father was a wicked Warlock. Ventorroh followed in his father's footsteps and practiced dark sorcery. He studied at *AMLA* many years before moving back to Draekidell. Eventually, he decided to move to Earth, where he became known as the infamous leader of the Dark Earth Legion (*DEL*).

"Zandorah is not aggressive, and I believe, ultimately, we can conquer the planet. If she receives help from Alexis, that will change. Alexis has the AoE, which is fierce. We will not be able to match their might," reiterated Ventorroh.

Gilbort Hinderspelt jumped out of his seat. "Sir, my scout informed me she is planning to send AoE, SAoW, and a handful of her Dark Guardian Wizzards. Are we sure we can face off against them?"

"Well, Gilbort, that is your job. Not mine. You are the Army Commander in charge. If you feel we are not prepared, I would expect you to present us with other options," Ventorroh hissed with annoyance. He despised incompetence, and he wanted to punch Gilbort for acting cowardly.

"Unfortunately, we do not have that many W3s in our command. Currently, we sit at 1200. They are by no means equipped to face the AoE or Dark Guardians. We require more spells, potions, and equipment," Gilbort retorted, defending his status.

"No more excuses, Gilbort. Handle it. I do not care what it takes. We must be ready to engage within the next 12 hours, or it will be too challenging to move forward with our existing plan." Ventorroh sat and folded his hands.

A young Wizzard rose to his feet. "Sir, my name is Flextin Grubly. A few years back, I worked indirectly for Alexis Snipperdoom under her husband, Armbruster. I can tell you we are not prepared. However, I know a few Warlocks on Alstromia who may be willing to aid our efforts for the right price," he smiled.

"Really? Well, why don't you have a chat with Gilbort and fill him in on what you know? See what you two can come up with, and once you have a plan of action, seek me out, and I will listen," Ventorroh bellowed.

He was tired of the conversation and wanted action. Perhaps this young Wizzard could aid them, providing them with an advantage to use against Queen Alexis and her sister, Zandorah.

Gilbort snatched the young Wizzard by the arm and roughly escorted him out of the room. He disliked his impromptu response and wanted him to know it wouldn't happen again. Once in the hallway, he began reprimanding the young Wizzard. "Listen, Flextin. Next time you wish to speak out of line, I suggest you chat with me first. This is not how things work in my chain of command. Do you hear me?" Gilbort shouted, inches from Flextin's face, causing the young Wizzard to flinch.

"I am sorry, Sir. I meant no disrespect. I was attempting to help," he explained.

"Fine. Do not ever let it happen again!"

"NO! Absolutely not. Now, may I tell you what I know?" Flextin offered. Of course, Gilbort was interested. He could not wait to hear what the young Wizzard had to say.

Alexis decided to leave all the military responses to Rammadar and Yarlen. Since Yarlen remained on Iriss, aiding her sister, she suggested Pauto and Andreh deal with anything army-related on Alstromia.

By now, it was late in the evening, and the Queen was eager to speak with Aerianna, asking her if she was ready to finalize the wedding plans. TheWinterFrost Festival was days away. She also hoped that by then, the threats against Iriss would have been handled. She did not need there to be drama during the festival in the City of Miccay. It was Alexis's favorite time of year. Now, the wedding would be taking place as well. There was no room for interruptions or attacks of any kind. She planned to ensure the safety of all participants and residents.

On Tullah Mountain, snow fell out of the sky, slowly blanketing the entire region. Before too long, most of Alstromia was white and sparkly. Christmas trees were decorated in icy blue and silver to enhance the festive atmosphere and were scattered throughout the Manor. Outside by the entryway of the building, several tall trees had been erected and decorated with clear, bright white lights. The Manor was also bustling with vendors preparing their stands in anticipation of the WinterFrost Festival.

Some of the events were held in Amaranteh, a northern, frigid region of Alstromia, famous for its intricate ice castles. It was also where the elite members of Alexis' staff lived during the Fourth-Season (Winter).

In the past, Amaranteh had been the hosting city of the Torrin-Pulled Sleigh races, but the Draghoon-Pulled Sleigh races replaced the event. The adrenaline rush from the races was unmatched, and people from all over the world flocked to the area to witness them.

However, due to the icy weather, the races were recently relocated to the track on Tullah Mountain, attached to the Manor. Even though some W3s felt the frigid environment was too cold for their liking, the sheer amount of attendees indicated their love for the sport. The pond near the Manor was used for daytime ice skating competitions and turned into a private skating event in the evenings. Every year, participants arrived from Earth, Draekidell, and Iriss, hoping to take home metals and Victor Coins.

This year, the Manor would host Aerianna and Pauto's wedding before the kick-off event of the WinterFost Festival. Alexis and Aerianna met inside the building to review the table settings and ensure everything had been completed to provide the most stunning backdrop for the nuptials.

Aerianna dressed in warm clothing and transported to the Manor, wishing to be on time for her meeting with Alexis. She felt energized and well for once, which made her quite happy.

"Alexis, it is gorgeous. Now that the snow has covered the grounds, it looks enchanting. How can Pauto and I ever thank you enough for all you've done for us?"

"Aerianna, it has been my pleasure. I am so happy you are thrilled with the results. Did you complete your final fitting of the gown?" asked Alexis.

"Yes. The sewists extended the gown's waist a tiny bit. It felt snug. Thank goodness it is done, and I am ready. Pauto has his outfit, and we're excited about the ceremony."

"Fabulous. The flowers have arrived from Earth. We are set. I cannot wait to witness your exchange of vows. Now, we need to head back to the Security Command Chamber. Zandorah and her planet still face threats, and our teams should be on the way to provide military reinforcement on Iriss. However, we should ensure Rammadar, Pauto, and Andreh have it handled."

"Agreed. Let us return swiftly to the Palace," Aerianna nodded, pounding her Ceptre to the ground and disappearing. Within seconds, she stood inside the Security Command Chamber, where her fiancé, Pauto, greeted her with a loving look.

Deeply hidden in the dense forest on Hexxton Mountain, the *Ninety-Nightlbade Brigade* (*NNB*) team members assembled to discuss their imminent attack on Alstromians. Their commander, Bryzorth Dreadstohn, paced around inside the rectangular-shaped tent, unable to remain still. He had received communication that it was almost time to begin the first wave of attacks.

Unfortunately, Bryzorth had not yet managed to capture the Witch, who would be tasked to aid them in using magic against Alexis Sniperdoom and Alstromia. The news relayed to Bryzorth stated that the Witch had been deployed to Iriss on a last-minute mission but was due to return shortly. Bryzorth would ensure his Second-in-Command, Cymone Wozzletin, would deliver her to him unharmed.

"Cy, do we have an update on the Witch?" bellowed Bryzorth, staring at Cymone, who lounged on a cot near him.

Instantly, the young Warlock sat up. "Yes, she should be back at the Palace of Snipperdoom. I have deployed two warriors to kidnap her. She will be here shortly, Sir!"

"Fantastic! We are to interrupt the opening ceremony of the WinterFrost Festival. So, we must ensure she is ready to aid us. If she refuses, kill her!"

"Understood, Commander! It will be done," Cymone reassured him. He jumped off the cot and ran outside to locate two of his team members, demanding an update on the Witch's current location.

Bryzorth was well aware of his competitor, Ventorroh Grimstock, who was attempting to overtake Iriss. Bryzorth wanted to ensure that

Alstromia would be unable to stop the violent takeover of Iriss. After Iriss' eventual surrender to Ventorroh, Bryzorth would approach him and ask to join forces. Together, they would set their eyes on the next prized planet, Draekidell!

Cazzandra marched from the Courtyard and headed toward the stairway to the basement. Suddenly, she felt an odd sensation run through her body, causing her to collapse. The two Warlocks lifted her off the cobblestones and placed a black silk bag over her head before knocking her out. They dragged her behind the building, slamming down their Ceptres, disappearing with their victim.

"Sir, she is here. I have her tied to a pole in the security tent. Do you wish to see her?" Cymone asked Bryzorth.

"Yes, lead the way. There is no time to waste."

Cazzandra opened her eyes. Everything looked fuzzy, and she was having difficulty focusing. There was a shrill screeching noise in her ears, making her want to puke. Her head pounded, and she smelled something strange. She cringed, realizing her hands were tied and that she could not summon her wand, which seemed to be elsewhere. A few minutes passed, and the dark, olive-green canvas tent door was pulled back, and a tall, handsome Warlock appeared.

"Ah, I see you are awake. How do you feel? Can I do something to help?" Bryzorth offered. He realized she would probably lash out at him, but he did not care.

"Umm, you could untie me and tell me why I am here. Who are you, and where am I?" Cazzandra demanded, glaring at him. Her eyes finally focused, and she saw his face.

"All in good time, dear. First, how is your head? I heard they whacked you quite hard. Do you require a Healing Warlock? I do not want you in pain. Rest assured, I need you healthy," his snide smirk made her want to scream.

"I am fine. Answer the questions. Why am I here? Where am I?" Cazzandra asked again, getting pissed.

He approached and stood before her, looking down. She sat on a Trimber stool, her hands securely tied to the tall Trimber pole supporting the tent, and she was helpless. Bryzorth loved her vulnerability, and an evil grin graced his rugged face as he stared at her.

"Listen, this will be so much better for you if you choose to cooperate. I need your skills to begin a campaign against the Queen and Alstromia. I understand you are one of Yarlen Raventon's apprentices. Supposedly, you are uniquely gifted. So, you will help me. Understand?"

"I will do no such thing," she screamed, exacerbating the booming sound in her head. She lunged forward and threw up. Embarrassed, she looked up at him.

"Well, you have to make a choice. You can aid us, or my Second-in-Command, Cymone Wozzletin, will kill you! Those are your only choices, dear," he announced, watching her reaction. "Here, let me wipe your face." Bryzorth cleaned her with a handkerchief and stepped back.

"You have chosen the wrong Witch. I will NOT rally against Alexis Snipperdoom and Alstromia. My allegiance is to her and the kingdom." Cazzandra closed her eyes. The nauseating pounding in her head hurt so badly that she thought she would pass out. It was also causing her stomach to churn, making her even more nauseous. She could taste bile making its way up her throat.

"No, on the contrary. I have chosen correctly. You are the one I need. Now, what will it take to make you understand you are in no position to negotiate? I am more than willing to provide you with something in exchange for your help. I am not stupid. I realize your services are valuable," Bryzorth continued.

"You are wrong. I do not want anything you have to offer except my freedom."

Bryzorth chuckled, finding her remark humorous. "Wrong! You will help. I do not wish to kill or harm you. After all, you are talented and extremely beautiful. Speaking of which, do you have a boyfriend? Girlfriend? Husband? If not, perhaps I might interest you?" Bryzorth added. He found himself highly aroused by her. She was stunning. Her long, unruly red hair and mesmerizing green eyes were precisely what he was attracted to.

Instantly, he turned away, feeling his cheeks become flush with desire for her. He was embarrassed and hoped she did not notice. He did not wish to come across as weak.

"Listen, you have not even told me your name." Cazzandra awaited his reply, hoping to steer the conversation in a different direction. His remark about her relationship status repulsed her.

"My name is Bryzorth Dreadstohn. I am the Commander of the Ninety-Nightblade Brigade." He turned around to face her, flashing a devious smile.

"I see. Nice to meet you," Cazzandra responded, wishing to come across as cooperative and courteous. "And no, I do not have a significant other, not that it matters," the young Witch retorted.

Cazzandra looked down, not wanting to maintain eye contact with him, as he made her uncomfortable.

"Oh, but it does matter. It gives me a glimmer of hope," Bryzorth added, smirking.

"So, get to the point. What do you believe I can do for you? I am a nobody. I am not extraordinarily gifted. I am not sure where you received your faulty information about me and my abilities," she added, hoping to derail his plan.

"Ha! Lies. I know exactly who you are and what you are capable of doing. Trust me. Well, I will have you moved to my tent, where we will continue this interesting conversation in private," he nodded to the Warlock, who untied Cazzandra. She remained seated.

Bryzorth advanced, grabbed her arm, and pulled her up. She managed to stand, feeling dizzy. She rubbed her aching skull, and he noticed. "Come, I will summon a Healing Warlock for you and insist he conducts a medical exam. After, we will finish our chat." Reluctantly, Cazzandra held his arm while he escorted her to the other tent at the end of the path, near a cave.

Bryzorth's tent was much smaller than the other. It was dark green and blended well into the forest. Once inside, he removed his cloak and draped it over a cot. She stood, unsteady, leaning against the pole, watching.

"Sir, how may I be of assistance?" the young Warlock shouted. He noticed the stunning redhead and nodded politely. Bryzorth moved aside, allowing the Healing Warlock to enter the tent.

"Please, tend to our guest. She has a head injury and is in pain," Bryzorth explained.

"Of course! It will be done," he announced, advancing Cazzandra. "Please, sit on the cot so that I can examine you," he instructed, dropping his black-and-red medical bag on the dirt floor. Reluctantly, she obeyed. She closed
her eyes as he stood before her, inspecting her head for wounds. There was a minimal amount of blood on the back of her skull, and the gash he located was superficial. He waved his wand and chanted. Seconds later, she felt relieved. The pain was finally gone. It was wonderful, and she managed a crooked smile.

"There you go," he announced as he glanced at the Witch. "Sir, summon me if you need anything else. I wish to continue working on the project," Jordann Mazkin, the Healing Warlock, announced.

"Thank you. Yes, please complete the task," Bryzorth agreed.

After Jordann's departure, the tent was eerily quiet. Bryzorth observed Cazzandra, who nervously fiddled with her hands. She wondered if he would force her to work against the Queen. The thought elicited a panic attack, and she bent over, trying to catch her breath.

Bryzorth noticed her condition but chose to ignore it. "Cazzandra, it is time. We must finish our discussion. Please, be wise and agree to aid me. It will be in your best interest. I am sure you have noticed that I have cast a spell that disables your magic. You are unable to summon anyone. You cannot beckon your wand either," Bryzorth reassured her, knowing she wanted to fight him, noticing the stern look on her face.

"What is it you want from me? Be specific," Cazzandra inquired hesitantly. She fumed with anger, perturbed at his persistence. He made his overwhelming control apparent, attempting to intimidate her. It was working.

"First, I will explain my detailed plan, and then, we will discuss your part," Bryzorth confirmed. "I promise you will be compensated for your help." He sat beside her, ready to share his vision.

CHAPTER 19

In the middle of the night, another powerful snowstorm hit Alstromia. The relentless whistling sound from the strong winds woke Alexis. She pushed Andreh's arm off her waist and jumped out of bed, quickly walking toward the window, pulling back the heavy curtains to peek outside.

She waved her hands, chanting, reigniting the fireplace flames, hoping to warm the freezing chamber. Her feet were ice cold, and she sprinted back to bed, pulling the cover over her shivering body.

"Are you okay, Luv?" Andreh asked, sounding groggy.

"Yes, the storm woke me. It is still snowing. It is beautiful, but it makes the Palace cold. The fire should warm up the chamber shortly," Alexis explained. She looked over and saw Andreh had fallen back asleep. He had not heard a word she said to him.

Alexis shook her head, staring up at the ceiling and wondering about the wedding about to take place. She had already picked out a gown to wear. It was a stunning, icy-blue, and made from a sheer, flowing material. She planned to pair it with high heels and a silver cape with a fluffy, white faux-fur collar. It would keep her warm.

The Queen had also already commissioned her own wedding dress. The sewist was busy creating it. Alexis wanted it to be perfect, insisting the pearls and crystals were sewn by hand. She opted for a white and silver gown with a matching veil. The bottom of the dress was embroidered with pale pink flowers. Six months would pass quickly, and she would finally marry Andreh! Alexis giggled at the thought as she lovingly watched him sleeping.

As she lay in bed, wide awake, she wondered about Lilah. Her mother had picked her up and was now staying on Iriss. Instantly, Alexis bolted upright in bed. "Oh, my God! What have I done? What if Iriss is attacked? My daughter is there!" she screamed, waking Andreh again.

"What? What about Iriss?" he asked, sounding irritated, rubbing his eyes and attempting to become more aware of what was happening.

"Mother picked up Lilah and brought her to Iriss. I should have asked her to take Lilah to Earth. With the threats against Iriss, it is unwise for my daughter to be there. I must contact Mother and insist she move my child immediately! It would be best if they stayed with Magorr. He will ensure their safety," Alexis reiterated nervously.

"I agree. Move the child! I am not sure why Lorthana thought it was wise to bring Lilah to Iriss, given the situation," Andreh concurred.

Alexis jumped out of bed. She approached the table and grabbed her wand, waving it wildly through the air as she chanted. It took almost an hour before Lorthana appeared, wearing her nightgown, and she looked mad, with a frown on her face.

"Goodness! What is it, Alexis? Do you know what time it is? Everyone is asleep. You are lucky I was able to contact Yarlen to have him temporarily remove the protective shield. Otherwise, I would not have been able to leave Iriss. Why have you summoned me at this hour?"Lorthana complained. She stared at Andreh, furious that he was in her daughter's bed. Andreh sat up, listening to the conversation.

"Mother, you must immediately move Lilah to Earth for her safety. With the threats against Zandorah and Iriss, I feel uncomfortable leaving her there."

"I was already planning to take her in the morning. I spoke with Magorr, and he invited us to stay at his estate," Lorthana explained. "Is there anything else, or may I return to Lilah? Yarlen provided me with a ten-minute window. He insists I return right way for my safety."

"Oh, okay. Thank you, Mom. Sure, see if you can return. I love you, and thank you for taking care of Lilah." She hugged her mother and allowed her to depart, heading back to her daughter and Iriss.

Andreh jumped out of bed and approached. He took hold of her hands and pulled her into his arms. "Feel better? Can we please try to get some sleep?"

"Yes. I am quite relieved." Alexis accompanied Andreh back to bed. She waved her hand one more time, closing the curtains. He snuggled up against Alexis and nuzzled her neck, glad they were back in bed.

"I have a great way to relieve that stress," he whispered in a sexy tone.

She moaned, taking his hand and placing it on her breast. "Hmmm, show me, lover," she insisted, rubbing him as he panted heavily.

★ ˚. ★ ˚. ★ ˚. ★ ˚. ★

Morning finally arrived. It was the day before the Ceremonial Exchange and Aerianna and Pauto's much-anticipated wedding.

Alexis was eager to finalize a few minor details. Andreh was still asleep, snoring lightly. She opted to let him stay in bed while she dressed and headed out for the day. Before departing the chamber, she bent down and kissed Andreh on the lips. He woke up, snatching her hand.

"Mmmm, you should come back to bed. I believe you still need me to relieve your stress," he joked, hoping to make love to her.

"Nice try, Andreh. Sadly, I have urgent matters that require my attention. I will see you later in the Security Command Chamber. Do not forget about the briefing at 2 p.m."

Alexis sprinted out of the room before he could pull her back into bed, seducing her. She marched toward Aerianna's chamber, her cheeks still glowing from her romantic night with Andreh. Her heart overflowed with love for him. She treasured their relationship and was grateful to have him in her life.

Suddenly, she stopped as she passed Armbruster's room. She stared at the chamber door, daydreaming of him opening the door with a big and wonderful smile across his rugged face. Oh, how she missed him. Her heart pounded, feeling as if it was about to explode.

Guilt hit her, and she looked down at her feet, suddenly feeling dreadful. She shook her head and continued her walk, realizing the hurt was still fresh. Unexpectedly, she heard a commanding voice, *"It was MURDER! Avenge my death so I can rest."*

Frantically, Alexis spun around, searching for the source. It had sounded like Armbruster, just slightly more raspy. There was no denying it. Was she losing her mind? She pinched herself, ensuring she was awake. Alexis swallowed hard and ran toward Aerianna's room, frightened about the communication from the beyond. It sent chills through her, and she fought to breathe.

Alexis furiously pounded on the chamber door, "Aerianna, open up. Hurry!" She turned around to ensure no one was in the hallway.

"What has happened, Alexis?" Aerianna inquired. She stared at the Queen, who looked crazed. Alexis chewed on her bottom lip, and her hands shook. Aerianna grabbed her and pulled her into the room, swiftly locking the door and securing them inside the chamber. Alexis stumbled toward the bed, where she finally managed to sit, almost falling over.

Aerianna joined her, highly concerned. "Alexis, I am scared. What is it? Should I summon Pauto and the security team? Are we in danger? Please tell me what happened!" Aerianna insisted.

Alexis remained silent, looking around the room, appearing paranoid. Aerianna frowned, unsure about what was occurring.

"If you cannot answer me, I must summon Pauto," Aerianna boldly declared. She refused to wait for the Queen to come to her senses. Something awful must have transpired, and she was not willing to risk their lives.

"NO! DO NOT call Pauto or anyone else. Aerianna, I believe I am haunted by Armbruster."

Aerianna did not know whether to laugh or cry. Was Alexis insane? The thought of Armbruster coming from the beyond and haunting Alexis seemed doubtful. She had only heard of a few instances where the soul of someone deceased had to be avenged, and the dead haunted and tasked a loved one with finding a killer.

"How can that be? Alexis, maybe we should summon Edwinn. Perhaps the death has affected you more than you realize?" Aerianna reasoned.

"I am NOT crazy, Aerianna. I heard his voice. It happened the first time when I experienced a nightmare. This time, I heard him when I passed by his chamber. He is communicating with me and instructing me to catch his killer!" Alexis screamed.

"Okay, Alexis. Let's assume you are correct. Why does it matter if we find out who murdered him? It will not bring back Armbruster. What if the discovery causes other issues within the Clan? We must seriously consider all reasons why not to proceed."

"Are you advising me to drop this? That will NOT happen, Aerianna. You are my Second-in-Command and a good friend. I thought I could trust you with this secret. Did I make a mistake?" Alexis asked, perplexed.

Aerianna had no idea how to answer her. It seemed highly improbable that Armbruster was communicating with her. It was more likely that Alexis was experiencing a nervous breakdown, unable to deal with Armbruster's death. So, Aerianna chose to go along with her suggestion to see where it would lead. Later, she would secretly seek out medical advice from Edwinn.

"Okay, Alexis. I hear you. How do you suppose we locate his killer? We have zero clues other than the fact that someone gave him a toxic tea, which led to his untimely death."

"I know! But, regardless, we must try to find out more." Alexis stared at her friend, looking for support. She knew Aerianna was reluctant to get involved with such a time-consuming task, especially since she was about to get married and give birth to her first child.

Aerianna had already requested maternity leave, which would begin on the day her child was born and last a minimum of 3 months.

Alexis cupped her face and began sobbing. Aerianna felt sad, wanting to console her friend, but worried that doing so would encourage her friend's crazy ideas.

"So, what now, Alexis?"

"I am needed in the Security Command Chamber. You do not need to attend. I will also wrap up a few items for the wedding. I hear the village is abuzz with W3s. The WinterFrost Festival will be lively. I will insist Mom returns Lilah to the Palace after the wedding. I want her to be able to partake in the ice skating," Alexis added, changing the subject. She had witnessed the look on Aerianna's face, who clearly believed Alexis was hysterical and that she heard non-existent voices. Alexis refused to discuss the Armbruster matter anymore. She would figure out how to proceed without involving Aerianna.

"Great! Yes, I will stay behind and rest. I hope to see you at dinner," Aerianna replied.

Alexis spun around briefly while headed for the door. "Yes, we will meet for dinner." She quickly departed, making Armbruster's room her next destination. Aerianna and Pauto had not yet moved in. She wanted to spend time inside his chamber, hoping he would reach out again. Maybe she could actually speak with him. The thought intrigued her.

Aerianna collapsed onto the chair after the Queen's departure. She shook her head, confused. *'She cannot be serious. There is no way Armbruster is trying to communicate with her! I will find Edwinn and have a chat with him regarding Alexis and her erratic behavior,'* she said aloud, alone in the room.

In a hurry, Aerianna picked up her wand and dressed in a warm, furry cloak. As she approached Edwinn's office a few minutes later, she wondered how to begin the conversation. She could not just blurt out that the Queen was potentially losing her sanity!

That could start a process that could be cumbersome to undo. No, Aerianna had to choose her words wisely, asking for guidance but not being too specific as to elicit tricky questions from Edwinn.

Aerianna stood before his door. She could hear music playing inside the room. She did not realize that Edwinn enjoyed classical music compositions from Earth. Taking a deep breath, she mustered up the courage and knocked, planting a fake grin on her face.

"Well, hello, Aerianna. Did we have a meeting? Did I miss a scheduled pregnancy wellness appointment?"

"No, Edwinn. I am here because of a different, sensitive matter. May I enter?"

Edwinn acknowledged her request and allowed Aerianna to enter his office. He closed the door and pointed to the plush three-seater couch near the fireplace.

"So, what brings you here, child?" He noticed the worried look. She tried to hide it, but he could see through the facade. Edwinn sat across from her in a recliner, sitting on the edge of the seat, observing her behavior.

"Anything I tell you or ask will stay between us, confidential, correct?" she wanted to confirm before proceeding to tell him more.

"Of course. Always. Tell me why you are here. How may I be of assistance?" The older

Warlock offered. He was intrigued by the vagueness of her words.

"What I am about to tell you may sound crazy, but I need your medical guidance. I do not feel equipped to deal with the situation."

"Okay, that sounds serious. Go ahead, tell me. Do not leave out anything!"

Aerianna let out a deep sigh, clasped her hands together, and began to confide in Edwinn, hoping he could come up with a viable solution to the bizarre situation involving the Queen.

Alexis entered the Security Command Chamber, unaware of Aerianna's visit with Edwinn. Rammadar pulled her aside. "Your Majesty. We have a problem. At first, I did not want to mention it since the wedding will be taking place tomorrow, but we may be facing an imminent attack from a radical group!"

"What are you talking about, Rammadar? The *GRAW* has discontinued its assaults and given up. Gardone is dead. Iriss is the one in jeopardy, not us!" Alexis insisted, confused and wondering what he meant.

"Wrong, Your Highness. I have received intelligence that a new enemy has emerged and is already stationed on our planet. We have not yet located their camp. I have the

SAoW scouring the planet as we speak. Rest assured, we will find them if they are here."

"WHO is this new enemy? What do you know?" Alexis screeched, panicking. Pauto overheard their conversation and joined them.

"Your Majesty, we do not know enough for a thorough briefing," Pauto began, feeling that Rammadar's notice to her was premature.

"I want to know what you have on them. Who are they? What is their mission? What do they want?" Alexis grilled Pauto and Rammadar.

Andreh entered the chamber, catching the end of her interrogation. He stood beside Pauto, glaring at him. He wished someone had informed him about this newly discovered enemy before Alexis learned of the potential threat to Alstromia.

"My Queen," began Andreh. "Perhaps Rammadar and Pauto could gather more information and schedule a briefing as soon as they know more. In the meantime, why don't you finish the wedding plans? We will ensure the safety of the planet."

"Absolutely not. Do not speak to me in such a condescending tone, Andreh! I am not leaving until I gain information about this new enemy."

Rammadar pointed to the table, indicating it was best for everyone to be seated since the explanation could take some time.

Reluctantly, Andreh took a seat next to Pauto. He edged closer and whispered into his ear, "Did you know about this? Why did you not tell me? I feel blindsided. Alexis is clearly livid."

"So far, we have very little information. I planned to tell you once I knew more. Rammadar is ringing an alarm bell that cannot be retracted. He is making a grave mistake," Pauto explained angrily.

Rammadar waited for everyone to take a seat. Once he felt he had everyone's attention, he walked to the large map on the wall. "Our teams have searched this entire area," he drew an imaginary circle with his pointer finger. "We are searching this area of Hexxton Mountain next. Our teams will be returning by nightfall. We should have a better idea of where to continue the hunt next. Hopefully, our warriors will find clues. We must locate the elusive group of malevolent Warlocks."

Alexis jumped out of her chair. "Great. That still does not explain what they want. Who are they? How did you acquire this information, Rammadar?"

"My Queen, I found this note yesterday on the conference table inside this chamber." Rammadar reluctantly handed her a piece of paper with words scribbled in red.

It read, *'You are in danger. The Ninety-Nightblade Brigade has infiltrated your security*

*and is already hiding on Alstromia. They will
strike soon, take hostages, and murder innocent
W3s. Their ultimate goal will be to kill the Queen.
It will be a bloodbath. Prepare before it is too late!'*
It was signed X.

"Bullshit! Who would leave this note?
Surely, it is a joke. Who are the members of the
Ninety-Nightblade Brigade?" Alexis
bellowed, demanding an immediate answer.

Pauto stood. "I have asked a few friends
from Earth if they know anything. This is
what they told me about this new group. The
Nighty-Nightblade Brigade (NNB) is a small unit
comprised of ninety specialized mercenaries.
They were hired to kill you, the Queen, and
overtake the kingdom. Their commander and
head of the unit is Bryzorth Dreadstohn, a
good friend of Gardone's. He plans to finish
what Gardone and the *GRAW* failed to do."

"Okay, and WHY are they here?" Alexis
continued to grill Pauto.

"As I stated, they are here to assassinate
you and take the kingdom," Pauto reiterated
loudly, hoping to get his point across.

Rammadar shook his head and ordered
Pauto to take a seat. Andreh frowned,
disliking how this meeting was progressing.

"Your Majesty, it is a continued effort to
relieve you of your powers. Now that the King
is gone, the group may believe you are

vulnerable and unable to manage your kingdom. They must feel it is an opportune time to catch us off guard," Rammadar added.

Andreh refused to keep his mouth shut. "My Queen, allow our group to finish their intelligence gathering. It makes no sense to assume what will happen next. You are wise and know what I say is truthful. I have no reason to mislead you. Rammadar is right to inform you about the threat, but we should not stop our plans for the wedding or the WinterFrost Festival. We must proceed as planned. Changing course will only alert the *NNB* that we are on to them," Andreh added.

"Yes, you are correct, Andreh. We will NOT be altering our plans. Increase security. Scour the planet for the *NNB*. Once we have more information, we will meet again and discuss the next steps," Alexis agreed. She felt Andreh was the only one offering a reasonable suggestion.

Pauto bowed in agreement. Rammadar clenched his fists, trying to hide them behind his back, appearing furious.

Alexis made her way to Rammadar. "Join me on the Landing Deck, Rammadar. I insist," she hissed. He was about to object, but he noticed Andreh shaking his head, suggesting he do as ordered.

Once on the Landing Deck, the breeze was brisk, and the snowflakes hit Alexis in the face, causing her to flinch. She held tightly onto her cloak, which violently whipped around her.

"Rammadar, I thank you for your candor. However, from now on, I suggest you work with the team before sounding unnecessary alarms. You have a capable and intelligent group at your disposal. I urge you to utilize their services. Am I clear?"

"Of course, Your Majesty. I will do as you ask. I will enlist Pauto and Andreh to ensure we have a well-thought-out plan. When we have concrete intel, I will schedule a follow-up meeting with you. Will that suffice?" he sounded almost apologetic.

"Great, Rammadar. I appreciate your help. Have a great day." Alexis walked away, happy she had made her point. That would be the last time he would ever go rogue. He had to learn to become a team player, or he would be fired.

Armbruster's vision for his team was quite different from hers. She would not allow one individual to run the entire show, or in this case, the Security Command Team. These highly intelligent team members were instrumental in forming a powerful partnership. Each W3 added something of value. If Rammadar could not grasp that concept, he would be useless, and Alexis would no longer require his services.

Despite the drama of the day, Alexis wrapped up all urgent matters pertaining to security and the wedding. It was almost dinner time, and she planned to join Andreh, Pauto, and Aerianna for a meal before bedtime.

Forty minutes later, Alexis arrived at the dining hall, dressed in a long, slinky, dark gray gown, barely covered by a thin cloak. It seemed strange, considering how cold the building was, but she did not care. She wanted to feel sexy and enjoy her night before watching her best friends marry in the early afternoon the next day.

Andreh pulled out the chair, aiding Alexis. She looked around the room briefly and chose to sit, resting her hand on her lap as she waited for the staff to arrive with drinks and hors d'oeuvres.

Aerianna giggled while holding a conversation with her fiancé, Pauto. She looked blissfully in love, and Alexis could not help but be happy for them. She knew they were made for each other. There was no doubt about the deep affection they felt.

Andreh grabbed Alexis' hand from her lap and squeezed it, noticing how much she observed the other couple. He knew she was elated for them, but deep inside, she wanted to marry Andreh now. The moment he squeezed her hand, she turned her head and whispered into his ear, "I love you, Andreh. I cannot wait for our special day to arrive."

The waitstaff finally appeared, Trillays overflowing with drinks, potions, and snacks. Alexis nodded, allowing them to place the items in the center of the table. The smell was fabulous, and Alexis heard her stomach growling, realizing she had not eaten since breakfast.

Andreh stood, raising his glass. "I would like to make an announcement. Tonight, we celebrate your last night as a single W3! Tomorrow, you will unite your love and lives and become one. Here is to Pauto and Aerianna. We wish you a life full of happiness. Cheers!" Andreh took a swig of the Porting Wine.

Alexis jumped to her feet and spoke next. "Aerianna, I cannot express enough how much you mean to me. You are not just a work colleague but a sister. We may have our disagreements, but we always make up and hug each other. I am overjoyed that you have found the love of your life. I am eagerly looking forward to tomorrow. It will be a fantastic day. Pauto, you better take good care of my friend, or you will have to deal with me!" Alexis sat down, feeling overwhelmed with emotions. The group clapped and began eating and drinking.

CHAPTER 20

erianna opened her eyes and immediately felt a grin spring across her face. The day had arrived! She would finally hold a Ceremonial Exchange with Pauto. It was also bittersweet. She had no family left. Both her parents were deceased, and she was an only child.

So, today, Alexis would fill in as much as possible and become her adopted family member. Aerianna felt overwhelmingly grateful to the Queen for her love and support.

Pauto had chosen to sleep in Armbruster's old room, wishing to give Aerianna privacy the night before their nuptials. It was a silly gesture in a way, but he suggested it, and she accepted.

As he stretched, he glanced at the frosty window pane. It was also chilly inside the chamber. Pauto hopped off the tall bed and walked to the fireplace, rubbing his hands. Once he stood before it, he chanted, quickly reigniting the flames. When he finally felt the warmth, he smiled, anticipating the day's events. He was ready to marry his best friend, lover, and the mother of his soon-to-be-born child.

It was at that moment that Pauto realized how fortunate he was. Every struggle and lonely moment was instantly forgotten. He finally could look ahead with gratitude and love, ready to live out the rest of his life with a wife and child.

Pauto thought briefly about Andreh and hoped he would be able to feel the same in the future. He deserved it. No matter what had happened in the past, Andreh was a wonderful and loyal friend. He loved Alexis, and though Pauto initially felt it was a horrible idea for him to become involved with the Queen, it seemed they were deeply in love and destined to be together. So, Pauto decided he would support his friend and be there for him every step of the journey until he exchanged vows with Alexis Snipperdoom.

The Manor was lively with W3s. Many had arrived early to witness the Ceremonial Exchange between Pauto and Aerianna, while others planned to enjoy the WinterFrost Festival only. Nonetheless, the place was packed.

Aerianna met Alexis in her chamber. When she arrived, there was a breakfast buffet waiting. Aerianna was hungry, so she greatly appreciated the thoughtful gesture.

"Good morning, Alexis. Thank you so much for arranging the food. I suppose I should eat before we head out to the Manor. I am sooooo nervous!" Aerianna disclosed. She picked up a croissant and quickly devoured it. She noticed the petit fours and clapped.

"Goodness, how did you know I loved French-baked items? My favorite flavor of petit four is the pistachio."

"I know! You have told me this many times. That is why some of the food choices at the reception will be from Europe. I ensured the cooks and bakers arrived days in advance to prepare the wedding items. Wait until you see the cake," Alexis teased.

After filling up on delicious food, the Witches held hands as Alexis transported them to the Manor. Inside one of the dressing rooms, Alexis chose to lounge on the long sectional sofa. She observed Aerianna as she dressed in a gorgeous pink gown with the help of two chambermaids.

Ten minutes passed, and Alexis finally dressed, ready to head out to ensure everything was prepared for the momentous occasion.

"I will return shortly. By the time your makeup is touched up and your veil is secured to your head, I will be back," she advised, chuckling.

"Thank you, Alexis. Will you check on Pauto and ensure he is ready? I don't know if Andreh is assisting him."

"Yes, Andreh informed me he planned to arrive with Pauto and guarantee he was ready on time. But I will check, just to make sure. Stop worrying!" Alexis departed the chamber fully dressed, looking spectacular.

Pauto stood before the full-length mirror, adjusting his charcoal gray colored bow tie. Andreh leaned on the wall near him, watching.

"Are you nervous?" Andreh asked, noticing Pauto playing with his tie and running his hands through his thick, blonde hair.

"Of course. I have never been married. I do not want to screw up or ruin Aerianna's big moment. Can you imagine? There are hundreds of W3s in the main hall, ready to witness our I do's."

"Well, yes, you are both prominent staff members of the Palace. It is a big deal. It is probably the event of the year!" Andreh joked, trying to lighten the mood in the room.

"Exactly. I just pray I don't mess up my lines."

"Pauto, relax. It will be a beautiful and memorable Ceremonial Exchange. The reception will be fun. Believe me, Alexis worked her butt off to ensure everything was perfect for the event. She loves you both."

"Yes, we owe the Queen. She has gone above and beyond to make it an affair to remember! I hope all goes smoothly."

"You look handsome. Aerianna will approve."

"I cannot wait to marry her. Then, in a few months, we will welcome our child. Can you believe it? A year ago, I dreamt of having a family, and now my dreams and desires are coming true! I am a blessed Wizzard." Pauto gushed with excitement.

"Indeed, my friend. I am thrilled for you both. Now, let us head to the hall. I hear the music playing. It is almost time," Andreh suggested, leading the way to the door.

The terrace doors were wide open, and the crisp air filled the manor. Snowflakes gently drifted from the sky, creating a serene, picturesque backdrop. The soft blanket of glistening snow added a magical quality to the back terrace as the Ceremonial Exchange was about to commence.

The music switched, and Viollah Grackenbone softly sang a familiar song: *"Love eternal, forever in my heart."* The inside back doors opened, and Alexis appeared, holding a small bouquet. She strolled down the white carpet and headed toward the podium and pink arch adorned with white roses, Bloomitz, lavender (a nod to Aerianna's mother), eucalyptus, and baby's breath sprays. She stood on the left side of the terrace. Next, Andreh entered the room and quickly made his way to the platform. He finally stopped on the right side, nodding to Alexis.

Seconds later, Pauto appeared. He wore dark-gray slacks, a white shirt, a charcoal-gray bow tie, and a battle uniform dress jacket. His medals took up the entire right side of his chest.

Viollah stopped singing, and the orchestra hired from Earth began its rendition of Canon in D Major, the famous piece played on Earth at weddings. It was the bride's favorite.

Suddenly, oohs and aahs rang out throughout the room as Aerianna appeared. She wore the custom-created icy-pink sheer gown. A long, gold, and iridescent sparkly cape covered part of her, and it trailed behind. Her head was covered with a see-through veil, and her hair was pulled up with only a few unruly, long, golden blonde curls peeking out. She looked breathtakingly stunning. Her cheeks and lips were a matching soft pink color. Aerianna was known for her tremendously long eyelashes, which looked wispy and beautiful, accentuating her deep chestnut-colored eyes.

Pauto's heart skipped a beat the moment he saw her entering the room. He desperately tried not to cry as he was overcome with emotion at seeing his bride.

Aerianna sauntered toward the terrace, where she would join the rest of the wedding party. Friends and guests nodded and smiled approvingly, watching her in awe. Finally, she reached the platform. Pauto stepped forward and reached for her hand. He helped her up the two short stairs. Once standing and facing the terrace, Yarlen appeared, dressed in a dark-gray and silver cloak, holding the *Book of Memories* in his hands.

"Welcome, W3s. We are honored to have you here to witness this very special event — the long-awaited Ceremonial Exchange between Aerianna Arleenah Diamahnte and Pauto Krestohn Vexxorth. The couple has asked me to read from the *Book of Memories* before they share their self-written vows. Thank you for joining us on this joyous occasion." Yarlen flipped open the book, and Pauto and Aerianna held hands, listening to the old Wizzard as he read.

★ ˙. ★ ˙. ★ ˙. ★ ˙. ★ ˙. ★ ˙. ★ ˙. ★ ˙. ★ ˙. ★ ˙. ★

"Within the pages of the Book of Memories,
There lies a verse of love and eternity.
Where two hearts unite in marriage,
And find eternal happiness in each other's
carriage.
A love so pure, so true and divine,
That even time cannot tarnish its shine.
A bond that grows stronger with each
passing day,
And in each other's arms, they find their way.
Through the ups and downs, they stand tall,
Holding hands, they conquer it all.
Their love, a shining example to all,
Of a marriage built on trust, respect, and a
never-ending soulful call.
So let us cherish this verse of love,
And keep it close to our hearts like a dove.
For in the Book of Memories, it shall remain,
A testament to love, marriage, and eternal gain."

★ ˚. ★ ˚. ★ ˚. ★ ˚. ★ ˚. ★ ˚. ★ ˚. ★ ˚. ★ ˚. ★ ˚. ★

Yarlen closed the book and spoke to Aerianna. "Please, it is your turn." The Bride nodded and began her rehearsed vows.

★ ˚. ★ ˚. ★ ˚. ★ ˚. ★ ˚. ★ ˚. ★ ˚. ★ ˚. ★ ˚. ★ ˚. ★

"My beloved Warlock, as I stand before you on this enchanted day, my heart swells with love and magic. From the moment I met you, I knew that we were destined to be together. And now, as we unite in marriage, I vow to love you more fiercely than ever before.

I promise to hold your hand through all the adventures, to support you in your dreams and aspirations, and to cherish you every day with all my heart. My love for you is like a never-ending spell, enduring through all the trials and tribulations of life.

I vow to honor your individuality, to respect your choices, and to accept you for who you are. I shall be your companion, your friend, and your lover, walking beside you.

Pauto, you are the missing piece of my soul. With you by my side, I feel complete, and I know that we shall create a life filled with joy, magic, and eternal love. So, on this day of magic and romance, I take you as my husband."

★ ˚. ★ ˚. ★ ˚. ★ ˚. ★ ˚. ★ ˚. ★ ˚. ★ ˚. ★ ˚. ★ ˚. ★

Yarlen nodded and addressed Pauto. "It is your turn, Pauto." The old Wizzard stepped back, and Pauto recited his vows.

★ ⁎, ★ ⁎, ★ ⁎, ★ ⁎, ★ ⁎, ★ ⁎, ★ ⁎, ★ ⁎, ★ ⁎, ★ ⁎, ★

"My dearest Aerianna. As I stand here on this cold winter's day, my heart is warmed by the love and magic that surrounds us. As we unite in marriage, I vow to love you with all my heart, to cherish you every day, and to stand by your side through all the seasons of life.

I promise to honor your powers, to respect your choices, and to be your partner in every magical endeavor. Together, we shall create spells that light up the winter sky, brew potions that warm the soul, and conjure magic that will last a lifetime.

Even in the coldest of winters, my love for you shall burn like a warm fire, providing comfort and solace in all weathers. I shall be your rock, your support, and your confidant, walking with you hand in hand through all the joys and challenges of living. As we take our vows today, I pledge to be your loving husband, to stand by your side in every phase of our existence, and to create a life filled with love, magic, and everlasting happiness."

★ ⁎, ★ ⁎, ★ ⁎, ★ ⁎, ★ ⁎, ★ ⁎, ★ ⁎, ★ ⁎, ★ ⁎, ★ ⁎, ★

Yarlen received the ceremonial rings from Andreh. He lifted them into the air and boldly declared, "The rings you exchange today are not mere pieces of jewelry but rather symbols of the endless bond that unites you. As you wear them, may they serve as a reminder of the unending love and commitment to each other."

He handed the rings to the couple and nodded. "Pauto, place the ring on Aerianna's finger and repeat after me, *'Today, I bestow upon you this ceremonial ring as a symbol of our unending love. With this ring, we are now one, bound together by the magic of love and the respect we have for each other.'* "

After Pauto repeated the words and slid the platinum ring on her finger, Aerianna reciprocated. Seconds later, Yarlen enthusiastically announced, "W3s...please welcome the newlyweds, Pauto and Aerianna Vexxorth!" Yarlen clapped, and everyone in the room followed his lead.

Pink rose petals fell from the sky, mixed with snowflakes. It was an enchanting scene. The couple turned around and faced each other. Pauto lovingly pulled the veil back from his bride's face, kissing her passionately. The onlookers went wild, cheering ardently.

Andreh glanced at Alexis, who cried, wiping away the happy tears. He quickly approached and hugged her, whispering, "It is our turn next, beautiful." She looked down, acting coy, and chose to hold his arm as the pair followed Pauto and Aerianna out of the room, as the wedding guests tossed Victor Coins and flower petals at the wedding party. Yarlen left the podium, waving his hand and closing the two wide doors. He walked behind Alexis and Andreh, heading to the ballroom for the reception.

Pauto escorted Aerianna to the dressing room. She planned to change into a different dress for the reception. Alexis appeared, ready to help her friend.

Andreh and Pauto made their way to the reception, eager to eat, drink, dance, and enjoy the rest of the day.

The two Witches changed out of their long gowns, opting for shorter versions for the receptions. Aerianna stopped briefly. "Thank you again, Alexis. The ceremony was wonderful." Alexis nodded happily, thrilled that Aerianna was happy and finally married.

★ ˚. ★ ˚. ★ ˚. ★ ˚. ★

On Hexxton Mountain, inside the tent, Cazzandra ate dinner while staring at Bryzorth, who watched her every move, analyzing her.

"When you are done, we must conclude our previous discussion. I have ordered the attack to begin tomorrow. Now, you can either side with me and help, or as I previously stated, I will be forced to end your life."

Cazzandra took a large swig of the Porting Wine and slammed down the glass on the table, almost breaking it. Bryzorth jumped and glared at her. "Yeah, okay. As I told you before, I am unwilling to rally against the Queen. So, you might as well plan my murder if that is the route you plan to go." She wiped her mouth with the napkin and allowed it to drop onto the dirt floor. She pushed back the rickety chair and stared at him, done acting polite.

"That is your choice to make. I would suggest reconsidering your options," Bryzorth bellowed.

"I do not know what you expect of me. Why don't you get to the point?" Cazzandra chewed on her lip with impatience.

"I would like for you to agree to help me. Then, in exchange, I will release you when the takeover of Alstromia is complete," Bryzorth added.

"Ummm, no. I have nothing to offer you as far as help is concerned."

"Okay, have it your way, Cazzandra," he responded. He stepped out of the tent and quickly returned with two Warlocks. "Take her to the other tent and tie her up. I will come by later to update you with her disposal instructions," Bryzorth bellowed.

Cazzandra did not resist. She allowed the two Warlocks to move her to the tent next door. Once inside, she was forced onto a cot, and both her hands and feet were tied. The older Warlock pushed her down, flat. "You might as well rest. Enjoy your last few hours of living!" he chuckled, exiting the tent. Cazzandra squirmed around uncomfortably, wondering how she could get herself out of this mess. She contemplated whether Bryzorth was testing her to see if she would break down and agree to help him. However, that would never happen. She wouldn't give him the pleasure.

CHAPTER 21

The reception was spectacular. The food was over-the-top, and the guests devoured it while drinking various exotic potions provided by Henrii Snubberly and the BrewHaus. Music played softly in the background while Pauto and Aerianna sat in the center of the stage, surrounded by floral arrangements and floating candles.

The towering four-tier white wedding cake was elegantly adorned with delicate pink and opulent gold accents. The tiers glistened with exquisite crystalized flowers, adding a touch of ethereal sparkle to this magnificent creation. Each detail was crafted with the utmost precision, bringing together a stunning masterpiece that was sure to leave a lasting impression.

This delectable creation was not only a feast for the eyes but also a delight for the taste buds. Each layer was generously filled with four distinct and decadent cream fillings, adding an element of indulgence to this already exquisite confection. From luscious lavender and vanilla bean to rich chocolate ganache, pistachio, and caramel, every bite offered a symphony of flavors that perfectly complemented the heavenly exterior. This decadent combination of fillings elevated the entire cake to a level of pure culinary bliss, ensuring that every slice served was a moment of pure delight for all the W3s in attendance.

At the top of the grand cake rested a dazzling crown in gold and blue, a gift from Alexis Snipperdoom intended for Pauto and Aerianna's future child.

Alexis sat on the other side of Aerianna while Andreh sat beside Pauto. The four conversed, laughing, and having a splendid time. Sadly, the evening was about to be interrupted, and it would cause utter chaos.

Andreh frowned the second he spotted Rammadar entering the room with four security members. He wore his battle uniform and held a Mesmer Ceptre. Andreh jumped out of his seat and sprinted toward Rammadar to head him off. He did not want the wedding reception ruined.

"Sir, what are you doing? We are celebrating Aerianna and Pauto's union. Please, can this wait?" Andreh insisted, pulling him out of the room forcefully.

"Andreh, we must end the party early. I have received a verified threat. The *NNB* will strike tonight. I prefer that no one be hurt. Be reasonable. I am sure the W3s will understand," Rammadar explained.

"Let us speak with Alexis and allow her to make that decision, shall we?" Andreh retorted.

Before the words left his mouth, she appeared with a massive scowl on her face. "What the hell is going on? We are celebrating the wedding of two amazing W3s. Why are you here, Rammadar, with security to boot? I do not appreciate the way you invaded the room. Everyone noticed and is already on edge," Alexis hissed.

"My apologies, Your Highness. My intentions are to keep everyone secure. As I informed Andreh, we have received notification that the *NNB* is planning to strike Alstromia tonight. We must discontinue the celebration and lock down the planet."

"We will do no such thing! Rammadar, you and Andreh secure the planet. Seek out Cazzandra. She was absent from the wedding. She was supposed to help us with the magical showers, but was not in her room. We must not allow the *NNB* to bomb our planet or cast any spells against us. Get it done!" Alexis ran back to speak with Pauto and Aerianna to fill them in on what was transpiring.

By the time Alexis returned to the head table in the room, Aerianna was crying. She knew something horrible had happened. Pauto glared at Alexis and marched toward her.

"What is it, Alexis? Why did Rammadar interrupt our reception? I saw the security detail with him. I assume there is a danger? Aerianna is already horribly upset."

"Yes, we must shut down the party. I am so sorry. We will begin your couple's dance. Thereafter, you two will depart for your honeymoon on Earth. I will fill you in later on the rest of the details," Alexis announced. She hated having to share such awful news.

"Fine. I will take my bride and make my way to the dance floor. Please, after we begin, join us with Andreh so we can keep things as calm as possible."

Alexis nodded and walked off to locate Andreh. He was standing outside the room chatting with Rammadar.

Five minutes passed, and the music turned to one of Aerianna's favorite songs. Pauto took her hand and led her to the illuminated dancefloor. The two embraced, dancing and smiling. Andreh reached for Alexis' hand and escorted her to join the newlyweds. Soon, the dance floor was filled with W3s dancing and celebrating, forgetting about the brief interruption.

After the song ended, Pauto advanced the standing microphone. "Hello again. Aerianna and I wanted to thank everyone for joining us for this monumental occasion. We thank you for witnessing the Ceremonial Exchange. Now, we are off on our honeymoon! The Queen will address the crowd shortly. Have a wonderful rest of the night!"

Pauto walked toward Aerianna, and the two quickly left the building, heading to the carriage to fly back to the Palace. Their bags were already packed. They would change their attire and head to Earth, avoiding any potential catastrophe about to take place on

Alstromia. They realized it was best to leave, though guilt hit them both.

Aerianna disliked the idea of abandoning Alexis. However, she knew there was no way the Queen would allow her to stay now that she was married and about to honeymoon on Earth.

Alexis headed to the podium with Andreh by her side. "Well, wasn't that an amazing wedding? I am honored that so many of you have attended. Unfortunately, our festivities must be cut short due to an unforeseen emergency. We ask everyone to return home as soon as possible. We will be closing down the venue in thirty minutes for your safety. Thanks!"

Without waiting for a barrage of questions from the crowd, she ran off the stage while Andreh followed. Once in the hallway, he held her hand while chanting, waving his wand. Seconds later, the two appeared inside the Queen's chamber.

"Alexis, I suggest we change our attire and meet the others in the Security Command Chamber. We must prepare for the imminent attack," Andreh announced.

Alexis agreed. She swiftly changed into her battle uniform and unlocked her Ceptre from its stand. She tucked her Wand of Grimleah into her belt and nodded. The Queen was ready to face her enemies, and she would win!

Aerianna and Pauto assembled the suitcases. He smiled as he took her hand.

"Are you ready, love?"

"Absolutely! Let's begin that honeymoon, shall we?" Aerianna agreed, blushing.

Pauto waved his wand, and they disappeared, safely exiting Alstromia, ready to begin their lives as husband and wife.

In the Palace's dungeon, the security commoners searched for Cazzandra. Unfortunately, they were unable to locate her. Frustrated, they chose to head back to the Security Command Chamber to brief Rammadar and Andreh.

Hearing the news, Rammadar frowned. He wondered where Cazzandra was hiding. It was unlike her to be unavailable. Instantly, he panicked. *'What if something has happened to her?'*

Alexis and Andreh entered the chamber together. Both approached Rammadar, ready to hear his briefing.

"I am sorry, My Queen. We were unable to find Cazzandra. No one has seen her in a while. Has Yarlen heard from her? Do you know?" Rammadar inquired.

"No, I do not believe so. I spoke with Yarlen earlier, but he headed back to Iriss after the nuptials. Yarlen will stay a little longer to help Zandorah and her team secure the planet. He never mentioned Cazzandra. I can only assume she is here, on Alstromia. Last time I spoke with her, she planned to head to the laboratory to work on new spells and such," Alexis responded, feeling something was amiss.

Andreh stared at the ceiling, trying to make sense of the information. *'Why would Cazzandra be missing?'*

Alexis paced around the room, acting restless. She stopped a few times to stare out the window. Andreh and Rammadar observed but remained quiet, not wishing to interrupt her.

"My Queen, what would you suggest we do? Cazzandra is unavailable, and Yarlen is on Iriss. Now what? Do you think we should find someone else to aid our efforts? We cannot wait for help to arrive," Rammadar added.

"Yes, let's send someone to speak with Farla Summerstahr. After all, she previously agreed to help us in the future," suggested Alexis.

The decision was made, and Alexis announced she would retire to her chamber. She wished to stop by Armbruster's old room and look around, believing he would reach out and communicate with her.

Andreh chose to remain with Rammadar to help secure the planet. He spoke briefly with Alexis, reassuring her that he would see her at dinner.

On Hexxton Mountain, Cazzandra closed her eyes, her head resting on a flimsy pillow on the cot. She wondered when someone would return to the tent to speak with her. She assumed they would demand a final answer on whether she planned to aid them in overthrowing Alexis and Alstromia.

In a way, she wanted to help them in order to be returned to the Palace, but then she realized she would be labeled a traitor. She refused to spend the rest of her life in the High Tower, never able to practice magic again. So, instead, she decided to wait and see if Bryzorth would be willing to negotiate.

It did not take long for him to appear. He entered with a smug look on his face. He held a plate of food in one hand and a drink in the other.

"Awww, don't you look horribly uncomfortable," he began, placing the food and drink on a nearby table. "Here, let me help you sit up." He approached and untied her hands.

Cazzandra squinted her eyes, wishing he were dead. Reluctantly, she addressed him.

"I have been thinking. I do not wish to help you because if I do, I will be labeled a traitor, and that is something that cannot happen. So, what can we work out?"

Bryzorth handed her the plate of food and pointed to the drink on the small round table beside her. "Please, eat and drink. Once you are done, we will discuss your options." He looked arrogant as he glared at her.

Cazzandra wanted to decline his offer, but she was starving. Overwhelmed by hunger, she took a bite of the sandwich. It tasted amazing. She had not eaten in a long time. She quickly guzzled the drink and placed the empty glass on the table, choosing to speak up, "Fine, let's talk."

In another tent, not far away, twenty members of the *NNB* discussed the orders they had received from Bryzorth. A young Warlock stood at attention and announced, "Why are we waiting? We are wasting time. By now, we could have taken over Alstromia."

"Calm down, young one. Be patient. The time is almost upon us. There are a few details that must be worked out first. Bryzorth is attempting to rectify this as we speak," clarified Cymone Wozzletin.

Inside the Palace of Snipperdoom, Alexis remained edgy. She paced around in her room, attempting to figure out how to proceed. She did not wish for anyone to be harmed by the *NNB*, but she had no idea if they would strike. Perhaps they were simply bluffing. She hoped Andreh would join her in the chamber so she could bounce ideas off him and ask for his input. Unfortunately, he remained in the Security Command Chamber, aiding Rammadar.

Many things had changed since Armbruster's passing. With Pauto on his honeymoon, there was one less senior security officer on staff. As a result, Andreh had to devote more time to work, making him less available to Alexis. She strongly disliked it and planned to speak with him about it later.

Alexis knew he was loyal by stepping up when the kingdom needed his expertise, and she was proud of him. But she selfishly wanted more of his time, especially since Aerianna was unavailable, and she felt lonely.

Night crept up quickly, and the countryside became cold as it grew dark. Heavy snowfall resumed. Cazzandra trembled inside the tent, tugging the blanket up to her chin. She pondered Bryzorth's return, as he had left nearly an hour ago, mentioning that he needed to talk to his team. Now that they had reached an agreement, he promised to release her swiftly.

Feeling weary, she nestled into the cot, longing for her room in the Palace's dungeon. As she drifted off to sleep, thoughts of Alexis flooded her mind. She pondered how their relationship would change once she discovered what Cazzandra had done. The young Witch strongly disliked the agreement she reluctantly had made with Bryzorth, but realized it was the only way to ensure her own safety. She hoped that the Queen would be understanding and lenient. However, in her gut, she knew that was unlikely to happen.

"I have excellent news, Cazzandra," he shouted, entering the frigid tent. "I have arranged your return to the Palace. Are you ready to head back?" It seemed like a silly question to her, so she nodded and shrugged her shoulders. She wondered why he was willing to release her before the attack. That meant she was in jeopardy as much as all other Alstromians.

"I thought we agreed that for my help, I would be returned and kept safe? If I am back at the Palace, I will be just as vulnerable as the other W3s, and that is not okay. It is also not what we negotiated," yelled Cazzandra angrily.

"We never discussed your safety. I promised to release you. That is all. Take it or leave it. It is the only chance you have to get back to the Palace. What will it be?" Bryzorth retorted. He was furious with the Witch for challenging him.

"Alright, I'll take my chances at the Palace. Please take me back," Cazzandra agreed. Hopefully, once she was in the Palace, she would have the opportunity to speak with the Queen before the chaos began.

Cymone entered the tent, and he smashed his Ceptre into her gut, causing Cazzandra to howl in pain. Bryzorth watched as he punched her in the face using his fist.

Instantly, she felt warmth running down her cheek. She stared at him, confused. *'Why is he doing this?'* Cymone struck her leg, causing her to fall. He dragged her by her long, red hair out of the tent while she kicked and tried to free herself. As he neared the giant bonfire, he smiled.

"NOOOOO, please, do not burn me. I have already agreed to help!" Cazzandra begged for her life, convinced this was the end.

★ ˚. ★ ˚. ★ ˚. ★ ˚. ★

Alexis and her staff remained oblivious as hundreds of warriors stood in formation, arranged in rows of ten, clad in battle uniforms and armed with wands, spells, swords, and arrows. They eagerly awaited their attack orders, ready to launch magical assaults and begin hand-to-hand combat against the Queen and her kingdom.

They were prepared to give up their lives to seize control of Alstromia and proclaim it as *NNB Territory*, with Bryzorth Dreadstohn as its new ruler.

CHAPTER 22

lexis heard screaming and commotion outside her bedroom door. She almost fell out of bed, attempting to reach for her wand. Once she held it in her hand, Alexis expeditiously cast a spell to illuminate her dark chamber. Andreh plowed through the bedroom door, out of breath. "Alexis, the assaults have begun, and they are more severe than the previous attacks by Gardone and the *GRAW*!" he screeched, panicked.

"What do you mean?"

Andreh ran toward the window and pulled back the heavy curtains. "Look outside!"

Alexis joined him, and her jaw dropped. Tullah Mountain was on fire, with the sky blazing colors of red, purple, and orange. Black smoke billowed from buildings in the Valley.

"Oh, my God! Is it the *NNB?* Do we know? Where is Rammadar? Has anyone asked Cazzandra for help? We must protect the Palace. Thank goodness Lilah is on Earth with my mother and Magorr." Alexis' mind raced, panicking.

"We must head to the Security Command Chamber to form a Chant Circle and protect the building," Andreh acknowledged. He briefly gazed at the fallout and realized the enemy used a variety of weapons. It made the entire situation more difficult to handle. Minutes later, Alexis and Andreh transported to the Security Command Chamber, ready to speak with Rammadar.

Once inside the secure room, Alexis began grilling Rammadar. "What do we know?" She tapped her foot, staring out the open window. She heard loud booming noises and shrill screams, which caused her to jump.

"Your Majesty, we have been unable to locate Cazzandra. No one has seen her. Perhaps it is time to ask Yarlen to return to

Alstromia. We could use his help!" Rammadar added, hopeful to convince the Queen.

Andreh interrupted. "No, Yarlen must remain on Iriss. It is too late for him to aid us. The attacks are underway. Once we lock down the perimeter, he will be unable to penetrate the protection layer. He might as well remain on Iriss for now."

"Again, do we know...was it the *NNB* who began this barrage?" Alexis demanded clarification.

Rammadar nodded. "Yes, we believe so. The previous communication and warning imply so. Now, what will we do next, My Queen?"

"We will enact the Chant Circle and secure the Palace. Once we are safe, we must find a way to protect all of Alstromia. However, since we are being attacked from within, I am not sure how to proceed. Does anyone have any ideas?" Alexis asked. She wished Armbruster were around since it was his area of expertise. He would have known how to handle it. Now, she would have to rely on Andreh and Rammadar for guidance. She wondered if Aerianna and Pauto had been informed about the attack on Alstromia.

Unexpectedly, three security officers entered the room. One was out of breath, quickly bowing the moment he spotted the

Queen. "The Palace has been infiltrated. What are your orders?" he screamed.

"What? Are you sure?" Rammadar asked, now hysterical.

"Yes, they are using chants, weapons, physical assaults inside, and battle Draghoons in the sky! Where is the AoE? The SAoW is in the sky and on the ground, battling the enemy. Can we activate the Dark Guardians?" The young security commer screeched.

Alexis approached and placed her arm on his shoulder. "Yes, we will handle it. Please keep the enemy out of the Security Command Chamber as long as possible. We need time! Do you understand?"

"Yes, Your Majesty. It will be done!" he nodded and left with the other two commoners.

Alexis slumped in the chair by the conference table. She heard screaming and saw sparks raining from the sky as he glanced out the window. She knew it was a battle for the planet and the Palace. Andreh slipped into the seat beside her, taking her hand, ready to hear her orders.

Outside the Palace, the AoE assembled, tracking down the *NNB*. They had previously been briefed on the possibility of their imminent attack on the Palace. However, it seemed as if more than just ninety individuals were attacking.

An AoE member surveyed the sky and observed over 100 Draghoons flying above the area, ridden by the adversary. On the ground, multiple groups of twenty-five or more engaged in physical combat using swords, machetes, and various other weapons, slaughtering innocent commoners and warriors. It truly was a bloodbath, as had been warned.

Several large Draghoons soared over buildings, breathing fire and engulfing the Valley in flames. Tragically, the Vizzork Community Center and many commoner huts burned to the ground. Blood-curdling screams were heard as lives were ended violently. Some victims were burned, while others were decapitated. Some had their magical abilities stripped using dark magical chants, courtesy of Bryzorth and Cazzandra Whiddletoad.

Andreh released the Queen's hand and nudged her. "Alexis, we must do something. We do not have the luxury of waiting. The enemy will be here soon!"

The Queen bobbed her head up and down and exhaled deeply. "Rammadar, join Andreh and me. I will begin the chant. We must hold hands and make a circle. It cannot be broken. NO ONE moves until I tell you. If we break the circle before the chant is complete, it will not work and can backfire.

We cannot risk it! Close your eyes and get ready!"

The three W3s held hands and formed a tight circle near the window, closing their eyes. Alexis began the chant.

"By the strength of stone and ancient might,
Protect this Palace day and night.
Shield the Wizzards, Warlocks, and Witches,
too,
With magic strong, pure, and true!
A line of protection, firm and bold,
A shield around, no harm can hold!
And enemies within, shall meet their fate,
Terminated now, by this spell so great!"

The candlelight flickered in the room. There was an odd screeching and hissing noise, and everyone grasped firmly onto the other. Alexis felt a force trying to pull them apart. She squeezed their hands to the point of pain, attempting to keep the bond connected while screaming, "HOLD on! It is working. DO NOT LET GO!!"

Alexis opened her eyes, hearing a thunderous sound coming down the corridor. Alexis knew it was the enemy about to penetrate the room. Nervously, she shouted the chant again, worried she had not completed it correctly.

The chamber door exploded, and Trimber pieces flew into the room, some bouncing off the walls and hitting the window.

The three W3s released their grips and ducked. Alexis believed it was the enemy and figured the three in the chamber were about to be murdered. Then, a miracle happened. She looked up and saw him! She sighed with relief, nervously laughing.

"My Queen, I thought you may need help. I am here!" He was covered in blood. Alexis assumed it was not his and probably that of their rival.

"Yarlen! You are amazing. I have missed you and your magic! Where is the adversary? Did you see them on your way into the Palace? I am surprised you were able to make it past the protective shield we enacted."

"There are several dead W3s in the hallway and outside the chamber. Did you cast a spell? Because it worked!" Yarlen explained, holding onto his Ceptre of Argin. He looked tired, wiping his forehead, which was splattered with blood. His white beard was soaked, too, now turning a dark-pink color. "I arrived before there was a force field in play!"

Alexis approached the old Warlock. "Yes. I enacted the Chant Circle since you were not here, and we have not yet found Cazzandra. Do you have any idea where she is hiding? Gosh, I hope she is okay!"

"I was under the impression she was in the dungeon, working to aid you and the Security Command Team. I need to locate her. Perhaps a *Reveal Spell* will work. Let me attempt that now," Yarlen responded. He felt uneasy about the young Witch not being around. It was unlike Cazzandra to leave without informing anyone. Her sudden disappearance seemed suspicious, and he was afraid of what might have happened.

As Yarlen began his *Reveal Spell*, Alexis heard another voice becoming louder. It sounded familiar. She frowned, wondering who would enter the room.

"I do not care! Move aside! I must speak with the Queen now," the Witch demanded.

Cazzandra entered the building. Her cloak and dress were tattered, and she had black smudge marks around her face and hands. Her thigh was exposed, and a large cut, gushed blood, running down her pale leg. She limped into the room, barely able to speak. Her lips were split in half, and her eyes were black and blue as if someone had viciously punched her. She looked as if she had just survived a horrendous battle. She squinted, unable to see well with her eyes so swollen, but she recognized Yarlen's voice and began to sob.

Yarlen ran toward her and held her as she attempted to sit down, screaming out in pain.

"My Queen, it was Bryzorth Dreadstohn and the *NNB*. I was kidnapped. He wanted me to aid him with the attack against you, but I refused. So, he and his team beat me up, leaving me for dead. I managed to get away, but they will try to find me. They will kill me!!!!"

The group of friends stared at each other. Yarlen released Cazzandra's hand. "What did you do? Tell me! I protect you if you refuse to be honest." Yarlen glared at her.

"I told you...Bryzorth did this. He used the *NNB* plus the Blud-Trackers. They have killed many. You know how excellent they are at hunting. They pulled their forces away from Iriss to focus on Alstromia and the Palace. He will not stop until he sits on the Queen's throne. Your magic will not be strong enough!"

"Why do you believe we cannot outsmart him? We have powerful magic. What are you not telling us, Cazzandra?" Rammadar retorted. He was convinced she was lying. Perhaps she was part of Bryzorth's group, maybe even a planted W3 to gain inside information! He approached her, snatching her by her arm. Forcefully, he pulled her out of the chair. "You are lying! Are you part of this? Confess!!"

Cazzandra began to cry. The acidic tears burned her chaffed skin. Frustrated, she wiped her face with her hand. "He told me I would die! I had to protect myself. What did you want me to do? I had no choice!"

Rammadar released her, and she fell to the ground, shrieking in pain. Yarlen stood over her and shook his head.

"How could you betray us? Cazzandra, I believed in you." He walked away disgusted, unable to look at her.

Andreh shouted for a security commoner in the hallway. He arrived within a few seconds. "Take her away and lock her in the High Tower. See that no one gets near her. Keep her secured. If anything happens to her, I will hold you responsible!"

"Yes, Sir!" bellowed the commoner, and he quickly apprehended his prisoner. He bound her hands with Mystic Shackles and dragged her toward the High Tower. Cazzandra did not resist. She was too tired, injured, and embarrassed. Plus, in a way, she figured at least she would be safe in the High Tower, guarded by the security commoners.

Rammadar glared at Yarlen. "Did you know? How much of our security measures have you disclosed to that traitorous Witch?"

Yarlen rolled his eyes. He felt Alexis' wrath about to be unleashed. "I had no idea. I trusted her. She was like my granddaughter. I feel just as betrayed as the rest of you! Now, let us not forget that she is not the enemy.

Bryzorth is! She was given no choice. You heard her. Let's allow things to calm down, and then we will properly interrogate her to get more information. We cannot jump to conclusions. She is right about one thing. Bryzorth will not stop unless we destroy and disband his group."

Andreh agreed with Yarlen's assessment of the situation. "Alexis, we should find out what is happening outside. Is the Palace a safe zone? Do we have control?"

Alexis knew this was not the end. The team would have to respond quickly to ensure that the *NNB* and the Blud-Trackers could not continue waging war against the Clan members of Alstromia. The town was filled with visitors for the WinterFrost Festival, too. It was the worst time for such a catastrophe to be unleashed.

In the High Tower, Cazzandra was allowed to bathe. Edwinn Shivvers appeared shortly after in her prison cell and tended to her wounds. He looked at her with disbelief. It was hard to comprehend that she could have rallied against the kingdom and aided the dark W3s. Sympathetically, he began talking to her. "Cazzandra, how did you get into this mess? Please, I want to help you!"

"I was kidnapped, beaten, and basically left for dead. I am lucky to have escaped their ruthlessness. I gave them very little. I wanted to stay alive, believe me. I never planned to betray anyone." She sobbed as Edwinn cast a spell to heal her wounds. The swelling quickly subsided, and, magically, she was able to see again. The old Warlock felt horrible for the young Witch. He believed that she had been forced to take the action she did, and he intended to support her in her case. He planned to seek assistance from Head Legal Counsel (HLC) Shorttar.

Battles raged on in the Valley and the City of Miccay. Hexxton, Sunthrone, and Tullah Mountain were ablaze, prompting creatures to flee down the hills in search of refuge away from the fiery mountainside.

Preemptively, Essten moved all the Torrins from the Royal Stables with the help of Marittaz, his wife, and four other commoners. The Torrins were flown to Trominniah, the western region of Alstromia. The royals owned several properties hidden in the tropical forests. There, the beasts could rest in the stable, away from the conflict and evil sorcery.

Yarlen entered the High Tower, wishing to speak with Cazzandra. He knew she was a victim and wanted to prove it to the Queen. When he saw Edwinn, he felt relieved.

"Yarlen, I am done. She is resting comfortably. I have summoned HLC Shorttar. I wish to speak with him about her case. Her wounds were severe. She fought back."

"I know. That is why I am here. I want to help Cazzandra. I need to know what she gave them. Once I have more information, I will have a better understanding of how I can assist her with her case," Yarlen explained.

Jamessihn Shorttar appeared, wearing his black and dark green cloak and holding a thick, old book. "I am here, Edwinn. Please brief me on the case before you depart." Edwinn complied, filling him in on what he knew.

Yarlen sat beside Cazzandra on the narrow, uncomfortable metal cot. The mattress was thin, and he could feel the Ozar springs poking his butt. Cazzandra looked up, tears dripping off her face. He felt awful. "It is okay, Cazzie. I will not abandon you. I promise. I will be there every step of the trial! We will prove you were a victim of circumstance."

"No, Yarlen. I gave them the spell. It was from your book. You know which one!" She closed her eyes, feeling shame.

"Awww, no, Cazzie. You didn't. That is how they knew our weakness. Damn it! Okay, we will figure this out. What else did you disclose?"

"Nothing. I told Bryzorth I would rather die than give him more information. After his minions beat me up to the point where I could barely breathe, he decided to leave me alive for some crazy reason."

"WHO? Bryzorth?"

"Yes. He and his Second-in-Command, Cymone Wozzletin."

"I see. Why did they choose you?"

"They knew I studied under you and probably hoped I had access to your books and spells. They were right. I am so sorry, Yarlen!"

"I will need to speak with Andreh and get his feedback. I will not involve Rammadar. He likes to jump to conclusions. It may take some time to help prove the coercion caused your participation. In the end, we will win. Please believe that. I will be back." He hugged her carefully so as not to hurt her further. She still sobbed, embarrassed and scared.

HLC Shorttar approached. "Cazzandra, please, fill me in on every detail. I need to know what transpired while you were held captive and what led up to you aiding the enemy. It is the only way I can attempt to help you legally." She nodded and began divulging everything.

On Earth, Lorthana and Magorr received the devastating news that Alstromia was under siege. Lorthana was grateful that Lilah was safe with them, but deeply worried about her daughter.

"What can we do, Magorr?" Lorthana inquired while he held her hand, supporting her during such tragic times. He realized she was overwhelmed with emotions.

"My love, there is not much we can do. We must keep the child safe for Alexis. In the meantime, I will attempt to identify the Blud-Trackers who betrayed all of us and are aiding Bryzorth. It is unconscionable."

"Who is Bryzorth? Have you ever dealt with him in any way?" Lorthana feared his power.

"No. I have never personally interacted with him. However, I have heard of his exploits. He is vicious and refuses to surrender once he begins an assault. I heard he attempted to take over Draekidell years earlier but was destroyed by their formidable army. It took him some time to rebuild his forces and amass followers," Magorr explained.

"Well, that does not make me feel any better, but I assume Alexis has handled it. She will prevail. However, I am sure she is beside herself with worry, wondering what is happening with Lilah."

The two remained silent, observing the sleeping Princess. She lay on the couch across from them, blissfully unaware of the tragedy.

It did not take long for the news about the bombardments on Alstromia to reach Aerianna and Pauto. It was all the clan members discussed on Earth. Some were worried that war would be brought to them, but realized it was unlikely since the Council of Peace & War wouldn't allow such actions.

"Pauto, perhaps we should cut our honeymoon short and return to Alstromia. Alexis and Rammadar will need our assistance. I know how much we want to enjoy our time, but I believe it would be negligent if we choose to remain here, not aiding the kingdom."

"First off, I doubt we can enter Alstromia. I believe it is completely locked down by now. Second, no, we should not end our honeymoon. You require rest, and I don't feel it is negligent for us to remain here," Pauto rebutted. He refused to get involved in the conflict. His priority was his wife and unborn child.

"I suppose you are right. I feel a twinge of guilt. Nonetheless, I do enjoy the time away. The weather has been wonderful, and it has been fun catching up with our friends here.

Let's see how things proceed before making any hasty decisions," Aerianna concurred.

The newlyweds strolled out onto the balcony with a view of the Grand Canal in Venice. The gondolas were packed with tourists, and Aerianna felt a sense of joy, realizing that Italy was a beautiful refuge from the troubles back in Alstromia. Pauto stood behind her, his arms encircling her waist. She reached out to touch his hand, and he tenderly kissed her neck. They were thankful for a day filled with love and peace.

Sadly, nothing was safe or blissful on Alstromia. Alexis attempted to communicate with her mother by summoning her, but after several failed attempts, she resorted to using the Eternal Mirror. After spending an hour unable to reach her mother and receiving no update on her daughter, Alexis lost her temper. She began screaming and pounding her fists on the nearby table.

Andreh remained in the Security Command Chamber with Rammadar and others. Yarlen was present, though he seemed otherwise preoccupied and unattentive to the conversation occurring.

"We are in agreement. The AoE, Dark Guardians, and SAoW seem to have the situation under control. It seems that the enemy is withdrawing. We need to dispatch groups of civilians to recover the injured and the deceased. Once we have confirmed the security of Alstromia, the Queen will likely want to conduct a ceremony," declared Rammadar firmly.

Andreh nodded and said, "I will be heading back to speak with the Queen now. You know where to find me." He quickly excused himself to join Alexis, realizing he had been absent for too long.

CHAPTER 23

ndreh entered the dimly lit chamber. He heard snoring. Alexis had fallen asleep, so he snuck up the bed and sat on the edge. The moment she felt the weight beside her, she opened her eyes.

445

"You're here! I missed you. Andreh, I have not heard from Mother. Do you believe Lilah is safe?" she asked him apprehensively.

Alexis contemplated whether the enemy would resort to sending scouts to Earth to seek out any members of the royal family to harm or kidnap them.

"I have no doubt that Magorr and Lorthana are able to protect Lilah. Do not worry, dear. Let us focus on what must be done here so we can bring her back. What do you say?"

"I suppose you are correct. What updates do you have to share with me?"

Andreh began divulging the news. He explained what the Security Command Team intended to do and what was occurring. Alexis listened attentively, nodding. Once in a while, she furrowed her eyebrows, appearing disturbed.

At the same time, outside the Palace, Bryzorth supervised the attacks. He remained standing beside Cymone as he shouted, trying to rally the forces against the kingdom of Alstromia.

"Sir, I feel the time has come," began Cymone.

"The time for what, Cymone?"

"Sir, it is time to retreat. We cannot match the forces the Queen has established on

Alstromia. We are losing too many of our members," explained Cymone. He was unhappy about having to share such unwelcome information, but preferred to head back to Earth as soon as possible.

"We are not done!" bellowed Bryzorth, advancing and looking Cymone in the eyes.

Cymone stepped back. "I understand it is not what you want to hear. Nonetheless, we should save the unharmed warriors. Retreating now will allow us the opportunity to rebuild and rethink our strategy."

Bryzorth was furious. He did not know how to respond appropriately to his Second-in-Command.

"Sir, I think we should have stayed focused on Iriss. We could have easily defeated the Supreme Ruler's army. They wouldn't have stood a chance. Why did we switch our strategy and attack Alstromia?" Cymone inquired in a complaining tone. He was driven by the desire to win. Engaging with Alstromia seemed like a losing proposition from the start, in his opinion.

Cymone's negative, whiny attitude did not go unnoticed. "I see. Now you want to second-guess our plans? Yes, we could have destroyed Iriss. However, I wanted Alstromia. We can still attack Iriss once our troops have recovered. Plus, we need to enlist more. I do not believe we had enough soldiers for our raid on Alstromia. That is YOUR fault," Bryzorth screamed, making it clear Cymone would be held making it clear that Cymone would be held responsible for their withdrawal.

"I understand. I will be happy to bear the burden of responsibility for the failed mission," Cymone yelled. He was furious and knew this day would come. Bryzorth never accepted responsibility for his failed actions.

"Fine. Withdraw our troops. Let's fall back to Troficcah. The mountains are on fire, and I am sure our camps have been destroyed. We will remain there until we know that it is possible to depart the planet. I am sure there is still a force field keeping W3s out, which means we cannot leave either. Troficcah has several resorts. I know of one owned by a friend. We can hide out there. Plus, it is a nice tropical area. We could use a break and a little relaxation!"

"Sir, it will be done," agreed Cymone.

Bryzorth watched as Cymone shared the orders. Then the two stood side by side, and seconds later, they disappeared, heading to Troficcah, the expansive southern region of Alstromia. They would attempt to contact Ventorroh Grimstock and formulate a plan to make Iriss their next target, joining forces.

Rammadar clapped. "Great job, everyone! I knew we would force them to abandon their mission! I am eternally grateful to everyone." He stood on a rocky ledge outside the Palace, addressing the warriors. They were exhausted and bloody. Yet, realizing they had won, they mustered up the energy to clap, stomp, and yell with excitement.

Andreh, Alexis, and Yarlen joined the boisterous crowd. The Queen quickly made her way to stand beside Rammadar. She addressed the brave warriors who had courageously and selflessly defended the kingdom and all of Alstromia.

"Today marks our victory! It was a hard-fought battle, and although we mourn the loss of many comrades, the enemy has retreated. Your efforts have safeguarded our planet and kingdom, and for that, I am immensely grateful. Now, return to your families and take the time to rest. We will work together to rebuild. Yarlen and his team will commence casting spells to extinguish the burning mountains, and our beloved Alstromia will be restored to its former glory!" Alexis raised her hands into the air. "For the kingdom! For all Alstromians!"

Andreh began clapping. Soon, the large gathered crowd joined in and shouted, "ALL HAIL QUEEN ALEXIS! Glory to Alstromia!" Their voices were loud and supportive.

Before too long, the group disbanded. The armies headed back to their units, hopeful to be released to return to their families.

Rammadar, Yarlen, Alexis, and Andreh briefly gathered in the Security Command Chamber. Alexis instructed Yarlen to deactivate the security shield and encouraged him to talk to Cazzandra to gather more information about what she had revealed to the Bryzorth. Alexis wanted to believe that Cazzandra had been forced to aid them. She still liked the Witch.

Yarlen spoke. "Alexis, I am working with HLC Shorttar. We will find out what we can. He will press charges against Cazzandra if it is appropriate to do so. In the meantime, let us focus on the current situation of rebuilding Alstromia and aiding Iriss in case Bryzorth decides to attack them."

Rammadar agreed. It was the best plan, given that the enemy had fled the scene. No one knew whether they had managed to retreat to Earth or were still hiding on Alstromia. Rammadar planned to send out scout units to try to locate them if they were still seeking refuge on the planet. It would, however, take time.

Alexis and Andreh excused themselves, feeling relieved. They headed to their chamber, wishing to retire early. Once sitting on the bed, Andreh gently took Alexis' hand.

"Why don't you summon Lorthana? I know you want Lilah back with us. It will make you feel better, sweetie."

"Yes, I was thinking the same thing!"

Unexpectedly, there was a loud pounding noise on the chamber door. "Come in," yelled Alexis, wondering about the visitor.

Aerianna and Pauto appeared. Alexis jumped off the bed and ran toward her friend. "Oh my gosh, what are you doing here? You are supposed to be on your honeymoon!"

"Pauto and I agreed that we could not stay away, knowing you were under attack. I am so glad to hear the enemy is gone. We ran into Yarlen, and he updated us on everything."

Pauto joined Andreh, and the two conversed while the Witches laughed and enjoyed their time together.

After about an hour, Pauto and Aerianna excused themselves to head to their chamber to rest for the night. They were tired and noticed that Alexis and Andreh seemed to want privacy.

In the Village of Miccay, Henrii Snubberly opened the BrewHaus to anyone wishing to celebrate the victory over the enemy. HLC Shorttar and Edwinn Shivvers sat on barstools beside each other, chatting.

"I have been thinking," Edwinn began.

"About Cazzandra?"

"Yes. I am fairly certain she was coerced. Can you prove it?"

Jamessihn Shorttar shrugged his shoulders. "I really hope I can. She does seem like a victim. Perhaps I can speak with the Queen and attempt to reason with her, pointing out the obvious...the young Witch was forced into aiding Bryzorth, or she would have perished."

"The Queen has been known to be reasonable at times," Edwinn retorted.

"Well, let's drink a few more potions and brews, and maybe we will come up with a brilliant plan. What do you say, Edwinn?" The two remained at the BrewHaus for hours, hoping to develop a plan to save Cazzandra Whiddletoad.

Inside the Palace, alone in their chamber, Alexis smiled at Andreh. She closed her eyes, summoning her mother, and contemplated how long it would take for her to appear as she waited for Andreh to change into more comfortable clothing after he showered.

Andreh was about to slip into bed when he heard voices outside the chamber door. Alexis dashed to the door, eager to see if it was Lorthana with Lilah.

"MOMMY!" Lilah yelled with excitement.

"Oh my gosh, come here, Lilah!" Alexis said, embracing her daughter and feeling relieved. "I am so glad you are safe and back at home."

Magorr stood next to Lorthana. "Alexis, we kept the child safe. You had nothing to worry about! Your mother was strong and caring, ensuring Lilah had love, support, and safety during your absence. Lorthana desperately wanted to return to Alstromia with Lilah, but knew we had to wait to hear from you. We came as soon as you summoned her."

"Magorr, I am thankful for your help." Alexis shook his hand, and surprisingly, he pulled her into his arms and gave her a bear hug.

"Alexis, we are basically family. I don't shake hands with loved ones," he said, laughing.

Lorthana approached Andreh. "Thank you!"

"For what?" he asked, confused.

"For protecting my daughter and loving her. I am sorry, I have been doubtful of your intentions toward her. I can see how much you love her. Armbruster's death has changed all of our lives. However, if you wish to marry my daughter, please know that you have my support." Then she did something surprising.

Lorthana embraced Andreh, and he smiled, overjoyed that she had finally accepted him.

The family members remained inside Alexis' chamber for hours, catching up and enjoying their time. After some time, Lorthana and Magorr took Alexis up on the offer to stay in the Palace for a few days. They headed to one of the guest chambers a few doors down.

When Alexis had finally tucked Lilah into bed, she returned to her chamber to find Andreh in bed waiting for her.

"You are glowing! I can see how happy you are, my love. See, everything worked out."

"Yes, Mother spoke with Zandorah, and she is well, and her planet is secure. I understand we are keeping some of our AoE there for protection. That is a wise plan."

"I am delighted things are the way they should be," Andreh announced.

Alexis pulled back the top sheet of the bed and snuggled against Andreh. He pulled her close to him.

"Your mother gave us her blessing to marry. Did you know that?" Andreh figured Alexis would be thrilled to hear such good news.

Alexis sat up in bed and turned to look at Andreh. "Really? WOW, I am shocked. However, I am ecstatic she has come around and recognized how much you mean to me.

Well, hopefully, the next six months will go by quickly, and we can hold our Ceremonial Exchange. I cannot wait. I will be counting down each day until we say our vows."

Alexis exhaled with relief. She was still stunned that her mother supported their union. In the past, Lorthana had been adamant that Alexis would find a different suitor, someone more her age. Now, she must have come to her senses and realized that Alexis and Andreh were made for each other.

Andreh leaned over and kissed her. Then, he looked at her lovingly. "Let's get our rest, shall we? There's much to do to rebuild."

"Hmmm, before we sleep, maybe we should hold a private celebration in bed?" Alexis teased as she jumped on top of him, pinning Andreh down.

"Well, if you insist," he replied, giving in to her. She nuzzled his neck, breathing heavily, "Make love to me, Andreh."

After their intimate time together, Andreh fell asleep. Just as Alexis was about to drift off, she heard it. Instantly, her heart pounded, and she quickly sat up in bed, chewing her nails nervously. She gazed around the room, bewildered.

"It was MURDER! Find the one responsible so that I may rest!" The voice forcefully commanded.

Alexis knew it was Armbruster, and she began trembling. He had returned from the beyond and was begging for her help. She stared at Andreh, wondering why he was still asleep. *'Did he not hear the voice?'*

Frustrated, Alexis continued visually inspecting the room, searching for any sign of life. Her eyes almost bugged out of her head when she noticed a bright, light-blue glow in the corner of the room.

Disbelieving over what she was witnessing, she quickly rubbed her eyes, shaking her head. Squinting, she tried to make out what was happening. The glow began morphing before her.

The swirling light transformed into a ghostly figure that resembled a blurry version of Armbruster. His tattered robe trailed behind him as he floated above the chair in the corner of the room, casting an eerie silhouette. With dark, hollow eyes, he pointed his finger menacingly at Alexis, his face twisted into a fierce, angry expression.

"Avenge me! Do it now, Alexis!"

THE END,
FOR NOW

TO BE CONTINUED

Dearest Reader:

I want to express my sincere gratitude for taking the time to read my book. Your support means the world to me, and I hope that you enjoyed the journey it took you on. If you found the book entertaining, I kindly ask that you consider leaving a review. Your feedback is invaluable and helps other readers discover the book. Thank you once again for being a part of this literary adventure.